THE
SEDUCER
IT IS HARD
TO DIE IN DIEPPE

by the same author

The Man Who Wanted to be Guilty
The Road to Lagoa Santa

THE
SEDUCER

IT IS HARD
TO DIE IN DIEPPE

a novel by
HENRIK
STANGERUP

translated
from the Danish by
SEAN MARTIN

Marion Boyars · London · New York

Published in Great Britain and in the United States
in 1990 by Marion Boyars Publishers
24 Lacy Road London SW15 1NL
26 East 33rd Street New York NY 10016

Distributed in the United States and in Canada by
Rizzoli International Publications, New York

Distributed in Australia by
Wild and Woolley, Glebe NSW

Originally published in 1985 by
Gyldendal, Copenhagen as
Det er Svaert at Dø I Dieppe

© Henrik Stangerup, 1985
© English translation, Marion Boyars Publishers, 1990

British Library Cataloguing in Publication Data
Stangerup, Henrik, *1937—*
The seducer.: it is hard to die in Dieppe: a novel.
1. Fiction in Danish, 1985 — English texts
I. Title   II. Det er svaert at do i Dieppe. *English*
839.8'1374 [F]

Library of Congress Cataloging-in-Publication Data
Stangerup, Henrik
[Det er svært at dø i Dieppe. English]
The seducer: it's hard to die in Dieppe: a novel/by Henrik
Stangerup: translated from the Danish by Sean Martin.
Translation of: Det er svært at dø i Dieppe.
I. Title
PT8176.29. T3D4   1990
839.8'1374—dc20   89–22243

ISBN 0–7145–2894–3 Cloth

Typeset in 11/13pt Baskerville and Futura by
Ann Buchan (Typesetters), Shepperton
Printed in Great Britain by
Biddles Ltd, Guildford and King's Lynn

AUX JEUNES GENS
D'AUJOURD'HUI
FATIGUÉS DE LA LITTÉRATURE
POUR LEUR PROUVER
QU'UN ROMAN
PEUT AUSSI ÊTRE UN ACTE

Blaise Cendrars, *Rhum*

To Ellen Olsen Madsen and
Uffe Andreasen whose enthusiasm
encouraged the start of this novel.

To Susanne
whose love carried it through

Marienborg/St.-Jean-de-Luz/Paris
January 84 – January 85

The publishers gratefully acknowledge the kind assistance received from the following organizations towards the publication of this book:
The Peter Augustinus Foundation, Copenhagen
The Wheatland Foundation
The European Commission

preface
to the English edition

Peder Ludvig Møller was the leading Danish literary critic in the first half of the nineteenth century, the first to recognize Hans Christian Andersen's greatness. He inspired Meïr Aron Goldschmidt, Karen Blixen's favourite Danish author, to make his debut with a novel of incredible daring, considering the age in which it was written: *A Jew* — so modern that it might have been written by a Philip Roth or a Saul Bellow. Although a child of the prevailing spirit of romanticism, Møller nevertheless fought against it when he realized that it had degenerated into national self-glorification. His *Critical Sketches* (1847), in two volumes, display an elegance and enthusiasm virtually unmatched in Danish critical writing. Like Kierkegaard, Møller fought against Hegel and his horde of Danish imitators who were led by a certain Professor Heiberg, but whereas Kierkegaard wanted subjectivity and, later, religious idealism, Møller set his sights on realism. And, perhaps most important of all, while Kierkegaard was content to write about — and to — women (mainly his former fiancée, Regine Olsen), Møller became the seducer incarnate, a man whom no Copenhagen professor dared invite home if his daughters' virtue and reputations were to remain untarnished.

The divergence led to an open clash between these two ardent anti-Hegelians: two bears sharing the same territory. Møller criticized Kierkegaard for turning life into a 'dissection room', with poor Regine as the most tormented victim of the scalpel, following his own unmerciful dissection as the sadistic Johannes in *The Seducer's Diary*. The polemic conducted between Møller and Kierkegaard is possibly the most ruthless in Scandinavian literature. Both parties were mortally wounded. Møller, who had already incurred the wrath of the Copenhagen establishment for his vitriolic attacks on repressive, idealistic Danish romanticism by comparing it with such European precedents as Byron, Heine, Hugo, Musset and Pushkin, was forced into exile. When Kierkegaard brutally revealed his anonymous involvement in Goldschmidt's dreaded republican and egalitarian weekly, *The Corsair*, Møller, the handsome critic with the famous wolfish smile, eternally handicapped by his proletarian background and constant poverty, had lost any chance of getting a permanent position at the University of Copenhagen. Meanwhile the wealthy, awkward Kierkegaard retreated behind the drawn shutters of his apartment in Copenhagen and devoted his energies to religious writing. In a very real sense, each adversary succeeded in stealing the other's body, while the always unblemished Goldschmidt fled in terror.

Kierkegaard's second phase is amply documented. It resulted in a new flow of work and the final heroic, suicidal attack on the stultified and bourgeois Established Danish Church — the Lutheran Evangelical. Møller, by contrast, left little apart from a batch of articles written during his fifteen years of exile, especially in Paris where he eked out an existence as an impecunious Don Juan. Since his death in 1865, ten years after Kierkegaard's, his survival has continued to be fraught with difficulty. Danish literary history — traditional or Marxist — has despised and reviled him, or simply reduced him to a footnote; an obvious object of scorn and hatred to orthodox Kierkegaardians; despised by the bourgeoisie, conservative and radical, as a derelict, because he was so thoroughly unconventional, so wild. There is no Møller biography, nor any definitive anthology of his essays and articles, although he figures in a handful of seminal 19th century novels as a peerless demon — a Lermontov's *Hero of our Time* — and has indirectly achieved worldwide fame as the reluctant model for *The Seducer's Diary*. The eternally inquisitive Karen Blixen occasionally asked: 'Whatever happened to that man Møller?'

One day I sat with the transcripts of words found in brown paper bags at The Royal Library in Copenhagen: Møller's legacy in the form of torn letters, fragments of drafts for articles, unpaid bills and unfinished poems. There were also brief coffee-stained notes from the *grisettes* and *lorettes* who had paraded under the arcades of the Rue de Rivoli. Bags filled with an unsolved riddle. What happened to Møller after his departure from Denmark with Kierkegaard's dagger in his breast? That was the puzzle I concentrated on when I had finished the novel about his diametrical antithesis — naturalist, ascetic and ethicist (in the true Kierkegaardian sense) Peter Wilhelm Lund who also 'stayed away' — in remote Brazil. Lund's fate prompted *The Road to Lagoa Santa*. After *The Road* I considered a new novel on Kierkegaard, only to discover that it was impossible since Kierkegaard himself had written it, over and over again. Instead, and in close association with Roger Poole, I cut and spliced together a kind of Kierkegaard reader of his own writings (*The Laughter Is on My Side, 1989*), for the sheer pleasure of showing what a happy and all-embracing writer Kierkegaard was, especially in his first phase. But Møller?

Whereas P. W. Lund, Kierkegaard's beloved relation, lived to the ripe old age of 79, long reconciled with all his defeats in Lagoa Santa, a tiny village in Minas Gerais, P.L. Møller died a miserable death as a syphilitic wreck in a lunatic asylum in Normandy, at the early age of 51. Could I write 'his novel' as I had written the novel about Lund, but also contrast the two figures? *Either/Or:* either Lund's long road to reconciliation or Møller's wayward dance to and beyond the brink of the abyss. . .

The Seducer is a novel, not a biography disguised as a novel. A novel in the same way, I hope, that *The Road to Lagoa Santa* is a novel. Both contain authentic biographical material, the result of painstaking research. Whenever I use quotation marks for Møller's utterances, they are taken straight out of his few books or letters or from the coffee-stained scraps found in those brown paper bags. I have traced their footsteps — Lund's and Møller's — both victims of the 19th century's intellectual drama which is still in full spate. Møller, the myth, this Danish Richard Savage, perhaps did not after all demand a biography, but — as in the case of Lund — a 'fantasy' where Kierkegaard's Johannes the Seducer might also walk and talk and act. And Møller's own *Janus* from his one and only novella, a romantic, nihilistic work about a seducer who is tormented by guilt and self-hatred and ends up committing suicide. Kierkegaard's sadistic seducer seen from beneath the skin, when the wolves are howling at three o'clock in the morning.

With the approval of my publisher, Marion Boyars, I have decided to include a glossary at the end of the book, even though many readers will choose not to consult it at all. I myself enjoy reading novels with names and references which I am forced to tackle letter by letter. This makes characters and settings remote. Delightfully remote — for a novel.

Henrik Stangerup
Langebaek, 1989

prologue

'He did not overexert himself in facing up to reality. He was not too weak to endure it. No, he was too strong; but that strength was a disease. As soon as reality had lost its importance as a stimulus, he was disarmed; that was the essence of the evil in him. He was aware of this himself at the moment of stimulation, and in this awareness lay the evil.'

Søren Kierkegaard, *The Seducer's Diary*

'. . . anyone who wishes to feel the uncertainty, the lack of fulfilment and also the agony of his existence, need only read *Janus* and give it some thought. Without himself being aware of it — at least fully aware of it — he says there about himself: I wish to meet death in mute desperation rather than grovel to the Cross.'

Meïr Aron Goldschmidt
Life's Reminiscences and Results

'I listened with rapt attention when he talked about his audacious hunting expeditions and adventures with ladies of the night and yet, as I listened, I sometimes felt a painful foreboding that what had originally been capable of developing into a noble nature in him would fall short of its goal. . . Even when engaged in his bouts of dissipation, he was at heart naive and innocent as a child. On these skirmishes, which were to the detriment of his own equanimity, he was not, of course, alone; he had an army of confrères, whom, however, I seldom met, as he sought their company only when he was bent on going berserk. Often, while they were indulging in these orgies, he would suddenly leap up and scream: "I hate you all, I despise you, and I despise myself for being in your company." Then he would dash out and return to his lodgings, where he would isolate himself for some time, only again to allow himself to be tortured by the relentless Eumenides and lapse into inconsolable remorse.'

Peder Ludvig Møller, *Janus* (*Gaea*, 1846)

'How odd indeed that this man should be an object of hatred and badly spoken of, even in his early student days here in Denmark. And what had he done? Well, the only accusation they could make was: "He is a bad man." — Perhaps — . . . Møller was the only one who dared express a different opinion, and that is why he was subjected to hatred.'

Hans Christian Andersen, *Letter to Jonas Collin*

one

The maidens form a circle and begin to sing:

Here shall you dwell, and here remain
Here shall you find lost peace again!

The nymph's palm presses against his forehead. The pressure grows, as though she is about to lose balance, one knee already touching the grass. As her arm slides down, round his neck, a sudden surge of intense warmth pervades his body. He melts, in a state of bliss he has never before experienced, not even in his dreams. Then the surface of the lake parts once more, a glittering palace emerges and glides along the crests of the waves; as it nears the shore, greenclad huntsmen with guns and game bags dart out from the fringe of the forest. Each huntsman seizes one of the chanting naiads and carries her off to a deep sylvan glade. The palace comes closer and closer, rises imperceptibly, and then, glowing and shimmering, gently sinks to rest, over him, round him. The walls and the pillars are limpid, like crystal, but he gradually realizes that the crystal is nothing but ice. The scarlet blush, slowly fading from the nymph's cheek, turns into a transparent film of ice, through which he now sees her, as cold and as stiff and as pale as one of the statues in Fredensborg Gardens.

He feels as if he too is turning into a pillar of ice. The chill creeps slowly through his limbs. Before it finally reaches his heart, he musters his flagging spirits to keep it at bay.

The candle has gone out, and the chill November wind persists in forcing its way through the chinks and cracks of this godforsaken rooming house; with mouse droppings everywhere; with its soot-encrusted, tattered wallpaper and the stench of sweaty feet nauseously trapped for years in the mouldy carpets. And that fat Flemish landlord, sprawled in his bed two floors down, emitting snores that resound in the farthest nook and cranny — snoring away in his torpor, pleased with life, the miserable huckster and his precious francs, relentlessly extorted from penurious tenants, and now securely lodged upon the bed's two bug-infested mattresses. The monotonous, thump-thump of crass inanity, hell's own pulsebeat, the dull percussion of excruciating, everlasting boredom. Snoring their lives away — that's what they all do here in Dieppe, even that malicious Jackal, Monsieur Lachambre, the quack pharmacist who has deliberately given him an overdose of quinine, and the priests he sent for and then dismissed from his sickbed, in a fit of fury, telling them to go back to their god, when he realized that they were incapable of offering a single word of inspiration to usher him over death's threshold.

For the past fortnight he has eaten virtually nothing, suffering from constant diarrhoea. With quinine, opium and ether as his only sustenance. — '*Hélas, que je ne peux écrire un poème sur l'éther, quel thême!*' — He gets it down on paper, in a scrawl. Thanks to the ether he has been able to go on writing right up to the end; testamentary provisions, the odd article for publication at home in Denmark, an entry on Norwegian authors for a French encyclopaedia, a few passages to be translated, and the letter — its pages scattered all over the floor, mingling with all the other scraps of writing, the letter to Jeanne, Jeanne the tart, Jeanne the faithful Parisian *grisette*. '*Madame Jeanne, 36, Monthabor . . . il est difficile de mourir à Dieppe*' . . . ether, opium, quinine; quinine, opium, ether . . .

No, even if he lights the candle again or moves over to the moonlight he will scarcely be able to read what he wrote to Jeanne a while ago, when he suddenly felt that his sight, at least the sight of one eye, had improved a bit. '*Je meurs d'insomnie, empoisonné par un pharmacien — . . . pardonnez mon crayon au dernier moment de la mort. Jeanne!*' Or was it Matilda he had written to, Matilda, at home in farflung Nordic climes? Aunt Tilda, sister Tilda, *nostrissima*, my dearly beloved, my dear sensible Tilda, my sweetly naughty, my naughtily sweet Tilda, *ma brava, signorina, inamorata*, awful Aunt Tilda, *mia cara*, O, incorrigible chatterbox, Aunt Teacosy, *ma 'bonne vieille'*, *chère bonne*, poor, fire-scarred Tilda. . .

He lurches around the floor, now he's down on all fours, trying to find the letter. Of course it's that fat bastard of a Flemish landlord who has pinched it, intent on persecuting him up to his very last gasp.

Jeanne Balaresque! Matilda Leiner! *Gehaben Sie sich wohl! Sempre il inconstante P.L. Møller.* . .

Hôtel de Newhaven, Dieppe — the night between the twenty-sixth and twenty-seventh of November, 1865. Møller runs out of his squalid room, stark naked, forgetting to shut the door, and dashes down the stairs. Driven frantically onwards, downwards, by the pain; the sudden stabs, the crippling spasms. No relief now from the ether, not even from the opium. As he passes the snoring landlord's room he lashes out with his foot at the mangy mongrel, curled up in front of his master's door; kicking so savagely that the slobbering, deranged brute bares his teeth and snarls before cringingly retreating, as Møller resumes his headlong flight towards the front door. He wrenches the glass door open with such force that one of the greasy panes falls out of its cracked putty casing. Møller plunges on towards the harbour but suddenly loses his bearings, missing several familiar sidestreets to the nearby waterfront. Streets, market squares, church squares — whichever way he turns, there is no familiar landmark; no local butcher shop nor friendly bistro, no crêperie, nor ships' chandler, nor hotel. He races down blind alleys, along cobbled pavements, oblivious of direction, wracked with pain. The wind howls in every chimney, through every cavernous warehouse, now reaching hurricane force and smashing cheese-sellers' flimsy stalls, flinging gates open, and releasing a cacophony from the cats, from every cat in Dieppe, and from scurrying rats, squealing for mercy beneath the scabrous moon as it races along, directly above the tattered clouds, almost matching his pace until, at last, he can tell from which direction the tang of coiled rope and acrid tar hits his nostrils.

The streets of Dieppe at night are deserted, apart from two drunken English sailors, staggering out of a brothel, the last customers to leave, and a priest, muttering to himself on his way home after administering the last rites; the priest, with toothless upper jaw and eyes gleaming like white-hot coals, clutches his cassock and turns to catch a glimpse of the naked apparition. The seamen smugly hurl raucous abuse at him before turning down a sidestreet where they casually kick in the door of their hotel. There it is at last, the harbour. There is a creaking sound as one ship moves against another. Møller keeps on running. But now it is as though the pain is relenting, as though he is being borne aloft, as though the clouds are settling, as though the world is smiling at him, a world that smells of new-mown hay. He slackens his pace, he thinks he sees her. Over there . . .? No, over there, lurking behind a stack of fish crates. He catches a glimpse of her purple cloak. Then, suddenly, she's behind him. He hears her muted voice with its touch of irony:

'*Cherchez et trouvez!*'

When he turns round she has vanished. But she's not far away; so near, in fact, that he knows he can find her. And now, as the steamer slowly draws alongside, the huntsmen all emerge from the depths of the forest; they are clad in green, with game bags and guns and hunting horns. The barefoot naiads run among the huntsmen. The steamer's passengers wave their straw hats at them, but Møller has no time to join in, for he has to catch her before she disembarks. He must get her address, so that they can meet again in Paris. All roads lead to Paris, the goal of all his yearnings, right from when he was a boy, dreaming that he rode with Napoleon. Yearnings that have only been rekindled and refuelled during his sojourn, his forced exile, in Hamburg — Hamburg, now a rancid memory of mashed potatoes, stodgy meat soup, the unspeakable *Eisbein mit Sauerkraut* and vast quantities of insipid beer.

She came to him as he stood on the steamer's afterdeck, passing to and fro, twice, right in front of him, smiling at him, darkly, as though from behind an invisible fan. She was alone, and, as an exquisite tingling sensation rippled from his neck down his spine, he wondered how he had failed to notice her earlier. Observing the Victor Hugo volume in his hand, she raised a quizzical eyebrow:

'Vous êtes français?'

'Qui est français, qui le veut!,' he replied, as though quoting a line from *Le roi s'amuse*, with which he simultaneously smacked his thigh. He took pride in the purity of his diction, and found it easy to confide in her, without any mawkish preliminaries. His tales of low life in sordid Hamburg elicited gales of laughter from her as she stood there, neck proudly arched. At one point she made a sweeping motion with her hand, as though forced by the exhilaration of the moment, she wanted to toss her invisible fan overboard, into the churning wake of the steamer. Then the boat docked, and she was gone.

A while later he once more catches a glimpse of her, in her purple cloak, now on dry land, ecstatically grabbing a huntsman's hand and disappearing into the forest, without as much as a single backward glance, closely pursued by the other huntsmen and the chanting naiads. He rushes across the deck, but, just as he reaches the exit, the gangway is hauled aboard. Then the steamer resumes its voyage down the Elbe to Magdeburg, from where he plans to travel by the recently inaugurated rail route to Leipzig, and then the rest of the way right down through Berlin, Frankfurt, over the Alps and up to Paris. There it is Sunday, late in the afternoon, in the Closerie des Lilas, on a boulevard on the outermost fringe of Montparnasse, and Jeanne Balaresque is ecstatic because he has torn himself away from his hotel room, where he has spent a week shackled to his desk — vainly invoking an absent muse — to take her out to where the students from *le pays latin* and the girls from all quarters of Paris dance the magic contredanse, pepping things up with the can-can. The contredanse has caught on and spread like a contagion, and, like the can-can itself, relies on the dancer's ability to improvise, on talent, on agility — or rather on loose-jointed limbs. The gentleman has the major role, which, precisely as Møller has explained in a gratifyingly provocative article published at home in Denmark, requires him, while retaining his balance and facing his lady, to contort his face into the most tasteless sequence of grimaces without the slightest regard to relevance or meaning, apart from emulating the other gentlemen in absurd facial contortions, but with due observance of a variation restricted to the can-can, consisting of hammering dents in one's hat and creating a state of artistic disarray in one's attire. And all these ridiculous grimaces are to be contrived while maintaining an outwardly serious countenance, as waiters scurry about, carrying beer and wine, as the lilacs burst into bloom in their arch above the entrance and the citizenry of Paris arrives in throngs, to mingle with the cream of the aristocracy and admire the long-stemmed meerschaums. Known as the Holy Battalion, its members would never dream of participating in the gyrations, preferring to observe such vulgar diversions from a safe distance, yelling sarcastic comments at the gentlemen and bawdy encouragement at the girls.

The contredanse! Ladies and gentlemen, take your places! Dance yourself beyond all recognition, into a state of oblivion, in the can-can! Wriggle your hips, shake a leg, in any direction! Banish all your cares in the swirl of the dance, cock a snook at the world — it deserves no better! 'And lift that leg!' he hears his own exhortation mingled with the lusty shouts of the crowd, 'Lift that leg, Jeanne! Now I can see you as nature intended! Lift, Jeanne, lift! Higher, Jeanne, higher!' And he tears at his clothes, pulls one trouser leg above his knee, turns his pockets inside out, and soon he doesn't even know who he is. He is all that is most repulsive in the whole wide world; he is transmuted from lizard to toad, from giant insect to dwarf, from dwarf back to lizard with swishing tail, until all the repressed hatred suddenly wells up in him and he is Søren Aabye Kierkegaard, with the unsated eyes, the truculent snout, the pert chin, the ostentatious gesticulations, the peacock strut. And Møller twitches and kicks his heels as high as he can, hair dishevelled, as though locked in combat with thousands of indecipherable hieroglyphics, as though everything is just a matter of grey cells and black ink, and the body a corkscrew, the legs stilts, the arms matchsticks, the head a ball and the heart a steel spring that has unleashed itself and chops everything in its random path to bloody shreds. And never before has Jeanne Balaresque experienced such ecstasy. Suffused with pride in her partner's dazzling performance — he's by far the best at the contredanse, never mind that he happens to be twenty years older than the students. She stands there, rapt in admiration. And the waiters stop to watch this mad dervish who has become unhinged. Even the Holy Battalion roars in approval.

Then, from somewhere behind him, he hears:

'*Cherchez et trouvez!*'

With trousers in tatters, hair jutting out through the rent in his hat, aching in every joint, the heels of his boots worn to a frazzle, he turns round. But she's already reached the exit, with its lilac-crowned arch. She turns, looks at him, tosses her hair sensuously and smiles, making the myriad garden lights sparkle in her gleaming teeth, two perfect rows meeting as though in a languorous bite into a succulent peach. She goes through the mime routine of dropping an invisible, make-believe handkerchief. Then she vanishes through the lilac-crowned arch of the lilac-strewn Closerie des Lilas.

He chases her, for hours, through most of *le pays latin*, oblivious of the puzzled, indignant stares of the stolid bourgeoisie, of the crass obscenities of the street urchins. He reaches the Right Bank, runs in the general direction of Boulevard du Temple with all its theatres and the open-air folk pantomime. Late evening succumbs to early night, and on several occasions he narrowly avoids being run over by an omnibus or bashing his head against one of those climbing poles erected all over the place by boisterous youngsters, until, finally, several hours after the invisible handkerchief fluttered gently to the ground, and without knowing which bridge he has crossed, he finds himself on the flat, rectangular plain of the Champs du Mars, tree-lined on three sides, the fourth sloping down to the murky Seine. Still not a trace of her. Still no call from any hunting horn, no dancing naiads to lead him to her. He is cold. He aches in every joint. Paris closed its shutters and climbed into bed hours ago, and now, on the verge of exhaustion, he trudges off towards his hotel, far from the Champs du Mars, on the corner of Rue de Rohan and Rue de Rivoli. Beginning only now to worry about his appearance, he puts his pockets right, lets down his trouser leg and with numb fingers combs his ruffled hair into some semblance of order. When he reaches the hotel, Jeanne Balaresque is sitting on the steps, in the first light of dawn, holding a shoe in her hand: she has kicked the other one into the gutter. She has been crying for so long that her cheeks are marred with streaks of eye make-up. He takes her by the hand. She snatches it away, spitting at him, but then clings to his thighs, nestling her forehead against his crotch, shuddering in a new outburst of sobbing. She sobs all the way up to his room where she sits on his bed and disconsolately picks up a manuscript, written in a language she is painfully struggling to learn.

But her anger returns. Year after year: the same scene where she screws his manuscripts into a baton, paces to and fro across the room, and then attacks him with fury, battering him as he lies exhausted on the bed. Now it's in this hotel in Rue de Bellechasse down by the Seine, and he dreams of getting away from it all, far away, to Dieppe or Etretat or Fécamp with their hot seaweed baths and their saltwater baths and their sulphur baths, to ward off that vile disease first mentioned in a poem by Fracastorius, in 1530. There he can also find the medicines and diets which will restore his stomach to health after all that coffee, always stronger and stronger, which he has been consuming in recent years. His room is littered with coffee cups, as was his room at home in Copenhagen, at the end of Store Kongensgade, right above the snaps distillery. If anyone wants to trace his steps, all he has to do is to follow the trail of coffee cups he has left behind, black on the inside for want of washing, blue on the outside from inky fingers.

He takes hardly any notice now when Jeanne Balaresque stops hitting him, stops twisting his manuscripts, and begins to scour his cups with coarse salt, scrubbing away at the hand-basin in the corner. After all, those manuscripts won't earn enough to keep body and soul together from one day to the next. Manuscripts and coffee cups, coffee cups and manuscripts and ink, ink, ink; the cheapest ink that money can buy, to put on the cheapest French paper of a quality too poor even for school children. Not that it matters very much now that he is back in Normandy where he is beginning to feel the good of the hot seaweed baths and the long, long walks on the beach, along the shore, where the Manneporte cliff stretches its rust-coloured, dreamlike tentacle seawards. And the words come to him, even if he doesn't quite know why: *bain complet, linge fourni. Fécamp, Houlgate, Veulettes et Yport. Fauteuil . . . 15 centimes. Place sur un siège portant abri contre le soleil . . . 20 centimes . . .* He inhales the sea air. The gulls screech, and he stops now and then to pick up a snail or a mussel, or to strike a bargain with a fisherman over a lobster. He thinks of the woman in the purple cloak, recalling how much that ugly little marquise's voice reminds him of hers, as he stands outside a hut, having decided to buy the lobster and about to pay the fisherman for it when the arrogant marquise comes up to them, studies 'the hideous thing', lets a gold coin drop into the fisherman's hand, stating *'c'est pour moi!'* — and then departs, quite unabashed, to join her party, while the fisherman consoles him with a shrug of token apology.

Wherever he goes, he constantly hears her voice in other women's voices, but he is not destined to see her ever again. And if he should happen to see her he would not want it to have happened, for he is now twelve whole years older than he was on that late Sunday afternoon in the lilac-strewn Closerie des Lilas, and he is bald and sunken-cheeked and nearly blind. His knees tremble, his clothes are shabby and out of fashion, and the coarse socks he wears were bought with what was left of Jeanne Balaresque's savings. His world is now the hotel room in Paris, Café de la Régence, and those baths in Normandy when the torrid heat of Paris prevents him from writing and writing and writing. The pangs of hunger bring on fits of dizziness, and Matilda Leiner bombards him with dolorous pleas to return home to Denmark, to her teacosy, to her muffs and the waxed linoleum, to nauseating evenings with the university choral society, to the servility of audiences graciously granted by the ineffable landed gentry, to the latest Danish novels and anthologies of verse, meretricious trash — pleas that are furtively slid under his door, written in her neat copperplate, sealed in envelopes bearing the dull Danish stamps, pleas that cast an evil spell on his room for days on end, making him peevish, brittle with friend and foe alike, even with the kindhearted tradesmen who often allow him credit.

He has debts everywhere. And back home in Denmark all they want to do is cheat him, wrench articles from his tormented brain without ever sending him the encouraging double fee he so badly needs, while at the same time boasting of their long friendship with him, dating back to those days in the forties when he had his regular table in the corner of the student union's dining room and was renowned for his scintillating wit. Oh yes, he had given them his whole life!

And now they just took it.

He strides on, still sticking close to the shore, but has no idea where he's going. He indulges in a bit of timorous bathing, wishing that the merciless tide would mercifully sweep him away. He is hungry, but has nothing to eat apart from snails and mussels, which he forces open with his little pocket knife. He has done a moonlight flit from all the hotels, bills unpaid, and every room at every hotel is still littered with manuscripts, notes and drafts of poems, to convey the impression that somehow a real P.L. Møller still occupies that very room in that very hotel. Are the police on his tail? He doesn't know, and soon it won't make any difference whether they are or not. He is freezing because he is not wearing any clothes, and night has fallen and he is back in Dieppe. The disease has now begun to affect his nervous system, and he screams with pain as he lumbers along the quay until he suddenly feels as though he is being borne aloft, as though the air is pervaded with the smell of new-mown hay, while the greenclad huntsmen join the throng, each grabbing a naiad by the hand, and the steamer draws alongside the pier and is transformed into a shimmering fairy palace which is imperceptibly lifted up, hovering for a moment, and then gently sinking to rest, over him, round him, the shimmering palace with walls and pillars of pure crystal. And she comes in from the depths of the forest and in a single graceful movement sheds the purple cloak. She smiles at him as she did in the lilac-strewn Closerie des Lilas, and now she is coming straight towards him, while the maidens form a circle and sing:

> Here shall you dwell, and here remain
> Here shall you find lost peace again!

The nymph's palm presses against his forehead. The pressure grows, as though she is about to lose balance, one knee already touching the grass. The scarlet blush slowly fades from the nymph's cheek. Her gown turns into a transparent film of ice through which he now sees her, as cold and as stiff and as pale as one of the statues in Fredensborg Gardens.

two

Kaarsberg, Testrup, Rovlund, Brix, Slamberg, Hastrup, Hoffmand, Schack, G. Hansen, Bock, Mørch, Steenstrup, Schierup, Møller and all the other pupils in the upper and junior forms, dressed in their cassocks, have assembled in the hall of the Cathedral School of Aalborg to celebrate the headmaster, Professor Tauber's, birthday. Peder Ludvig Møller has not only contributed two rigsdaler. He has also been in charge of the collection, which was so successful that it has been possible to go out and buy the silver goblet, richly decorated with a cluster of oak leaves, which is now to be handed over to Professor Tauber as a token of the joy felt by the assembled scholars at his return to the school following a lengthy absence caused by a bout of illness.

'And to you too — our *polemicus ferox* with the lupine smile! — to you too I wish to extend my gratitude,' says Professor Tauber to Møller as they shake hands, in such an air of ambiguity that Møller will never know whether the words were uttered in a spirit of amity or condescension. The others will continue to make him the butt of their crude jibes and sneers, with that despicable Slamberg braying loudest of all — slobbering, dimwitted Slamberg with the toadlike lower lip and the shrimp-sized brain and those sweaty wisps of hair in his armpits that stink like putrid seaweed through the silk-trimmed dress shirt.

Peder Ludvig Møller, a prize pupil with distinctions in all subjects, son of the merchant Eric Møller — who has been forced to abandon the unlucrative trade of freighting goods to and from Norway and can now barely support the family — realizes, not for the first time, that scholastic pursuits represent his sole, albeit slender chance of retaining any independence, any *gravitas*, in his mode of thought, any chance of transcending the crude cynicism that pervades the school and nourishes the evil demons lurking in his soul, so that — as the verbose headmaster proceeds with outstretched palms — he cannot help parodying the lot of them. He deplores, with upturned eyes, their ineffable stupidity, now ranking the lisping, slavering Rovlund as only marginally less dimwitted than the abominable Slamberg, and Schierup as easily the most ridiculous figure of the sad lot, that silly Schierup, standing over there in the corner, ramrod stiff, with burning ears and lolling tongue, thrilled at having just shaken the headmaster's hand.

They are all paralyzed — and Møller knows this full well — by an inner loathing, but this loathing will find no expression, will not explode in any flurry of overt rebellion, and if one of them were ever to betray his true inner sense of outrage, of decency, such honesty would evoke howls of fear and lead to savage beatings during the school breaks. And yet another cruel nickname will be branded on the soul, more savage, because more accurate, than Bully Bock or Shitty Shack: Pennyless Peder.

It seems that this agony is to go on for years and years, at least for months and months, until he can escape to Copenhagen and master the intricacies of ottava rima and terza rima, canzonet and sonnet, hexameter and elegy, poetic Edda and prose Edda and Gregorian stanza. And as his reverie brings back a parade of classical poets and heroic generals, he is suddenly gripped by the realization that he who has once been granted the gift of the gods will always retain that divine spark. After all, had he not scored a triumph at the age of eight years? When no one believed that he would, he recovered from attacks of scarlet fever, at Marengo, at Austerlitz and Jena, along with Napoleon! And had he not marched by his side through the Brandenburg Gate?

And had he not already written his first poem at the age of ten?

Beloved old Steward, Lord of Beasts and Hay,
Long before your Prime, you sadly passed away.

Peder Ludvig Møller struts through the winding, sloping streets of Aalborg, chuckling at the clumsy effort of the child poet, while the fire brigade conducts a routine drill within hose-reach of Budolfi Kirke. On past the main gate, the customs house, the workhouse, Nyhavn. It is raining, and this is the sort of weather Møller loves — no better weather for his hours of after-school trudging, while he thinks of his grandmother in Aaby vicarage who was charmed by his poem and had given him a fine sketchbook so that he might take lessons from Herr Kjølstrup, the sexton. Then he can learn to draw what caught his eye on his outings to Møllen and Børglum Kloster and Sandelsbjerg and Skeelslund Wood, all remote dots on the horizon of the vast tract of countryside surrounding the vicarage, *Aaby praestegaard*, with its linens and woollens, cartwhips and capes, battered umbrellas, four rooms, each with its own special smell, and each smell varying with the season, and scores of faded prints depicting Belgian ports and the works of Luther, Hans Tausen, Rousseau, Tordenskjold and Frederik IV. His grandmother, Maren Laurentin Kanneworff — oh, how often he had dreamed of writing a poem for her, a poem with several lines artfully wrought to rhyme with Kanneworff, because ten years ago she had given him the sketchbook and persuaded Herr Kjølstrup, with his impeccably brushed coat, his thick-soled clogs and his persistent tapping on his tobacco tin, to teach him the rudiments of perspective, without ever entering the magic world of watercolours which Herr Kjølstrup to this day still believes to be unforgivably modern. But the rhymes never rhyme, he never gets farther than norf, korf, snorf, borf, sounds that would be sure to offend the delicate sensibilities of his grandmother. She is always as prim and proper as a peeled egg, always greets him with a bow, a curtsy, a handshake, like a ghost from Brorson's godfearing era. Everything within her domain is weighed and measured to a nicety, the mussel shells on the floor, mealtimes, the tea and the tiny biscuits which can be made to last from one year to the next. She always addresses him as 'my dear Per' — thus avoiding the rustic clang of 'Peder' — and it was 'to my dear Per' that, ten years ago now, she dedicated the sketchbook, adding her favourite maxim: 'if it is across the ocean of life you happen to be sailing, you should never learn to swim, because that will only prolong the agony.'

Møllen, Børglum Kloster, Sandelsbjerg. When he thinks back to all the drab and glorious Sundays he has spent out there, during weekends at the vicarage, with sketchbook, a sheaf of pencils, Indian ink and, nearly from the earliest days, small glass plates on which, as the sexton hobbled home to attend to his churchly duties, he etched in colour, imbued with a feeling of newfound bliss now that he could paint an azure sky and a golden meadow, he feels in a more cheerful mood. He banishes all regrets, all thoughts of school; Slamberg's taunts, Schierup's envy and all the backbiting belong to a different world, a nether world. Everything he can see and touch and feel is plainly good — Budolfi is the church of churches, the sky above Aalborg is the vault in a palace of crystal, pushing back the clouds and allowing the rain to cease and the late autumnal sun to sparkle like a diamond in every leaded window pane. Then, when he reaches the harbour and stands on the quayside, dreaming of all the countries that the ships will carry him to, he hears, from behind him, the raucous braying:

'Pennyless Peder! Polemicus! Ludvig Lupus!'

And the ugly brawl begins. There are five of them, led by the despicable Slamberg, and fists lash out at him from all angles. A nasty blow to his neck, a punch in the stomach, and when he's down in the mud he gets four kicks in the kidneys. The pain leaves him gasping, but even when he gets a heavy blow above the eye from a stick, he refuses to cry. The flow of blood blurs his vision. And they've got him in the kneecap. It hurts so badly that he feels he can swivel it right round. He lies there for a long time, aware of the screeching of the gulls out over the fjord.

Night has begun to fall when he finally manages to stand upright, his body pierced with a thousand needles, his face smeared with caked blood, and he achingly tries to find the way to the parade ground, which he will struggle across and then easily make his way home to Nørre Tranders where he won't quite know what to tell his brothers and sisters, let alone his father who has entered his second week of huddling in a dark corner, brooding over his shattered dream of getting back on his feet again financially by making a handsome profit on a consignment of Edam cheeses. Once more the family are faced with the prospect of surviving a winter with nothing to sustain them apart from the most meagre diet, fuel for only one stove out of three and on top of this privation the sanctimonious, self-righteous recriminations of the grand-father with the long-stemmed pipe out there in Aaby vicarage, in whose opinion everything in this world is regulated by a mechanism that works like a Swiss clock and is called 'just desserts'. If Pennyless Peder tells them about the assault, Frederik Christian, his younger brother, will gloat until he collapses with the hiccups, Henriette Rudolphine and Birgitte Marie will pucker their lips, his father will work up a fit of rage over the torn trousers and his mother will spend the rest of the day piteously sobbing, hiding her face in her hands. The delights of Mariendal.

A woman walks towards him. As she draws closer, he sees that she must be well into her thirties. She has deepset, yellowish green, greenish yellow eyes, a ring in one ear, hair swept back, as though hastily combed with splayed fingers, and the dress which she wears under the shoddy, unbuttoned raincoat looks tattered. As they draw closer and closer, he gets a strident whiff of attar of roses, and she suddenly walks round him, with palms turned outwards and head tilted to one side, lasciviously surveying him from head to toe:

'But, my boy, what happened to you?'

She takes him by the hand. She tells him she lives in a small sidestreet near the workhouse, and asks him to take no notice of the dreadful mess in her home and just step outside and wait on the doorstep if a visitor arrives, because these visits don't last all that long in this part of town. And it seems that the pains are all gone, that he can once more draw himself up straight when she plunges a hand deep into his trouser pocket, gives his hand an affectionate squeeze, pulls out a handkerchief and stoops and wets it in a puddle. She pats and dabs and wipes the blood off his face, and now he can really see how beautiful she is. Her very slight accent is enough to tell him that she is certainly not a native of Aalborg, nor even of Denmark, but may very well hail from some Romany tribe, or from deep down in the forests of Poland, or she may stem from Wendic stock and Svantevit.

He does not care that his family are waiting for him, postponing dinner, those miserable dumplings, the lumpy gruel and the brackish water from the well. When the woman gives him a friendly prod between the shoulder-blades as they reach her front door — just a single step above street level, the paint peeling and faded, a pinkish picture of Jesus above the lintel — he enters a world of enchantment that takes his breath away; the double bed littered with cushions in every colour of the rainbow; the table in the middle of the room with the crimson tablecloth and a vase of nearly jet black roses and a casket that is transformed into a jewel box made of the finest burnished silver, packed to the brim with precious stones and hearts of pure gold. The wreath of roses over the bed becomes a solid chain of diamonds from Peru, all the cushions are now covered with gold brocade, and her dresses, hanging on nails driven into the wall at random points around the room are evening gowns from the court of the Sun King. Her Persian perfumes on the bedside table, the unguents from Egypt; powder puffs from Paris, the shoes under the bed, lined up in a row, all gilded in pure gold, and her dolls on the window sill all smile at him, radiating a blend of desire and love, as though delighted that he, Peder Ludvig, is now to be initiated in this temple. It is as though never again will there be a recurrence of what happened a couple of years ago when he was sitting in the vicarage with Herr Kjølstrup's housekeeper shelling peas, when he suddenly had an attack of dizziness and she drew him down on top of her as he fell, giggling so loud that his mother came from the pastor's study and screamed with rage at what she called her 'disgusting discovery', thus surrounding him with coldness and loathing.

The woman from the Wendic forests with the yellowish green eyes is standing right behind him, holding him by the hips, and he turns round when he has finished washing himself at her handbasin which is made of richly grained Ferrara marble and shaped like a swan, with golden faucets which release a cascade of clear, sparkling Nile water. He kisses her. He has regained all his strength. He is elegantly dressed in the latest fashions from Strøget in Copenhagen. Then he lifts her up, still with his lips pressed against hers, and carries her over to the cushions, and as Saint Budolfi's clock strikes the full hour she helps him undress her.

And this time his mother will not come in and start caterwauling about his disgusting intentions, so that years from now she can denounce him to the girl he is then in love with, and has been for many years — a love affair that culminated on a summer's evening when the girl kissed him gently on the cheek, while, shaking with anxiety, he took her by the hand and asked her if she would deign to accept a poem he had written to her. She softly replied that she would cherish it forever and a day, keeping it in a small heart-shaped mother-of-pearl box bound with a silken ribbon. Then gaily, naiad-like, she danced across the meadow that shimmered with the evening dew, clutching the poem in her pale hand, into the evening mist, only to declare their relationship, their affair, to be finished two months later, at the promptings of his mother. Shortly afterwards she was formally engaged to another man, and he, Peder Ludvig, ever the perfect gentleman, had felt constrained to offer her his congratulations. When she saw him walking past the living room window, she dashed out, flung herself around his neck and cried until the tears ran down her cheeks and mingled with his, and gave him the first kiss he'd ever had, the kiss he had been yearning for. But the engagement had deprived her of all her virginal lustre, and that same evening, when he was introduced, over a cup of cocoa, to her ten years older, blotchy-faced, oddly tongue-tied lover, he suffered all the pangs of jealousy. All the time he kept seeing her sitting on her lover's knee, kissing him, caressing him, dressed in his imaginings as she is now, in dappled Flanders linen, emanating a spirit of celebration and triumph. If only he could succeed in making a cuckold of that landed nonentity, already an object of derision in his green huntsman's uniform, the laced-up boots and Bavarian hat! But the couple soon left the district, leaving him to his misery in Mariendal, with his lachrymose mother, repository of all virtue, the saintly, even 'virginal' Georgine Sofie Magdalene Kanneworff Møller, with the wrinkled hands, the closely pared nails, with eyes perpetually downcast through fear of incurring the wrath of her husband when yet another tortuously contrived business scheme went wrong.

If his mother only knew what cards she has dealt him, how she has virtually packed his trunk, booked his passage! Now there is nothing to restrain him, here in this temple. Now he is about to reap the reward for all the punishment she has inflicted on him. No more languishing in the oblivion of leaden sleep. He kisses the woman's breasts while firmly seizing her by the thighs. Soon he finds himself kissing her belly, the navel, the inner thigh, and his nostrils quiver with delight. Feminine fragrance — no, this is what a woman *smells* like, and with his tongue he finds her sex. The golden cushions, the gushing Nile water, the perfumes of Persia, the dolls — they have all leapt out of Oehlenschläger's *Aladdin*, and as he spreads the woman's legs and strikes, with the darting tip of his tongue, a strange, jutting, resilient spot just above the entrance, the portal to this bower of fragrance, this smell of woman, making her quiver in ecstasy, as though he has between his lips a sort of snail that writhes and swells and fills the harder he licks, he thinks of all the times Oehlenschläger has driven him wild with excitement. He raises his head. The flames lick upwards from the Aladdin's lamp, as though drawing on some magical force hidden in the oil; Odin's magnetic sceptre makes the room vibrate, suspended between light and darkness, force and matter, life and death. Suddenly the room is peopled with Hakon and Baldur and Mjølner and Thor. Then comes line after line from the man who is the Danish Goethe, Schiller and Shakespeare, the Greek, Roman and Edda poet, the Christian troubador; simultaneously embodied in the one and the same being, his hero, his unattainable ideal, who over twenty-five years ago set Copenhagen ablaze, while Aalborg still languishes in the obscurity of the last century. Line after line sounds in his ears, to the accompaniment of a clangorous blare of 'The Golden Horns':

. . . ablaze, ferocious and untamed, Udgaardloke's crimson locks, and the solitary eye casts its greenish, narrow, sidelong gaze. . .'

And the same unearthly voice, accompanied by the same golden horns:

Through din and quake and thunder
God Thor in copper strode
With Mjølner on his shoulder
Nor faltering spirit show'd
Nor was Loke encumbr'd,
Light of heel advancing
With black locks abundant
Gainst gleam of mail flowing

'What on earth are you raving about?' the woman asks, clinging to the hair on the back of his neck, as the nectar is poured into golden goblets, and the incense smoulders, and the heathens gambol before Svantevit in the Rügen moonlight. And he feels that he will never escape from the nectarine valley of her thighs and the black downy hair that goes all the way up to the navel, and reaches down to her inner thighs.

'*Quiet!*' he shouts. 'What bliss! — What tinge of rosy dawn on yon bleak and barren horizon! Oh, what bliss! — What scintillating rays to banish the gloom of night, to invigorate the flagging spirit!'

The woman is softly weeping:

'Why do you carry on like that?'

He thinks she is weeping with sheer joy as she sits up in the bed with a jerk and runs splayed fingers through her hair. He rolls round onto his stomach and presses his face down into the bedspread, and every single strand of gold exudes the rich fragrance of her body. He keeps on pressing, down into the mattress, into the darkness, until he sees the sparks fly and he is carried away to the Paris of Napoleon, and he is strolling along the banks of the Seine with Oehlenschläger who is overcome with grief upon hearing of the bombardment of Copenhagen and the loss of the fleet, but who with one manly effort that fills his handsome face with new hope composes *Palnatoke*, which rises verse after verse against the stifling plague of the day. The woman is still crying in short, nervous sobs, but a while later she lies down beside him, but with her face in line with his feet which she now seizes with both hands and frenetically rubs against her forehead. She moves back. She rolls him over onto his back, grabbing his balls as she fiercely gobbles his member. And now it is no longer the fragrant mattress that makes the sparks fly before his eyes. Now everything is vibrant and shimmering like the luminous vault above Børglum Kloster on a clear frosty night. He feels that he too is about to burst into tears, overcome by this unknown bliss.

She shakes him roughly:

'You mustn't say that sort of thing!'

'But it's a poem!'

Her whole body shudders and she sits at the edge of the bed: 'I don't *understand* it. I just don't *understand*. . .'

He sits up and wriggles his way to the edge of the bed. He takes her hand and plants small kisses in the tiny valleys between her knuckles. He kisses the back of her hand, all the way out to her fingertips. He is eager to teach her all about Adam Oehlenschläger. To read aloud to her, quietly, page after page. To explain all about the metre, calmly, line after line. To gaze into her eyes confidently, while he translates the difficult words and tells her who all the gods are. Nordic gods, gods of the North. Not that worn-eaten tree-stump Svantevit, but Baldur whom no arrow can wound, the North, as it once was, home of free women and doughty men. And this verse, so

subtly veiled, can't she hear the music?: '*Gently lulled by th'
soft airs of summer's eve, I sank into the meadow's flower-decked
arms. . .*'.

'No, you mustn't!' she shrieks.

And she lashes out at him. At first he thinks it's just for fun,
but soon her rage takes possession of her, and she hits him
with every object within reach; a shoe, a shoehorn, a
candlestick. But it's not her blows that hurt him. It's the
transformation of the room. Over there, where her expensive
evening gowns hung in stately array, there's nothing but rags
and tatters. The handbasin is not a graceful swan executed in
Ferrara marble, but a chipped tureen, and the water in the
rusty bowl on the floor is muddy, because it also serves as her
chamber pot. The wallpaper is tattered, the roses ashen-hued,
the dolls hang in the window, eye-sockets vacantly gaping.
And the woman is old and nearly toothless, the woman lying
on the bed, hammering the bug-ridden mattress with the
crude brass candlestick in a fit of impotent rage. He averts his
eyes as she dresses. For Peder Ludvig Møller she will forever
exude the perfumes of Arabia, forever beckon with greenish
yellow eyes. Again he feels as though his clothes are from the
most expensive tailor's in Copenhagen, and he crosses the
floor, stoops, gently lifts her right foot and softly kisses it on
the arched instep. He places a rag rug over her trembling
body.

'Are you leaving?'

'Only to hasten my return to you, my love,' he replies.

'Liar. . .'

He leans over her and whispers, right into her ear:

*Against dappled pane thrusting,
Green bough by deep roots fed;
With rich abundance bursting,
Of cherries ripe and red.*

'Now that *was* a pretty poem,' she whispers in sad and
puzzled admiration.

She hides her face behind her hands as he softly moves to
the door and lets himself out to the autumnal balm of
Aalborg's moonlit streets.

In his fetid imagination the houses have all been reinforced with triple fortifications and buttresses, to withstand the fury of any storm. The cellars bulge with stocks of victuals that will be allowed to rot rather than fill the bellies of Aalborg's needy. Barrels of pickled herring, saddles of venison, row after row of game bird, neatly hooked to the sagging beams. And towering padlocked cupboards filled with bottles of the finest burgundy that no one will drink. Nothing short of the most cunningly devised military strategem could ever threaten these fortresses with their impenetrable oak portals and the empty, empty windows. And the unspeakable custodians, who spend their days snatching life away from the less fortunate and less deserving, are now slumbering, with their chins resting on their chests, snoring away, with heaving potbellies and sagging jowls, and the women all have blisters on their blue-veined feet, and the overbred lapdogs, stretched out in front of the still glowing stove, scratch themselves.

The better houses, which his mother always speaks of in a dazed rapture and his father in inchoate rage, fuelled by his own abysmal sense of failure. Not a single beautiful house, Møller convinces himself, as he heads for the parade ground. Cheek by jowl, these unlovely edifices, squatting there in the moonlight, dismally trying to resemble Antwerp or Lübeck where elegantly dressed citizens graciously greet each other. He lets out a laugh, so highpitched that he himself is frightened, because it sounds like the howling of a wolf. Rounding the next corner he lets out another laugh, this time bellowing, and he continues to bellow as the hairs on the back of his neck begin to stand on end and he hears the counterwailing of the overbred dogs from the impregnable houses that fail to realize that he, Pennyless Peder, sees through all their sham. This is the tame, grovelling town of Snotty Slamberg and Bully Bock and Runty Rovlund, and it's never going to be anything but just that, dragged down into the mire of *the majority*. Comforted by his vengeful act, he suddenly feels that time races, that the drab present races into the glorious future, and as he strides along the final stretch towards Mariendal and home he knows that soon, very soon, he will get away, leaving it all behind.

And winter comes, and then it's early summer. At school none of his fellow pupils speak to him, but they no longer tease him, as though they realize that the beating was more than he deserved. The teachers are still full of respect for him, because they know how little time Peder Ludvig Møller devotes to his studies while easily retaining his status as the school's most accomplished student. They are preparing for 'Studentereksamen', the diploma of admission to higher seats of learning. And he is so sure of passing with distinction that he can confidently rehearse the *festsang* which Tauber, the headmaster, has commissioned him to write on behalf of the school to mark the return of his Majesty the King and His Royal Highness Prince Christian from their visit to North West Jutland.

Now and then he thinks of the woman from the harbour, but he never sees her again, not even when he drives through her street one sunny afternoon and wonders why the fading, pink-coloured Jesus no longer hangs above her door. He is filled with dire forebodings and momentarily considers going out and buying paints of the richest texture and warmest hues and merrily marching up to paint her door, the door to the most beautiful house in Aalborg, but then a harbour lout bumps into him and, reeking of alcohol and drooling plug tobacco, hisses at him, letting him know in plain words that he can't just stand there with hands in silk-lined pockets and look like he owns the whole bloody world.

'Clear off! — and that means now!'

Towards the end of June 1832, his agonies are over, and he is tempted to believe that it is solely in his honour that all Aalborg is ablaze with flags and bunting. An enormous throng has assembled to line the banks of the fjord and wave at the King and the Crown Prince as they sail out from Sundby, acknowledging the enthusiasm of their subjects from the gleaming deck of the royal yacht which is escorted, from a respectable distance, by a vast fleet of less magnificent vessels. The occasion is marked by further ostentation the same evening — a stately convoy of pleasure craft in the fjord, led by four torch-lit boats, followed by another gaily decked craft for the brass band. The bank of the fjord is also brightly illuminated by a string of flickering torches. Across the rippling water, Sundby glows in joyous celebration and the giant bonfire in the Sankt Hans Hills sends flames high into the darkening sky. The stately procession is now and then illuminated by a bluish-tinged flash of light, and the whole panoply is best surveyed from the palace bridge which is bedecked with beech branches, flowers and Chinese lanterns, and the best vantage point of all on the bridge is precisely that now occupied by Peder Ludvig Møller with the wind in his hair and an odd feeling that up to this very moment all that has happened is a matter of total and sublime indifference.

When it gets a bit chilly, he wends his way back to the palace yard of Aalborghus, where all his fellow pupils have assembled under the stern supervision of their teachers, to receive the King and the Crown Prince. And the sole author of every syllable of the song commissioned by the headmaster, the song which will be published in full in tomorrow's *Aalborg Stiftstidende*, is P.L. Møller. And soon the words and the notes rise in the evening air, all the disciples singing in harmonious unison, led by Kaarsberg, Testrup, Rovlund, Brix and Slamberg:

> *Great monarch hear our simple lay,*
> *Our plea we raise!*
> *With favour, benign father, pray*
> *cast thy gaze 'pon this array,*
> *thy subjects blending voices gay*
> *in paeans of praise.*

Headmaster Tauber fusses with his buttonhole and nods at the young laureate. The teachers look at him with frank admiration, and when the rendition is complete his fellow pupils send Slamberg over to express their appreciation — now that it doesn't matter one iota. Peder Ludvig Møller has left.

three

'So you *too* are a writer?'

The question is barbed, and P.L. Møller, student of theology, feels that this is an encroachment on his secret territory, or, even worse, that the strings of his harp have just been broken.

He has abandoned his medical studies, although a skeleton still looms grotesquely in a corner of his room in Regensen, that royal hall of residence built in Copenhagen nearly two centuries ago and now charitably accommodating P.L. Møller in compliance with a ponderously phrased request of Professor Tauber. The inverted skull is mockingly made to serve as a candlestick, artfully placed on a stack of medical tomes which have so far remained unsold. Theology has long since lost all its allure, but he sticks to it because, despite the drudgery and the stultification, it can pave the way to a sinecure as an ecclesiastic or tutor. He has mastered Hebrew for his own pleasure so that, whenever the mood seizes him, he can look up a passage in the *Song of Solomon* and be transported to another world, to a land of figs, tender grapes and pomegranates; and the azure Mediterranean gathering to its bosom all the countries that might claim to be truly cultured. Seated at his desk in the reading room of the University library, or the Royal Library, he scrutinizes the ancient texts, and he feels that he can almost *hear* how they spoke in those days — not the mournful, whining passed off as Hebrew, Greek or Latin here at the university where the only language with any stamp of authenticity is that spoken by the peasant students from stormswept Iceland, but a living, vibrant language with a register of light tones when fortune smiles and with sombre cello tones when sorrow prevails, with undertones of deep secrets, of subtle hints when danger is in the air and with gentle sighs of contentment and wellbeing when love, carnal love, makes man and woman cleave in fleshly union.

This is his world. He opens folios ignored by the other louts, from Averroës to lesser known theologians of ancient Greece, often ordering tomes whose leather slip cases show that they had not been opened since the seventeenth century. Toledo, Granada, Valencia. These are his cities. The square, the agora, where Jew and Moslem and Christian engage in the thrust and parry of theological duel, with the King of Spain as the supreme and impartial arbiter. The unbounded vista that had captured the imagination of Rasmus Rask and the other great philologists, mountain slopes clad in eternal snows, with secluded grottoes where the earliest people still dwell, fashioning primitive sounds into the grammatical and syntactical complexities of language, a world that spans all ages and where immortality is the reward of those who persevere. The rest is trivial, especially the tedious daily intrigues conducted at the ridiculous Regensen where complaints against him are constantly registered in the ledger of vilification, today for one infraction, tomorrow for another. And then the daily vying for supremacy among his fellow undergraduates and now this question — 'So you *too* are a writer?' However hard he tries to ignore it, the question gnaws at him, even though he pretends to shrug it off while he turns the world into his own world, thus making Frue Plads the square where he recently stood on marble paving, at the rim of a gushing fountain, studying the visage of Averroës who addressed an assembly of about one hundred worthies, expounding his thoughts on the lack of coherence in the incoherence of *Tahafut al-tahafut*.

But that dry, waspish tone. The piercing blue eyes, staring

at him without a trace of mercy. The lips that suck upon every syllable as though it were a fishbone. A head full of hair in arrogant disarray. Above all, those eyes.

Søren Aabye Kierkegaard, student of theology.

'So you *too* are a writer?'

'Pray, why do you ask?'

'Come come, Møller, a man must know his curs by their yelp.'

'Thus making *me* one of *your* curs?'

'Purely out of interest, Møller, that's why I ask. Surely there's nothing reprehensible in that?'

But reprehensible it is, for this is the question that he has been dying to ask for months, little Søren, who cannot bear to think that anybody might know more than he, now gloating to himself in smug self-satisfaction: '. . . I've got you, Møller, at last I've ferretted out your precious secret, after all the pain of being outshone by you, time and again, at street corner harangues, in the Academic Society, and in Madame Fouchanée's eating house in Vestergade where you arrived in your shabby cloak and conquered the whole clique'. That slight stress on the word, '*too*'. That's what's tormenting the malicious Søren Aabye Kierkegaard, now that he has had an article published in *Kjøbenhavns flyvende Post*, 'In Defence of the Higher Origins of Woman', and has acquired a more confident gait.

'Yes, Kierkegaard, I write *too*, but not, as you do, about woman. I elect to cultivate woman elsewhere — far removed, shall we say, from the murky confines of my . . . *inkwell*.'

'Thereby implying?'

'Oh, no implication at all, my dear Kierkegaard . . . nothing in particular.'

Kierkegaard's eyes, burning with longing for experience. The huge hands, itching to clutch his desk and tear it asunder. The dwarfish, tensed body. Møller has inflicted yet another defeat.

'But do join us, Kierkegaard, should the spirit so move you!'

'At another of those dinners down in Vestergade?'

'*In Defence of the Higher Origins of Post-Prandial Diversions?* Oh, no, obviously the pleasures of the table hold no immediate attraction for either of us. . .'

Møller's most earnest wish is that the girls are all at home, and that he can sneak into the house in Lavendelstraede where they receive gentlemen callers, that the girls will all bestow a welcoming smile upon him, that Jenny will plant a huge, wet kiss on his lips, that Marie will give him a peck on both cheeks, that Johanne-Louise will wrap her arms around his neck and cling to him, that Sussi will take him by the arm and admire the shiny new buttons, while Norway Kate — lacing up a black, high-heeled boot, the foot tantalizingly resting on the arm of a chair, thus allowing a glimpse of her thigh — stares in disapproving puzzlement at his fellow student, Søren Aabye Kierkegaard, student of theology and evinces not even the faintest desire to give the dwarfish Jack-in-the-box with his pretentious cane a peck on the cheek, let alone a kiss on the mouth. And he wishes that he, Peder Ludvig, will then slowly and appreciatively wink at Norway Kate, while the other girls drag him onto the sofa, so that she understands that an arduous task lies ahead, which she undertakes solely as a token of old friendship, of absolute trust.

It's Saturday, and all the girls are dressed in their finest gowns. There are freshly cut flowers that fill the room with the perfume of Provence, and, as though obeying Møller's own stage directions, Norway Kate, more ravishing than ever and with dark invitation flashing in her dark eyes, takes Søren Kierkegaard by the arm, allowing him to carry the dainty silver tray from Harzen on which stands the chilled champagne and two, only two, fluted glasses, and leads him into the holy of holies while Møller himself succumbs to the blandishments of the other four girls, apologizing that due to temporary financial embarrassment he is reluctantly forced to postpone taking his pleasure with Jenny, his favourite, his treasure, whom he smothers in kisses. And he hopes that when the midget Søren has finished he, Møller, will not once more collapse with exhaustion and loathing at having to continue as master of the revels.

But exhaustion wins, confirming his worst fears. Suddenly Kierkegaard comes bouncing out, crimson-faced, hair dishevelled, and places his champagne glass on a sideboard with such crass clumsiness that the slender stem snaps. He turns round, and their eyes meet. Once more Møller relives the barbed interrogation he suffered at Frue Plads, once more his harp is broken, and as he draws Jenny to him, making her snuggle against his shoulder, he knows that it is himself he wants to horsewhip, to lash into a pulp, because he has let himself be swept away from his noble train of thought, let himself be loutishly diverted by some opinionated but unspeakably ordinary student of theology with his 'In Defence of the Higher Origins of Woman' — this plebeian upstart who wouldn't as much as dare sniff at the same exalted female's underwear!

Møller fumes with suppressed rage, struggling for control, but manages sufficient composure to blurt out: 'O, noble Grecian youth! O, blue-eyed favourite of muses less richly endowed! What ill-conceived inquiry hath escaped thine lips?'

And Kierkegaard has vanished, as though swept away by a whirlwind, the cane left behind on the sofa, while Møller turns all the legions of wrath against himself. He laughs, mockingly, persuading the girls to join in the scorn — and feels his loathing grow within him, like some indigestible gruel, while Norway Kate seats herself before a frosted Empire mirror and lets her hair tumble down, covering her face, and relates how the dwarfish Jack-in-the-box had sat gingerly on the edge of her bed and simply *looked* at her as she lay there with outstretched arms, virtually naked, waiting — until he suddenly went amok, in a wild frenzy of kisses that made her believe she was being ravished by a drooling ape, and then, with equal abruptness, leaped up, although now himself virtually naked, hastily dressed and dashed out as though an earthquake were imminent.

Møller is in the slough of despond.

In Gothergade's army drill hall he is initiated, along with all the others smiled upon by the relevant muses, into the martial arts. He comes to regard this period as the most excruciatingly boring he has spent in Copenhagen, and he vainly hopes to be granted an exemption from service. Partly as a gesture of defiance, he is reluctant to acquire the regulation uniform, and for the three weeks of induction he trudges along the streets wearing the shabby cloak from his days of tutelage in Aalborg, almost strangled by the musket so awkwardly slung over his shoulder. The only escape from the tedium is the hour and a half of rest, during which the reluctant warriors huddle round the table in the mess where he develops a particular weakness for those sugar-dusted delights, the pastries from the baker's in Møntergade. The drill routines for the platoon to which Møller has been assigned are the least rigorous of all, and he soon assumes the rank of anarchist-in-chief. He seduces his comrades-in-arms to open insubordination: when commanded to order arms, all present arms; when barked at to march straight ahead, they disperse in an unseemly jumble; when ordered to halt, they all charge bravely forward, plunging bared bayonets into the wall. The slightest opportunity of rebellion is a call to arms, and the rafters of drill hall ring with his mocking laughter when he has succeeded in creating total confusion, which often reaches fever pitch infecting adjoining platoons.

Then his stint in his majesty's service is at an end, and it's back to Regensen and bouts of drinking with Lynnerup and Ploug and Pedersen and Trap and Tøxen and Sylow and Visby and Walther and Bøjesen and all the others who always have one complaint or another indelibly lodged against him in the huge ledger, complaints that are unexpected, unwarranted. It may be a complaint about his nocturnal fits of laughter that shatter all sleep, laughter that pours out of him when he lies there, wide awake, prevented from sleep by the countless cups of coffee, staring at the faintly illuminated

window until, in a flash, it seems that everything is turned
upside down and inside out: that the outer wall of the
neighbouring house now faces inwards, while Regensen's
outer wall is papered in a floral pattern and richly hung with
deep-toned oil paintings, prints and silhouettographs; that
the clouds are falling down out of the sky and racing along
Store Kannikestraede while Regensen's copper roof floats
upwards and into the sky; and that the last nighttime
stragglers are walking on their hands so that the gentlemen
lose their tophats and the ladies' skirts trail along the
cobblestones, revealing their long, full creamy-white thighs.
And if it's not his laughter that incurs their wrath, it's his
heavily veiled sarcasm when he has wounded Lynnerup or
Ploug or Pedersen or one of the others with utterances whose
deeper meaning reveals itself to the victim only hours later. Or
it may be all the times he has been guilty of pinching sugar,
tea, coffee or bread and butter when once again the pittance
from Aalborg fails to arrive, when his application for a grant
has again been rejected and he suffers agonizing pangs of
hunger. And despite this grossly offensive behaviour he's the
one whose opinions and skills are solicited when they're trying
to organize a fancy dress ball or to devise a list of new works to
be added to the library. Come on now, Møller, you're so well
informed! Say something! Set the town on *fire*, Møller!

He is infinitely contemptuous of this uncouth student life,
with unrewarding outings to debate issues of spiritual and
temporal import — out to Frederiksberg and back to
Rosenborg, and from Det Nordiske Museum all the way out to
Christianshavn and back again. No manly duelling, as in
Germany, no *Gemütlichkeit*, no public spirit. Instead of free
flights of poetic fancy, vapid witticisms and a pledge-bound
brotherhood whose sole ritual consists of nobly lending a
small sum to a student in need, as long as that student is
anybody but the needy P.L. Møller. And in the drawer of his
desk: a stack of unpublished poems and articles, all returned
with rejection slips by editors he has approached, often with
the desperation of a grovelling beggar.

'So you are a writer *too*?' He might as well stuff the whole

Møller canon into the corner stove where his poems would at least do some good. When doubt rears its ugly head, it's not like a pang of conscience or a passing dizzy spell. It pervades every fibre of his body, courses like a feverish tremor under his skin, and if he has at the same time been starving for a week or more, the only confidante left is the night. Not the night spent in bed, on sheets wet with sperm, nor the night spent at the desk when the reigning chaos mocks him, as though the books were trying to tell him: don't bother yourself with all this, for the secret of the printed word will never be yours! As though the glue pot were trying to tell him: ha, ha! drink me now that your belly is empty! As though the scissors are whispering to him: snip-snap, snip-snap, you'll *never ever* cut yourself free!

But this night is the Copenhagen night. It understands him. He drapes his cloak over his shoulders and briefly considers his appearance; his socks are unwashed, his shoes full of holes, his trousers shabby and unpressed; no tailor is willing to extend him credit. He has no qualms about sneaking out. He can no longer seriously concern himself with the complaints ledger, whose pages seem to have been ripped out and stuffed deep down his throat, and he contemptuously slams his own door and later the massive outer door. Outside the clouds are still racing along Kannikestraede, and he is suffused with strength and renewed courage as he catches a whiff of the breeze that sweeps in from the harbour, redolent of seaweed and salt from the sound and of fresh pine needles from the endless Swedish forests where the free wolf people howl at the full moon. Now he is at ease, masterful P.L. Møller, firmly in control, at ease with his own body, with glands, sinews, muscles and cells, and by walking, always walking, he gradually escapes from his hunger; he is sweating all over, and he sees everything, hears everything, from Oehlenschläger, who is propped up in his huge bed with the embroidered counter pane and pillows in a torment of doubt and frustration because inspiration will not return, to the mice scuttling behind the woodwork of every house that he passes and the rats in the sewers and down in the harbour and the worms pushing their way through the earth in a relentless quest to undermine every foundation.

And he dreams of an entirely new literature, a new *novel*, written with such force that the shop signboards leap out of the text and hit the reader in the neck, the mice gnaw their way through the pages and every chapter has its rats, but at random intervals, so that they can surprise the reader, sticking out their snouts and biting his fingers till they bleed. Everything is to be recorded in this novel, the rainswept cobblestones he's walking on which mirror the universe, the cats scurrying up the treetrunks, the horses chafing against their bridles in the stables and the cries of the night watchman, and not just his odd rhymes, but his appearance too, down to the tiniest stubble of his moustache and every scrap of memory, right from that night in the previous century, in some humble cottage in some distant rural parish when he was ejected with a scream of terror from his mother's womb. And all the girls are to be there, ladies of quality and the lavender lovelies from Lavendelstraede; those who lie with twisted lace handkerchiefs weeping because of love unre-quited; and the ladies of the night, denizens of the houses of pleasure, with Jenny the tiger lily and forget-me-not Sussi and buttercup Johanne-Louise and Marie, the marguerite and Norway Kate, the musk rose, the most beautiful of all. And the smell of their armpits and their sex and their perfumes and soaps, the sounds as they slowly undress and as the comb with a crisp magnetic crackle moves steadily through their hair. . .

Pleasure and joy must have their place, but also the despair that spreads its blight like old sperm in the sheets. The rumbling bellyaches of professors, the Sunday typesetters when they have to work overtime, brains bent on cogitation, desks gathering dust, the draught under the roof of Frue Kirke, the howling of the wind and the thousands of secret, hidden worlds behind the world in Det Kongelige Bibliotek and the university library. He contains and encompasses all this, and he could write with both hands, dipping into pots of ink, on walls and on rooftops, he would write it all down as he walks and walks and listens to his heartbeat pounding, and a while later he sees himself emerging from Klosterstraede and crossing his own path, wearing the same cloak casually slung over his shoulders, the same holed shoes, the same unwashed socks, with the same shabby trousers and dishevelled hair.

And he follows his own footsteps, and if it had been snowing, he would step into his own footprints, the holes of his shoes landing on the blotches he left there a moment ago. And now he turns and looks back at himself. His lips reveal the jagged teeth, poised as though ready to bite, and in the night his eyes have a yellowish gleam:

'Catch me and put me in your novel!'

He begins to run, in desperate pursuit, reaching out when for an instant he imagines that he can clutch at his own back. Janus is the name — Janus who can look forward and backward at the same time.

'Wait!' he shouts, and already he sees the first page of the novel where Janus wakes up one morning in Regensen, in effervescent mood, gets up, dons the most elegant apparel and goes out to enjoy Copenhagen's brilliant sunshine.

'What's happening? Tell me!' — he shouts and runs still faster after himself, but once more he's alone. Dawn is about to break over Gammel Strand where the fishwives have their stalls. He catches sight of himself, reflected in a window pane, unshaven, loutish. All his strength deserts him and, while Copenhagen wakens, he trudges listlessly to the university without worrying about all the indignant passers-by he nearly bumps into. When he enters the theology reading room, the first students are already seated, poring over treatises on dogmatics. He moves from shelf to shelf, like a somnambulist, choosing volume after volume, stacking them one by one on a table, forming a stack that will soon reach the ceiling. None of the others takes any notice of his odd behaviour until he suddenly pulls out the bottom book so that the whole stack tumbles down, spilling over the table onto the floor with a deafening crash. And now he is no longer himself, but Janus with the gleaming yellowish eyes that see through everything, and with teeth ready to bite. And he just sticks his hands into his pockets and walks out and slowly heads for Regensen, kicks in the front door, climbs up to his room and flings himself, face down, onto the bed.

Deep within there is a voice telling him that he must regenerate himself, and that this can be done only if he leaves the city and rents a room in a rural vicarage and completes his studies in six months.

From the window of his room in the vicarage, through a clearing in the wood, he can see Lake Esrum and, beyond the lake, on to Nødebo. For the past two months he has got up every morning at eight o'clock. He is making rapid progress with his studies, and before lunch or late in the afternoon he wanders along the shore of the lake on the constant lookout for the animals half-hidden in the foliage and behind the trees, or he sits on a gnarled log out among the rushes and lights up his pipe. Now and then a wild duck flies past, almost brushing his head. The place abounds with life, and the mist assumes strange shapes on the surface of the lake. He has never felt such peace.

> *Retain, Lord, alone Thy Heavenly realm,*
> *If I may but retain my Esrum!*

. . . he says, aloud, and he walks slowly home to his meal and to the pastor and his wife and to his beautiful, blind daughter. None of these three utters a word as the food is taken; the pastor looks steadfastly at his plate, while scratching his flowing, uncombed beard. If soup is served, the pastor has already slurped it down before the ladling ceremony is complete. If saddle of venison is served, he demands a portion twice as big as anyone else's. The only dish served up with any sense of egality is the turgid mass of Swedish meatballs which he does not especially favour. Now and then he looks up at the ceiling, clears his throat and appears to be addressing himself to some matter that has been neglected or forgotten. His wife is as pale as asparagus, but she is always attentive when Møller talks of Copenhagen, and the daughter, who otherwise just sits there staring vacantly into space with her milky-white vacant pupils, can enter the proceedings with sudden, shattering peals of laughter, as though she lived exclusively in a world of her own where people play leapfrog and dance around the maypole. This is how mealtimes are observed at the vicarage, and hardly has the last hunk of cheese been consumed before the pastor, with a jerk, pushes his chair back and rushes to the confines of his study. The weeks pass, and soon Møller has covered half of the required syllabus in the perpetual chill of the attic guest room. And day after day he looks forward, with a sense of growing rapture, to his stroll along the shores of Lake Esrum.

One morning the pastor slides a little note under his door, reminding him, in plain language, that he has failed to pay the stipulated quarterly rent. Møller knows that the money will arrive, if not from his impecunious father then from the vicarage in Aaby, especially now that his ecclesiastical grandfather is pleased that graduation is only a matter of months away, and he goes down to inform the pastor. But the pastor demands instant settlement of amounts outstanding. The terms of their agreement must be duly observed, otherwise Møller must leave. He gives him twelve hours.

'But I . . . you. . .' Møller stammers.

'But me this or but me that,' the pastor replies and buries himself in his Sunday sermon. 'Buts have never put food on any man's table!'

The following morning, when the money again fails to arrive from Aaby or Aalborg, Møller makes his departure. He has stuffed his textbooks into a knapsack. All day and all night he wanders around the lake in a state of dejection and confusion. From time to time he gives vent to a horrendous bellow of despair. At one point he is so hungry that he hurls himself to the ground and chews his way through a tuft of grass. He smells cow-dung but he continues to tug at the stubborn grass with his teeth and keeps on munching. He looks up, and there is the church. He stands up, seized by a violent urge to walk right up to it, to tear it apart, brick by brick, seized by a manic urge to hurl the bricks one after the other into the depths of the now placid Lake Esrum. In the distance he hears the blare of hunting horns and the baying of hounds. The sun begins to shine again, everywhere the fog is lifting, except over the lake where it has now taken on the shape of a fairy palace that glides gently over the waves, rises briefly and then settles over him, round him, as he reaches the shore of Lake Esrum, exhausted, to let his body sink against the yielding rushes.

The water seeps into his clothes, down into his boots. He cradles his forehead in his right arm, and his mother has come back to him. He is suffused with life and love, but when he tries to approach his mother, she steps back and upbraids him for not always having been like this. Then he feels once more that since he was first tarnished all has been lost, he feels that where the slightest scratch has been inflicted there can be no healing. He turns round, softly, and he recognizes this feeling as one of acknowledgement rather than sorrow. Beside him huddles the pastor's half-grown daughter, blind, weak and sickly. She belongs to him. Against her he has never sinned, and he loves her more than anything else in the whole wide world. All the others regard her as silly, but to him she is everything. She looks at him with her vacant milky-white pupils, with that strange smile that sick children wear, the smile that often appears to bring childhood back to the faces of the old. He speaks to her and she becomes happy. And now he begins to tell her things that children are told, without sticking to any subject, just letting the words tell of pretty things.

He places himself close up against her while the blare of the hunting horn gets nearer and nearer, and she goes on looking at him, just looking, without ever uttering a single word.

four

Copenhagen, Athens of the North! Oh, yes. But with no resurrected Lord Byron from Cephalonia and his club foot and his menagerie of ten horses, eight huge hounds, five cats, an eagle, a crow, a falcon, a goose. And his horde of demons and his women. Within its ramparts there is no place for such poetic, half mad drunkenness between the sea and the mountain for everything in Copenhagen conspires to stifle this beautiful night in sleep, as if no one has ever heard the lines:

> *Most glorious Night!*
> *Thou were not sent for slumber! let me be*
> *a sharer in thy fierce and far delight —*

Pauvre Louis — for as such P.L. Møller signs himself for a period — has long since realized that life in the capital which had fed his dreams and yearnings only ten years ago in Aalborg, has dwindled into little blocks of respectable houses. He depicts it in detail in *Arena*, the 'polemical-aesthetic' journal he founded in 1843. He takes an impish delight in aptly choosing the word that will inflict the deepest wound on this narrow bourgeois soul, which, like the dear families who gather round their tables in the Deer Park form one single faultless tribe. This quasi-official cabal, he reports in *Arena*, conducts its regular business in Copenhagen's coffee houses and at private tea parties, where some of its members regurgitate tired anecdotes and outmoded witticisms, with one old crony passing the snuff, while another, with an expression of profound gravity, polishes his spectacles. Within these safe confines everybody knows everybody else and literature is criticized *en famille*; over an innocuous game of dominoes trivial items of news are exchanged and characters are assassinated. And nobody escapes.

And of course it is not in the least surprising to find the writers of the day at their leisure at these gatherings, and all fear the rapier barbs of *Pauvre Louis*, failed student of theology, erstwhile resident of Regensen and author of a volume of euphonious *Lyrical Poems* (whose slightly excessive euphonious euphony evokes less rapture in him now that he has recovered from the heady days of his literary debut, although he is still delighted with the Latin typefaces which he himself chose) and of *A History of the Art of Printing* (with spicy digressions all the way south to distant Algeria, to Egypt and to the remoteness of Coptic Abyssinia, a work of over two hundred pages, published by 'The Society for the Proper Use of the Right to Print' and printed on a high-speed press at Bianco Luno's printing works). And he is the winner of further laurels, the University's gold medal for his entry, 'Has good taste and appreciation of poetry in France improved or deteriorated in recent years?' (Improved, of course!) 'And for what reason?' (La France!) For a year he was editor of *Nordisk Maanedsskrift*, a monthly journal in which he endeavoured to introduce Rasmus Rask's use of Danish art terms, had a spell as literary critic for *Berlingske Tidende*, the national daily, and is now sole editor of the dreaded *Arena*.

Pauvre Louis has an encyclopaedic knowledge of contemporary Danish writing, and he often ends up in a violent controversy with authors when he employs expressions such as 'insipid, waffling gibberish'. Having read his invective aloud to himself in a booming voice, audible far beyond the bounds of his tiny rented room, his humble ground floor room at Nørregade number forty-six, bouncing with glee in his chair, he describes how in the old days literature was produced by men dressed in rags and sold for a pittance, barely enough to buy a bottle of snaps, whereas today it is produced by sleek, fastidiously attired men, not for a measly rigsdaler, but for *diners, soirées* — and *smiles. Pauvre Louis*'s attacks become more and more vehement: whenever one of Copenhagen's literary luminaries scribbles a line or utters a syllable — according to *Arena* — he can spend the next month in triumph, as the various members of those family table coteries shower him with expressions of gratitude, paeons of praise and entreaties to write a sequel, to enlarge the canon, and as there are certain risks involved in declaring a man to be nothing less than a genius, prudence demands the exercise of a seemly measure of reserve. The code of behaviour urges the scribbler to have himself frequently hailed as a *poet*, to have himself described as a *poet*, to have himself styled and addressed as *poet*.

And woe unto him who dares criticize the *poet* for squandering his talents or for wittingly plagiarizing foreign antecedents. Like a latter-day Abraham, the *poet* musters his minions — and he may very well have three hundred and eighteen at his beck and call — and marches righteously forth to flush out and destroy the presumptuous foolhardy critic. A secret police force is formed, the bloodhounds are sent sniffing in all directions. When the dossier is complete, due procedure is set in motion for a hearing on criminal charges, while rumours are spread about the 'evil character' of the bounder, the 'depravity of his way of life', and pernicious accusations are hurled at him, of having penned the most scurrilous anonymous articles. And for months and months he is not allowed a peaceful stroll down Strøget or through Vestergade without exposure to extreme harassment:

'Well, Møller, that malicious piece in Georg Carstensen's *Nye Intelligensblade* — that was your hand, wasn't it?'

'Indeed?'

'There you are, so you admit it?'

'Certainly not, by no means!'

'Come, come, Møller! Of course you're the author — who on earth else would put a shabby *nom de plume* to such revolting rubbish! Besides, I have it from the most impeccable sources.'

'May I repeat: I am *not* the author. Not that what *you* choose to think bothers me in the least!'

'There it is again, Møller — you've just admitted it!'

'Balderdash! You now maintain that I've ad. . .'

'Of course you have, Møller. And now I can inform one and all that the author himself has confessed!'

The Emperor of Det Kongelige Teater, writer *and* professor, Johan Ludvig Heiberg, author of *The Philosophy of Philosophy*, upholder of censorship and opponent of both Shakespeare and pleasure gardens in Copenhagen, is not a person but a concept. And even more perplexingly, a concept within a concept within a concept, who incurs the growing wrath of *Pauvre Louis*.

Without even once having raised his visor, without ever having associated with anyone who was not a member of the all-powerful Heiberg cabal, year after year the professor retreats further and further into the arcane world of the spontaneous evolution of ideas, with particular reference to the art of writing, which he himself would rather have practised without any roar of acclaim, without any weeping and gnashing of teeth, and certainly without any trace of mud or rude noise at all hours when the ungainly wagons of the Dutch market gardeners trundle into Copenhagen from nearby insular Amager. The Paris revolution he once applauded has been consigned to oblivion. In the silent solitude of his observatory, as the pages of *Urania*, his yearbook, devoted to aesthetics and philosophy, softly flutter down around him, the professor sorts literature into his own Hegelian trinity; the *lyrical*, the *epic* and the *dramatic*. Avoiding the bent nails and maimed thumbs, and sacrificially depriving himself of the songs of workers, Heiberg fits together the very scaffolding of literature. In the discreet elegance of his apartments in His Majesty's Naval Armoury, he builds layer upon layer, from sturdy oak floor up through the open dome of the observatory, reaching towards stars and galaxies and eternity itself.

Ariadne's magic thread is used to measure with, calipers wear doll's ballet shoes to describe graceful arcs; soundless planes plane away; silken saws are used and pincers and screwdrivers wrought from abstract thought. And all the professor's hired writers smile at one another rapturously, as the scaffolding grows higher and higher from the *lyrical* to the *epic* to the *dramatic*, while sub-scaffoldings along which some of the auxiliaries bear the *ode* aloft towards the *elegy*, from which a highly polished spiral staircase leads upwards to the *idyll*, while other scribes wheel *romance*, up towards the *epic* which is then hoisted via an intricate system of pulleys and cogwheels up towards the *novel*. Some of the builder-scribes totter along the plankwork, wearing hoops, with boxes of nails and rulers jutting out of their overall pockets, wondering which direction to take in their journey from *drama* to *tragedy* and thence to *comedy*, while the good professor, clad in a flowing crimson kimono — and precisely at the predetermined junction in the scaffolding from which drama has found the path to tragedy and comedy and from which low comedy, via a well-honed plank has made its way to high comedy and thence, via a steep ladder, to universal comedy — has found *his* way upwards, from the prepenultimate step to the penultimate to the ultimate peak, where the steps leave *opera* and *melodrama* in the mists below and ascend to the vantage point of vantage points, the good professor's own *vaudeville*.

This mammoth scaffolding has attracted the willing services of every writer in Copenhagen with any hope of advancement from triad to triad. Decked out in their best Sunday suits they have arrived at the base of the professor's monument, bearing their works, which they hope to have hung at the tip of one of the triads, so that when they awake from a brief and untroubled noontime nap, the sacred muse will be present to prod them upwards to the next triad. The whole scaffolding and all its substations and promontories are bedecked with manuscripts, swaying gently in the late afternoon breeze: first draft and bound folio side by side, a towering monument to the written word, visible to the naked eye from all parts of His Majesty's capital. There hangs a rhapsody, complete and personally approved by Johan

Ludvig Heiberg, writer *and* professor to boot. There hangs a *singspiel*, in three acts, inspired by the Tyrolean tradition. And there is a novelette on the struggle of the spirit against substance. And the writers painstakingly dust their pages, using sand to remove the last traces of ink blots, while the initiated, those seated closest to the professor's feet, recite passage after passage, inaudibly. Kisses vainly planted without lips on the insubstantial air.

But now and then a writer falls all the way down, through the ribs of the scaffolding, ending in a crumpled heap on the floor, just as Oehlenschläger did when his new play — and now his earlier play too which had earned the unstinting admiration of the then younger professor — suffered banishment from the grand triad, the *dramatic*, to a lesser triad, the *lyrical*. For the good professor is less than pleased with some details of Oehlenschläger's plays. *And* with their structure. *And* with their execution. Steen Steensen Blicher has experienced similar difficulty before being invited to join the ranks of authors of the high novel, he must first demonstrate his aptitude for the low *fairytale*, the genre in which Hans Christian Andersen may have qualified for admission. But still only 'may have': Andersen has much to learn, according to the professor.

With arms interlinked, Oehlenschläger and Blicher and Andersen make a stumbling, shameful exit from the Royal Naval Armoury, and in Copenhagen there is no other critic to pick them up, to bandage their wounds and to restore their courage. That is, no other critic apart from the 'self-appointed' *Pauvre Louis* in his garret, first in Stormgade, then in Kronprinsessegade, then in Store Kongensgade, and now in Nørregade forty-six, littered with stacks of paper and books, on the desk, on the floor, at the foot of the bed, on the bedside table, on the window sill and on every rickety secondhand chair. And on the tiled stove his indispensable coffee, kept hot in the dented tin coffeepot, all day and all night — when he is not lured from his work by the omnipresent demons — *Pauvre Louis* composes translation after translation and article after article, while he dreams of an entirely new way of writing, no longer thinking of the novel he conceived that night when he slammed the gate of Regensen behind him, but criticism. Literary criticism.

The good criticism, the *new* criticism: bold enough to introduce common sense and to consider the single work as an independent entity; never letting itself be led by the airy abstractions of charlatans to grossly distorted conclusions; no longer to subject a writer to the horrors of a torture chamber as a prerequisite for advancement in the system, that is if it truly is a writer who can survive without being addressed in public as one: criticism with a simple injunction to see with one's own eyes, to hear with one's own ears. The literature of any age, writes *Pauvre Louis* in *Arena*, is at the same time a glance backward and a mirror in which the future is reflected. And turning his vitriolic attack on the Royal Naval Armoury: it is futile to lay down any laws of beauty for poetry, insofar as poetry itself, the art of literary composition, even in its earliest infancy, before the power of words brought heaven down to earth, had already dictated these laws. *The mysterious union* of form and content, of thought and expression — that is the union *Pauvre Louis* seeks to inspire in his new work, provisionally entitled *The Danish Tone*, a compendium of the essence of Denmark for which he incessantly jots down notes whether sitting or walking. Suddenly, while crossing mud-bespattered Knippelsbro, he stops in midstride to scribble a few words about its wooden railing, totally indifferent as to whether he gets pushed in the back or yelled at. In restaurants he gets a sudden urge to push the plates to one side, oblivious of his surroundings, of the boring discourse with one of Copenhagen's cigar-chewing literary editors, as he forces himself to remember his most scathing phrases.

The venom of his attacks on the literary poseurs is more than amply matched by the warmth that surges through him when, as critic or as contributor to the instructive almanacs of the day or to *Dansk Pantheon*, he writes about those whom he regards with affection, from Holberg and Wessel, whose works he makes available to a broader readership, taking **pains** to produce an illustrated edition, to Aarestrup,

Kaalund, Christian Winther and on to Oehlenschläger, Blicher and Andersen.

He writes of Oehlenschläger:

'Oehlenschläger's most distinctive merit is that of simplicity . . . confidence in his conviction that the essentially human factor will never fail to exert its effect when it is presented with the sure touch of the artist. All who wish to do so may repeat *ad nauseam* the over-inflated coterie-propagated drivel: Oehlenschläger has outlived himself, his genius has faded. . .'

And of Blicher:

'For centuries people have been tramping the moors of Jutland, gazing at the dunes, listening to the North Sea, passing the old manor houses and the brown, woodclad hills, without ever giving them a thought, while ream upon ream of verse gets written about the natural beauty of Funen and Sealand and the other islands . . . Steen Steensen Blicher has wrought poetry out of Jutland, out of its scenic beauty and the character of its inhabitants.'

And of Hans Christian Andersen:

'The only real writer among us to have emerged from the rank and file of the people.'

And of 'The Red Shoes':

'The brightest jewel in the crown of fairytale literature.'

The Danish Tone. Møller hears it. It is not French, nor German, nor English, but something entirely different. It is capable of being grasped by all those who have not wreaked havoc in their souls by aping foreign writers. Chateaubriand, Goethe, Byron — they can never be Danish, and how perfectly ridiculous they seem with their Copenhagen nightcaps, disguised as writers intent on climbing Heiberg's literary scaffolding at the Royal Naval Armoury, hiding under pseudonyms like Ploug and Sivertsen and Heen and Huldgaard and Jens Peter Quill-pen or whatever they now choose to call themselves, names that slip off the tongue like axle grease.

The Danish tone reaches its apogee at the end of 'The Red

Shoes,' when the church 'comes home' to little Karen. It is in
Blicher's pathos, like a whiff of the purple heather on the
moorlands and the intoxicating tang of the North Sea, Peder
Ludvig Møller's own native Jutland with muddy roads and
Sunday outings to Børgum Kloster and Sandelsbjerg and the
little wood at Skeelslund with Hr Kjølstrup, his ecclesiastical
uncle's sexton, endlessly tapping the lid of his tobacco tin. The
Danish tone is the fleecy sky above Limfjord, or the North
Sealand mist that rises like a fairy palace above the unruffled
surface of Lake Esrum as the dawn breaks. It is the slightest
motion of the rushes, but also the sound of hunting horns and
boisterous guffaws, the eternal *ho-ho-ho* from the bustling
courtyards of the rich merchant houses. It is the thud-thud of
clogs on worn earth floor and the sound of bulls as they break
chains and uproot the hedges, but also of pale, blind girls who
lie in bed and smile as though transported to another world.

The Danish Tone. Is literature vital for a nation like
Denmark, so tiny, so surrounded by adversaries, so corroded
from within by killjoy scruples? Møller gets it all down on a
new scrap of paper stained with coffee — or is it Madam
Fouchanée's famous chicken soup? Isn't literature in a sense a
treasure twice sacred, because it embodies visible evidence of
a society vibrant with life and which deserves to live? Ah, yes.
If a new generation of writers would only have the courage
and fantasy to raise this nation from the dead, bringing it back
to life, raising every single blade of grass, ruffling every tuft of
every meadow, grabbing clouds in flight, riding the waves of
the tree-fringed lakes, entering the houses, sitting down to
meals with peasants and Copenhageners, listening to the
variety of their dialects.

There is a difference between the speech of Lolland and that
of adjacent Falster, even down to a simple 'no'. And Møn,
forgotten island of ancient royal warhorses, of Fanefjord
church and dolls-castle Liselund; Møn, with all its chalky
white ghosts dancing on the shores of the Baltic — how do
they speak there? How do the isolated inhabitants of
stormswept Fanø greet one another? Why are Holbaek people
so tightlipped? And if you write down the speech of Skagen's

fishermen, how will it read? How will it sound when read aloud in Nyboder inside Copenhagen? Surely different from the expressions Møller has already picked up when he went there after nightfall to listen to the sailors and their children: 'I will only marry someone I have an *appetite* for.' Or '*Gottes Donner*. I will go out and throw some fireworks under the Hawker's chair, so I will.'

The Danish Tone, as Møller hears it, is the Danish of the 'Skovsers' — fishermen and fishwives from Skovshoved, a morning's drive or an afternoon's sailing from Copenhagen — of 'Christianhavnere', the traders and artisans who captivate Møller with their peculiarities of speech. It is the Danish spoken by the lowest orders and it is the Danish of Pauline, who speaks and writes only with difficulty when she visits him twice a week, coming straight from the factory. He teaches her how to spell and yet cannot help thinking how beautiful it sounds when she hands him the sheet on which he has asked her to put down the first thing that comes into her mind and writes it as a letter to him with a little heart neatly drawn between every two words and begins 'To my only deerest' and goes on to say how much 'she wud like to have a littel boy the spitin imidge of him who is to be batised and chrissend Ludwig Ollsen and he is to be the pritiest most bewteeful boy in the hole wid worl and evry evnin he wil sit on hur lap in thier littel hom wher he will rite all his buks.' And Møller gives her a hug, lifts her up and sits her down on the desk and doesn't feel in the least like correcting her language. For a brief moment he forgets the vow he made to himself: to break off all connection with her before long because day by day her dependence grows. She is convinced that they are going to be married when the beech trees burst into bloom, whereas the only thing he has ever had in mind since first meeting her one autumn evening on the embankment is an uncomplicated flirtation.

'Tell me you luv me, Møller!' And she runs her fingers through her thick brown hair.

'Spell it first!'

'Y-o-u-l-u-v-m-e!'

'Another try!' It galls him to realize that the tendency to play schoolmaster lies so deeply rooted in him, and springs so easily to the surface when she hangs her head and the soft, round cheeks are suffused in a blush of crimson and her hands are entwined in shame, dug deeply into her lap. She is on the verge of tears.

'Pauline?' — a now mellowing, apologetic Møller.

'Yes . . .'

'Say something. . .'

'I l-u-v. . .'

'And I love *you* too!'

And she leaps down from the desk and cheerfully humming an idle tune begins to pack his books now that he is to fold his tent and move yet again, this time to the outer reaches of Store Kongensgade, to number two hundred and seventy-one, just above the most popular snaps distillery in town. She handles each volume as though it were made of the most fragile china, and now and then she thumbs the pages and declares that one day he will no longer have to feel ashamed of her when she has worked her way through his entire library, at least all the works written in Danish. And he doesn't know what to reply, especially when she tells him how much all the girls at the factory appreciated his articles in the newspaper on 'The Incorporation of Women in Culture.' The article in which he describes the horrors of all the diseases that strike at women, and destroy their youth; heart spasms and rickets . . . outbreaks of rashes and hysteria and toothache and feet that refuse to grow and — Pauline giggles — the article where he writes about those confounded corsets that all the doctors disapprove of, adding that women might simply collapse into a heap or be cut in two once freed from them.

'Oh, do read it to me, Møller, you have such a beautiful voice when you read your own words!'

And there is no way of refusing her. He has to go and find the articles among all the mess and he knows the bits she likes best. She's already sitting on his bed with legs crossed, cheek cradled in the palm of her hand. And he reads aloud:

'Just take one look at these young girls who already seem to

have lost half their bloom, take a look at those cheeks, those
eyes sunk in black-rimmed hollows. . .'

And now she begins to laugh because she knows the next bit
by heart.

'. . . and that flat chest. . . And yet a well-rounded bosom is
one of woman's greatest treasures, just as it is one of the surest
signs of good health.'

'In that case *I'm* healthy, Møller, isn't that so? And clean!
I'm always clean, I am so, just like you say in the article it's so
important to be. . .'

And she asks him to let her have the article so that she can
read those lines again, just those lines. Tracing the words with
her forefinger she begins to read, in a brave staccato, nodding
in pleased recognition and staring at him in unabashed
wonderment. The time of the big move comes, and Pauline
helps him most of the day, installing him in the new garret
above the snaps still. He no longer bothers about what he's
going to do with her in the future when they're finished, now
that the books have been arranged in a new, inspiring
sequence on the rough planks he has hammered together, a
new coffeepot which Pauline gave him as a house-warming
present stands proudly in the window sill and reams of fresh
paper from the stationer's in Vimmelskaftet are stacked on the
desk, waiting for Møller's muse, for Møller's ink. And they go
to bed together, and afterwards, as usual, he can't fall asleep
although Pauline falls into a profound slumber, her brown
hair flowing over the pillow. It occurs to him that he should
launch a new journal, bigger and better than *Arena*. Or a
yearbook with illustrations for every poem and every
novelette, illustrations which will surpass in beauty anything
yet seen in Copenhagen.

And the names Andersen and Blicher will loom large in its
table of contents.

Over in Aalborg, his mother lives on in her widow's weeds,
following his father's death some years ago, having elected not
to divide the deceased's estate among the bereaved, but to

remain in sole control of the family fortune. Møller doesn't receive a penny from her, nor from the vicarage in Aaby, now that he has long since abandoned theology. But Hans Christian Andersen — *Der dänische Dichter*, as he now refers to himself in a letter to Møller, following the recognition he has won throughout Europe — and Steen Steensen Blicher both promise to produce pieces for the yearbook. He is no longer in any doubt about the title; it is to be called *Gaea*. Oehlenschläger recommends him as a teacher of literature at Copenhagen's institutes of higher learning, more and more articles are accepted for publication in the newspapers, and at night, whether he is alone or whether Pauline sleeps with him, he translates Heinrich Heine's poems as though they had flowed from his own pen:

> *Years come and go, yellow leaves wither;*
> *I would fain once more behold my mother.*
> *Twelve years have passed of trials dire,*
> *Far deeper now my loss and soul's desire.*

His own last twelve years. His own desire to see his mother again. His own fears and trials and tribulations. His own sense of loss, the yearnings and desires of his own soul. And once more he trudges through the streets of nighttime Copenhagen, as the melting snowflakes fall. There is a stillness all round, and Heine's *Ein Wintermärchen* strikes a chord deep within him.

Pauvre Louis knows that something has to happen, and happen soon. He has just reached the age of thirty.

five

'Get it *down*. That's what the pen's for!'

'I'm quite aware of that, but has one the *right*?'

'Has one the damned right . . . of course one has the damned right!'

'No call for another fit of rage, Møller.'

'*Shema israel!* Or whatever it is you lot say. You're going to regret it, Goldschmidt, if you don't get it down.'

'But will they take it in the right spirit?'

'Will who take it in the right spirit?'

'The Christian community.'

'My dear Goldschmidt, are you suffering from the illusion that we're meant to be coddled and cossetted? The right spirit! What a grovelling sentiment to issue from the mouth of a revolutionary. Rubbish!'

'That may very well be so, Møller, but it's a mighty leap for me. . .'

'Then go ahead and *leap*, and break your neck if that's the price . . . or become a writer. I'm no lily-livered youth, Goldschmidt.'

'True enough, I will admit, when it comes to expressing your own opinions.'

'You're utterly contemptible, Golle. . . You have a great novel in you, the kind of novel that's never been written in this country! And you can safely forget all that drivel about the Christians, the *Kemech*, as you call them. They simply don't exist.'

'What do you mean, Møller? No Christians?'

'Well, at the very most an occasional Syrian Catholic, a Copt on a column, a fasting Moscovite in Constantinople, but not a single specimen, believe me, up here in this North Germanic penal settlement for self-besmirching schoolmasters and ecclesiastics incapable of raising anything where it might do some good. And you just stand there and talk about Christians! The *Ohs*'ers — isn't that what you call them? Carrion flesh! Men of evil! *Beheimo*'s! Nitwits! Send the whole despicable lot of them scurrying into some Levantine wilderness to the blast of trumpets and the clang of cymbals! Tell them that Jesus is your Jesus, a peripatetic rabbi with a weakness for Egyptian magic! Bring the walls of Jericho crashing down on their puny heads, bury them in marble slabs from the ruins of Copenhagen Cathedral! Out with your *rage*, Goldschmidt, let's hear the sound of your fury, and this time not from Goldschmidt the newspaper publisher, but from Goldschmidt the writer, doing what a writer's supposed to do!'

'You make it all sound nearly like me.'

'*Hramor*, fool! I *am* you, Goldschmidt, at this very moment, here in the small hours, sitting at your hearth. And I call upon all the gods I bow to, whoever they may be, to bear witness. You will write the novel just as you told it here and now, ablaze with conviction and passion — at least in those chapters you went through tonight — when at last you cast off those shackles . . . *Shema israel!*'

The young host had intended to travel to Lolland to attend to some family matters and had invited Møller to accompany him. But when they reached the pier the sailing was cancelled — a broken camshaft — and Møller had accompanied Goldschmidt to his home instead. The conversation had commenced when Møller, throwing wide his arms, asked:

'Is this the full extent of your princely abode?'

'Yes, why do you ask?'

'Because on the occasion of an earlier visit it occurred to me that you might have a concealed room.'

'What are you getting at, Møller?'

'I was simply referring to the room, sire, from which you emerge to assail people with the pertinent but awkward question: what do I hope to achieve by moving among you?'

Seven hours later the title was forged — seven hours spent in mental anguish and feverish pacing. *An Outcast, A Stranger, Ahasverus, Not of their Kind, Not Kith and Kin, And yet not a true Dane* — that night they had produced enough titles to paper the wall, until, suddenly, Møller began to pace to and fro, bombarded Goldschmidt with questions, became silent, tugged at the back of his neck to restore the flow of life to his nearly-numbed brain and massaged his temples until he saw sparks fly, oblivious of the fug of stale tobacco smoke and the flat wine and the tepid coffee, his stomach rumbling in protest at the paucity of the fare stocked in Goldschmidt's larder — a crust of stale bread.

'*Heureka!* I have your title!'

'You mean. . .'

'It is etched in furrows of pain in every feature of your face, it is branded on your forehead, it smoulders, like *Eimo*, like angst, in your eyes! You *yourself* are the title!'

'You mean something like *I, Meïr Aron Goldschmidt?*'

'. . .!'

'Don't tantalize me like that, Møller. I'm all ears.'

'*A Jew!*'

And Goldschmidt flung himself on the sofa, collapsing in a fit of laughter, wan from the relief of it all, and then perched himself at the edge, slapping his thighs:

'That was a real *Masaul!*'

'I've never heard that one before.'

'A real *fluke, stroke of good luck.*'

'Then let us enter the solemn covenant, Goldschmidt, you and I!'

'Yes, now I know it. You are my friend! Now I shall write that novel!'

'You're wrong. I'm nobody's friend. Remember that we

duel. For the sake of the beauty of literature we duel, and if it should happen that one day one of us pricks the other, let it be *in majorem literaturae gloriam!*'

For a year or more P.L. Møller has been living with *A Jew*. He has already written every single page of the book in his head as he waits for Goldschmidt's final result. He can see — down to the last comma — how the opening and closing sentence of every chapter should be phrased, where reflective passages should be inserted and where action sequences should take over from the more leisurely descriptions, and when dialogue should pave the way for peaks of drama. He knows many expressions used by Jews in the Levant. He pores over the tattered pages of an erudite compendium on Judaism, published in Leipzig by a secret society, 'The Tears of Ishmael', so that he now knows how Jacob, Goldschmidt's main character, must have felt, right from his earliest childhood, when the Christian world turned its prejudiced back and averted its hypocritical gaze rather than meet the burning eyes of the impoverished, wandering Polish Jews when they visited a home to narrate their stories about the child Moses who held fire above gold and burnt his fingers; or about the battle cry raised by the sons of Jacob, a cry powerful enough to dethrone a mighty monarch; or about the white-shrouded death that spreads dismay among the tiny community, night after night.

Møller grows up with Jacob in the childhood home so scorned and so despised by all, where the uncle is forever going amok. He shares Jacob's pain when he is jilted by the gentile girl he met on the slopes of Skamlingsbanken, just as Goldschmidt himself was jilted in his most muted chapter, and he accompanies Jacob when he moves to Paris and signs on for service in the Franco-Algerian war and later takes up arms again to join in Poland's struggle for freedom against the Russians — and suffers yet another rejection, another banishment.

Møller shares the trials and triumphs of the Jacob character most vividly when he swears to wreak revenge on the world of the gentile by kissing the swords of his vanquished arch enemies or when — having interpreted the arcane message of the Tarot — he secretly builds his own *Golem*, the legendary seventh century Jewish figure, the character in the novel that Møller awaits with diabolical glee, rubbing his hands in anticipation: a figure that can be all or nothing, neither man nor woman, imprisoned in a mound of clay and pebbles. It can bring happiness or misery in equal measure to its owner and if only the latter can shove the magic number from the *Kabbalah* into its mouth, he can suddenly move with incredible violence, gifted with powers capable of pulling down anything built by the hand of man, whether it be the University of Copenhagen, or the cathedral, or Professor Heiberg's scaffolding in the Royal Naval Armoury, or the fortifications of the capital.

And Møller speaks Yiddish to himself, constructing sentences short and long, or electrifying commands to the Golem, and, when he is especially upset at what Goldschmidt tells him, he goes so far as to waken Jenny and Sussi and Norway Kate at Lavendelstraede with shouts of:
'*Shabbas hättest du'n Baunensupp bei mir essen sollen koscher!*'

Or the Jewish joke that appeals to him most:
'*Das letzt' Hemd muss man verkafen um'n Kohtzin zu werren*, you should sell your last shirt to become a rich man.'

A great novel is waiting to be acclaimed by Copenhagen.

It was *The Corsair*, Denmark's most widely read and most feared weekly, with a circulation of three thousand, that brought Peder Ludvig Møller, failed student of theology, wearing a blue tailcoat and light grey trousers, to exert a gentle pressure on Meïr Aron Goldschmidt's bell wire. Møller had just returned from a short stay in Norway where writers had told him that *The Corsair* was so excellent that it deserved to be Norwegian. Both before and after this voyage of reaffirmation he had defended Goldschmidt, especially following the sentence imposed by the High Court for insulting the royal house, although that august house's own tribunal and the city court had both previously acquitted him on the same charges. In *Arena* Møller demonstrated his sympathy for Goldschmidt, narrating the story of his life, from the days when he set South Sealand alight as a mere eighteen-year old by publishing a satirical weekly — *Naestved Ugeblad* — until he received notice of his prison sentence in Sweden, where he was enthusiastically received by rebellious Swedish students. And it was Møller himself who had sailed across the sound to Malmö as bearer of the ill tidings which Goldschmidt had received with monumental calm, simply stating that he would take no steps to avoid incarceration.

Today, just as in his *Naestved* days, when he attacks the abuse of power, lashing out at a bailiff's official, citizens of standing and privilege see red at the mention of the name Goldschmidt. It is a name synonomous with sedition of the worst sort, and now at this first meeting in Goldschmidt's home Møller expects to find a Jacobin with his feet on the table, adding a name or two to his death roll, surrounded by Verginaud, Danton, Hébert, Saint-Just, Merlin de Thionville and Camille Desmoulins enthusiastically executing all adversaries like dolls in toy guillotines, while the troupe of touring Parisian actors, *Les Montagnards*, so grossly misrepresented by Copenhagen newspapers as 'The Mountain Singers', line up on either side of the steps, all the way up to the platform, waving their tricolours and singing the forbidden *Marseillaise*, waiting with bated breath for the editor himself to announce the hour appointed for the execution of Christian the Eighth on The Common.

Instead Møller found a pale and lonely Meïr Aron Goldschmidt, with a steel-nibbed pen, his sole weapon, lying on his desk.

'Are you here under constraint?' Goldschmidt asked, interrupting his proof-reading and looking up with his dark, intelligent eyes.

'What an irrational question to put. . . No, the purpose of my visit is to extend to you filial and collegial greetings from young Norway.'

'In recognition of my serious articles on political issues?'

'No, in recognition of *The Corsair*'s aesthetic distinction.'

And Møller knew instantly that the man sitting opposite him was by no stretch of the imagination a writer with political convictions, let alone a bloodthirsty Jacobin, but a downy youth who was hardly aware of the consequences of his actions — five years his junior, obsessed with the dream of having his name writ large in the annals of literature. The way Goldschmidt swept the proofs aside, leaped to his feet, and rapturously shoved the chair back with his heel; the way he marched over to the stove, opened a hatch to puff at the dull coals, slammed it shut and then gently caressed the enamelled carousel of circus horses decorating the top of the stove. And the way he turned round, brushed a bit of fluff from his shoulder and looked straight at Møller, who had remained immobile throughout the exchange.

'So they like my way of writing up there, do they? My "comical compositions"?' he asked, speaking so softly as to quell any suggestion of revolution. 'And you . . . I mean yourself?'

'Your article on that New Year's spot of bother, I read it at my barber's,' Møller replied. 'It was an appropriate accompaniment to the lukewarm lathering and nearly appropriate for the sloppy bit of work with the blunt razor, right up to the final part of the ritual when I nearly incurred a gash in my snout because I performed an acrobatic leap in the barber's chair on account of what I'm now about to tell you . . . on account of your article which, towards the very end, also performs an acrobatic *leap* right into the sphere of what you term "comical composition".'

'Praise the Lord!' Goldschmidt whispered.

'Retain some sense of proportion! I haven't come to sing the *Te Deum*!'

'Then why have you come?'

'To brandish my pen along with your own!'

And Møller knew that all it needed now was just one little step more — a single deft move — and he could write whatever he liked in *The Corsair*. They met again a few weeks later, and that single step proved to be a remark from Møller when Goldschmidt had been speaking of Goethe's *Werther*; he had felt repelled by the ending; he thought that Werther was unworthy of Lotte's love and that Werther had behaved in an ugly and repulsive manner by shooting himself in her presence.

Møller turned in Goldschmidt's doorway, on his way out:

'You're just a child. You've failed to grasp what the book's all about. It's a protest against society. And society is always wrong.'

From that day onwards they were inseparable, attending the first performance of Mozart's *Don Juan* together at The Royal Theatre, together in The Student Union and the Academic Reading Rooms and in the editorial office of *The Corsair* which Goldschmidt, hotly pursued by police spies, was frequently forced to move. For nearly three years now they had been the talk of the town. The dark changeling, the would-be author, the king's worst enemy, with explosives under the bed, but, if a terrorist, certainly not beyond enjoying a saunter down Strøget in his new overcoat from the fashionable Fahrner's, the most expensive tailor's in town; a coat of navy cloth, trimmed with fur and with strings rather than buttons and rich braiding on the chest. And then there was the fairhaired mischiefmaker from Aalborg, the proletarian with mortgages on a score of will-o'-the-wisp castles, the cantankerous profligate rumoured to mark his cards, to seek the company of harlots and smugglers from Holstein, to sell — in deepest stealth — hashish from Morocco potent enough to drive a man mad at the first whiff; rumoured to owe money to all and sundry and to wear garments bought from a pawnbroker with the paltry sums offered against temporary or final surrender of his remaining books — garments which he will soon return to the pawnbroker's mothballs when the pangs of hunger begin to gnaw at the pit of his stomach. What devilish plot is afoot? And all these hacks they take on for a pittance, mere stooges, in the editorial office of their scurrilous rag, conferring titles on them such as 'informateur' and 'pattern designer' and 'decorative painter'? When will the two of them show their true colours and inflame the masses with Parisian exhortations to break down walls and tear up cobblestones and pour slops on the heads of the King's Guard?

What Copenhagen's earthly and spiritual powers fail to grasp is that conditions in the capital are only rarely the subject of discourse between the two. No pastor need fear that his altar will be desecrated, no aristocrat need fear that his windows will be shattered. For they talk about literature, and Møller spends hour after arduous hour zealously trying to remedy his new acquaintance's pitiful ignorance of the subject, with zeal soon deteriorating into peevish irritability. He lists, in order of merit, the hierarchy of French writers, he introduces his apprentice to the latest plays, with a timely reference to *Sakuntala*. . .

'*Sakuntala*, what's that?' Goldschmidt asks.

Møller revels in the irony of his measured reply:

'*Sakuntala* happens to be a serial narrative currently being penned by Herr Pattern Designer Olsen.'

'Amazing! Do tell me what it's all about!'

'*Sakuntala* is a composition, my dear Goldschmidt, a major composition, a drama whose sole distinction is that of not yet having reached the eyes or ears of Denmark's leading exponent of the scathing lampoon. It has so far failed to attract the attention of the distinguished editor of *The Corsair*. It also happens to be an Indian drama, a flower that bloomed in the days of the beatific Lord Vikramaditja. The work is available to initiates — on the shelves of the University Library. Come with me, Goldschmidt, and I shall lead you to the veritable fount of amoral wisdom. And under no circumstances neglect to send me that first draft. You promised to. . .'

'I know, Møller, but the ethical dimension, the *ethical*. . .'

And Møller snarls and mimics Goldschmidt's quirkish speech, the hesitant utterances, the squishy sounds that almost choke every expression — 'democracy' and 'mankind' and 'you must have ideals and be true to them' and 'you must develop your mind until you become an outstanding human being, fit to join the ranks of those who serve the republic and promote progress and contribute to the propagation of divine justice throughout the world'. What on earth has all this to do with *Sakuntala*? And what about the *Bhagavadgita*, that cruel Hindu epic, the work most treasured by young Germans, an epic that teaches lessons of fire and destruction and redemption by the sword alone — mercilessly slaying the enemy, preferably four of them in one foul swoop, cleaving skulls and chopping limbs? *Sakuntala* and democracy! Tantamount to mixing vintage wine with tepid ale! A free constitution, 'government by the people'? Poor Goldschmidt! And then the *Bhagavadgita*! As bad as emptying the spittoon into a flagon of pre-revolution cognac!

And the ridiculous idea of forcing citizens to pay tax 'according to their incomes' and all the other whims that possess Goldschmidt's brain! No, the king's sole mistakes are — Møller gets excited, momentarily forgetting his own sympathy with the opposition — that he has failed to replenish the state coffers by seizing a colony or two, following the excellent example set by the English; that he has failed to display the ferocity of Ivan the Terrible or a Turkish despot; and that he has failed to entertain the public with executions every Saturday morning, or better still, every morning, right at the spot where the monument had been raised to perpetuate the treason and infamy of Corfitz Ulfeldt, mingling afterwards in disguise with the mob, to hear whether the morning's performance has been sufficiently frightening. 'Forget all about the public good!' Møller preaches, as Goldschmidt becomes more and more paralyzed.

'But justice, Møller, haven't you the slightest concern for *justice*?' Goldschmidt enquires, and Møller is forced to admit that nothing interests him less.

'Such sentiments belong to Frederik the Sixth's past,' Goldschmidt adds.

Møller lashes out at a wall with his stick:

'Past, do you say! Then just let me tell you a bit about your future. Yes, your future! Oh yes, you'll get your democracy all right, no doubt about that. . .' And while he momentarily

does not quite know why he is exhausting all that energy on
his disciple while his loathing of his own self wells up again,
loathing of his failure to let things be as they are and to
comport himself like any ordinary pedestrian among other
pedestrians — displaying that convivial manner, casually
nodding to one and all — Møller portrays how the future will
take shape with its much-vaunted democracy. The citizen
may very well come to shake the hand of every other citizen,
but not with warmth and friendship. No, the handshake will
be reduced to a signal: 'So I can rely on you and your vote at
the next committee meeting in the chambers of the city
council.' Every citizen will represent every other citizen.
People will pay their taxes and levies. Life expectancy will be
increased, without expectations, without life. Copenhagen
will dwindle into a miasma of bleak stage settings. Hoist them
up and let them drop. How do you do and goodbye. And we all
walk round one another, look forward to renewing our
acquaintance, don't forget your brolly, and you too are
receiving a decoration on Thursday. No action, no call to
arms, only what are we *now* going to vote about? What colour
to paint the mailboxes? What to put into the sausages? And
newspapers. By all means let us have newspapers, so that we
can all read about one another, reducing one neighbour by
exposing his idiosyncrasies, exalting another with a flattering
headline, a column for every citizen, with his latest domestic
titbits. The good pastor who has his Jesus, a Jesus who will
also wish to cast his vote and sit down alongside the bishops.
No *casus belli*, no vision — only details, details, details. A
sensation: to puff at a feather. A drama in three acts: to rub
your mother's back. An epic: to repair your watch. Dwell
securely in the mind of your fellow citizen, with meeting after
meeting, spending hours working towards the grand climax:
whether the meeting is to be reported on Finnish or Swedish
handmade paper. And no writers, but all over the country
thousands of Royal Danish Literary Practitioners with the
status of civil servants of appropriate rank, who spy on one
another and proudly publish their observations and accompanying exegesis in a slim volume of vapidity at intervals of

ten years — an ode to the potato, the miracle of the carrot, lullaby to a piglet. . .

'May I reiterate my position, my dear Goldschmidt. I'm in *favour* of the death penalty for lack of talent! You may quote me. . .'

And the pangs of hunger come and the words throb like a dull migraine in his temples and at the back of his eyes, and his feet have grown cold, his fingertips are now numb in the wafer-thin gloves and for several days he has had nothing to eat apart from a few coarse biscuits, some cheese and jam. He feels that it is ink and not blood that courses through his veins and he suddenly resorts to the crude device of edging Goldschmidt into a restaurant, demanding dinner on the spot, the choicest items on the menu with the best wines, and Goldschmidt acquiesces while Møller continues to speak, drawing heavily on quotations, dredged up specially for use that evening. He snatches the menu from the waiter's hands and surveys the room. Yes, that's Holst the writer over there, obscured in a cloud of smoke, blatantly pretending to be oblivious of Møller's presence; and that's Ploug the writer, drinking a fulsome toast with a group of national liberals to a future in which academics will rule the roost; and over there sits a third writer, demanding Hungarian goulash instead of his dish of lobscouse. While back in the far corner, bereft of all human company, with his hat and new English cane placed beside him on a chair, sits Victor Eremita, whom Goldschmidt and Møller have often intended to invite to a Greek symposium — Copenhagen's most talented writer (intentionally shielded by *The Corsair*), master of Socratic irony, the writer whose *Either/Or* Møller had regarded as something out of the ordinary when he saw it on display in Reitzel's bookshop, went in and bought a copy and read it cover to cover on the way home to the outer reaches of Store Kongensgade. He found it hard to believe that this was the same writer who as a young student of theology with thirsting eyes had expounded his 'In Defence of the Higher Origins of Woman'. And yet there is still something about Kierkegaard that annoys Møller, possibly — and in particular — the way he used his broken engagement to Regine Olsen in *The Seducer's Diary*, which according to wagging tongues, embodies features and characteristics borrowed by and large from him — *Pauvre Louis*.

Their eyes meet, a shadow passes over Kierkegaard's face. Møller forgets Goldschmidt, forgets his hunger, and he feels that he has turned into a butterfly whose wings are unfeelingly wiped and dusted by huge, gnarled fingers stained with ink up to the knuckles. He is crudely dropped onto the meaningless vastness of the centre page of a hefty tome. And then the abysmal darkness and suffocation as the book is closed with a final slam. Any remaining vestige of life is squeezed out of him. The words he utters are not his words, but abject squeaks that escape — flattened and distorted — through the outer edges of his two-dimensional dungeon. The now malevolent Herr Doktor Kierkegaard creeps into his insides, his fingers, his eyes. The mouth turns into a snout. That recent affectation, the neatly trimmed goatee, jabs spikily into his lap and his ears blush crimson with anxiety about Pauline and Jenny and Sussi and Norway Kate. The malevolent midget has never felt a woman's body, never smelled the secret cusp, never kissed warmly damp armpits or shapely feet — nor will he ever, down all his drab days. He has nothing but himself and his own oversized member that grows and grows every time he seizes it, flinging himself wildly about on the mattress and moaning with desire until release finally comes, making everything slimy as he sinks into the black pit of despair and remorse.

Then Victor Eremita rises, shoving his chair back while studiously averting his gaze from Møller's direction, places the top hat on his head and departs, the cane held forward, downward, like a divining-rod, passing right behind Goldschmidt who has failed to notice him. Møller regains his composure and the eyes he now peers into are Goldschmidt's, and, suddenly brimming at the expectation of the early arrival of the chop and the claret, he launches into a discourse on women. Goldschmidt is still not prepared to reveal whether he has known any women apart from the gentile he met at

Skamlingsbanken, the woman who let him down, but he nevertheless listens attentively — with an occasional quizzical smile — as Møller describes his amorous conquests.

And Møller tells him all about Pauline, the little dandelion that sprouted up from the cracks between the cobblestones, the Pauline he can't bring himself to leave. Not that they ever have any lengthy spiritual conversations on lofty themes. But in bed, yes, my dear Goldschmidt, that's it, *in bed* . . . how does it go in French: '*La femme la plus naïve est la meilleure à opposer à l'homme le plus retors*. . .' His migraine disappears, the chill leaves his body, and as the wine forces the blood to his head he initiates Goldschmidt into his latest adventures at the girls' school where he has been taken on as a temporary teacher.

'A girls' school!' Goldschmidt is ecstatic. 'I've never heard the like of it. Just fancy that! . . . the salivating old wolf preening himself as he sits there admonishing the tender lambs. But surely the very acceptance of a position of trust must in itself impose some measure of self-restraint?'

'By no means! What you call a position of trust I find removes all restraint. I am impartial, like a gardener whose only pleasures are his small flowers.'

Møller intentionally raises his voice so that his words are audible to the surrounding tables. Here he is truly in his element:

'A few of those maidens are really like the buds in May . . . crimson leaf in a sheath of green. There is something frankly wholesome about them, something rare and beautiful, the suggestion of unreleased heat. I see all that is best in woman, folded up, just waiting for the passage of time and the glow of the sun to make that bud spread. Of course, I will agree that most of them are merely green, disgustingly green. Frankly, I'd rather put up with the most depraved boy any day than a woman who fails to bloom. . .'

Møller hesitates for a moment and then resumes the tale:

'Recently, Goldschmidt, we came across a word in a German lesson, in German a totally innocuous word, but when properly uttered in Danish, nothing less than filthy. Now do you think I could get even one of those young madams to pronounce it properly? Not if their virtue depended on it, that's how well brought up they are, even without the benefits of my tutelage. Then I calmly requested one of my little darlings . . . retaining all my magisterial composure . . . to read the word aloud. And she went ahead and pronounced it with such simple innocence, lowered eyelashes concealing her knowledge, and I had an urge to embrace her and shower kisses on her. Which, my dear Goldschmidt, is precisely what I did . . . later, on the way home.'

'Møller?'

'Yes?'

'It occurred to me that something odd came over you — just when we entered this place. Was it an attack of something or other?'

'No, no . . . it was nothing, nothing. . . Come, let's go. And do tell me about your novel. Have you reached my special friend, my *Golem*? And have you wreaked vengeance on the true cruelty of the Old Testament and crushed that gentile viper? *Nebbich*, you miserable wretch!'

When they reach the street, there is a gentle drizzle. The biting Siberian wind has nearly abated, as though at precisely that hour spring has decided to announce its arrival. As they saunter down Vimmelskaftet, Goldschmidt reports that he is making splendid progress with the novel, and asks if Møller will read a few chapters.

'I would appeal to you to take on the sole liability for any folly you may commit, so that you can't come back and lay the blame at my door. You have two possibilities. Your *Jew* can either be as exciting as sparkling champagne or as dull as stale beer.'

'Isn't there something in between the two?'

'Art doesn't know any in-betweens.'

Møller feels ill at ease, feels that mere exchange of words is not enough. Right ahead of them is Gammel Torv's still splashing fountain. He sprints towards it.

'Come on, Goldschmidt! Last one in's a sissy!'

Møller flings himself into the basin and shudders as the chill hits him, but he enjoys it, even getting drenched in the foaming spray — like being engulfed in cold fire. He stands upright, glistening, and raises his arms to embrace the night sky.

'You'll catch pneumonia!' he hears behind him.

'On certain magic nights, my dear Goldschmidt, I'm absolutely invulnerable against slings and arrows and fountains and adders and all the rest of it,' Møller replies, patting his clothes and squirting small jets of water in all directions.

'Nemesis,' Goldschmidt whispers.

'A biblical fig for you and your vile nemesis! Come along, let's raise the curtain on Act Two.'

And Møller walks up the steps to Frue Kirke, opens the huge door, enters through the gloom where he senses the presence of all Thorvaldsen's apostles and Jesus with outstretched arms at the far end of the cathedral. He strides up the aisle with firm, rapid steps, turning only when he has reached the altar. Far down the aisle he can discern Goldschmidt's outline. Instead of freezing after his immersion, Møller feels his limbs glow with cold fire. His skin is taut, vibrant — no arrow can pierce it. He stretches out his arms, like the Jesus on the cross behind him. He emits a roar which makes an echo drum against the walls — an incoherent, meaningless sound in search of a meaning, as though called forth from the fossilized memory of a million years, sounds from the age when the first man discovered the rudiments of language. If only he could find those altar candles he would light them. If only he had a bundle of fireworks, he would make the nave explode in a myriad of dazzling stars. And if only he could push the magic numbers up into his palate, right behind the teeth, he would certainly do so, taking ponderous, measured steps backwards, shoving the walls aside, still stepping backwards into night-time Copenhagen, surrounded by dazzling showers of sparks on all sides.

Goldschmidt is now right in front of him, and he appears to be less than one foot tall.

'Meyer A-a-a-a-aron!' Møller roars, feeling that he can lift the roof off the cathedral with his shoulders.

'Yes?' The sound comes from some place far below him. 'Tell me, are *you* my literary creation, or am *I* yours?'

Towards the end of spring 1846, Møller has read *A Jew* for the third time, and he can only repeat to Goldschmidt his earlier opinion: it's a competent novel, the best Danish book of the recent crop. But Goldschmidt's failure to wreak vengeance tenfold on the gentile girl and her despicable family and — even worse — his failure to introduce the Golem figure can only be regarded as unforgivable. And increasingly so. The pensive Møller sits alone, carefully protected from glare rather than heat by a tilted parasol, at an outdoor table in the Tivoli Gardens. No, he has no reason to retract his assessment. He is exhausted, oddly empty, following a prolonged quarrel with Pauline, which nearly ended in a brawl when she had suddenly vandalized all his bookshelves, flinging books and manuscripts all over the place until, by coincidence if not accident, he was hit in the back of the neck by *A Jew*. She cannot understand why he still refuses to move in with her, permanently, to become man and wife, with ring and the blessings of the church and room in the corner for a cradle.

The Gardens bring about a slight improvement in his mood. He derives quiet pleasure from Georg Carstensen's Copenhagen Summer-Tivoli. Although Møller is hardly inclined to praise Carstensen's paltry efforts as a publisher of trashy magazines and pipe dreams, despite his unstinting admiration of a man who drinks the most expensive wines, smokes the best cigars and wears a new pair of white gloves every day — he feels quite at home here in the glittering greenery, the old artillery range which His Majesty allocated, by means of a royal *privilegium*, to create his pleasure gardens according to Carstensen's whim, in the belief and hope that swings and roundabouts and Chinese lanterns would quench all passion for revolution in the hearts and minds of Copenhageners.

Møller muses, how reminiscent it all is of Carstensen's childhood in Algiers as the son of the Danish consul. Carstensen has always had an African soul, and that — Møller agrees — is precisely what drab Copenhagen needs: lottery-ticket booths, toffee-makers, a fortune teller's tent, sword eaters, the crazy kitchen, water that defies gravity by running up into taps rather than flowing out of them, magic carpets and the Indian rope trick and Aladdin's magic lamp, to be rubbed by all the children, and genii trapped in bottles. The muddy site has been transformed into a replica of the bazaar in Oran or Tangiers, with headless chickens performing weird gyrations, and stealthy pickpockets and hidden entrances to harems and nightlong discussions between Moslem and Jew on the lack of coherence in incoherence. Over there is the mighty giant from the depths of a Ukrainian forest, sticking awls right through his arm. And over there is a stall where you can go fishing for your happiness with bamboo rods and line and hook, and some leave stooped in defeat while others continue ever faithful to lady luck. He sits there with his beer glass, studying the tarot pack gratefully tendered by Goldschmidt in memory of the night Møller hit upon the title for his novel. He spreads the cards out on the table, twenty-two Major Arcana, exactly the number of letters in the Hebraic alphabet. 'Can one *convert* to Judaism?' Møller had asked Goldschmidt one night, and there had been no reply.

Twenty-two Major Arcana, and he feels that not one of them has been dealt to him. Judgement, Death, Hierophant, Devil, The Hanged Man, which card is his? It is as though he has become incapable of movement, as though he is helplessly sinking deeper and deeper into his own self, like an amorphous heap of earth and gravel. He deals the first card in the game — man as the first figure in his own picture book. Aleph, the first letter, based on the human figure, with one hand pointing heavenwards and the other downwards, as though the letter were trying to say: as it is above, so is it below, as it is below, so is it above. And the figure on the card becomes Janus, and Janus looks at him with his yellow eyes and steps out of the card and now sits before him. Janus stands up, with jeering expression and mocking laughter:

'Catch me, *Hramor*! Catch me for *your* novel, nitwit!'

Janus disappears into the bazaar without once turning round. Camels lumber past. The Jews hide in their synagogues, the Arabs will soon burn all in their path while the Christians of England and France prepare for the crusades. The rain suddenly comes tumbling down. The Tarot cards sail on the table in crazy patterns while Møller feels that he is floating, swept away over the edge of the flooded table to become one with the drenched grass and churning mud.

six

When it's not raining in Sorø, which it usually is, the sun shines; the cows graze, the bees buzz, and summer has arrived in the only place in the kingdom where you can find famous men. That is, of course, apart from Copenhagen and Kiel.

This is the place where Saxo Grammaticus wrote his chronicle in the Middle Ages, this was the seat of Holberg's barony, and here dwell some of Denmark's leading men of science and *beaux-esprits* — *lektor* and writer Carsten Hauch, *lektor* and writer Bernhard Severin Ingemann, *lektor* Steenstrup, creator of an epoch in the history of Danish peat, *lektor* Peder Hjort, famous for his twelve paragraphs and *The Danish Child's Friend*, *lektor* Lütken, renowned as a philosopher of the new school — the sceptics ('Where nothing has been established, nothing ought to be said.'), *adjunkt* Paludan-Møller, famous because his brother is a writer, and *rektor* Bojesen, famous for the errors in his Roman history, errors he has refused to remove because they have been drawn to his attention by a Copenhagen professor.

These dignitaries are all on the staff of *Sorø Akademi*, and are regarded in the area as men of such distinction as to merit being addressed as professor, and all, with the exception of the psalmist Ingemann, live in Sorø itself, a town consisting of one main road and a few side streets. Ingemann lives outside the town, as does Bredahl, the impoverished peasant dramatist, who has written a number of rebellious plays in the grand Shakespearean style, and although he has his avid supporters, among them Peder Ludvig Møller, no Copenhagen bookseller is brave enough to send the plays to the printers. Not far from Sorø, in the village of Pedersborg, *pastor* Peter Christian Kierkegaard, Victor Eremita's elder brother, preaches a gospel of fire and brimstone to a packed church.

At the very end of the main street there is a sinister, arched portal, the remains of the monastery, corresponding exactly to the writers' definition of the romantic, because it evokes a feeling without ever satisfying it. And a bit beyond that is the church, with the coats of arms of the steward Peder Hoseøl and the other nobles painted in fresco, the tombstone with Bishop Absalon hewn in life size, and the altarpiece depicting the nativity for which the twelve apostles, according to local rumour, were originally to have been modelled on Sorø's twelve distinguished professors, until each of them in turn declined to lend figure and visage to Judas Iscariot, whereupon twelve peasants were recruited, and the one who had volunteered to sit as model for the traitor who implanted the kiss of death degenerated into all sorts of ungodliness and came to a sorry end. Here in the church the professors have their own pews, beside those of the royal family. And parallel to the church is the new academy building with its famous corridors. Sorø is Denmark's Oxford, and it is to Sorø that P.L. Møller buys a coach ticket on a brilliant day in late September.

Even if half of the literati of Sealand have more than a sneaking suspicion that Møller is one of *The Corsair*'s anonymous contributors, and though the organ continues to wring tears from the angels and mocking laughter from the forces of evil, his reputation as an aesthetician and critic is steadily growing, with the acclaim of the first volume of his annual, *Gaea*. Published by himself, with financial support from The Society for the Advancement of the Sciences of Beauty and Utility and printed at the *Berlingske*'s works in exquisite Gothic type, large for prose pieces, smaller for poetry, it is illustrated with lithographs, stylographs, and wood engravings of pieces produced by the country's leading artists: Jens Juel and Frølich and Marstrand, Skovgaard and Bertel Thorvaldsen. Møller has himself spent days and nights supervising the setting of every single page, with the illustrations winding like arabesques in between the poems so that a garland of apple-blossom kisses a line especially rich in inspiration, and in the printer's shop the typesetters hailed him one night as the only writer in the country who displayed such enthusiasm for their craft, for the *art* of the printer. They had all read his book on the subject, the single copy tattered and dog-eared and stained, and glowed with pride when they reached the chapter on famous book printers in which they could read that one of their very own had been burnt at the stake, the brave Stephen Doletus, back in 1546.

In the company of these typesetters Møller feels a sense of security he has never known before. Even his eternal restlessness seems to have been cured. He absorbs the scene with all his senses, thrilled by the atmosphere of the workshop, fascinated by the gradual emergence of a wood engraving, the hammering and stretching of a sheet of type to the accompaniment of the latest broadsheet ballad, sung with gusto by a young apprentice. The smell of Dutch shag and coarse working clothes, of lead and printer's ink — and then the healthy faces of the printers, happy in their ignorance of the pain so often involved in every page of a manuscript, of the pang of doubt before every nervous dip into the inkwell and the accusing silence when inspiration dries up, the sand flying in the eyes and the white sheet staring triumphantly at the writer, whether he be Oehlenschläger or Blicher or Andersen, all contributors to *Gaea* — Andersen with 'The Elder-Tree Mother', the annual's shining pearl, illustrated with a drawing etched on copper by Frølich himself.

The likes of *Gaea* has never been seen before in Danish.

In Sorø the arrival of P.L. Møller is the occasion of some excitement. The luminaries await the lively brain that continues to challenge Professor Heiberg's position; await the stylist who (never mind what they say about his way of life;

idle gossip, utter rubbish concocted in a town where everyone snoops shamelessly on everyone else) has now shown a sure touch as a poet. And he has a mastery of the not-so-readily accessible essay form practised by Montaigne and the English writers, now that they have had a chance to read an excerpt from his prize-winning entry on French poetry in *Gaea*. This work elicits nods of grave approval in Sorø; that medal, minted from the king's own gold, was certainly deserved, and the Sorø luminaries order banquets to be served in their tiny houses with the neatly trimmed back gardens when they receive the caustic aesthete at the coach stop, when he arrives to commission material for his next annual, to be published early in the new year, 1846.

Møller, encouraged now that he has been awarded a grant which makes it possible for him to eke out an existence and a bit more (Goldschmidt remarked with a snarl that Louis XVI will probably soon receive him in audience at *Sans Souci* palace), muses as he travels in the lumbering, bouncing coach along the country roads, half-blinded by the swirling dust, acknowledging the cheerful waves of peasant girls, . . . who can tell, there might just be a position for *him* in Sorø, in the service of the state, or — a stone causes the coach to bounce suddenly — even at the University of Copenhagen itself, when Oehlenschläger's chair in aesthetics becomes vacant in a few years. Now that would be a goal well worth his new green jacket, impeccably cut and stitched by master tailor Fahrner, his cream-coloured ducks, his boots with the special resilient soles that give a spring to his step, the white gloves and the leather suitcase from London with room for every item in its own enclosed compartment: the silver-backed hairbrush, the nail scissors, the shaving kit, the talc and the scent, pencils and stationery, notepads and traveller's ink, cigars, a pocket chess set and board and the little phial of laudanum drops secretly prepared by his youngest brother, Marenus Laurentin — apprentice since last year in the Vajsenhus pharmacy.

And he thinks of her — Gerda Petrine with the swan neck, *royal* actress, no less, and the short, ruffled hair, the boyish fingers, the soft complexion and the thinnish lips that betray a slight element of bitterness; her long, well rounded thighs, the perfection of her legs and feet and that oblique, downward, almost retiring glance when she smiles, as though she is concerned about something far removed from the words she happens to be saying now. The noble proportions, the chandelier, the high ceiling — everything about her apartment impresses him: not a speck of dust, not a single stray hair from the yelping brindle pup tugging at her skirts. And the tasteful silhouettes on the walls, with a whole stack of as yet unframed, newly commissioned pieces casually awaiting her favour on the window sill, the salmon pink curtains, and his own *Lyrical Poems* resting on a little mahogany table by the sofa when he first visited her in Bredgade, a mere stone's throw from Nyhavn. She momentarily glanced downwards, persuading him to believe that it was just for the joy of looking at the new Grecian-patterned linoleum floor, the latest craze in Copenhagen, rumoured to have been conceived by her ladyship from The Royal Naval Armoury, Johanne Luise Heiberg — to the universal delight of the professor's literary hirelings.

Darkness was about to fall. She lit the oil lamp, produced a bottle of hock from a cupboard richly adorned with motifs from ancient Egypt, apologizing for having had the gross impertinence to write to him, but then she could hardly have restrained herself, for she had always thought highly of all his writings, especially his articles, or rather his *poetry* — she added the abrupt correction with a brief outburst of dark, mocking laughter. And now that she had seen him so often, in the next street when out for a stroll with the puppy at her heels, or at Kongens Nytorv on her way home from the theatre, she simply had to make his acquaintance. Would he try to excuse her indiscretion in writing to him? Behaviour incompatible with her gender and station. And then, without once pausing for breath, she had told him all about her life, since she — a hapless orphan — had toured provincial theatres as a child prodigy, had been adopted by an aunt who also happened to be on the stage, up to the days when she had begun to attract the attention of the critics in a piece by Kotzebue and then on to her debut at The Royal Theatre, as Fanchette in *The Two Grenadiers* — and her subsequent appointment as a permanent member of the ensemble.

He took her gently by the hand after the first glass, and she made no effort to withdraw it. He put his arm around her waist and noted that she was wearing nothing beneath the gown, and he drew her to him and kissed her on the shoulder and at the nape of the neck, and then she said:

'What haste. . .' and he replied:

'My only regret is that we haven't met earlier. . .' and she said:

'Better late than never', and led him to the bedroom. Hours later, when he lay adrift in a profound sleep, she woke him roughly, tugging at him.

'Go!' she shrieked, thumping him on the chest, 'Get out of here!'

He dressed without the faintest notion as to why she was suddenly behaving like this. Had he not made love to her as a woman wants? Had she not writhed and jerked her whole body, sobbing with pleasure, devouring him with kisses before their ardours had reached a climax, before exhaustion and the blissful sleep? For months on end after that she failed to greet him when they met. He often saw her arm in arm with one of Bournonville's young solo dancers, and as they drew nearer and Møller tried to catch her eye, she broke into a gale of wild laughter, whatever the dancer happened to be talking about, or she embraced him and hugged him until the poor youth blushed with the embarrassment of it all. But one morning, when Møller had been working most of the night putting Blicher's novelettes together in the edition that would finally open the eyes of the reading public to the true greatness of the bard of Jutland, he received another missive from her, written in red ink. A note of apology. If only he knew how much she had missed him. But surely he would understand. Would forgive. Her sea of troubles. And down at the theatre where they *whispered* in corners — with Fru Heiberg the worst culprit. Despite her callousness, wouldn't he visit her once more? And he called that same evening, and on the little mahogany table lay a copy of *Gaea*, opened at one of his own poems, 'The last hours of Lord Byron', and the brindle boxer, now fully grown, was firmly leashed to a brass hook in the hall. When she clasped both his hands in hers, she once more glanced obliquely, downwards, at the linoleum floor. He knew that she wore nothing beneath the ankle-length dressing gown, and that night he slept with her, leaving as the faint morning light penetrated the heavy hangings.

He loves her, he loves her not? He doesn't know, but he sees it all before his eyes as the coach lumbers on, now past Ringsted: their life together in a spacious, sunny apartment in Kronprinsessegade. A view over Rosenborg castle. His study with all the books he — as *Pauvre Louis* — has coveted for years, now easily affordable on his professor's salary. Gerda Petrine as hostess. Gerda Petrine when she awakes, stretching languorously so that her breasts flatten out. Gerda Petrine, when she comes home from the theatre, smiling, after another stunning performance, and he has bought her a bouquet or a tasteful nosegay. . . Travel to distant parts — Berlin, Paris. . .

Gerda Petrine Møller. Never! Nonsense! He drives the thought out of his head. And yet . . . he begins to whistle.

And he arrives in Sorø.

Within the next few days he has visited most of the 'professors'; his biggest problem is gluttony. *Lektor* Stenstrup's saddle of venison, *Lektor* Wegener's sagging layer cake, and then Ingemann's mountain of cakes and cascades of cream-topped chocolate. At Carsten Hauch's he is treated to the best crayfish soup he has ever tasted, served with fresh crayfish boiled alive a few minutes before in a huge vat, the whole gargantuan meal served solely for the delectation of the gentlemen by the taciturn Fru Rinna, known in literary circles for her socialist sympathies and as an advocate of total emancipation for women. Yes, of course, she has read Møller's articles on 'The Incorporation of Woman in Culture', she mumbles, adding that, *post prandium*, the gentlemen themselves are to shape the course of the evening's pleasures. Carsten Hauch stomps his wooden leg on the floor, but abandons all moroseness when Møller begins to *interview* (Møller takes a special delight in using the imported term) him about literature. Oehlenschläger? Believe in a man once, believe in him for ever — that's Hauch's comment. Aarestrup? The two concur in their positive opinion. Kierkegaard . . . the philosopher with all the names . . . most recently Hilarius Bookbinder, publisher of *Stages on Life's Way*. Around the oval table all are silent. Then Hauch clears his throat:

'. . . or Peregrinus Proteus, as I call him. Surely he can't possibly expect people with other duties and interests to remember all the outlandish names he puts on those books of his!'

Words that are music to Møller's ears. Words that require a few words of his own. He pushes his plate to one side. He grabs the fork and jabs it fiercely into the damask tablecloth. Regine, poor Regine! Just listen to Søren himself, Søren Bookbinder, Søren Inkpot, Søren Leap-into-print, and Møller quotes from the back of his mind, this is not literature, it's sheer madness. Just listen, and all at the oval table listen: 'Today a year ago. Well!' And Møller works himself into a frenzy, shall we take that last bit again, emphasizing the exquisite, affected, conceited '*Well!*' 'Today a year ago. *Well!*' Then what? 'Then I became engaged. She is truly winsome, but confound the silly maiden; she fails to grasp that I wish both to be engaged and to delve . . . she fails to realize that our betrothal is dialectical. . .' Dia-lect-i-cal, and Møller repeats the word: dialectical, dialectical, dia. . . 'A *dialectical* engagement, I ask you? Isn't there something called common sense, human reason? Very well, now we all know, from Skagen to Lauenborg, that this Victor Eremita or Hilarius Bookbinder or Constantin Constantius or Vigilius Haufniensis regards life as a dissecting room and himself as . . . why doesn't the man come right out with it: as a *cadaver. Well!* I too have become a cadaver, and let it all cease now, Søren, indulge in all the flagellation you like, as long as nobody else gets involved the police won't bother you. But . . .' and the 'professors' listen attentively to Møller who feels that he has never before achieved such mastery, such adroit control of his often suppressed eloquence . . . 'but to trap a fellow human being in your miserable spider's web, to cut him open while he still breathes and feels, or to hack his soul away with blunt scalpel, droplet by droplet, purely in the interests of an *experiment*, to fulfil some dialectical precept, only insects have the legitimate right to do that . . . and probably not legitimate. . .'

'You speak well!' The 'professors' are not beyond giving praise.

'You are certainly moved by the spirit, Møller!' Hauch chimes in.

'It's true enough, he's right,' adds Rinna Hauch, passing through the room to attend to some menial chore.

'Who, Kierkegaard?' Carsten Hauch asks, nervously scratching his wooden leg.

'*Carsten!*'

And Rinna Hauch nods to Møller, and he continues his diatribe against the petulant midget, using words like 'inquisition' and 'mental torture' and Regine . . . yes, after being subjected to one of those ungodly, unhuman sessions it would be quite fitting if she hurled herself off some parapet into the swirling, murky waters, thus providing Kierkegaard with material for another book. No! Søren Leap-into-print should have left that book in his bottom drawer, while he still boasts about addressing his work solely to that 'solitary reader', that 'single one'.

'Are you going to publish your opinion?' Hauch asks.

'You can wager your life on it!'

'I warn you, you're up against Denmark's most brilliant — excuse the term — *dialectician*.'

'Then I fling down the gauntlet!' Møller says defiantly, smiling at Rinna Hauch. And he scoffs another dozen crayfish. The old rage wells up within him, and has not dissipated as he coils up tensely on the narrow bed in the spare room. He turns over onto his back and looks at the moon, and he has an urge to howl at it. Then he drifts into sleep, to dream of Kierkegaard as he struts down Østergade, coming towards him, and this Kierkegaard is a fleshless skeleton. In his capacious pockets Møller carries a vast quantity of raw meat. It oozes blood, down along his thighs and onto his ankles. When the two meet, Kierkegaard nods so that his hat falls off his hairless skull. Møller stoops to pick it up, but Kierkegaard seizes the opportunity to plunge the bony fingers into his pocket and, leaving a trail of blood-dripping meat behind him, he runs along towards Nytorv, with a ghostly clickety-clack as the skeletal feet hit the cobblestones. He next sees him squatting on a rooftop, flinging hunks of the oozing meat down on the pavement. The sky turns red. Møller stands there with Kierkegaard's hat and doesn't know what to do with it, and the blood continues to trickle down his thighs and legs, now in a gushing stream.

The following day he journeys back to Copenhagen, this time in the even rougher comfort of a freight wagon. He has an article ready inside his head, and he is impatient to get back to Store Kongensgade. He hopes that Pauline won't turn up, and he has no intention of seeing Gerda Petrine until he has written the last line. Summer has swollen into early autumn, the storm tears the first leaves from the treetops and now there are no buxom peasant girls to wave as the wagon trundles towards the market. His trousers have become grubby from all the shifting about on the seat beside the driver, but he is no longer worried about the elegance of his attire. He knows that the visit to Sorø has been a success, and that not one of the luminaries will stand in his way.

That same evening he makes a detour, avoiding all the potential traps, on his way back to his garret. He has no wish to meet any of his cronies. He lets himself in. A stale odour of tobacco, old socks and something else he can't quite place — possibly the sweat produced by the soul. He writes. Nobody to disturb him, and he calls the article for *Gaea* 'A visit to Sorø'. He describes his visits to the Academy's teachers, devoting most space to the visit to Hauch, quoting verbatim his own words about Kierkegaard until the last crayfish has been cracked open and he says: 'let us then, gentlemen — *Well!* — move on to a different subject and conclude that Kierkegaard is the example of an author who under other circumstances might have gone far. Now he is in his dotage; an unusually powerful intellect blemished by a sickly imagination.'

Møller is in the mood to do a bit of writing, and he goes on to correct the rough draft of a novelette which has been lying untouched for months, a novelette about two young students who are not yet twenty. He himself is the anonymous narrator, while the main character is the university's worst troublemaker, and when the main character and the narrator have been called up for military service in Gothersgade and later, when they go on a hike to Lake Esrum, he manages to turn every event inside out and upside down. He, the main character, is always in the best of high spirits, is always ready to deliver a scathing remark, and the narrator feels that life without him is as boring as Copenhagen in March. He respects nobody, women adore him, but something, the narrator senses, pains him. Pains Janus.

What dark secret is Janus clinging to? The narrator is simply aware of it, and it is not — as in most novels of the genre — a case of unrequited love. Emptiness perhaps? Maybe the excruciating banality of it all? Maybe this: the ability to predict every situation, the constant absence of surprise, an inability to forget himself once in a while? A sense of sadness derived from what? Childhood? Adolescence? Møller cannot find the answer, and for a moment he is angry with the narrator for not having taken the trouble to probe the depths of his companion's soul. Does it suffice to state that the main character has a worm that gnaws at his breast? And isn't the ending a bit too abrupt when Janus decides to embark upon a new life, rents a room in a vicarage to complete his theology studies — and then early one morning shoots himself because he can't pay the rent? But through several long passages of the book Møller is still in love with his Lake Esrum, full of descriptions of the scenery — the fog that lifts like an illuminated fairy palace, the sound of hunting horns, the dance of the naiads. . .

The novelette is up to *Gaea* standard. Møller is now tired. Then behind him he hears:

'So you thought you could get rid of me just like that?'

He turns round, rubbing his eyes. There stands Janus with the yellow eyes. And the blood oozes from his pockets, dripping down his trouser legs.

The answer comes to him in a flash. Three days before the ushering in of 1846, a week after stacks of the new *Gaea* have been delivered to the booksellers, Frater Taciturnus, Centurion of the Third Division of *Stages on Life's Way* issues a reply. Møller reads *Faedrelandet* in serene peace. He knows that there are many who agree with him in his criticism of Kierkegaard, he has even received a greeting from Regine Olsen who since publication of the book has hardly dared show her face in the streets for fear of ridicule. Ha! ha! So the bashful maiden did not, after all, walk up the aisle wearing a veil, did not marry into the wealth of the Kierkegaard mills where cloth and ideas are spun with the same profound disdain! Life is a bit easier now, but she occasionally relapses into spells of nervous depression which no bleeding can alleviate. Yes, Møller notes with growing satisfaction that Søren has been painstaking in shaping his reply, since his famous irony is now far from Socratic. But, as he reaches the end of the reply, Møller bolts upright in his chair, causing consternation at the tables of the coffeehouse in Gammel Strand.

'Is anything the matter, sir?'

Or:

'Can we be of assistance, sir?'

Møller doesn't reply. Every line now goes straight into him, and he knows that nothing can be done about it. What is at stake is not his career as a writer, but his very bread and butter. At a single stroke the road veers abruptly away from the cul-de-sac that leads to a faculty chair or lectureship, the road ahead is not lined with sheltering trees but is full of jagged stones and gaping holes that no Sorø coach could ever negotiate. '*Ubi spiritus, ibi ecclesia*': the jagged stones are treacherously placed by Brother Taciturnus' own skeletal hand, and Møller knows what is to come. He clears his throat and looks sternly at the other denizens of the coffeehouse, who by now are beginning to stare. He again holds the newspaper up to the dim light, and the words leap off the page into his face: '*Ubi P.L. Møller, ibi*', no, of course not the excellent *Gaea*, but the vulgar *Corsair*. The rest is obvious, can only be an anticlimax. The rapier has been wiped clean at home in Frater Taciturnus' abode at Nytorv, but what about adding a little salt to the open wound for good measure: sentences stating that he, Møller, is a *vagrant*, and that he has discommoded *respectable* men who in *honest* obscurity follow their vocations in *the service of the state*. Clever, clever, Møller thinks . . . clever to the end! In the service of the state! The station in life for which no vagabond is worthy.

Søren Aabye Kierkegaard has a solitary, explicit request: a cessation of the practice of treating him as the only writer not to be lampooned in *The Corsair*, and Møller swears on the honour of his grandmother, Maren Laurentin Kanneworff, to comply with the request. It is no longer a case of article against article, now it is body against body, a duel to the death where all means are fair. And on his way home to Store Kongensgade, Møller repeats the word — *all* — while thinking of Klaestrup, the painter, this tiny, unsuccessful genius, Goldschmidt's Indian ink magician who was rejected at the Academy of Fine Arts by Master Eckersberg and whose antecedents merit only a single measly line in any reputable biographical compendium, utter snob and arch enemy of anyone whose talent matches his ambition. Klaestrup is his black-hooded executioner, gleefully whetting the blade of the guillotine, and for the first issue of the year Møller has commissioned a series of Kierkegaard caricatures as appropriate embellishment for his own satirical articles which he will write either in *The Corsair*'s dingy editorial offices or in the comparative sumptuousness of Lavendelstraede, with Sussi and Jenny and Norway Kate as eager, if unlettered, muses. For the time being Møller has no intention of setting foot in Store Kongensgade: it now seems like a thousand years ago since his fortunes took a turn for the better when he sat down there to write and edit *Gaea*.

Møller calls the first article 'How the Wandering Philosopher found the True Wandering Editor of *The Corsair*,' which is mainly a description of how Taciturnus burst breathless and flushed into the editorial offices of *Faedrelandet* to reveal the true identity of the anonymous editor of the scurrilous *Corsair*. In the next issue the screw is tightened; Kierkegaard is lambasted as a ridiculous philosopher and landowner, but in the third issue Klaestrup's skills add the desired touch of sweet malice, with cartoons of 'Kjerkegaard' astride Regine's back, 'Kjerkegaard' as a preening stork looking askance at a maiden of humble origin because he believes her to be nothing more than a common harlot, and 'Kjerkegaard' as Michael Leonard Taciturnus arrogantly strutting into the jaws of *The Corsair*, convinced of his invulnerability, only to find himself, in the next cartoon, on his arse on the pavement, having been shown the door. And Møller eggs Klaestrup on to more vicious efforts: depict 'Kjerkegaard' with one leg shorter than the other! As a hunchback! Show him with the hat flying off his head and his hair standing on end as though he had just seen the spirit of the universe pass by on horseback! Or draw him as an ineffable jackass on a pedestal from which he bestows his collected works, bound in morocco, to the gaping Danish peasantry! Render him as the conceited, dialectical principle that governs the universe, but as miserly as a Shylock! Draw him! *Kill* him!

With every new issue of *The Corsair* Møller banishes Kierkegaard from the city that the wandering philosopher regards as his own. Kierkegaard has to cede street after street, square after square, to his foe. Victor Eremita no longer haunts Østergade and Vestergade, he no longer engages passers-by in erudite conversation, as though he fears being hit on the forehead by a squishy tomato. And gradually Johannes de Silentio shrinks from appearing in the side streets, Klosterstraede and Mikkel Bryggersgade, where he used to wander in the small hours, addressing himself and his concepts to stray mongrels and Copenhagen's bibulous night owls. Johannes the Seducer, no longer in the guise of P.L. Møller, but as the midget philosopher himself, provokes titters in every coffeehouse, and gales of outright laughter whenever he happens to pass a house of pleasure, essentially Sussi's, Jenny's and Norway Kate's in Lavendelstraede. Constantin Constantius doesn't dare show his proboscis in Gammel Strand, for fear of slipping on the codfish heads flung in his path: and the rumour goes that Johannes Climacus cannot replenish his wardrobe, as his tailor is afraid of offending other clients; Vigilius Haufniensis is held to have come under what amounted to a physical assault as he walked through Kattesundet, and Nicolaus Notabene can no longer stroll along the embankment and go for an ill-balanced slide along the tracks left by the children's sleds, one of his favourite pastimes when he happens to be in an especially good mood. Street by street, door by door, war rages, and *The Corsair* has only to snap its inky fingers to recruit volunteer reinforcements — growing numbers of street boys and drunken sailors who can, with a single crude insult, send Kierkegaard reeling home to his last bastion, the apartment at Nytorv beside the Town Hall. Within its confines Hilarius Bookbinder and Frater Taciturnus cringe behind drawn shutters and bolted doors, like a pair of frightened twins, only rarely visible, peering timidly through a chink in the curtain.

Møller knows it: if Klaestrup is capable of banishing Kierkegaard from the streets, his own articles are capable of keeping the philosopher awake night after sleepless night, and he often reads his material aloud to Jenny and Norway Kate before sending it to the printers. He leans back on their new sofa, purchased with money suddenly lavished upon them by a Turkish diplomat before his recall, and Norway Kate has lit the incense, while Jenny, pale in the cheeks, opens a bottle of claret. They are angry that Kierkegaard has let Copenhagen know that *The Corsair* is akin to . . . a common harlot.

'And I would thus beseech you to receive these deliciously perfumed black stockings on your balding pate, my dear Søren,' Møller shouts, and quotes for Jenny: '*Magister artium* Søren Aabye Kierkegaard, my lord bishops, ladies and gentlemen, is a mere mortal who treads the earth just like any other mortal. . . He comes walking down Gothersgade, and a man falls and breaks his leg outside the grocer's. The *magister* remains aloof, observing the man's agony when he struggles to get up and notices that one leg refuses to obey, because it is fractured. . .'

Norway Kate is blissful. Jenny smiles in appreciation.

'Shall we also send him to bed wearing a pair of naughty red harlot's highheeled boots?' Møller asks, and continues to quote from his own article:' ". . . The proper moment had come at which to step in and help the man, if only the second phase of the observation had not intruded on the observer's mission of mercy: 1) the comical hustle and bustle and perplexity of the throng; 2) their questions to the sufferer, and arguing over the best method of transferring him to a place of treatment; 3) the foul curses heaped on negligent city fathers and on houseowners who had failed to spread cinders on the slippery pavement." '

'And then what?' Norway Kate is rising up on the sofa.

'Well, our *magister* toddles off home to sit down and write seven hundred pages . . . no, you wouldn't get the point even if I give you a parody of them. Wait a minute! A sinful corset for tiny Søren! And perfume, let's spray him with perfume! Roll him in tar and then drown him in feathers from your beloved eiderdowns!'

But Jenny is tired. She coughs. She leaves them to go to her own room, paler now. Norway Kate, full of concern and fear, runs after her, and Møller sits alone, under instructions to keep any callers at bay by declaring all the lovelies to be busy. Johanne-Louise, Sussi and Marie are not due to arrive until later. Møller places the manuscript in an envelope. A few more issues of *The Corsair* and then he will be sated. He is wide awake, but has no idea how to occupy himself. Gerda Petrine has resumed her affair with her ballet dancer, and in a letter sent to Store Kongensgade she apologizes yet again: it will be best if they break it all off. But he must understand. He must forgive. All her problems. Goldschmidt avoids him, turning up at the office only at times when he knows that he will be undisturbed by the presence of others, and the changeling has spread the news about town that he plans to sell *The Corsair* and spend some time travelling abroad. And Pauline has at last moved into Store Kongensgade as a permanent resident and refuses to eat or drink until Møller has fulfilled his promise and marries her. And now Norway Kate comes back and tells him that Jenny's in a bad way. She's coughing up blood. Møller goes to her, sits down on the edge of the bed, takes her gently by the hand and whispers tenderly to her, urging her not to give up. She has been ailing for months, and no doctor has been able to help.

'How terrible for poor Regine. . .' she whispers.

Møller takes a room at a nearby hotel. The next day, when he returns to Lavendelstraede, Norway Kate receives him with tears in her eyes. Møller takes a swig from the phial prepared for him by his brother, the apothecary's assistant. The opium has its effect. He feels that he is walking on cushions, all his worries are over, and he knows that Jenny cannot be really dead; she's just sleeping, content in the knowledge that men love her. In front of him the tree-lined avenue leading up to the portals of the University of Copenhagen beckons, and there is Oehlenschläger himself to receive him.

Three medical students come in and address him. They ask him about Jenny, if they can take her to the hospital and keep her there. After all, she has no relatives. Møller shrugs his shoulders. The medical students produce a sheet of paper and indicate where he and Norway Kate are to sign. Møller scribbles a signature, but Norway Kate collapses before adding her surname. The students snatch the paper and soon carry Jenny out, wrapped in a sheet.

Møller empties the laudanum phial. Now he sees his own mother too. Then he collapses onto the sofa. He knows that Jenny, his tiger lily, will arise from the dead and sit in the front row with Pauline and Gerda Petrine and Sussi and Norway Kate when he delivers his inaugural address as professor.

But it was not to be. *The Corsair* was beginning to exact retribution.

seven

'I am Janus.'

Pauvre Louis turns round in the narrow corridor.

'Who?'

'Janus, I am Janus.' — A mere whisper.

It's the effect of the hashish again. It's the incessant burst of laughter, the torrent of meaningless words echoing uselessly within him. It's Pauline's sobbing and all these days and nights and all these weeks — even months — when he hasn't put pen to paper, spending all his time smoking hashish and drinking and spouting streams of words that now churn and seethe as the chicken struggles to escape from his grip, down onto the earthen floor and into the freedom of the darkness. He kicks out futilely after the bird. He bruises his big toe against the wall and the pain shoots right up to his thigh. He cannot grope his way to the door to Amagergade and make his way down to Pauline and all the others down in *The Elephants' Graveyard*, an illicit dive, but only bangs his head against the narrow staircase with the diseased, mouldy steps leading up to the decrepit first floor. Now the hen is right behind him. It's here, there and everywhere at one and the same time, it seems to him, and it just grows and grows.

'Cluck-cluck-cockatoo,' he half hisses, half intones.

And to Janus:

'Shush! Shush! You're dead! Go back to the shadows where you belong!'

And for a brief moment he sees the dance of the naiads, the fairy palace. Then Møller flings himself over the hen and just manages to grab it with both hands before it again wriggles free. He feels as though he is choking on a bundle of feathers, that his nostrils are stuffed with chicken shit and drunkard's piss. The rats are all over the place. He hears them, all the giant rats in Christianshavn, black and brown and grey and piebald, the sick and the healthy, the blind and the seeing, and all their slimy, disgusting offspring, omniverous, half rodent, half human foetuses, soiled with parturitional blood which they ecstatically lick off each others' backs as they grow to adulthood in a few minutes and spawn new offspring so that the harbour and the canals soon become a loathesome, heaving mass of unstoppable, everspreading, all-devouring, self-propagating evil. And up on the first floor the deaf old skipper has once more started to beat his pale wife, hammering mercilessly at her, after puking his guts onto the dingy floor, just as Møller has vomited words for hours on end to a heedless audience in *The Elephants' Graveyard*, before he was chosen, after a drunken drawing of lots, to go out and chop the head off some chicken, any chicken, for the evening meal. *The Elephants' Graveyard*: meeting place for failed theologians, artists and medical students, where colours are not something one mixes on a palette, but a heap of mire rubbed into faces, and words are not something one searches for, pen in hand, but sounds to be stuffed down the other man's gullet, to flatter him into silence or to drive him out of his wits.

A quotation from one of the great Renaissance painters — often a quotation invented for the occasion by Møller himself — and Pete the Painter manages to coax his fat carcass into something resembling a swagger, beaming in appreciation at Møller and blushing with gratitude at such a favourable comparison, until he believes that it is a brush between his fingers and not a bottle. Tappernøje-Jørgen ceases to have any doubts about his talent when Møller expatiates on his formidable sense of language: though virtually incoherent, he manages to make it clear to one and all, through swollen lips, that tomorrow morning, at the crack of dawn, he will be at his desk, getting the first magic phrase down on a clean sheet of paper. And throughout all this mockery of life, Møller's loathing of these rejects' lack of self-criticism grows, until he lets them have the full blast of his incisiveness, his brutal accuracy, sparing only Pete the Painter, knowing that this will make his comments about the others more credible, more hurtful.

'A pack of children!' he sneers, regretting the word, for he knows that children are by far superior in wisdom and common sense to this dissolute, spineless, cretinous pack of infants posing as adults. No vision, no will to fight against all the vicissitudes that drag them down into the bottomless pit of anonymity, down there where everything is in an amorphous, muddied mess and no individuality is allowed. It is as though Møller, peeping over their shoulders, can see their paralyzed mothers vainly whispering to them that the days when they might rightfully expect mollycoddling and spoon-feeding are long, long past. 'A bunch of nitwits, oafs, hulking louts! Have my words penetrated your thick skulls! Do you seriously believe for one minute that there is as much as a tiny spark of talent left in your addled brains, in your bankrupt souls?'

And it never fails to turn into a free-for-all, with everybody fighting everybody else. Tappernøje-Jørgen vents his anger on poor Glud, the would-be writer; Glud melts into tears; Heen, another writer who failed to find favour in the good professor's Royal Naval Armoury, rubs his bloodshot eyes, seizes a bottle by the neck and bashes the hapless Glud while two failed theologians and Matthisen, who as a medical student can always lay hands on a stock of hashish, chuckle with glee as they pass the pipe round in hilarious formality. And over there, sitting demurely in the corner, is Pauline, saying little and sucking her thumb. Sob-sob Pauline, as Møller has dubbed her in his mind. Or when he happens to be in a black mood: Pauline Nothing, Pauline Zero.

'Møller,' she speaks with her eyes when he has finally

succeeded in flaying the already vanquished assembly. 'Stop it, Møller!'

This is how time passes — hours and days and weeks of utter futility. And Møller can no longer put up with it all and soon reaches the point where he forgets that he can no longer put up with it. He has succeeded in getting out a collected edition of Blicher's novelettes and two volumes of his poetry. He is still editor of *Gaea*, and soon he will complete a new volume of poems and two volumes of *Critical Sketches* covering 1840–47, prefaced with an extensive quotation from Sainte-Beuve's *Vérités sur la littérature*. It is a thousand years ago since he concerned himself with that sort of thing! Another world. A world where he used to take pains to uphold the merits of the aesthetic criticism of a new age against mere speculative perception. And now there are broad hints that he is soon to be allocated a public grant to enable him to travel abroad. Oehlenschläger is his most loyal advocate, but Møller is no longer interested in literature. Neither reading nor writing has any appeal, the magic phrase evokes no flash of recognition, no quiet thrill; the landscape stretches into an infinity of bleakness, stacks of paper wrenched out of fevered brains incapable of creating any ripple in any tiny pond, never mind this world, nor its fearful lack of meaning, incapable of preventing the world's jarring daily stab at the consciousness. Literature: *rien, nothing, Scheisse*. Nausea.

At home in Store Kongensgade everything is in a mess, and Pauline has long since abandoned any thought of looking after him and has decided instead to follow him as he makes his way across the bridge for his daily pleasures in *The Elephants' Graveyard*. Møller sets off for the one part of Copenhagen that has refused to move with the times, passed over by the vagaries of fashion and progress — drives past the Royal Naval Armoury and descends gradually to the dregs of the populace, there, where no page is turned, where no poem is penned, where no rosy dawn heralds any coming day, where infant mortality is the highest in the country, where the air reeks of raw snaps and stale beer, where gypsy fortune tellers gaze at the cards — three of clubs, deuce of hearts, queen of diamonds, king of spades — foretelling death and dire accidents, where gypsies sell purloined silver, where children bawl with hunger, and the bankrupt talents of the University of Copenhagen — faces that Møller clearly recalls from ten or fifteen years ago and which he now enjoys meeting in sweet victory — seek oblivion in the bosoms of the cheapest whores in town. Dronningensgade, Prinsensgade, Amagergade and Sankt Annegade, which runs from the old warehouses to the point in Copenhagen's fortifications where 'The Pea Kettle', Christianhavn's own answer to fashionable Langelinie, begins. This is the district in which P.L. Møller — poet, editor, friend of talent, enemy of posturing — plans to reside.

This is the place where he does his drinking. And here he need not worry about the cut of his coat, nor the state of his trousers. Nor is there any need here for a great show of manly indignation, of wounded pride, when Pauline leans over his shoulder and entreats him to head for home on his own. Solitude. No histrionics here, just a shrug of resignation. She has been an experiment in his life, in all essentials a figure of dependence, living proof that a man can give birth to a woman as long as he sticks rigidly to the rules, never letting her know that the truth of the matter is that it is he who secretly guides her steps, luring her from the unconscious to the conscious. From a being barely capable of reading her own name to having an insatiable appetite for books and newspapers; from being a blind adherent of the creed of predestination to becoming — under his tutelage — a believer in her own free will, an apostle of the inalienable right of woman to full and equal participation in what she has hitherto regarded as an admirable but unattainable pursuit: 'culture'. From an utter and pitiable lack of dress sense to deftly cutting and stitching her own clothes, copying the latest fashions from French magazines. From a gawkish and even slovenly comportment to pride in her posture, in her straight back, in her manner of sitting down, or getting up, or crossing a room, or serving coffee. From blind impetuosity to a tranquil enjoyment of any beautiful landscape, blissfully unaware that it is he who has drawn her attention to the beauty of summer meadows, mountains, valleys, snow-clad fields; landscapes within herself, nurtured in her soul, and her imagination. From being incapable of distinguishing between dross and gold, never knowing whether to say yes or no, to confidence in her ability to call things by their right names. She then had an air of maturity and a becoming measure of restraint, her controlled blush, warm eyes and full lips a subtle tribute to nights of passion and ardour. In short, from being a little waif she had become a woman in all her ways, even in suddenly turning her rage and frustration on him, just as women do in the latest French novels.

And as they do also in the most secret pages of his diary, written in invisible ink. Everything delicately poised, ready to come tumbling down, starting her long fall through the various stages, down to the most primitive one of all, more lowly than when he first met her on the embankment: down to an existence where limp strands of hair are left bedraggled, where nails are bitten down to the quick, where swollen, black-rimmed eyes glower in sullen despair and the only gesture left, *her* only gesture, is to suck her thumb and stare at him, with anxiety like a grey, sodden veil draped over her face. That's what it's like to be a nonentity, that's what it's like in the land where no grass grows, where no ray of light penetrates — his own landscape of blackened treetrunks and barren fields and the ashes of indifference in his soul. *Rien n'existe. Rien n'arrive.* And right now a piteous wail of anguish, the strangled scream of mortal pain.

'Cluck-cluck-cockatoo!'

Muck and dirt. Upstairs the skipper's wife is screaming with pain, yelling for mercy, beaten to a pulp. The unbearable stench of shit and ammonia. The chicken always just managing to escape his desperate lunges. And then it seems that everything is bathed in a blaze of light. Møller looks up from where he has fallen and listens to the squealing of the rats of Christianshavn. There stands Janus, right before him, a black cape casually slung over his shoulders, hair brushed down over his ears, a gold ring glinting on his little finger, scarlet boots reaching up to his thighs. His face is of bronze, and a goatee droops far below his chin. He points behind him, at two doors standing alone on a vast plain where no blade of grass can grow, each door resting on its hinges, with a bronze face mounted above the lintel. The face of Janus. Both doors are open, leading from nowhere to nowhere, Møller thinks — until Janus tells him that the doors beneath the bronze-cast face lead to places he cannot glimpse until he comes right up to them. And if he looks closely, he will see more doors. There are doors everywhere. And Møller gets to his feet, clutching the hen, which is now so exhausted that it hangs limply in his grasp. Møller approaches the first door and can see nothing but the mist; he steps back, eager to know what lies beyond the other threshold. He approaches the next door and looks down into a deep grotto and hears a gang of blacksmiths raining blow after blow on their anvils; and then he discerns their sweat-drenched backs glistening in the flickering blaze of the furnaces. He steps back, makes his way to yet another door, steps under the lintel and now glimpses. . .

'Are you going through?' Janus asks from behind, with a note of warning in his voice. Møller tries to regain control of his senses:

'Pray be silent! You are literature. You are n-o-t-h-i-n-g!'

Now a lake emerges, and soon he sees himself lying lifeless in the reeds. Beside him is his knapsack, bulging with all his theology textbooks. He withdraws and moves on to the next door.

'What do you see?' Janus asks.

Møller sees a lane, a house, a vase, a key lying in the middle of the road, a bear, water and, beyond them, a wall.

'Tell me about the lane,' Janus prompts.

'It's a country lane. A place in Jutland. It's a winding lane, and it's steaming, because there has just been a shower of rain. It's a beautiful lane.'

'Tell me about the house and what you're going to do when you reach it.'

'It's brightly lit. They're celebrating something. I'm going in to join the festivities.'

'And the vase? Tell me about it and what you're going to do with it.'

'It's antique. And very beautiful. I'll take it with me.'

'And the key? What does it look like and what are you going to do with it?'

'It's golden. And now it's gleaming in the sunshine after the rain. I'm going to stoop down and pick it up. Maybe I'll drop it into the vase.'

'And the bear? What does it look like? What are you going to do when you meet the bear?'

'It's huge and full of menace. I'll look it straight in the eye and then just walk round it.'

'And the water? What are you going to do when you reach the edge?'

'The water is a tempestuous sea. I'll plunge in and swim for a long time. Then I'll step ashore again in a state of bliss.'

'And the wall? What does it look like?'

'It's covered with moss, and it's part of the ruins of a castle. There's a point in the middle of the wall, or maybe a bit to the left, where I can climb over it.'

'Close your eyes,' Janus says.

And Møller closes his eyes.

'What do you see on the other side of the wall?' Janus asks.

'An endless meadow decked with flowers. I'm going to walk across it. I'm happy.'

'Then go through that door,' Janus says. 'You have told me about your life and about your death, and you have nothing to fear. The beautiful lane is your wandering. The house is other people, and you feel like being among them. The vase is love, and you are taking it with you, just as you are taking the key, which is wisdom. The bear is your own problems, which you bravely face before calmly walking round them. The water is carnal love, in which you blissfully cavort, and the wall — the wall is death, and you climb over the wall and are reborn on the other side in a meadow decked with flowers. Go now! This is your life, this is your death. You wish it so. . .'

Møller is gripped by a chill, and at the very moment that he tries to cross the threshold there is something that holds him back. He looks up at the bronze face with the beard that reaches down to its throat and the mouth that hangs half open, as though caught in mid-sentence, and the eyes that, milky white, stare ahead, and instantly he knows that the face is also on the opposite side. Maybe there will be nothing if he passes through the doorway, just as now, when he is standing in the middle of nowhere, befuddled, exhausted. Or . . . no, it's the books that have gone to his head. Or if he now crossed the threshold, never again to be able to find the way back if it turns out that. . .

'Turns out that what?' Janus asks behind him.

'That everything would be otherwise. . .'

'What do you mean?'

'If the lane should. . .'

'. . . be strewn with stones and thorns?'

'And the house. . .'

'. . . is a ruin inhabited by people with vulture-heads?'

'And the vase. . .'

'. . . is smashed into a thousand fragments?'

'And the key. . .'

'. . . is rusty and fits no lock?'

'You snatch the questions out of my mouth! You think my thoughts!' Møller hisses at him, and once again looks into the void beyond the door. And now the lane is strewn with jagged stones, and the house is a ruin inhabited by people with vulture-heads who scowl at him, with puss oozing from their eyes and blood seeping through their boots, and the vase has exploded into a thousand fragments, and the key is rusty and the bear charges towards him, foaming at the mouth, and the water is a frozen lake where the swans are trapped in the ice, slowly dying of hunger, and the wall is covered in a shroud of black soot and reaches from earth up to the sky, without ever admitting a chink of light. Møller beats a hasty retreat. He stumbles in panic from door to door, and through every door he can see the same lane strewn with jagged stones and thorns, coming to an abrupt halt against the black wall. Then it is not Janus he hears, but old Pan. He stands in front of the last door — so heaped with mud that one can hardly discern his evil, hairy body and face beckoning to Møller. Full of relief at recognizing him, Møller hurries over towards him and through the doorway, the smallest doorway of all, with the bronze head reduced to quarter size, like one of those shrunken heads in a museum of anthropology.

'Welcome back!' Old Pan rumbles, shaking off the layers of mud. Møller takes in his surroundings. Over there, playing dice at the long table, is Pete the Painter and Heen the writer. And over at the other table, dealing the cards, sitting at their regular table by the shelf with the rancid sausages and the mouldy cheeses, are Glud the writer and Tappernøje-Jørgen and Matthisen the medical student. In the corner, sitting on the floor with legs crossed in front of the fire, is Pauline. Her hair is bedraggled, her thumb thrust into her mouth. She permits the two theologians to kiss her chastely on the neck, on the cheek. Møller brutally wrenches the hen by the neck and flings it into her lap. Then he goes over to the counter and pounds on it. The owner emerges from the foul-smelling kitchen and pours more wine.

'Honourable members of the Fraternity of Bacchus!' Møller yells, before lowering his voice to a whisper: 'Are you plagued by the satanic beast? After all, you sit there like a bunch of undertakers, your eyes are reddened with the tears of misery, not with the glory of the grape. And soon you will succeed in moving me too to tears, for a man unhappy in love is forced to endure an unhappy lot. But right now I am a man *happy* in love, and wish to remain in that blissful state. . .'

He seizes Pauline by the hand, dragging her to her feet and drawing her close to him. He clutches at her dress, smothering her with kisses. Perplexed by the onslaught, she wraps her arms around his neck, and now she's crying. The two theologians eye her avariciously, and one of them, salivating, crawls over to her and begins to cover her ankle with kisses. Night has fallen in *The Elephants' Graveyard*, and the boorish host moves from table to table with a fresh supply of tallow candles. Pauline's fit of shuddering is so violent that Møller is convinced that she will collapse like a rag doll if he releases her from his desperate embrace. At the door, right under the shrunken Janus face, stands Old Pan, leering. Then Møller lets go of Pauline. She slides to the bare floor, collapsing in a graceless heap. He raises his arm in the manner of a Roman orator and continues:

'We have passion enough to have ideals, taste enough to clink glasses and join in a lusty toast, the intelligence to exercise a measure of restraint and break off just as death does, rage enough to return to the fount of pleasure — that's when we are beloved of gods and women. But what are these words here?'

He glances towards the door where Old Pan nods at him, urging him on. Møller feels unable to continue his diatribe and departs through the door, but changes his mind and re-enters *The Elephants' Graveyard*.

'How ghastly for poor Pauline!' one of the theologians mutters, ineptly trying to revive her. Confused, Møller looks at Old Pan as he steps into the smoke-filled room where Tappernøje-Jørgen greets his early return with a bellow of laughter:

'The way you come and go, Møller!'

The other boors share the pointless humour. Then Mattisen asks:

'Did you actually *sell* her skeleton?'

And Møller turns deathly pale. Once more he stands there, unable to recall what exactly happened when the medical students came to Lavendelstraede and carried Jenny away, wrapped in a sheet. Well, yes, he had sat on the girls' expensive new sofa; he had affixed his signature to a scrap of paper; he had awoken early next morning and tried to console Norway Kate, who had spent most of the night in a welter of grief; he had gone home to his own place; he had written a poem; he had torn it into shreds; he had rewritten it; he had been savage in his treatment of Pauline when she kept on pestering him, asking him where he had been and why he was so silent; he had sent Pauline away; he had again torn the poem into pieces. He had made up his mind to forget — until the ugly rumour had surfaced a week later, and there is nothing he can do to quash it, for even he himself in moments of weakness believes it to be true, when he has over-exerted himself, or at night when he lies awake, or when, as now, he has squandered days and weeks on mad binges. After the fourth bottle of wine he vainly tries to recall what exactly happened after the medical students had handed him that scrap of paper which he and Norway Kate had signed. He remembers nothing. But he can still produce the spellbinding torrent of words:

'An appreciation of the sheer pleasure of being cuckolded, without actually being cuckolded, is a closed book to all — apart from the eroticist. . .'

Or:

'This is how a woman seduces. . . She exists, she is there, physically present, in close proximity, and yet she is infinitely remote, hidden in modesty, until she herself betrays her hiding place, how, she doesn't quite know, she has had no part in it, life itself has been the wily informer. . .'

Then the host growls that it is closing time, and Møller is kicked out by his companions. The hen will have to wait till tomorrow. The air is bitingly cold when he again reaches Amagergade, and he feels a fit of nausea coming on. He coughs. Later he vomits onto a snowdrift as the others disappear into the darkness. Pauline has stayed behind in *The Elephants' Graveyard*; it's the host's turn to have a bit of fun with her, if she is by now not too far gone, Møller muses, his breath rising like some floating spectre.

'*Contre moi il n'y a pas de remèdes!*' he shouts into the muffled night.

Nostrissima! My dearest, sweetest *Fräulein Vernunft! Ma brava!* Sister Tilda! My primly naughty, my naughtily prim! *Signorina! Ma chère!* This is how P.L. Møller addresses Matilda Leiner, school mistress, of Store Kongensgade 233, in his long letters to her, letters which he writes with particular care, because he is aware of her deep love of language, especially when it is peppered with bits of French and Italian. The letters range from the teasing mood to the poetic, but are usually a blend of the two: 'What is *Nostrissima* occupying

herself with these days? Is she awake or does she sleep? Do
bewitching dreams ripple with delectation through the dark
riches of the black grape, or does she belong to the wideawake
reality that may fill her lustrous eyes with salt tears? Let those
tears cease! Let tranquillity embrace her in its tender folds
and banish all care, so that tomorrow *Nostrissima*'s eyes will
tell no sad tale of a sleepless night!' The letters are often
accusing in tone: 'Remember that when you reach the point
where you wish to understand me, to judge me fairly, you
must avoid doing so on the basis of the bigoted, conventional
notions which have gained such currency that they virtually
constitute the atmosphere in which woman's heart is formed.'

Or the letters are full of self-recrimination: 'I'm a miserable
proletarian, an owner of fairy tale castles, a mere observer at
life's feast!' And Møller thinks of *The Elephants' Graveyard*: 'Can
you comprehend the misfortune of being a creature of fantasy?
Of having feelings turned into fantasy, of having fantasy
turned into feeling? That is the embodiment of the poetic in
man. That is what prevents him from abandoning himself, as
a child in his lack of awareness or a woman in her lack of
experience, to the full enjoyment of life. He is never capable of
simply enjoying, he must also produce, and the moment that
pleasure intrudes on reality, he has long ago experienced it,
enjoyed it in his fantasy, and has progressed far, far beyond
that fusion of pleasure and reality. . .' '*Votre victime* or *Votre
escabeau écrivant*. . .'

Matilda Leiner, daughter of Johan Jacob Leiner, outside
broker and translator of Swiss extraction, lives with her sister
Constance, music teacher, who often has pupils when Møller
arrives, a few minutes after leaving his garret in the same
street, to beg Matilda to translate an article or a poem from
the French, the language he dreams of one day being able to
speak without any trace of a foreign accent, and preferably in
Paris where his new lady friend has recently been pursuing
her studies. He made her acquaintance one evening in the
Tivoli Gardens, invited her shortly afterwards to the theatre
— to see Henrik Hertz' *King René's Daughter* — and he has
joined the family on excursions to Frederiksdal. He has

presented her with dedicated copies of *The History of Printing* and *Lyrical Poems*, having marked with a cross the poems he himself regards as worth reading and, now and then, he goes so far as to send her new poems, although never poems in which he makes any profound declarations of love because something keeps him from wanting to achieve a total conquest; maybe her incurable common sense, the stolid materialism living in paradoxical harness with her passion for language and literature. And on top of that, there is all her wool. Woollen rugs, woollen curtains, woollen dresses, woollen stockings, her tea-cosies made of wool, coffee and tea canisters encased in wool — everything surrounding her and everything on her is made of wool so that even Constance's pupils have difficulty in making the piano sound a note.

Nevertheless, he is drawn to her, especially during the periods when everything seems to join in one vast conspiracy against him, so that he hardly knows which way to turn to avoid the rumours circulated about him. If he utters a few words about a recently published book, it is soon maintained that he is jealous of the author and intends to seduce his daughter; when he visits the professors to request them to support his application for permanent employment at the university, they are content to receive him in an outer chamber, and Madame Fouchanée refuses to serve him chicken soup on credit because she has heard rumours that he loves to chase round Sealand, hoping to witness a particularly gruesome execution. And now that story about the skeleton which within its short lifetime has been embroidered, the current version being that he brazenly marched right up to the hospital to demand payment. He finds little consolation in the fact that his *Critical Sketches* have now at last been printed. On the contrary, they are used against him, used as a whetting stone to sharpen the animosity towards him in the coffeehouses. Goldschmidt, just returned from his travels abroad, has sent him the manuscript of his review of the two volumes intended for publication in Goldschmidt's new journal *North and South* where — and Møller does not forget to tease him mercilessly about this when they run into one another a few days later in Vestergade — the tone is to be more elevating than that of *The Corsair*.

'More *sanctimonious*, Meyer Aron, that's the essence of it, isn't it?' Møller asked, quoting from an article that amounted to an inflated valediction to him. And Goldschmidt, all rigged out in his new clothes and the expensive shoes from Berlin, was about to bring up the matter about the skeleton.

'By the way, Møller, it has come to my notice that. . .' he said tartly, with a sour expression on his face.

'And, *by the way*, it has also come to mine. . .' Møller interrupted, quoting so loudly from the article that some passers-by stopped to listen. 'Now what words of magic leap off the page to hit my unbelieving eyes. . .? It reads thus: "Herr P.L. Møller is an aesthete in the broadest sense of that term. His ideal in literature is the beautiful, and only the beautiful. But the beautiful without the good, the aesthetic without the ethical. . ." What, in fact, is that?' And Møller guffawed and continued:' "The beautiful — the beautiful is a beautiful word. . ." and, if I read aright, Golle, it goes on: "but only a vain attempt to aspire to heaven without ethical wings." Goldschmidt, do you seriously claim to be on speaking terms with Heaven itself? Bishop Mynster can now start quoting you. No doubt you will soon be a candidate for canonization, and the faithful will flock to the shrine where your Christianized bones are preserved.'

Goldschmidt: 'Just tell me, Møller, what have you yourself achieved by choosing to adopt this negative attitude? Where are the fruits of your precious aesthetics? A while ago it was *my* fate to sit with parched mouth hearing all about your happiness, about your pleasures, about your torrid nights of delight and rapture, and to leave you when some veiled lady with a most beautifully turned ankle entered. I left, although God knows it pained me to leave to return to my only consolation, a *Corsair* article, while you dallied with the most voluptuous pair of breasts you could find amongst the *grisettes* of Copenhagen.'

'So they really say so!'

'But, as you probably don't know, there is also something called divine retribution. Remember, we duel, as you yourself once so memorably pointed out!' And Goldschmidt stamps his foot: 'If we wound one another, it will be *in majorem litteraturae gloriam!*'

'You have learnt your lesson, *Nebbich*! Then let us enter combat! I can have an opportunity of saying much, observing the scene from my perspective! But don't forget the armchair I won from you in that wager. I would gladly have spared you that bitter memory. . .'

Møller pays another visit to Matilda Leiner:

'But I *created* him!'

'There you have the explanation, *Pauvre Louis!*' Constance Leiner replies, pouring another cup of tea, while telling him that, regrettably, her sister has still not returned from Paris, and for a moment she faces him with a look in her eyes that he oddly fears, that look that is also Matilda's. There is no accusation there, no suggestion of superiority. They are wise eyes, they plead without currying favour; they say: 'Møller, we two might make a couple!' and Møller feels as though he has been shoved under a woollen rug. He experiences a choking sensation and suddenly he begins pacing to and fro in the sisters' drawing room. The old energy wells up in him again. He will be forever doomed to walk about in ever narrowing circles in Copenhagen, and the gift of tranquillity and inner calm that the sisters bestow on him is worse than a dollop of treacle. Stultification. Woollen mittens, woollen bonnets, wool in the soul — the things that his mother dreams of when she sends him worried letters, always ending by telling him that the room that was his as a child is still there for him, and he can resume occupation whenever he decides to abandon Copenhagen. There he will have peace and quiet, 'safe from the scurrilous rumours'. He can, in other words, forget all about literature, forget about writing, whiling the days away like an overgrown schoolboy, sluggishly passing through the various stages — paunch, gout, middle-aged lechery, geriatric impotency — to his dotage and the cold embrace of the grave. Dullard. And grandfather would turn up every fortnight, tapping his long-stemmed pipe, and look into his room and blame him for giving up theology. . .

'Matilda. . .'

'My name is Constance!'

'I've composed a whole novel stretching years ahead into the future, only to see it exchanged tonight for another. And when I have another bout of sleeplessness — there will be another which will tomorrow in due turn yield to yet a third version of the same novel. Can you grasp, or just sense, what it's like to go through the sufferings of a poet? Can you, Constance?'

'Yes. . .'

'I want to walk along the beach, to still my throbbing heart in winter, and just to touch the rejuvenating fount — and then I'm swept away out into the deep sea, and the waves are closing over my head. . . *ma brava*! Do you understand?'

'I do!'

'Ah, my dear *Fräulein Vernunft*!'

And Møller has made his exit. He has reached an irrevocable decision. He is going to cast off his shackles, he is going to travel. He can survive for some months abroad, far from the choking confines of Copenhagen, on the grants he has been awarded, and he has heard that personages in high places would be pleased if he could address his eloquence to the defence of Denmark's position in the conflict with Schleswig-Holstein, by writing in the German newspapers. He has packed his belongings into the shabby trunks, leaving boxes crammed with his most treasured books to his brother Marenus Laurentin. On New Year's Eve, 1847, he loads his two trunks onto a cart and makes his way along the cobbled streets down to the harbour, to get a berth on a boat to Lübeck. Shafts of bright yellow light emanate from every house along his route — and from Gerda Petrine's bay windows . At this very moment she is probably entertaining her young ballet dancer. Møller smiles. He feels that he is passing through innumerable doors, each one firmly slammed behind him. At some point in the future — he can't make out the exact location — he sees a beautiful country lane, and through the autumnal haze a half-timbered house brimming with people and conviviality. He wants to join them. He catches a glimpse of an antique vase, a golden key and a bear he won't be afraid of. He hears waves lapping on a sandy shore, in the distance he can see a wall, covered with velvety moss, so low that he can easily climb over it.

The snowfall is thicker now, the sounds more distant, the lights dimmer, and more and more doors slam behind him. Three paces behind him walks Janus, tracing his footsteps, taking them with him. Soon every trace of P.L. Møller will be obliterated. *Pauvre Louis* feels light of heart, he is only thirty-three. *L'anarchie entre les hommes de talent est complète*; he recalls Sainte-Beuve's words, as the snow continues to fall. It is as though Copenhagen is softly sinking into nothingness.

eight

The Danes have suffered a crushing defeat at the town of Schleswig. The Dannevirke has been smashed, the army has fled in panic through the streets of Flensborg. But at this moment, as Wrangel, the Prussian general, crosses Kongeåen, Denmark is made to realize that its fate is, after all, not a matter of total indifference to the major powers. The Russian envoy in Berlin delivers a note: if the Prussians cross the borders of South Jutland and threaten Denmark, this transgression will inevitably lead to a rupture of relations between Russia and Prussia. General Wrangel immediately withdraws his troops in such haste that he fails to collect the war taxes he has just levied on the Jutlanders.

Towards the end of May, the Danes make their move, from Als to Sundeved, and attack the German federal troops. The victories at Dybbøl and Nybøl restore Danish pride and bolster the belief that Schleswig will never fall into the hands of the Holstein rebels. The summer of 1848 has come, and 'now that even the most stubborn cosmopolitan is obliged to consider national and patriotic prerogatives, it is fitting that I should commence by informing you of some matters pertaining to war and politics. . .' writes P.L. Møller from his lodgings in Hamburg in one of a lengthy series of 'Letters from the Elbe' to *Kjøbenhavnsposten*. He has temporarily interrupted his flow of portraits of Danish writers for publication in German newspapers with the intention of compiling and editing them to produce a comprehensive history of Danish literature for German readers. In his capacity as official scribe of Hamburg's Scandinavian Society he dashes off a letter of encouragement to the Danish war minister and virtually, as the first shot of the war is fired, he composes a Marseillaise for the Jutland infantry, with the following description of the enemy's officers:

Like gangs of strutting turkey cocks
they cry out to the sky
but when it comes to take hard knocks
they turn their tails and fly.

Hamburg is rife with rumour: the newspapers constantly issue special bulletins with the latest news from the front. One day the banner headline reads: RÜSTUNGEN ZU EINER GROSS-EN SCHLACHT! And the following day: DIE REPUBLIK PRO-KLAMIERT IN DÄNEMARK! Or: EXTRA VON DEM KANONEN-DONNER! And the day after that: AUSWANDERUNG DER DEUTSCHEN VON SCHWEDEN! Møller can only laugh when passing on to his Danish readers the rumour that a hundred thousand Danish soldiers have fallen at Fredericia, while only one German has been wounded. Møller is an eager, prolific correspondent and writing these despatches is his best daily dose of medicine to combat the boredom of a city that has struck no chord of sympathy in him since his arrival. Admittedly the houses are impressive and the surrounding landscape has beauty, but houses and landscape are inhabited by countless narrow-minded *Biederdeutschen* who evince a blind faith in all that is proclaimed in the sheets of the special bulletins from the chancery and from the front. When Møller can tug himself away to observe the noble and free Hanseatic capital, or rather the elegantly clad male population of Hamburg, he notes that power and influence are shared by two groupings; the merchants and the lawyers.

The merchants, who are subdivided into stock exchange traders, stock exchange runners and apprentices, are easily in the majority. Whatever the place, whatever the time of day or night, a deal is being struck, a speculative investment is in progress, or fraud, or the amassing of profit, or usury or downright theft. The thefts, Møller notes, are, of course, conducted in the forms sanctioned by law, and anyone who fails to master the techniques of transferring money from his neighbour's pocket into his own is regarded as a useless creature, a social excrescence.

La propriété, c'est la propriété. Everything in Hamburg derives its justification, its very breath of life, solely from this edict. Brains which in any other sphere of human activity are not worth a tinker's curse (and here Møller is thinking of Matthisen the medical student and Pete the Painter and Heen the writer and the rest of that lot in the squalid gloom of *The Elephants' Graveyard*) often seem quite capable of notable accomplishments. 'Just as the blind who use touch to perceive the most fragile, barely perceptible objects,' he writes, 'in the same way here you find scores of wandering vegetables who have never before had a sensible thought in their skulls, but who, by virtue of a wondrous instinct, discover the most lucrative, most invisible way to reap a profit.' And the women? So bored to death with their own men that Møller has only to give them a sidelong glance to make them turn round, elicit longing and desire.

On this point Møller can assure Copenhagen, as he fills his pages with matters of greater and lesser import: Hamburg is in all respects a worthy capital for Holstein, the most prosaic nation in the world. The children sing, without a note in their heads, the national anthem, *Schleswig-Holstein meerum-schlungen*, wearing swords and spiked helmets. The Danish prisoners of war who travel from Altona are robbed of their lunch and the seven marks they had been promised. A Schleswig-Holstein ship with a cargo of cannons from Hull has limped past the frigate 'Gefion'. The Schleswig-Holsteiners want to occupy the Danish islands and march on Copenhagen. According to their Münchhausen stories during their siege the capital will starve to death for want of . . . yes, Schleswig-Holstein butter! A mercenary from Kollen boasts that he shot a wounded Danish volunteer who asked for mercy. In Rendsborg, where there is an acute shortage of uniforms, they have dragged the garments off the backs of captured cavalrymen and made them wear, for God's sake, their own tattered red clothes instead. He reports the indignation felt in Hamburg at the news of ladies of that city dancing at a ball with Danish prisoners — even though no ball had been held in the city. Revolt in Altona. A mobile brigade consisting of fifteen-year old boys who have stormed five barricades, conquered five standards and downed five rebels. A Major Brockdorff of the Schleswig-Holstein dragoons has shot himself, realizing that he has broken his oath to the Danish king. Altona is in flames; a magnificent sight — the flames above the Steinthor shooting up into the sky. Socialists? Radical communists? The *Bremer Zeitung* maintains that the Danish army consists of fifty-year old peasants in clogs.

Later: *cholera is socialist* — even the well padded citizens of Hamburg are not immune. The Frankfurt troops marching homewards from the front remind one of the French imperial guard, the Baden infantry of the Russians, the Nassaus of the Swedes, the Hanoverians of the English, but not a single corps puts one in mind of German troops. A renowned *Kulturdoktor*, Theodor Mommsen, utters a few words — in the people's permanent assembly in Kiel — which sound unpleasant to the Schleswig-Holsteiners, with the result that they shamelessly take to punishing the genuine *Landeskind*. A Holsteiner is widely believed to have fired the revolution in Frankfurt. The Schleswig-Holsteiners criticize the Danish song, 'The Brave Infantryman', regarding it as evidence of the low cultural level of the Danes. And a Schleswig-Holsteiner has made the discovery — a 'scientific discovery', no less — that mendacity is an essential feature of the Danish national character.

And what is one to say to that? That people in Schleswig-Holstein are neither more or less mendacious than people elsewhere, Møller writes, now getting tired of these letters from the Elbe, adding that 'the lie' is most widely used by correspondents, the mercenaries of literature. One of these, and an especially despicable example, is a certain Herr M. who in the proper old 'sea-girt' style published in an article in the *Kieler Correspondenzblatt* states the opinion that Danish literature is *ein schlechter Abklatsch deutscher Missformen*. And Møller takes up the cudgel, spitting out the despicable word *Abklatsch*, these choked consonants, these sloppy vowels — indulging in a wild polemic, fully aware that he is doing so, but he has, he feels, a duty to tell things as they are, even if it is for the benefit of a distant Danish readership which agrees with his views.

What does this Herr M., this puffed-up schoolmaster, who doesn't understand a word of Danish, know about Holberg, who was never inspired by as much as a single line of German? What does this doctor of incomprehensibility, who probably suffered a paroxysm of delight at seeing his few paltry sentiments in print, know about Brorson, Wessel, Ewald, Oehlenschläger, Blicher, Aarestrup, Andersen? He might at least have taken the trouble of reading the work of the latter — *Der dänische Dichter* — in translation! And again the yearning wells up in Møller, the urge to write the major history of Danish literature, so that one and all will realize — anyone with the faculty of hearing — that *The Danish Tone* strikes the ear as entirely different from the German tone. Not to mention the 'New German'.

A solitary Danish aesthete in Hamburg and Altona whose only solace is a visit to the opera to hear Meyerbeer's *Robert le Diable* and *The Huguenots*, Møller experiences a growing depression at the thought of what will happen if the repeated New German ambition to turn Denmark into *Admiralstaat Dänemark* should become a reality, with Danish banned from all schools. Never again will a youth lying with a mature woman with yellowish-green eyes, late one afternoon, watch through the window pane how the sky rises like a crystal vault over a fairy castle, hearing in his mind words with such an intensity that he has to speak them:

Against dappled pane thrusting,
Green boughs by deep roots fed;
With rich abundance bursting,
Of cherries ripe and red.

. . . so that the bell of Budolfi church in Aalborg chimes and
the woman whispers into the boy's ear:
'Now that *was* a pretty poem. . .'

Møller is fed up to the teeth with this surfeit of Teutonic
bombast and vulgarity. Wherever he goes he hears the
rumbling of a Germany which is nothing but a gigantic
stomach with entrails that slither out in all directions like the
arms of an octopus. The food is abominable, but the German
stomach receives it delightedly. To each day its own dose of
'German blobs', meat soup with monstrous grains and split
peas all served as one hideous, solid mash. Dimwitted, clumsy
and loutish, boys with the reddest rash of outsize pimples he
has ever seen, their genitals bulging from lack of satisfaction in
coarse woollen trousers, the men with deepset eyes,
pudding-bowl haircuts and hands like shovels, belching and
farting, slobbering beer down their chins, the women more
and more debilitated, with piss-coloured hair and their gross
feet, too large for the fine high heels of their Parisian shoes
which fall apart on the hazardous streets. That's how Møller
sees the Germans when seized by a mood of depression, and
he feels forced to write more and more letters, because he has
not yet received full remuneration from the Foreign Office for
his toil in presenting the Danish case in the German
newspapers.

This enormous collection of tribes, on which the Romans
never succeeded in conferring the benefits of civilization, is
bent on teaching the world the blessings of the revolution, not
a revolution in the French spirit (and Møller feels a burst of
amicability as he thinks of Goldschmidt), but in the *lumpen*
Germanic spirit. Night after night Møller sits in his lodgings,

now bored to death with writing about towns which would not otherwise concern him one whit. One day there is a 'revolution' in Gera, next day in Schleitz, and then in Bovende (now where can that be?), in Glückstadt, in Krase; Fulda wants to secede from Hessen-Kassel, and the people of Fulda refer to themselves as 'repealers'; the town of Stotel (can there really be such a place?) is also in a state of revolt, and six of the town's luminaries advocate a new manner of shouting hurrah. Møller feels that he is being gobbled alive, drawn deeper and deeper down the gullet into the German stomach where blobs of grain and chunks of sausage and cracked chicken bones thresh about in a viscous meat soup, occasionally sending a stinking beer bubble into the craw before he again plummets downwards and bumps his head against a reactionary lump of dumpling or a revolutionary mass of stodge.

He rocks sluggishly to and fro in his chair, smoking far too much and drinking one pot of coffee after the other, causing his heart to jump up like a Jack-in-the-box. Revolutionary? Reactionary? What's the difference? The German gut wants to consume everything in its path, its innumerable tentacles want to clutch most of Europe, if ever Germany first succeeds in uniting. When his bile rises, Møller often hurls his pen at the wall, aiming at the heart of Hamburg. Here he sits, wasting precious time, simply because once upon a time there was a beatific Duke Christian, who, speaking of Schleswig-Holstein, stated, 'They should forever remain together and united'. Words doubtlessly uttered when drunk, with his feet stuck in a basin of lukewarm mud.

Møller dashes off a huge batch of personal letters, to his mother, to his brothers (in one letter claiming to have travelled to Bolivia to become a specialist in natural medicine), to Matilda Leiner who is now at home in Store Kongensgade surrounded by all her wool ('I would, however, greatly appreciate it if you could devise some method of determining how my letters have been received by the more intelligent among the populace of Copenhagen, and let me know the results of your soundings, so that I can decide whether to continue with my penmanship or to abandon my inkwell with a clear conscience. The issue is one of little import to me. . .' and: '. . . before thinking of visiting the writers in Paris whose personal acquaintance I should like to make, I shall probably require a few months' daily association with one or more of the lovable Parisian ladies referred to as *grisettes, lorettes* and so forth.'). And when he next finds a rubber band, he will wrap it round the letters he has received. But rubber bands never last long, and he flicked the last one across the room when his eye reached the last few lines of one of these letters, referring to the amount he is to pay for the love child that had finally arrived. The letter was posted to him the same day that he had written his words of encouragement to the war minister.

Finally Møller forces himself to read the letter from beginning to end, and now he does not shake his head in resignation at the multitude of spelling errors:

Copenhagen
18 April
1848

Dearly beloved

It is a long time since you have Received Any letter from me, I wated and wated to be Abel to send you Glad Teidings, but I shuddint have wated, I doan no if you have got the letter my Sister Rote, so I will repete same, the 28 March I gave berth to a Luvly littel boy the spittin imidge of you I was happy I dooan denai it, it was only a lone. the 4 April he was batised and cald Ludvig Ollsen we got a Very good fauster mother for 8 days I had him my self, I began to give him the breast you Shud see him at the breast you wud have Luvd him strate away, I luvd him hyer than my oan sole, thats whai god let me down as ushel, its the lass taim Ill ever ask him for anny thing, for 14 days our Luvly littel chile was helty, the 15st day I was to go over and see him, my Sister had bin there evry day, he was stil alrite and ful of Life, I was so trilld abaut going to see him, but Ill never forget the Site, he had kramps the nite befor I will not tell you how it had Changd him the Only thing I doan

unnerstan is how I remane sane I sent strate away for
dokter Hassing he come two taims a day to him he layd in
kramp from Tuesday evnin till Friday nite between 3 and 4
it was all over, my Sister and I watchd over him till the wery
end, she cudn be comfortit, Henrijete was the only one who
didn shed a tier on Saturday evenin I went hom to my
payrents in a wery Poor state I had to go strate to bed I have
a terribel bad leg the Doktor thinks its the Milk as has setld
som place in the leg it will take a long taim maybe I woan
get wel at all. What have I to sho for all I have bin tru, a
littel Grave it will be my Only konsolayshun if I get well,
this evenin my Sister is goan to Dress my littel son for the
lass taim I hav made the clos for him on Wednesday he will
be berit in the charity semetri, now I have nothing moar to
tell you I have Only a Lot to ask you for you must rite to me
woan you my dear sweethart Møller now doan you forget.
May I also have some of the monee you had put 1 side for
the chile I have had to boro to pay for evry thing, Wollf
Gave me the Order for 6 rigsdaler he cudn get it payd out so
he Gave me 2 from his own poket to Give to the fauster
mother doan forget to Rite to Doktor Hassing to thank him
for commin to the baby, my payrents no evry thing and they
are no way hard on me, they two wer very Happy about the
littel boy but that doesn make up for what I loss, Rite to me
what you think and feel but you doan no how big a loss we
have sufrd doan stay away longer than you pland and stay
well away from the Wor — goodby Møller Maybe Ill die
   Your devoted Pauline

'Ha! ha! Wedding. You talk about a wedding? Well you'll get
your wedding, don't you worry, *mein Liebling! Mein Müller!
Mein Dummdäne!'*
   '*Deutschland, bleiche Mutter,*' Møller whispers, trying to
commit Pauline's letter to oblivion.
   The woman's armpits stink, her nails are black, her
laughter is so hoarse and thundering that it threatens the

ceiling's plasterwork, and when she coughs, it's as though her lungs have been shattered, and she's spewing the pieces out of her mouth. She ceaselessly licks her lips, darting out the huge, scarlet, furrowed tongue. For Møller, however, her main attraction is her sex. The chicken-coloured pubic hair extends far down her thighs, and upwards it sprouts like a shrubbery on the base of her belly. Her breasts flop uselessly against her midriff, and when Møller, befuddled with alcohol, goes down on his knees in front of her and parts her thighs, she clamps them round his neck, bellowing with laughter as she pours a tankard of beer over him and rains a barrage of blows on his unprotected shoulders.

Møller has sunk as low as he can possibly go. It hasn't taken him long to pack his pens, pencils, paper, ink and all the rest of it into a suitcase, and to jam the last of his Elbe letters into an envelope. The letters are about the old Prussian officers from Waterloo who firmly maintain that that battle had nothing to offer compared with the assault of the Danish infantry at Nybøl and Dybbøl, and about the robber stories circulating in Schleswig-Holstein — like the one about the Hanoverian soldiers who, during the harvest in Schleswig, had found six of their comrades, bound hand and foot and gagged, but without any sign of violence. This is how the Danish peasants are supposed to have starved them to death — Møller doubts the veracity of the account. Finis. The very word 'Elbe' is sufficient to give him the shivers, and for days he has been staggering round the streets of Hamburg until he was ensnared by this woman in the poorest street in the most squalid district in all Hamburg. He has discovered the route straight down into the pit of Germany's gut. Here he can forget.

Several times a day he thrusts his head between the woman's legs, while he jabs his fingers deep into the fat, hairy thighs. He experiences a strange security in the darkness beneath her skirts, in the stench of stale urine, secure in the darkness of her room with the rotten floorboards and secure in the dank, foggy, autumnal darkness seeping in from the street where drunken seamen lie stretched out along the walls, sleeping off the effects of huge quantities of snaps. He no longer washes himself, and now and then he pisses in his trousers. He no longer cares. And that's how Anna, or Irmgard, or Hulda, or whatever she's called, likes it. When she has got her satisfaction from pressing her sex against his mouth, she flings herself on him with a shriek of delight, rips off his trousers and licks him clean.

Møller feels that now he will never manage to escape from Germany's stomach and intestines. His willpower has been sapped, and he threshes aimlessly about among the hunks of half-digested sausage, the coarse grain and the split peas, and he is brown, clammy and filthy. The gut sends a putrid pile of new hunks of sausage and split peas tumbling around his head as he lies on the floor, and there, floating groggily in the sea of putrefaction, are Doktor Mommsen's umbrella and Doktor Hassing's stethoscope. His own manuscripts are borne away, while, like flotsam, empty inkwells emit bubbling, bluish, poisonous acid to tinge the sea of brown. If he opens his mouth, it is instantly filled with excrement, and he is forced to swallow it or suffocate.

When the woman is finished with her licking, she rushes him off to the bed with the filthy bedspread and the torn mattress from which cruel spikes of straw jut out to pierce his skin. Here he can get some fitful sleep and try to recover from his binge until tomorrow morning when the woman will again put a bottle of the cheapest, rawest snaps on the floor, within easy reach.

'*Mein Müllerchen! Mein Müllerchen!*' she clucks, straddling him with her bulk.

And one morning he groans in delirium: 'You must belong to me, I shall have the banns read from the pulpit! Tomorrow evening I shall explain everything to you! Up the kitchen stairs, first door on the left, and straight ahead that's the kitchen door! *Auf Wiedersehen*, my adorable Pauline! Let nobody notice that you have seen me out here, or spoken with me, you probably know my secret!'

And the woman heaps kisses on him as he continues:

'*Wirklich schön ist sie*! Something could be made of her. When

I secure a footing in her chamber, then I myself shall proclaim the banns three times from the pulpit! I have always tried to develop the beautiful Greek *autarkeia*, and especially to render a pastor superfluous!'

'Of course, *mein Müller!* Render the pastor superfluous!'

And the woman dashes out of her room, onto the street. A while later she returns with four or five drunken seamen. More join the little crowd, each clutching a bottle. The woman calls the rowdy assembly to order by clapping her hands, using her huge belly to shove the table against the wall, thus leaving space in the middle of the room for a chair. She places her brimming chamber pot on the chair, two seamen heave Møller onto the pot, and they all dance drunkenly round the tableau, lurching, arm-in-arm. The woman leaves the room and comes back with a black, crocheted garment which she forces over the head of one of the seamen.

'Our pastor, Müller!' she says, in a low voice, blushing like a timid schoolgirl.

And as the woman takes her place beside the chair and takes his hand, the seaman, oddly at ease in the folds of the ample black garment, confers a triple blessing on them by invoking Satan. Another seaman supports Møller from behind to prevent him from toppling backwards. When the mock nuptials have been brought to an end, the woman opens his trousers and gobbles his member to a chorus of lusty applause from the seamen. Rising from the nape of his neck, Møller feels the excruciatingly painful throb of the worst headache he has ever suffered. His throat is as dry as sawdust and before his eyes everything appears in a grainy, distorted whirl. One seaman has lost an arm, another has only one finger on his left hand, a third has no nose. Is all this real? Møller wonders. An army of ants crawls out of the gaping cavity and down over his mouth and chin. The woman lowers her huge bulk to the floor, pulls up her dress and begins to caress her pubic hair, banging her heels against the floor as a crude signal to the seamen who lie down to kiss her, on the mouth, between the thighs. One of the seamen unscrews his wooden leg and rams it into the wall, bringing down a shower of plaster and gravelly filling. Children come in to look on, all with sunken cheeks and lifeless eyes. Already living in the land of the dead, it occurs to Møller. They have nothing left on their skulls, apart from a thin film of pallid skin, and they stretch out their hands in silent supplication, hoping for something to eat. One boy is carrying his own tombstone under his arm, and he looks Møller straight in the face without a trace of anger or accusation, as though to say, 'Well, it wasn't your fault, was it?'

The woman continues to roar with laughter. She gets up and takes the boy by one hand and Møller by the other.

'Come on, my pretties, put your best foot forward! We're going to dance, the three of us, all day long!'

Then a shot rings out, and three mobile guards enter and clear the premises. One seaman gets a bayonet in the stomach. The woman is knocked unconscious by a rifle butt. The guards, who are no older than sixteen, are obviously obsessed with the desire for action. The woman is lying with her head against the pot. Horror-stricken, Møller looks at her: like a mass of pudding, her gross body sprawls over the floor, while the blood of the dead seaman trickles under her thigh. The place is like one huge mire of mud, excrement, blood, plaster, broken bottles, rotten floorboards and crushed cigar stubs. From outside, Møller dimly hears shouting and more shots as he gradually regains his senses. The events of the past few days flit through his consciousness, moving from here and now to the beginning of it all, when he read the letter from Pauline and dried the ink on the last page of his last Elbe letter. He tries to dry his face on his shirt front, but it is coated with excrement and he makes things even worse. He walks out, onto the street. People are running wildly in all directions, screaming. In front of him is a rearing horse, a snarling cur is biting another dog in the neck. A disorderly bunch of very young mobile guards have breached a barricade at the end of the street and are charging forward, eager to join the fray.

Møller is in the middle of the crowd. He doesn't know how he managed to reach the other end of the street, the safe end.

Wherever he looks he sees the mobile guards on the attack, jabbing a bayonet into a rebel's groin. Children too are dropping dead. A child seizes his trouser leg, but when he is about to take her by the hand to lift her up, she slides down his leg and rolls into the gutter.

'They've shot Robert Blum! *They've shot Robert Blum in Vienna!*' The shout is audible above the din of the fighting; an old woman throws herself to the ground. Now the rebels are fighting with even greater ferocity, abandoning any thought of surrender.

Møller struggles through the mob until he reaches a deserted street and makes his way home to his lodgings. He stares at the two packed trunks, waiting to be conveyed to Leipzig, where his history of Danish literature should generate some interest.

The surroundings and the comparative calm make him painfully aware of his frightful state, of his appearance and the foul stench. The women make a point of steering a wide path as they pass.

nine

'*Cherchez et trouvez!*' . . . is all she replies when he asks for her address, and she moves further along the deck in her purple cloak and vanishes. A vague jasmine scent hangs in the air, and Møller is aware of a subtle, but unmistakable sensation of longing. And now the greenclad huntsmen join the eager throng, as the steamer draws alongside the pier. They emerge from the depths of the forest, with their bags and horns and guns. The mist obscures the scene, as an unexpected warm breeze transforms it into strange shapes. At one point it forms an Alpine mountain peak, at another an enormous grotto with stalagmites and stalactites and at the edge it catches the first rays of morning sunshine in the palace of the fairy king where the naiads are dancing.

Although it is November now, winter is reluctant to make its appearance. It is as though nature is rebelling, as though spring has arrived four months early, and the passengers let their padded coats hang open as they greet the huntsmen, whose boots glisten with the early morning dew. Møller has no time to exchange greetings with them, for he has to locate the woman and have a talk with her before she disembarks. He dashes along the deck as fast as he can run, and while he pauses for breath, the smell of the meadows urges him on. But just as he is about to step onto the gangplank a seaman drags him back, and soon the steamer resumes its voyage down the Elbe to Magdeburg where he will take the recently opened railway route to Leipzig.

How long did they spend together? Two minutes? Ten? Five? She came up to him as he stood on the rear deck while the dawn slowly broke, and it was as though she had an invisible fan to hide her slow, dark smile, as she not just once but twice moved to and fro in front of him. She was alone, her only luggage the crocodile handbag. When she observed that he was holding a copy of Victor Hugo's *Le Roi s'amuse*, she enquired:

'*Vous êtes français?*'

'*Qui est français, qui le veut,*' he replied, absurdly proud of his pronunciation.

She asked him what he did for a living, and he told her that he was a Danish writer fleeing from the boredom of Hamburg, ironically adding that it had been intimated in the highest places that he would be well advised to acquire a doctorate, that universal levy imposed by the Germans on travellers of any apparent standing. The woman laughed out loud as he ridiculed the German doctorate which — and here he pursed his lips and spoke in low, confessional tones — can be had in Berlin and Leipzig for a paltry two hundred Prussian talers, while less affluent seekers of appropriately lesser academic distinction can knock on the door of the second class doctorate factories in Jena, where the price is as low as seventy talers. Then the steamer drew alongside, and the woman again vanished, as swiftly and as imperceptibly as she had appeared.

Now once more he catches sight of her purple cloak on the shore. She casually takes one of the huntsmen by the hand, ecstatically swinging her bag in front of her. Once, just once, she turns round, but at the moment Møller captures her glance and waves to her, the sunshine hits her eyes, causing her to wince. Then the other huntsmen gather round her and sweep her joyously off into the depths of the woods. Møller hears the distant baying of hounds, the blaring of horns. For a long time he can hear the receding sounds of the hunting

party, as the sun rises higher and higher and spring
relentlessly moves one day closer to the chill of winter. Until
late afternoon he paces the deck, all appetite gone, and Victor
Hugo now fails to arouse his curiosity. The passengers loll in
deckchairs, enjoying the unexpected burst of sunshine, and
afternoon fades into evening. Soon, Møller thinks, the sun will
orbit the earth, the lamb will lie with the tiger and the dove
with the snake.

'If this beautiful weather continues, you know what to
expect. ∴.' an elderly woman remarks to him as he leans over
the rail, staring at the water.

'And what, madam, are we to expect?' he asks distractedly.

'Doomsday, my good man, doomsday!'

The flowers along the river bank are blooming. Fish leap up
to catch midges. Møller thinks he can still hear, faintly, the
sounds of the hunting party.

'Look, they never give a thought to the fate that awaits
them, the evil days to come. They don't know that the bitter
cold and cruelty of winter is nigh,' says the elderly woman,
pointing at the birds mating in the sedge.

In Leipzig, doomsday is truly drawing near. People are
concerned about the heat that persists, long after it should
have subsided. The issue is discussed in the modest offices of
the *Nordischer Telegraph* where Møller soon gains employment,
offices that exude an odd blend of punch, stamp pads, shag
tobacco and the nauseatingly sweet hair oil used by publisher
Lorck's assistant. Then, in the middle of November 1848, the
weather changes, and with a vengeance, from one hour to the
next. A crashing, blinding storm of thunder and lightning,
with streaks of fork lightning lacerating the darkening sky,
even the cloudless patches. The winter gloom becomes an
invisible hand drawn in a flash over the sky, and the hailstones
pelt down and then form sheets of opaque ice, forcing the birds
to abandon their nestbuilding and the flowers to creep back
into the soil. As the streets and parks take on a threatening,
frosty sheen, the populace has reached boiling point upon
hearing news of the brutal shooting of Robert Blum, Leipzig's
highly esteemed member of the parliament in Frankfurt, and

Møller exudes rabid condemnation — and enthusiasm for a common cause — at meetings called to express revulsion and indignation. In this situation there is only one stance he can adopt: staunch support for the democrats and revolutionaries against the forces of reaction. 'Whatever you think of the man's aims,' writes Møller, '. . . it is now evident that his beliefs amounted to a conviction, to a faith, a virtue usually lacking in the leaders of the era in which we live. It was this burning faith that gave him strength and confidence, that raised him to the level of a contemporary hero, but also rendered him unable to cope with the practical demands imposed by that same era.'

Impractical, but utterly unshakable in his inviolability as a member of the Frankfurt parliament, a man who enjoyed sitting in Vienna's coffeehouses, right up to the day before he was shot, following a court-martial, smiling to all and sundry, convinced that democracy would triumph as tomorrow's form of government, an adherent of the people's right to self-determination. In Møller's opinion the Frankfurt parliament can have had no more distinguished member than Robert Blum. The indignation at his execution following the occupation of Vienna by the imperial troops is so widespread among the meek citizens of Leipzig that even democratic and socialist factions, hitherto engaged in internecine strife, manage to unite. Irrespective of class, the people of Leipzig admire Blum, although, Møller notes, the womenfolk at one stage contemplated a revolution against him, a sort of Sicilian vendetta to punish him for enticing their men to linger in the ale-houses after ten o'clock in the evening.

Møller strikes up acquaintanceships and soon speaks and writes German so well that he is taken for a native left-wing democrat who, with his grey eyes, his sarcastic, wolfish smile, his air of being just about to pounce on his prey, his erect carriage, his impeccable attire and firm handshake, send a tremor of fear through the entire Junker party. From the Foreign Office in Copenhagen he now finally receives a quarterly remuneration of one hundred and fifty rigsdalers, in recognition of his services in defending Denmark, with the printed and spoken word, whenever he has a chance of reaching the eyes or ears of men of influence. In the offices of the *Nordischer Telegraph*, Lorck, aided by his jam-loving assistant — whose hair is glued to his forehead by his sweet syrupy hair oil, something which has annoyed Møller from the start — enthusiastically prints such lengthy treatises as Møller's *Kritische Bemerkungen zu der vom Frankfurter Reichsminis-terium in Sachen des Waffenstillstandes mit Dänemark erlassenen Denkschrift*. Møller feels as though he is writing an exam paper on a compulsory subject where every detail must be committed to memory and regurgitated, paragraph by paragraph. All the while, the publisher's assistant, convinced that a new European renaissance will emerge from 'the tiny, enchanting Germanic border states', Holland-Denmark and Sweden-Norway, dances round him like a tornado, opening yet another pot of jam into which he dips a soggy biscuit. Sometimes, and the sight of it makes Møller sick, he smooths down his sticky hair with the palm of his hand and licks it, exclaiming: 'Oh, Amsterdam! The boundless tracts of the west! Ah, Copenhagen, my emerald heart mounted in filigree copper!' or 'Stockholm, my sunken Caroline Venice!'

Møller finally succeeds in having his first articles on Danish literature printed, and he enters the golden flush of a period of sustained inspiration. Another year and *The Danish Tone* will be finished, a work that can restore his hopes of being chosen to fill the chair vacated by Oehlenschläger at the University of Copenhagen. The printer's fount is augmented to introduce Wessel, Paludan-Møller, Christian Winther, Henrik Hertz and Oehlenschläger *als Epiker* to German readers before the manuscripts are used as wrapping for jampots. And the reputation of the Danish writers spreads, reaching as far as Vienna, an achievement which Møller does not fail to report to his mentor in a letter which also describes how inspiration flies out the window as poverty creeps under the door. Is there no possibility of extracting a pittance from the bulging university coffers? To which Oehlenschläger replies that he will do all in his power to help his promising young friend.

When he feels that he can no longer suffer the nauseating

stench of jam mixed with syrupy hair oil, and he grows tired of
a defence of Denmark's position which he realizes will be read
and understood only by those already converted to the cause,
when *The Danish Tone* suddenly becomes inaudible simply
because he cannot lay hands on his source material, the books,
when his frustration at not being able to afford a new overcoat
or even a pair of new boots begins to gnaw at him, and he
alternately suffers fits of shivering and sneezing, Møller seeks
escape and solace in the company of one of the most famous
figures to grace the Leipzig scene. The poet, novelist, theatre
critic and humorist, Harlosssohn, is always available for a
discourse on weighty or trivial matters in the town's dingiest
ale-house where Harlosssohn, who loves to speak of himself in
the third person, drinks tankard after tankard of ale, whiling
the time away by engaging in exquisitely banal exchanges
with the coarsest philistines who can never be too obtuse. One
inane remark, a single mispronunciation, a grammatical
solecism, and Harlosssohn pounces:

'Harlos . . . *with three s's, gentlemen, I pray you!* Harlosssohn
now apparently believes in the partition of Germany! And
more than that! The partitioned areas are to be further
divided! A post office for every farmhouse! A theatre for every
hamlet! A revolutionary parliament for every village!' he
shouts one evening, provoking anger all about him. The
following evening, however, he whispers almost inaudibly:

'Last night, gentlemen, Harlosssohn had a dream, nay, a
vision! Silence! A Germany stretching from Narvik to the
sunny land of the Basques! And what's more, Harlosssohn
can speak the Basque tongue, should anyone present happen
to doubt the matter. *Gar dembora edera!* Which, of course,
means: today the weather is clement, as, gentlemen, it
happens not to be today in this sad city. And down in their
sunny climes the Basques use the sun sign as their escutcheon.
Our ancient swastika!'

Harlosssohn spews out his flood of nonsense as rapidly as he
guzzles the ale, while waiting for the actors to arrive so that
they can give him the gist of the play in which they are
appearing. At eleven o'clock, when the ale-house closes, he

goes home and writes his ten or twelve lines of drunken criticism which will be published tomorrow in the *Tageblatt* as dramatic criticism, and Møller cannot recall ever having read such utter drivel about the theatre as Harlosssohn's eternal garlands of praise and rapture, nor can he refrain from informing the worthy critic of his opinion.

'Harlosssohn knows that, he *knows* that!' Harlosssohn laments, looking at Møller in despair, the only one in the room who never provokes his outbursts, this odd expatriate whom he helps with a stack of letters of introduction to the most attractive actresses in Leipzig. 'But remember, my Nordic friend, Harlosssohn is paid only a paltry eight groschen for an article,' and he clutches his stomach in agony, contorted by the pain that can drive him staggering into the backyard with tears welling up in his eyes, where he stays for half an hour, then comes back, apparently recovered, wriggling his nose into place and patting his huge belly until he utters a rumbling belch — this man who only a few years ago was one of Germany's most widely read, most admired writers, a man possessed of sensibility, of a sense of humour and of what Møller refers to as inventive genius, capable of keeping five or six booksellers in business. Now the blabbering hulk can no longer infuse an element of life into a single sentence.

Harlosssohn grabs Møller by the arm, squeezing as hard as he can with his podgy fingers:

'Freedom of the press, Doktor Müller, that's what I'm telling you. Freedom of the press will be the death of Harlosssohn! Now they're all going to come down like a wolf on the fold! Watch them, Müller!'

He hesitates for a moment, and his gaze becomes forlorn. It is as though he is peering into himself, or even worse, into his own inner well of emptiness. Then he resumes, as he does night after night:

'Do you know, Müller, the difference between a poisonous toad and the writer Harlosssohn sitting here on the other side of this table? No, and how on earth could you know! Then listen to this: the poisonous toad is more human than Harlosssohn. . .'

One night 'the Triple-S' fails to appear. For a week ot two,
his absence is noted with regret in the offices of the *Tageblatt*
and the ale-house. Then life just goes on as though he had
never existed.

Around this time Møller is informed that his services as
writer and translator are required at the Danish legation in
Berlin.

He once more packs his trunks.

'*Vous êtes français?*'

'*Qui est français, qui. . .*' he is about to reply. But P.L. Møller
hates to repeat himself, especially now when for the first time
in his life he is experiencing a reality that matches his dreams.

He always has the feeling of running after reality, but it
eludes him, because reality never corresponds to the picture it
presents of itself. In the remote distance, in the background of
the scene, he sees, as though through a fine film of gauze, a
world shimmering in the finest colours — lighter, more
ethereal than the real world. A world where flowers bloom,
but then, often with a violent jerk, when he tears the gauze
aside and enters that other world behind and stoops to pick a
flower, it instantly withers between his fingers and the other
world assumes the pallid colours of reality. Where he conjures
up castles, ruins sprawl. What he conceives of as the dwelling
place of airy spirits turns into Hamburg's foul gut, the
typesetter's sickening hair oil, Harlosssohn's shrunken corpse
and now the base, philistine tone pervading the Danish
legation in Berlin.

Something constantly signals him to keep his distance —
his distance from beauty. And he doesn't know what this
something is.

But the moment she opens the door and he looks straight
into her questioning eyes, he experiences it for the first time:
that which he has dreamed of comes vividly to life, brimming
with allure and charm. And Møller makes a sweeping bow,
blissfully happy, and proffers the bouquet of tiger lilies and
yellow roses, but he is no longer standing on the deck of the

steamer on an early, unreal November morning. He is in Berlin, and it is a warm summer's afternoon a year and a half later and he has trudged up and down the barren stretch of sand in front of the Brandenburg Gate, quenching his thirst with the few cherries he had in his pocket, and now he stands on the doorstep of her residence, while Bettina von Arnim continues to look steadily at him, and a taut nerve makes one cheek quiver. Møller kisses her hand and replies: '*Madame, je suis danois, et j'en suis fier!*'

For weeks he has been living in his lodgings in Charité-strasse reading her letters to Goethe. Not one of them is superfluous, each vibrates with her delight in art and culture, vibrates with a wisdom unnatural in a girl of such tender years, born of a Frankfurt family of geniuses and eccentrics related to the Italian Viscontis and the French de Laroches. *Goethes Briefwechsel mit einem Kinde* has resuscitated Møller's love of reading, and he wonders why he failed to acquire a copy of this unique and deeply poetic document when it was first published in 1835, when he was lounging in the torpor of Regensen. This is how beautiful the world can really be, so unspoilt by everything that drags a man down into the muddy clutches of Old Pan. Møller considers writing an exhaustive thesis on the letters, in which he will emphasize the girl's inexplicable intuition, which amounts to nothing less than sheer genius — the intuition which he would like to discuss with the woman who was once that very girl, if she will but grant him a quarter of an hour of her time. To all of which she replies with a peal of girlish laughter:

'My day is yours! And tomorrow too!'

And he sees the small, orphaned Bettina Elisabeth Katharina Ludovica Magdalena behind every feature of the older, white-haired woman who leads him into her solidly furnished drawing room which, complying with the whims of Berlin, is far too big. He sees her knock-knees, her narrow hips, her nervous hands and slightly inward-turning feet encased in child's shoes, while stark terror makes her eyes bulge in a fixed stare when she realizes that she is to be reared in a Westphalian convent on the Edder, a period she describes in a diary which forms a third of the letters exchanged with the Elderly Gentleman in Weimar. Isolated, she grows up as a smooth, brown, finely boned fawn, radiating an odd mixture of friendliness and indomitability, at one with nature, virtually on speaking terms with the flowers, the trees, the bees and the swallows. In one glimpse she climbs the trees in the convent grounds; in the next she sneaks into the freedom of the outdoors, untroubled by howling wind or torrents of rain, falling asleep in the grass or listening to a band of gypsies who have set up camp on the edge of the wood, on the other side of the river. And when he looks again he sees her in the convent garden, confronted with death as it suddenly overcomes an aged nun who was pruning her roses, which is almost as big a shock as being ordered to carry away, on a sacrificial platter, the long, thick tresses of a novice who was undergoing her initiation.

'I shall never forget it, the velvety hair . . . and that *platter*,' says Bettina von Arnim and asks Møller if she might offer him tea or coffee sprinkled lightly with chocolate, a beverage for which she has a particular liking. Sparkling with life, she forgets her offer and begins to pour him a glass of wine, imploring him to take the best armchair. She herself sits on a rickety chair, apparently made of sticks and straw, with tiny hearts and lavenders embroidered on the back, and tells him how she first saw herself in a mirror when she was thirteen and visited her grandmother. She holds her face in her hands and laughs: no such frivolous and useless object was allowed in the convent! To Møller, Bettina von Arnim is just as beautiful today as she must have been when she at last set eye on her own intense eyes, her smooth forehead and her tresses casually brushing against her cheeks, and spurred on by his avid interest she recalls scenes, incidents and details from the days when she was only a slip of a girl, and the relationship she had with Karoline von Günderode — the remote and ethereally beautiful woman from the cushioned classes, condemned to impending spinsterhood, real or illusory, to dwell, probably until her dying day, if circumstances so dictate, in an immaculately kept manor house, sustained only by her piano and books and embroidery and due observance of the ten commandments — a relationship which was the most important event in Bettina's life until, many years later, her meeting with Goethe himself.

'Do they read it in Denmark — my *Günderode?*' she asks. And she puts two fingers to her mouth, as a gesture of mock remorse at having been guilty of such colossal vanity.

Møller nods and tells in subdued tones — still afraid that the ramshackle chair will collapse under Bettina von Arnim — the story of how Günderode, this woman from a different, colder world where the flowers unfold without colour and the moon shines day and night, deliberately experimented with the callow, sensitive, enthusiastic and giddy Bettina Elisabeth who has run away from the convent on the banks of the Edder. Her magnetic powers of attraction compel the eight years younger Bettina to worship her as together they enter the chilly portals of wisdom. Philosophy, history, mathematics, music and poetry: Günderode the Aloof, Günderode the Melancholic tutors Bettina in all subjects. But not like a school teacher. Bettina's education is like a game played in a dream: step by step the girl is transformed from a neglected convent child into an animated writer capable of striking a chord of sympathy in Goethe, captivating him and making him ten years younger. Expelled by Günderode from her earlier communion with nature and flowers and swollen rivers, Bettina experiences one fantastic revelation after the other, on every subject except philosophy, which, requiring as it does nothing but pure brain work, makes her suffer sickening doubts and confusion. Günderode, ever watchful, ever sensitive to the moods of her ward, detects the doubts and abandons the strictness of Kant and the fury of Fichte while she — and suddenly Møller notices how the small hairs on the back of his neck are standing on end like bristles, a shiver runs down his spine and he lowers his voice to the merest whisper — while she, Günderode the Bitter, Günderode the Aggrieved, in some inexplicable manner becomes more and more aloof and cold, spurning her acolyte, as though. . .

'As though *what?*'

Bettina von Arnim stares at him, terror-stricken. The chair

is about to collapse beneath her, and Møller politely indicates to her that she is to join him on the sofa. She replenishes their glasses. The sun is about to set, and from the desert of sand they hear the distant shouts of boys playing. An unnatural chill pervades the room, and Bettina von Arnim clutches a crocheted rug as she tremulously places herself on the sofa, her eyes wide open and staring fixedly into space.

'. . . as though she *hates*,' Møller continues icily, '*hates* the transformation this child has undergone; *hates* to hear how she repeats her, Günderode's, own words of wisdom, but with greater beauty, greater animation; *hates* her unassailable innocence; *hates* her boundless zest for life to such an extent that she is seized with a consuming desire for a new experience that will take her all the way back to that primitive state of childish ignorance from which she — you — will never again ascend to reach for the fruits of perception, never, never again. Günderode. . .'

'My goodness! How astonishingly well you pronounce her name!' Bettina von Arnim says, cuddling into an even tighter ball in the folds of the rug, as the white locks dangle round her wrinkled cheeks. 'I can almost see her rising out of your magic cauldron! But I loved her, loved her beyond all measure. . .'

'I know you did,' Møller replies, relieved that some element of warmth has been restored and is coursing through him too, 'and that love is beautifully depicted in the book, especially in the chapter where. . .'

'Where?'

Møller is about to ask her, tenderly, if she has even the slightest recollection of what she has written, because she hangs on his every word like a little girl with goose pimples, shuddering in horror as a benign uncle reads a lurid fairy tale by flickering candlelight.

'The part where Günderode takes her own life by stabbing herself with a dagger and jumping into the river with a stone around her neck. . .'

'No, no, *I* had nothing to do with that! That was all on account of her tragic involvement with that miserable Professor Kreutzer from Marburg and his silly symbolism!'

'Have I in any way implied that it *was* your fault?'

'No, no, of course not. . .'

Bettina von Arnim wriggles nervously, letting the rug fall to the floor, and tugs at the bell pull to summon her valet. Beyond the heavy drapes darkness has fallen.

'Bettina. . .' Møller stops short of uttering her full name.

'Yes. . .'

'I love you. . .'

'No, my young Danish friend, now you just listen to what I have to say. . .'

And she turns to face him:

'I assume that you are not so much as one day over thirty years.'

'I am thirty-six, Madam, and I am yours.'

'All mine? A withered hag like me?'

The valet enters with a tray of oversweet refreshments and a message to the effect that the Danes have scored a surprise victory at Isted. Møller hardly hears the news. He brushes the fluff from his trousers, breathes on his nails and polishes them against his knees, lights a cigar and looks forward to the coffee which Bettina von Arnim herself has impulsively decided to brew for him, dispensing with the services of the surly valet. 'Strong as an ox, black as a raven and with a double sprinkling of chocolate from Bahia,' she says, sticking her head into the room, in a voice quivering with emotion. A few minutes later she returns with coffee and cups clattering on a delicate Indian copper tray engraved with a fierce and beautiful Shiva.

'A gift from Humboldt,' she giggles, attempting a stumbling curtsy so that she nearly tumbles into his lap. Is he not thrilled to hear of the Danish triumph? she asks, but Møller is reluctant to speak of martial matters. He wants to hear all about the Privy Councillor. And while the oil lamps are lit to dispel the gathering dusk, the valet withdraws with a noncommital bow and a vast silence settles over Berlin. Bettina von Arnim so vividly and persuasively describes it all that it is no mere chance shadow or illusion created by a play of light, but Goethe himself who sits there in a corner of the study, smiling as the double doors are flung open to allow him his first sight of his young penfriend. 'Do exactly as you please,

my dear,' he says, and Bettina Elisabeth runs up to him, with
her knock-knees shaking, hops up onto his lap and instantly
falls asleep, utterly spent after trundling in a wagon across
rugged roads, without a wink of sleep, for two days and two
nights.

'When I awakened, life had commenced,' she trills, 'in a
kaleidoscope of rich colours, a fanfare of celestial music.' She
returns to her position on the sofa, now tucking her legs
beneath her.

'Do you know eternity?' she asks.

'A process of repetition, that's what eternity is,' Møller
replies. 'Hope is a beckoning fruit that doesn't satiate,
remembrance is wretched sustenance for the traveller, but
repetition is the blessing of eternity.'

'How beautifully you put things! You must be a writer. . .'

He imagines her as she saunters through Weimar with the
Old Gentleman. In one scene he protects her from a spring
shower under his cape, in another he puts a ring on her finger,
and in the next he is out for an evening stroll with her, fondling
her arm, allowing her to peep into the ornate drawing rooms.
And the blessing of Goethe's mother, with whom Bettina has
entered a sacred pact, hovers over them wherever they go.
And Frau Rath is present in the room, and Møller quotes her,
while he finally begins to feel that he is no longer running after
reality, that this devotion is true:

'Dearest daughter! My son shall be your friend, your
brother, who so clearly loves you; and you are to call me
mother, today and all the days that the good Lord sees fit to
grant me. After all, Mother is the only name that embraces all
my happiness. . .'

Bettina von Arnim falls silent, overwhelmed by the
quotation, but only for a brief moment. Then she again
sparkles, radiant with life:

'But she also said, yes, she really did, that. . . "you must not
make life too confused for my son, let everything remain in its
proper place, in order" . . . Oh, that insistence on order, on
keeping things in their proper place!'

She gets to her feet, walks over to a wall lined with

bookshelves from floor to ceiling and a few minutes later Møller has been given a stack of her own books, over a dozen of them, including her correspondence with her brother, *Clemens Brentanos Frühlingskranz*, and *Dies Buch gehört dem König*, her political testament, where she becomes an advocate of socialism based on good will, the open mind and the warm heart — and making provisions for a monarch at the peak of the pyramid to supervise the conduct of the national economy.

'Is it too terribly much to ask for?' she asks with a sigh. 'Ah yes, if only His Majesty had listened to me!' And now there is anger in her soul as she tells how the king, who up to 1848 had regarded her as a personal friend and adviser, has given her the cold shoulder because she elected to take sides with the underprivileged against the Junkers.

'We *must* do something about the world, you and I and all our friends. The Grimm Brothers, whom I admire, say so too,' she continues, taking Møller by the hand, as though she is prepared there and then to dash out onto the streets and start building barricades with him labouring by her side. But she knows, and everybody else knows, that the age of revolution in Europe is dead and gone; law and order prevail, the martyrs are forgotten, even Robert Blum. The madness and the heady rush are forgotten, but also the exultation, and the best course· for a man who wants to get ahead is to join a party whose watchwords are prudence and moderation. Even Bettina von Arnim's son, the baron, has decided to support the reactionaries, and Møller has heard that he is on the verge of regarding his mother as a prematurely senile daydreamer whose pleas to kings and emperors to release prisoners only make things worse, dragging the family name through the mud.

'What an idea!' And Bettina von Arnim thumps the table with such force that the cups begin to clatter again. 'The son of Bettina von Arnim's flesh, and of Goethe's spirit, and what does he do? Shoots wild beasts with *silver* bullets when he goes out hunting and breaks into a rash with the sheer joy of reading the *Kreutzzeitung*. The name alone is enough to make one's blood run cold. Hell and damnation! That horrible

Ordnung, Ordnung muss sein! And yet she too was a sort of socialist. . .'

'Who?' Møller asks, realizing that Bettina von Arnim is now finding it more and more difficult to impose any coherence on her thoughts.

'That one there. . .'

'Frau Rath?'

'Yes. Oh God, my memory's like a sieve. No, you'd do much better to get yourself a girl of your own age.'

The oil lamps are beginning to dry up and flutter feebly as the first rays of dawn penetrate the drapes and strike against the sculptures which Bettina von Arnim works on when not absorbed in her writing. Soon all the cocks in Berlin begin to crow. A raven flies past, fluttering along the window sills. Møller leans back, allowing the impressions to filter through and fall into place, while Bettina von Arnim stretches out on the sofa and draws the rug over her shoulders, so exhausted now that she has lapsed into total silence. A short while later he gets up and walks along the shelves, looking at her books, her knick-knacks, sheets of music with her own compositions and the piles of sketches and drawings spread about the room. One of them shows a youth who has been slain by the demon alcohol. He lies there, half naked under a vaulted ceiling, surrounded by bulging casks of wine, depicted as rapacious monsters. Satyrs and baccanthes seize their victim, clasp him and kill him.

Bettina von Arnim is asleep. One arm droops over the edge of the sofa, and her hand hits the floor with a dull thud. Møller goes over to her, lifts her arm and draws the rug up, covering her cheeks. She smiles in her sleep, and he kisses her tenderly on her brow, softly reciting the lines from Goethe's 'Willkommen und Abschied':

Doch ach, schon mit der Morgensonne
Verengt der Abschied mir das Herz:
In deinen Küssen welche Wonne!
In deinem Auge welcher Schmerz!

ten

'Give me my wall!' he roars.

Møller thumps the bolster in sweaty desperation. Furious. It started out as a joke when he and Goldschmidt — who happened to be in Berlin for a few days, entrusted with the mission of supporting the two barons, Reedtz and Pechlin, in their efforts to prevent a resumption of hostilities — found themselves aboard a Potsdam pleasure steamer. They were out for a gentle cruise along the trim parks and round the pine-dotted islands, and now he is furious that this innocent outing should end in a nightmare that rudely shatters his sleep every night at precisely three o'clock, an hour when vitality is commonly held to be at its lowest ebb, when the sick and aged die like flies, and the wolves in the forests stand side by side in wide circles and howl at the moon. This is a poor substitute for the opposition that Møller desires. Here are no dire forebodings about that wall he knows he must one day face and climb, to be finally acclaimed — with bloodied nails and lacerated body and tattered clothes — as victor. No, this is ridiculous. This nightmare brings no endless expanse of impenetrable wall, but splinters of glass between his toes, or sand sprinkled grain by grain down into the tiniest cogs and wheels of his brain, to irritate them and knock them out of gear night after night and drive him gradually mad, destroying his sense of direction and making him forget all about his quest for the wall that awaits him.

During the early stages of the cruise they maintained a polite distance, as though they were strangers. Each in turn offered the other a cigar; each in turn mumbled 'after you, sir' as they paraded along the deck and negotiated steep gangways. Stepping over coiled ropes and stooping under low lintels they soon became engrossed in a discourse on the finer points of the storyteller's art. They exchanged viewpoints on how best to drive the point firmly home, and Goldschmidt, now plumper and sporting a new gold ring, hinted broadly to Møller that he would have every access to the columns of *North and South* if he should happen to write the perfect story. Idea: a rich countess adopts a pauper. What happens when the child, now an adult, suddenly gets to know of its origins? No, a burnt-out theme. Idea: a girl cannot help regarding everything in this world as beautiful and spiritual, even poverty, sickness and death. How this attitude drives all who know her to the brink of insanity. Or that perennial one about. . . '. . . swapping character,' they burst out in unison, looking into each other's eyes as they uttered the words. The steamer sailed into a lake where the evening mist, settling above the reed-fringed shore, reminded Møller of the distant charms of Lake Esrum.

Idea: *A description of a character born with a keen conscience. How a clever thief, born without a grain of conscience, uses devilish strategies to steal the conscience of the good man, under the guise of friendship and thirst for learning, so cunningly that the good man fails to detect the theft until it is too late.*

After a while:

'And then . . . how the unhappy good man, bereft of any semblance of conscience, now must make his way in the cruel world, hated and despised. . .' Goldschmidt embroidered.

'. . . searching for his lost conscience, his lost innocence,' Møller continued, as the steamer rounded a promontory and sailed from the dappled light into a dark patch of water cut off from the sunlight by a steep, pine-studded hill.

'. . . but without ever finding anything apart from the

remaining primeval instincts which will never elicit the recognition or approval of the educated public without which he can achieve neither happiness nor gratification,' Goldschmidt interrupted as the boat left the dark patch behind and sailed on through an interlocking maze of new lakes fringed with new woods and a few grassy slopes cleared to accommodate stately villas and humble farmhouses.

'While the man without conscience cashes in on his crime,' Møller added, lowering his voice and examining Goldschmidt's new ring as the cigar smoke curled upwards and drifted into the gathering darkness.

This development of the story was not immediately taken up by Goldschmidt who paused, cleared his throat and looked straight at Møller:

'You mean that the thief flaunts the purloined conscience and is regarded by the public, who fails to see through the ruse, as the very personification of the ethical concept?'

'The very personification of the ethical concept! My words, Meyer A-a-a-aron, my very words!'

The tone had turned sour. Møller's wound still festers.

'And the original good man, the man who originally possessed the shining conscience, Møller? Have you worked out his destiny too, with a flourish of your dripping pen?'

'Oh, I don't know, Goldschmidt, what fate to allocate him. Shouldn't we just let him die a tragic death among desert dwellers?'

'So far away! And before that he has probably been blinded by the fierce Algerian sun and struck dumb by his inability to produce well-turned rhymes in his mother tongue?'

'Of course, what a story. . .'

'Yes, what a story. A veritable *Masaul*. Write it for me!'

'That's what I'm doing, Goldschmidt. Another cigar?'

They disembarked and spent a few hours strolling around in silence. They made their way to the peak of Easter Mountain, and climbed to the top of the tower to survey all the lakes and islands down to Rauberschlange. They turned round, still maintaining silence, until on their way back to Berlin they reached an alley lined with taverns where the tumult and the sound of the dice filled Møller with an urge to hear the sound of his own voice again. He gave a polite cough, removed his hat and pointed with it towards the most bustling tavern.

'And *magister* Kierkegaard? What's he up to these days?' Møller ended the reign of silence with a sudden stab of awareness that these were hardly the appropriate words with which to cast off the story's evil spell. If only he had said: 'My ankle is beginning to give a spot of bother,' or 'Is there no end to that exasperating war?'

'My dear Møller, with your vitriolic pen you have cleverly consigned the *magister* to the regions of darkness where no candle gleams, where no words are spoken. Surely you're not surprised?'

And Møller was forced to resort to their joint creation for an apt quotation, as they entered the tavern and seated themselves at a table in the corner:

'Thus, undoubtedly, speaks the personification of the ethical concept!'

A red-haired peasant girl arrived at the table carrying a wooden tray laden with huge log-shaped hunks of cheese and two enormous pewter tankards of foaming ale. At the next table a group of Schleswig-Holsteiners were loudly predicting Denmark's imminent decline and fall. Møller and Gold-schmidt decided to ignore the intended or accidental provocation.

'Just call me a witness. Your witness. And Kjerkegaards', as you call him,' Goldschmidt replied, with his nose immersed in the beer. And Møller can still see the foam as he hammers the bolster.

'But, pray tell me, where does he live these days?'

'Always on the move, flitting from one part of town to another. They say he's entering an entirely new phase of his work, a different sort of stuff altogether.'

'Oh well, but I suppose he continues to write to the nation's pleasurable approval.'

'But his writing is black, Møller. *Black*, remember that. There is no hope.'

Møller drank the weak ale, leaving the pile of cheeses untouched. Again there was a wall of silence between them. Above the hubbub of the tavern they could hear noises from the alley: dogs barking, sheep bleating, wheels creaking. And the churning of a water mill.

'By the way, my dear Møller, do you intend to apply for Oehlenschläger's vacant chair?' Goldschmidt enquired when they were on their third tankard.

'Are *you*?' Møller asked, his voice quivering with irritation at the refusal of the story to fade into a fitting oblivion.

'Come, come, Møller. Remember, I asked first. And what we truly need is your passion for our national literature. All of which amounts to an answer to your question. No, Møller, my hat will not be in the ring. I am not an aesthetician, merely a dabbler on the fringes of literature.'

'But a dabbler with talent! Tell me about Oehlenschläger's funeral. You know how much I appreciate your feeling for detail.'

'Stop dodging the issue, Møller — but I'm not going to pester you any further!'

'A thousand thanks, Meyer. And as far as I'm concerned, you can forget all about Oehlenschläger's funeral. But some personal comments, Goldschmidt, some personal remarks! As a shareholder in your conscience I *cannot* shirk my duty of congratulating you on your progress in the sphere of ethics. Keep at it, and you will undoubtedly be capable of reaching the stage where you will die of a common cold, like Paludan-Müller's *Adam Homo*. A death far more horrible than being bitten by a poisonous adder under the glare of the desert sun! I have taken great pleasure, right from its very infancy, from the faltering beginnings in *North and South*, in observing this effort to promote the ethical concept so cherished by the populace of Copenhagen, and here I am not thinking only of my amicable altercation with your good self. Even Grundtvig has fallen into your trap and has stretched out to you, heir to Palestine, his ancient Christian hand in the spirit of a friendly tiff. How much did you have to pay the man?'

At these words, Goldschmidt jerked himself to his feet and poured a shower of coins from his purse onto the table as payment for his ale. And he also had the last word in this chapter of their story, which ended with Møller left alone at the table, as the logs of cheese rolled onto the sanded floor, as the Schleswig-Holsteiners bellowed with glee, and the creaking of the water mill became louder. And continues to turn and to creak, louder still and louder.

'Incidentally,' Goldschmidt said, in a matter-of-fact voice, 'it *has* been decided. Hauch has been awarded the chair. And deservedly so, in my opinion. . .'

'Sand!' Møller roars.

He flings off the eiderdown, gets out of bed and lights the lamp. When his eyes have grown accustomed to the light, he dashes over to the window and forces it wide open. He sits down at the desk, now itching all over, from the soles of his feet to the nape of his neck. He looks at his papers, knowing full well that he will get no sleep tonight either, and he gulps down the grainy remains of the cold coffee. His draft treatise on the Old-German heroic poem *Das Gudrun Lied*, which in language and metre resembles *Das Nibelungen Lied*, but with a far lighter, more Nordic outlook on life — as the beech wood in May is to the oak wood in a winter storm — a treatise he had been particularly eager to send to Oehlenschläger. *Sand*! His polemic in support of the Danish delegation at the negotiations, *Schleswig-Holstein vor dem Friedens-Kongress oder Biedermanns neue Utopia nebst einigen Allotrien*, forty-six pages littered with notes and notes on notes, some of which had taken him days to produce. *Sand*! And sand, sand, sand — his history of Danish literature is nothing but sand. . .

He is in a sanddrift. The sand is drifting into his eyes, his ears, his shoes, under his shirt and his pyjamas, down into his trousers, day and night, hour after hour. The sand from Schleswig-Holstein, alternately brown like excrement and grey like decaying skin, with thousands of sharp flint fragments, stumps of rusty cartridges, dead soldiers' skulls

and rotting scraps of Danish and rebel flags, comes flying from
the farthest horizon, piling up in front of him in towering
heaps so that he has to dig his way forward like a mole,
struggling towards what he believes to be a bright, smooth
country lane where he can walk upright for the rest of the
journey towards his wall. But as soon as he shakes off the sand
of one heap, a new heap forms, engulfing him, and he is on the
verge of collapse after all the wading and crawling — and is
not yet a single step nearer that smooth country lane.

And on top of the drifting sand from Schleswig-Holstein
there is the quicksand heaped in his path, barrow after
barrow, by the Danish delegation, following his affair with
Fru von L., as he used to call her in bed, *Fru Lensgrevinde*, the
countess, as she demanded to be called by day when she
assumed her customary mask of rectitude. He had captured
her at a ball in the Danish legation. He had initiated her into
the art of poetry and, later, into the secret of following one's
erotic inclinations. 'Just see yourself as loaded down by a
heavy trunk, the one that's been crushing you since the time
you were a little girl,' he had whispered to her as they danced.
'I see it,' she had replied. 'Well, put it down!' 'Is it all that
easy?' she had asked. '*That* easy,' he had replied, biting her ear
and soon divining her deepest passions. She preferred to visit
him wearing nothing beneath the flimsy summer coat,
carrying all her clothes in a bag. Gradually a pattern was
established, a procedure to be observed with unfailing
regularity on subsequent visits. She knocked three times on
his door and then made scratching noises on it with her long
nails, like a cat that wants to be let in. The moment he opened
the door she said: 'Sorry, I must have made a mistake!' and he
was supposed to stand there with his pen in one hand and a
sheet of paper in the other, his hair in artistic disarray, naked
and sweating from the waist up, chest and arms covered with
erotic tattoos — hastily drawn with his pen. And just as she
was about 'to flee in terror', he was supposed to draw himself
up to his full height so that she could get an unobstructed view
of the tattoos and throw herself into his arms, letting her bag
drop to the floor. And then he was supposed to step back a few

paces so that she, as though hypnotized, could step right into this hotel room, still pretending that he was a total stranger, fling herself onto his unmade bed with a sob of longing and shame, unbutton her coat, let her hair down, close her eyes and moan: 'Do with me as you please, wretched stranger! I am yours, nameless pauper, yours for this one night!'

Night after night.

But then the letters began to arrive, from Copenhagen and even Oslo, when it was rumoured that they were having an affair. Everyone warned her against him. Another week, another fortnight, and her own good name and her husband's good name would be forever blemished. And it was not the countess, but her husband, the negotiating count, who turned up late one afternoon, while Møller was working on a new series of articles for *Kjøbenhavnsposten*, flung the letters on the desk and in clipped, savage tones ordered him to put an end to the squalid affair. Whereupon Møller twirled his pen like a dart and sent it quivering into the floorboard and shouted at the count as he ran down the stairs:

'Admit it, admit that you actually enjoyed it! Night after night you've known that your wife came to me naked, *Herr Lensgreve*, yes, *naked*! Night after night you've been lying in your nobleman's sweat, thinking: "Oh, if only I could be there, sitting on a little stool, an ever so tiny nobleman's stool, with my delicate, folded hands and my big, wide eyes . . . looking on!"'

'Vengeance will be done, proletarian, mark my words! You loathsome trader in female skeletons!' the count continued to shout as he made his way out. And the next day the wheelbarrows of quicksand arrived. Even the Swedish legation sent loads so that Møller is sucked down into one black hole after the other whenever a Scandinavian comes within hailing distance. Glances that kill, the catalogue of abuse and their obvious pleasure when it is rumoured that he is plunging into bankruptcy. And if it is not the quicksand, it is the small, idiotic heaps placed in his path when he least expects them, the solid chunks that cause him to stumble and fall flat on his face. There is the court case that two

Schleswig-Holsteiners have brought against him because he has called them *Aufwiegler* and *Ruhestörer* — a fine of fifty talers and twenty-five talers for costs. And there are the letters from the University of Copenhagen: 'we regret, *Herr cand. phil.* P.L. Møller, that the University cannot consider your application for financial support towards your continued stay abroad, despite, *Herr cand. phil.* P.L. Møller, the appreciation expressed at the highest levels of your diligence in defending Denmark's cause and in disseminating knowledge of Danish literature.'

And now this nightmare that wakes him every night at three o'clock, with Goldschmidt intruding — arriving with reams of paper and requesting Møller to add his parts to their joint narrative, and when he has spent twelve or fourteen hours struggling with plot and characterization and semi-colons, Goldschmidt makes a neat stack of the sheets, places them in a huge, stiff envelope and returns to Copenhagen. There, sporting gold rings on every finger and his new coat from Fahrner's, he visits the most prominent booksellers in Vestergade and Østergade, offering them his latest piece, 'a work, if I may say so, of considerable merit': volume eight, volume nine, now at the printer's the tenth volume of the story of *Pauvre Louis*! Purchase, acquire your own copy! Follow Møller's story to the very end! And at the Royal Naval Armoury a ball is being held, and Professor Heiberg is executing graceful steps on the linoleum floors, waltzing with Gerda Petrine — the royal actress with the swan neck and the short, dishevelled hair. And in his spacious apartments at Nytorv, Victor Eremita flings all the windows wide open, jubilantly clapping his hands at the passing summer clouds and issuing invitations to one and all to join him for a twelve-course banquet.

'*Sand!*'

Møller scatters his manuscripts and hammers his fist against the thin wall separating him from the occupant of the adjacent room, an old woman, maybe sixty, or maybe well over eighty. She resumes her shouting, in a vain attempt to resurrect her long departed husband, while all her cats wail and claw at the dingy furniture.

'Give me my wall!' Møller shouts, and soon most of the hotel residents are awake. At one stage the usual delegation arrives — the old woman and her cats, a Protestant pastor and a rightwing Social Democrat bookkeeper from Sittensen in Niedersachsen — to demand instant silence. Møller, now stark naked, dances wildly round the room, kicking at the sheets of paper, knocking *Biedermann* under the door and sending *Gudrun* flying out through the open window; with impish malevolence he mimics each of the delegation in turn, the pastor with his pink, sagging cheeks and the saliva trickling down his chin and bulging belly, the stringy bookkeeper looming above the other two, with the jutting gooseneck and a corkscrew nose, and the shrivelled old woman with her dirt-caked neck encased in a frayed, greyish lace collar and the unmistakable odour of stale urine. 'You snake of a priest! You worn out leather bag! Get out! You're only sand! Sand in my head! Pisspot Polly sand! You Priest with your balls hanging low and spit on your thumb, counting money! Counting sand! You sand people! You non-people! Ugly ugly people! Go and burn in the fires of hell! Drown in German hellfire!'

'Calm yourself, calm yourself,' he hears his own silent admonition, and Møller sits down on the bed and listens to the deputation as it disperses, listens to the small grunts of disapproval, the creaking floorboards and squeaking hinges. He knows it: the only way he can avoid the sand is to lock himself in, to seal off all approaches, doing precisely what all Berliners do. If salvation in Hamburg consisted of floating about heavily anaesthetized in an endless network of guts and entrails, the key to salvation in this Prussian capital is to transform everything, the entire physical world, into thought, into a figment of the brain. On the stages in the theatres of Berlin there are no flesh and blood actors, only mobile sculptures; that's how far drama lags behind French drama in this city where the freedom of comedy is so strictly curtailed. No masquerade. No *commedia dell'arte*. But dour gravity, a relentless sense of the serious when *thought* condescends to open its little window to allow a glimpse of its own pompous interior of total nothingness. And the art scene offers the same barren perspectives. No surprising angles. No subtle or unsubtle play of colours. What the artists serve is the *thought* such as 'Twelve Pomeranian peasants make merry till the crack of dawn when the harvest is in' or 'Young maiden gazes out of the window and waits with longing for her father to return from the wars', and neither peasants nor tankards nor girl nor window are imbued with a single breath of life in even a single brush stroke.

From morning till evening the Berliners go about *thinking* themselves to one another, palely smiling, declining to shake hands for fear of being smitten with life, expatiating on how Heine and Börne have corrupted the youth of Germany, while the philosophers, elderly gentlemen with their sad, drooping eyelids, weak bladders and meticulous notes, maintain their regular benches in the parks and cling to their concern for the rules governing philosophy, suppressing any latent spark of genius by reiterating the merits of their own work and their razor-sharp deductions, snuffing out any sudden burst of enthusiasm, any life spark. '*Schön wäre es!*' they nod to one another, scratching the back of their heads where all their precious notes are stored, '*schön wäre es!*' . . . without having the slightest notion of what would be so beautiful.

And at the peak of this Parnassus Møller sees the thought that surpasses all other thoughts, the Prussian king who is worshipped as a deity. The alliance of men of faith and true hearts, founded by the greatest cowards among the Junkers, court functionaries, toadies, the worldly civil servants, a few disgruntled artisans and backstreet hucksters, now has its clammy hand on everything; and the ladies are not the least unwilling to take part in this divine cult. After worship they assume their proper stations in their drawing rooms, from which any trace of dust has been banished with the energy of a whirlwind, and read *Gott mit uns, Organ für Preussens Frauen und Jungfrauen*, edited by the Pomeranian Don Quixote, Otto Graf Schliffenbach, with whom Møller was nearly forced to duel because he, Møller, had once expressed his unedited opinions on the *Graf* and his organ late one evening in a pretentiously respectable ale-house. Bow and scrape and think, think yourself away from everything that matters. Lull yourself into sublime security in the recesses of the monarch's brain: *schön ist es!*

Møller stoops down to retrieve a sheet of paper. *Schön wäre es* if only he could regain hold of himself and his faculties sometime within the next few months. Then he could write his way out of Berlin with a new series of articles before becoming firmly stuck in the mud or sand, past all help, in the Prussian brain, and at a time like this when he must face the bitter reality that his pen, and only his pen, is from now on going to be his sole means of support, his only chance of keeping body and soul together. But will they understand him at home? Won't they simply go ahead and think that it's Copenhagen he's describing if he puts down what he really thinks of Berlin? 'Always the same old dirge!' With Goldschmidt conducting the chorus of disparagement. . .

Møller peers at the paper, trying to remember when he wrote the notes. Suddenly he recognizes them, smiles and gropes for the little silver pipe in the drawer of the bedside table:

'Hashish is a plant closely related to hemp, which it resembles, although from the root upwards, the stalk of the former has more branches. Used in ancient times by the Egyptians and later by Israeli princes to produce artificial intoxication and visions. Either the petals are boiled, with butter added, so as to mix the syrup in cakes enriched with aromatics or balsam, or it is smoked, mixed with tobacco.'

And below:

'The castrati always say I sing too loud. Heinrich Heine.'

Møller has put away the hashish pipe and has crept out of the hotel. As dawn breaks and the last dark clouds disappear in the west, he reaches the edge of a forest for which he has a particular affection. The sun sends broad swathes of light down through the tree-tops, and the young deer lope past him without showing any trace of fear. A hare sits in front of a log, giving him a friendly look, a snake wriggles in the undergrowth, and in the deepest hollow, in the heart of the forest, all the hedgehogs have assembled. The flowers unfold, exuding new scents far beyond the edges of the clearing; the perfume of the wild rose. Møller thrills to the colours of the forest, tangible colours which fill him with an urge to reach out and caress them, the shaggy brown with the faint scent of honey that the bears love, the pale green like transparent gauze of gowns for the most beautiful *grisettes* in Copenhagen, the bluish green like limpid salt water lapping over his feet as he stands on some distant shore. Is it the sound, heaving in the distance, a murmur of waves with millions of glinting rays of sunshine?

Møller has succeeded in thinking Goldschmidt down to minuscule size, down to the size he appeared to be that evening in Frue Kirke, at the most one foot tall. And even an hour ago or more, when Møller stepped out of the hotel, bustling with newfound energy, the changeling abandoned any idea of accompanying Møller on his morning stroll through the forest, totally exhausted by the effort of having to hop down the gigantic steps and risk the precipices on the way from the doormat down to the pavement. Heiberg has long since crept into his hammock on the uppermost tier of his scaffolding, suffering from agonizing hip pains after all that dancing, and Kierkegaard has once more closed his windows and is sitting down alone to eat his turkey. Møller shouts out loud and the trees respond:

> *Vermund in purple raiment*
> *said, as fray and battle sway'd:*
> *Once more I feel Skraep's bright blade*
> *Cause for joy or sad lament?*
> *Fore the King's seat, a herald boy*
> *tripped and trilled the gay refrain:*
> *Cleave the skull, slash him in twain!*
> *The Old Man then wept tears of joy. . .*

'*Uffe the Meek!*' he hears from somewhere nearby. Møller instantly knows who has taken up the cudgel on his behalf and is overjoyed. The young German revolutionaries never took to him, calling him 'Professor Backwards' because he ended his days as a pillar of conservatism; and admittedly the orthodox Lutheran theology from which he gained solace, both in Breslau and Berlin, has never appealed to Møller. But it is a part of New German history, not of the Danish history of those days when his faithful follower, then the philosopher of light and lightness, regularly held court, as 'The Kaiser', in *Bakkehuset*, the writer's house on the hill just outside Copenhagen. There he delivered flaming lectures to the students on the inner nature of man and its pact with the outer aspects and aroused the young Adam Oehlenschläger from his lethargy so that his will became a man's and his heart a boy's. And Møller feels as if he is flying above the forest floor when he replies to his faithful follower, while the forest now unfolds itself in its full morning glory:

> *The word, to which Spirit gives all might,*
> *where voice is heard, bestowing th' gift of sight,*
> *received breath of life, Steffens, here with thee!*
> *here with thee!*

Henrik Steffens laughs a young man's laugh, a shriek of unrestrained hilarity. From this early morning chance meeting until noon they walk, quoting huge chunks of Oehlenschläger. Then Steffens falls silent. For the first time Møller turns to face him, and what he sees now is an old man in nondescript grey clothes, shrunken but in good spirits, saying quietly to him: 'They were worth it, worth my whole life, those days. . .'

It is as though Steffens with a single stroke has obliterated everything that has happened since, and it is not 'Professor Backwards', but 'The Kaiser' who now follows a forest path and disappears beneath the branches of a giant oak. It is the philosopher of light returning to his grave, finally free to sleep in peace. The rustling trees salute him, the forest animals accompany him on his way.

Møller cannot remember when last he felt so blissfully happy. '*Cherchez et trouvez*,' he hears, and everything around him has turned purple. In a state of ecstasy he flings himself onto a pile of leaves and replies, as the naiads dance their way forward:

Cleave his skull, slash him in twain!
The Old Man then wept tears of joy.

Møller does not succeed in shaking the dust and sand of Berlin from his heels until well into 1851 and, on the way down through Germany, he dashes off one article after the other. He again finds himself in Leipzig, which is again in a state of revolution. The mayor cannot make up his mind which side to support, the king or the revolutionaries. The rebels want to build a bridge of ice to cross Slien and Trene, if a really hard winter should mercifully set in. The ladies of Leipzig have such a refined sense of economy that they copy the wording of a theatre poster rather than part with the purchase price — a measly groschen. All the women of Altenburg are brought up to serve as wet nurses. They wear Slavic costume, a short apron over an equally short skirt. Coffee and tea are not to be had for love or money. A less noxious coffee substitute is brewed of burnt carrots. Anyone who arrives home late is forced to pay a fine to the man of the house. Several writers have set themselves up as booksellers, peddling their own works. Few of them took time to attend Harlosssohn's funeral. An English lady creates a furore by describing Leipzig as the general headquarters for stodgy German professors and beer-guzzling students; a city of books, gilded youth, ale-houses and printing works where the fumes of half-digested knowledge blend with the fumes of beer and wine to form a reeking stench for which it is difficult to find a safety valve. A Polish woman pianist creates a furore by smoking cigars in the company of gentlemen until she wins the heart of a bookseller and marries him.

Møller writes to Matilda Leiner: 'I, who am incapable of killing a midge or a fly or any animal unless it is obviously intent on doing me some serious harm, cannot thus vote in favour of your proposal to destroy my letters, unless you should one day *truly* lie on your deathbed. Let them live, poor sad things, securely locked away for as long as they do no one any harm. As winter this year shows no signs of being particularly harsh, I hope that you will temporarily postpone any plans you have made for your death.'

Weimar. What a wretched town, Møller enters in his notebook. The atmosphere is polluted by beer, bad tobacco and even worse newspapers. Here, he remarks, as distinct from any country blessed with a few miles of honest coastline, it is only possible to lead a hair-raising philistine life. One can hardly meet a fellow human being with whom one can exchange two sensible words. So as to avoid falling into the clutches of insanity, Møller is forced to smoke black cigars all day long. And this is the town where Goethe lived, and Schiller and Herder and Wieland. And this is why the philistines of Weimar still insist, with comical solemnity, on calling their town 'the Athens of the Ilm'. The town's only figure of any significance is Doktor Liszt, as the citizens of Weimar call him because he was once awarded an honorary doctorate as a token of appreciation of a concert performance. The visiting stranger would be well advised to take to his heels and flee as soon as he has seen Goethe's and Schiller's houses, Møller writes. He goes so far as to say that if one hasn't seen with one's own eyes Goethe's home and its surroundings, it is difficult to form an accurate impression of the man's work. Without once seeing the small apartments, which strike the visitor as suitable only for the more limited homely pleasures of hearth and table, and the tiny vestibule, and the step with its one or two sculptures, and the study upstairs where he first received Bettina von Arnim, all so tightly boxed in and with such low ceilings that one has to stoop (Goethe was only of average height) — without having seen all this, and the small garden where it is difficult to breathe and fill one's lungs, it is impossible to understand the justification for the comment often made on *Der Alte*: that in his work, side by side with spiritual greatness, there is a large measure of ... yes, pettiness.

But poor Schiller! Møller feels an instant sympathy for the man: apart from the black-striped waistcoat and the curiosa in his cupboard (Goethe's inkwell, a pair of gloves, letters from Wieland) and the snuff boxes on his desk under which he had a basin of cold water to chase the blood from his head, his house can only boast of old copperplate engravings from Italy, to which he could never afford to travel and from which so many dunderheads came home sunburnt, without ever having experienced anything they could not have experienced in equal measure in their own cabbage patches.

A nightmare, Møller concludes: to end up as a provincial hack, a beer-swigging writer for *The Thüringer Railroad Times* or the *Weimar News* unfitted for this life or any other life, a spiritual cretin — a denizen of Weimar.

Eisenach. Luther's ramshackle house. The town's other houses are old but without any special historical or architectural distinction, apparently inhabited by tanners and shoemakers. The peasant girls wear their hair swept back, tied with a ribbon in a little black encasing on the crown of the head. They have small feet and are coquettish.

Møller's travelling bag, carelessly slung too close to a red-hot stove, catches fire, and his already meagre wardrobe is further depleted.

Frankfurt. Small slate-roofed houses. Two streets of importance in the history of the world. Eschenheimer Strasse and Judenstrasse. Judenstrasse is just about the most horrible place Møller has ever seen. A shudder of terror runs through him as he stands at the end of the street which is straight as a die. An oppressive atmosphere. Timber houses, all alike, with gables facing the street, pitch black and slated right down to the ground. The inhabitants are pale and sickly. At the far end of the street there is a house which has been given a coat of paint on one side. There is a plaque stating that Börne was born here. The street's other famous resident, Rothschild, has not yet been accorded similar recognition. The entrances to Frankfurt's churches are blocked by sausage stalls. A Catholic priest is preaching a sermon of such monumental stupidity that the congregation must regard it as Protestant. Shrove Monday is celebrated with the last masked ball at the theatre. The prize for the best mask was won by a Herr Hämpelmann. A few people stand brushing each other's clothes. Ah, probably a rain of confetti to mark the happy occasion? No, two Hämpelmanns had come too close to a sack of flour outside the shop owned by a third Hämpelmann. St Paul's Church is a beautiful rotunda with a simple tower. A local guide, called Frau Hämpelmann, points it out. She knows the history of the parliament by heart and knows all about the speeches Frankfurt's Hämpelmanns delivered there. Robert Blum's place is still there, and the visitors leave it bearing chips of its timbers as profane relics of a man they have elevated to sanctity. The asses bray every morning, and Møller dreams one night of an ass that drinks ale and writes constitutional articles. A striking resemblance between the ass and the German people, Møller notes — both are happy only when braying in misery. The truth of the matter probably is that when all is said and done the Germans can write only under the firm rein of censorship! The native Indian writer from Ontario, Kah-ge-qu-ga-bak, creates a stir in the town. He is bent on introducing his tribe to the delights enjoyed by the white brothers, quotes Lord Byron with only the slightest trace of an accent and retells the old legends of his people. Monsieur Benneville, a French professor, albeit employed on a temporary basis, who spent some time in Copenhagen over forty years ago, can still speak Danish and sings the old ballads written by P.A. Heiberg and Rahbek.

A certain Herr Hämpelmann intends to travel to Copenhagen to shoot the Danish war minister and wound the king in the elbow. Another Herr Hämpelmann refuses to believe that the mission will succeed, and this disagreement leads to considerable discord in the ale-houses.

Møller resumes his journey southwards.

Baden-Baden. Nature itself offers all the riches, all the variety
and all the invigoration one could wish for, Møller writes. All
the way down from Heidelberg the landscape is a rich mosaic
of fertile cornfields, interspersed with fields of maize and
hemp. As the shadows fall and the traveller approaches the
gay lights of the town twinkling down below in the sweeping
valley between the mountains, it is like entering an enchanted
world. All the inns look like real fairy palaces, with brightly
shining lights, flowers tumbling in colourful profusion over
the balconies and down the terraces. A Roman bath from the
third century has been excavated. The main spring reaches a
temperature of sixty or seventy degrees, and the butchers
scald their pigs in its waters. The ruins of Hohen-Baden stand
on a mountain peak, bare walls covered with forest vegetation
and creepers. The local people used to be tortured in the
dungeons, and the garden is supposed to be haunted because
the lord of the castle insisted on keeping all the fruit for
himself.

When the traveller has attended to the ablutions necessi-
tated by the coach journey and sampled the comforts of the
inn, the prime pleasure of the evening is to visit the
promenade and listen to the musical performances provided
by the inevitable Austrians, the most congenial German-
speaking people Møller has met. And mingling with the
German noblewomen he sees elegant French *lorettes* from
Strasbourg and Metz, especially at the gaming tables, where
they are continually losing their gloves or perfumed
handkerchiefs. Møller enjoys beginner's luck at roulette, but
soon abandons gambling, even the simplest *rouge ou noir*.

'Continuez à jouer, chéri!' the *lorette* smiles at him, on his third
visit to the casino. She drops her handkerchief and lowers her
gaze when he stoops to retrieve it. But she immediately gets up
and leaves.

Møller is tempted to believe that she never existed in the
flesh. He feels faint; for two days he has been fasting, taking

the baths and going for long walks to exorcize the past three years from his body. He too gets up and leaves the table and moves among the other gamblers and lookers-on. Some of them greet him, but he doesn't know why. Obviously none of them knows that he is staying at Baden-Baden's cheapest boarding house. As he leaves the casino, a thunder and lightning storm breaks loose. It draws closer, attracted by the range of mountain peaks, and continues to rumble and flash across the night sky. Then the lightning strikes, hitting the promenade a few yards in front of him, and all the promenading couples scream in terror. But not Bettina von Arnim. She comes towards him, smiling, from a bed of roses, and she is not more than twelve years old. When she is only a short distance away she breaks into a run. He lifts her up and swings her round and round. Then he hoists her up on his shoulders and shows her the delights of Baden-Baden. He points out the various fairy palaces and tells her all about the naiads living in them. The air is heavy with the rich smell of orange groves and exotic plants, and Møller gives Bettina a piece of the cake baked with crushed hashish, the bit left from the hunk he ate before going to the casino when he could no longer stand the hunger pains.

They continue their stroll along the promenade all the way up to the pavilions where the Austrians are playing, and then the warm, thrilling rain begins to pour down. The strollers open their umbrellas, the lights hanging from the boughs fizzle out with a hiss, and Møller leads Bettina to the shelter of the magnolia trees. As he continues to tell her fairy tales he deftly unhooks her dress and takes it off, and a quiver of delight runs through his arm when he notices the soft down on the nape of her neck. He asks her to let her hair down, and when the rain ceases they resume their stroll, both naked, farther on into the night, where no prying eyes will see the burning embrace of their love.

He dreams. He is a little boy, and for hours he has been running up and down between the two old ladies. One is

Goethe's mother, and the other is his grandmother from the vicarage, Maren Laurentin Kanneworff.

'What did you get from Bettina?' Frau Rath asks.

'A darning needle,' he replies.

'Where do you keep it?'

'I stuck it into a haystack.'

'That was silly of you, Møller. You should have stuck it into your sleeve.'

And he runs back to his grandmother. She is so old that she can hardly sit upright in the bed.

'What did you get from Bettina, my dear Per?'

'A knife.'

'Where do you keep it?'

'In my sleeve.'

'Now that was silly of you, my dear Per. You should have put it in your pocket.'

And he runs back to Frau Rath, who is polishing all the windows in her son's house in Weimar.

'What did you get from Bettina, Møller?'

'A goat.'

'Where do you keep it?'

'In my pocket.'

'That was silly of you, Møller. You should have tied it up with a rope.'

For days he has been running to and fro like this in one of the Grimms' nightmares, tossing and turning in his bed, soaked in sweat. Finally he awakes, but only to sense that somebody is sitting in his room. He leaps out of bed and lights a candle. There in the darkest corner sits Janus, filthy from head to toe, and on his lap sits Bettina Elisabeth Katharina Ludovica Magdelena von Arnim with eyes glazed and vacant, as though the 'experience' has taken her all the way back to the earliest stage of childhood from which she will never, ever, again waken to reach out and clasp the fruits of perception.

eleven

'*Zitto, mi pare sentir odor di femmina,*' P.L. Møller sings, in a manner unlikely to please Mozart, but in his voice there is a ring of freedom that elicits enthusiastic nods of amused approval from pedestrians on the Champs-Élysées, and a couple of performers from an Italian troupe accompany him for a few steps, executing sweeping bows and joining in with exaggerated bravura, as he pauses at a stall to buy his usual bag of honey and gingerbread from Rheims. Then he continues with Don Giovanni and Leporello — pleased that he has made his way from Switzerland to Paris, having abandoned his earlier plan to travel to Italy.

'*Zitto,*' he replies to himself, now singing in the voice he reserves for Leporello, '*zitto . . . di donn'Elvira — signor la voce io sento. . .*'

'*. . . se sentite come fa, Ta! Ta! Ta! Ta!*' the Italians sing, disappearing into the Champs-Élysées' permanent Tivoli, where there is hardly a seat to be had in the shade of the trees. Wherever he goes, people are eating and drinking, spending freely on waffles, on fried potatoes, on cakes of every description, on toys for children of all ages. The thirsty can try the mysterious new drink *coko* for half a sou a glass, or the simple lemonade, which turns out to be nothing more exotic than ordinary water with a few slices of lemon, lugged round in an ordinary bucket from which thirsty dogs occasionally take a drink. There is also 'democratic' ice-cream, sold in small, knobbledy glasses, and wines of the noblest vintage for the discriminating palates of the bourgeoisie. Rifle ranges, dolls' theatres, sword swallowers, fire eaters, a conjuror and his musicians dressed up as Red Indians. There, sitting on a stage elevated far above the competing attractions, is the famous Swiss lady with her long black beard, that was generally believed not to be her own until she had had the matter settled in court in her favour when one of the judges dragged her four times round the courtroom by it. And wherever he goes, Møller hears, above the shouts and the beating of drums, a cry that drowns all other cries:

'*Allons, Messieurs, qui est-ce qui veut boire? — À la fraîche, à la fraîche. . .*'

And . . . *zitto, mi pare* . . . women, especially the very young! In Møller's eyes so completely and differently natural, as compared with most of the women in Denmark and Germany, with a healthy degree of fleshiness, striking the ideal balance between Flemish grossness and Spanish leanness, flesh distributed in harmonious proportion to limbs that are supple, taut-muscled; small hands and feet, the attributes of a people who have not had to wrestle with frozen root crops and stubborn, unmalleable surroundings; hair neither jet black nor light blonde, but chestnut brown eyes; skin neither brown nor milky-white; faces not round, but oval — Møller takes unending delight in watching the Parisian girls. Their lips are not thick, but sensuously full, and they have no hesitation in opening them in a broad smile, no fear of degrading themselves, never phlegmatically lost in Nordic, Protestant introspection, in that something-for-nothing attitude that expects adventure to arrive on the doorstep free of charge, from without, uninvited, unencouraged, to redeem the mind from the frigid injunctions of the catechism and the sickly sweet boredom of Lutheran insipidity.

It is, of course, only among girls from the lower classes that Møller discovers and adores these qualities. As soon as the Frenchwoman begins to ascend the social ladder, the gaiety

and the good nature disappear, and along with them the will
to work and the delicate sense of honour. And it is only when
she reaches the upper echelons of the upper classes that she
regains her erotic charms, now as a marquise of decadent —
mainly Italian — descent. The wives of the new capitalists
and bourse magnates and railway engineers and textile
wholesalers nearly all look like Englishwomen, who are,
according to Møller, just about the most unfortunate in
Europe, that is, of course, apart from the women of
Schleswig-Holstein: dull, snobbish, red-nosed, always suffering from a cold, with thin, carroty hair, thighs between their
shoulders and legs crossed as though they are afraid that even
the tiniest, wayward breeze would pollute their sex. The *mould-
ing* itself, that's what's so hopelessly wrong with these
Englishwomen, who seize the opportunity offered by the post-
revolutionary period to invade Paris, dragging their husbands
and sons on a leash, Møller thinks, as he hears one of their
shrill, petulant voices:

'Charles, I told you, didn't I? Come here, Charles!' And all
the poetry of Paris is blown away like the dust beneath the
trees on the Champs-Élysées until again he hears:

'*Ce soir, chéri?*' And a *billet* imperceptibly slides into his
pocket.

For a few months Møller's sole occupation has been his
study of the behaviour of the young Parisian girls. Their shape
is a clear indication that most of them have not been born in
Paris, and have probably not even been brought up here.
They arrive from all parts of France, some obeying their own
desire or impulse, some lured by lovers who have since
betrayed them. In Paris they hope to find work, but they
cherish the secret wish that fortune will favour them and that
they will capture a tycoon and one day return to their native
village with all the trappings of unlimited wealth. But as work
is hard to find and tycoons are not plentiful, the girls are
forced instead to go dancing at the Prado. They develop a
taste for students and themselves become 'students' — one of
law, another of philosophy. And soon when she, the student
from Brittany's remote west coast or some Basque valley,

from Aveyron or Provence, from Lyon, Lille or Dunkerque, has acquired a little practice and a passable wardrobe, she often advances in social standing and is allowed to descend to the lowest floor of the Prado which is populated with more opulent males. They are prepared to entertain her until finally they help her on with her coat and they leave together.

As long as she dances on the upper floors, with her callow student boyfriend, her blushing and eternally hoarse Jean-Pierre or Jean-Claude, the young girl is modest in her demeanour and in her demands. This is true love; he is the only man she trusts. Her only worries are the dance steps and well-being of her lover, for whom she often harbours a motherly feeling, especially when he manages to get drunk on two or three glasses of wine and is forced to stumble out shame-faced and vomit in the back alley. But as soon as the girl has been admitted to the round room at the bottom of the curved staircase, she becomes infected with the shamelessness prevailing among the smartly dressed gentlemen there who have a greater faith in the bulging wallet than in academic laurels, and who fill their glasses to the brim.

As Møller makes his way among the habitués of the Prado's most exclusive section, he finds himself surrounded by diminutive mademoiselles, all yelling at the tops of their voices: 'Buy me a bouquet!' 'Buy me one of those *expensive* ice-creams!' 'Buy me a box of bonbons or a candied apple!' or 'Buy me the night, *chéri*, and I shall repay you so you won't forget it!' And if he wishes to avoid having his only decent evening wear torn to shreds, there is only one appropriate course of action, although he knows full well that it is the one thing he simply can't afford. And as the evening wears on he sees how the most beautiful Prado lovelies are snatched, one by one, by commission agents and others from the banking and bourse fraternity, *le pays Breda*.

In a short time the ones most favoured are magically turned into *lorettes*. They move into furnished apartments, and are showered with elegant clothes which they can sport in the Mabille, letting the hat tilt rakishly backwards, and speak with utter contempt of *le pays latin*. And they acquire new names, mostly taken from novels — Lelia, Indiana, Malvina and Rigolette, while their former female acquaintances, the students, have to struggle on with less romantic names like Celine Leather Boots, or Louise the Lush. But these latter girls, Møller assumes, are far happier than the former who, now they are well off, suffer from stultifying boredom, with nothing to do all day long but put themselves and their finery on parade, while their new lords and masters sweat blood in the bourse. It is widely held that Celeste Mogador, the most feted dancer ever to grace the floors of the Breda or the Mabille, and now an actress, no less, at the Variétés, longs so much for the days when she made her debut as a 'student' at the university in Paris, that she prowls around the Latin Quarter wearing disguise. . .

The girls for whom Møller feels the deepest affection are those with a regular job, the ordinary working girls — seamstresses, nursemaids, housemaids, waitresses, girls behind counters at the baker's or haberdasher's. One night, when he again gets the urge to write some poetry, he composes 'A French *ouvrière*', with one verse reading:

> *Fresh and free from all prudery,*
> *Quick she melts in the fires of feeling,*
> *Muscles of iron her only weapon*
> *against desires that are not hers.*

She is the true soul of France, and it is she who in later life, as a *matrone* in one of the dance halls, or as owner of a *parfumerie* or a restaurant, rules France with such a deft hand that any talk of 'the incorporation of women in culture' is unnecessary. It is she — the middle-aged, the elderly woman — who is to the fore at every political demonstration, whether it is a dance around the guillotine or, as today, erecting busts of the president, Louis Napoleon. She played a prominent part in 1848 when it was a question of introducing the social and democratic republic, and now she is to the fore again. On this occasion with the vociferous fishwives bearing the banner, she struggles to restore order and common sense instead of the chaos that threatens peace in France. It is a fact, Møller writes in *Kjøbenhavnsposten*, quivering with excitement as he again feels the urge to dip into ink, that in most respects the woman in France enjoys a higher status than the man. This makes it all the more regrettable that most other nations, 'simply because they once allowed themselves to be dazzled by the brilliance of a magnificent court', have for centuries aped French men, instead of choosing the infinitely more sensible course, by following the example set by the women of France.

. . . And again it is *she* — now appearing as a very young girl, seventeen, eighteen, certainly not a day over twenty-two — who sends notes to Møller which he finds every morning in his letterbox in the hotel on the corner of Rue de Rohan and Rue de Rivoli. Graceful letters, often on silk paper, often as a collage, written in red or invisible ink, signed Blosine, Elise, Clémence, Ernestine, Marie, Louise, Sylvie, Joséphine or *ton bibi d'autrefois* or *votre inconnue d'hier sous les arcades de Rue de Rivoli* . . . or *Jeanne* . . . that most French of all names where all the letters have found one another to form a picture that exudes unblemished feminity . . . Jeanne with the equally enchanting surname Balaresque, the little modiste from Rue Mont Thabor who loves to address him in English — *my love, my dearest Louis* — and wants him to call her Jane, for this makes her name sound even more beautiful: *Djinn*. That's what an English lieutenant from Sussex had called her, and that county must surely be terribly exciting if it is even half as naughty as its name suggests.

But to Møller she is Jeanne, and her surname in itself constitutes a poem that inspires him to versify in endless variations. *Ba, la, res, que!* And in every possible way she matches the infinite richness of her name, never tired and tetchy, never bored for more than a few minutes at a time if someone has upset her in the shop, firmly fleshed and with the deep brown eyes so exquisitely set in that oval, always radiant face which her hair obscures when she takes the floor for the *contredanse* and its can-can, exuberantly exploiting the narrow confines of his hotel room. He invariably opens *her* letters in a state of great expectation: '*Mon bien cher. Je suis desolée de vous faire attendre. Il m'est impossible de venir. Comptez sur moi pour demain 2 h 1/2. Toute à vous, mille baisers, Jane.*'

Or: '*A cinq heures et 1/2 je serai chez mon coiffeur. Vous pourrez m'y prendre.Le petit bouquet de violettes a une odeur suave. Merci pour votre gracieux souvenir. Sans adieu. A bientôt — Jane.'*

Is this what it's like *to come home?*

Every fibre in Møller's body thrills at the realization that is confirmed day after day: that until now his life has been wasted by staying in the wrong place, but that now he is precisely where he belongs. This is his true home. This is how a city should smell. This is how its dust should tickle the nostrils. This is how the urchins should heckle passers-by. This is how theatre troupes should draw the crowds. This is how food should taste, even the cheapest dishes like cow's stomach lining which in Hamburg would be a horrid nightmare, but which here is turned into a tasty *tripes à la normande* served in Calvados sauce, prepared on charcoal trays and accompanied by a bottle of strong cider. And this is how people should talk to one another, at the same time rapidly, lucidly and considerately, without any attempt to ferret out what's going on in the other man's mind — *à la fraîche!*

'To think,' Møller writes on a scrap of paper, slightly irritated at not having come here in his late twenties when Balzac was still alive, '. . . to think right is to me simply a matter of the immediate perception of the right result when it arrives, when it casually saunters into the room without any further ado. If, on the other hand, I wish to provoke it by a process of "sensible consideration", I want an immediate result. If it fails to put in an instant appearance, I am forced to say: "*Larira, larirette, allez, c'est parfait*" and then let come what may. To think,' he concludes, and looks over at the Louvre in the light of the late afternoon, '*is thus a matter of showing thought the door.*' And the noise of a city where heart and brain and stomach are one shatters the tranquillity of his hotel room.

And if he woke up in Alexandria in the second century, he would bathe himself in a similar recognition and naturally participate in dinners where lively minds played with the magic effect of the nought when added to the nine digits; if he were suddenly transported to Toledo in the Middle Ages and listened to disputes between Jew and Christian and Muslim on the lack of coherence in incoherence, he would recognize it all, he, Peder Ludvig Møller, in every fibre of his body, born of the great unknown that is mother of all things, born into the scent of thyme, wild roses, garlic, pigeons, oranges and the exciting sun-blackened earth, without any eyes peering down his back, no Janus to creep stealthily the eternal three paces behind him or to run ahead of him, trying to lure him into writing the unfinished story, which, five years ago, he had put into *Gaea*, into writing it right up to the point where . . . where what?

And Møller sees himself wave to the Christian brunette standing behind the tulle curtains in a window under the eaves of the most beautiful palace on the square. He approaches her, knowing that she will fling herself around his neck. If they should meet again, several centuries later, in Louis Napoleon's Paris at the beginning of the second half of the nineteenth century, they will know that they have known each other before. Jeanne Balaresque, convinced that she has lived four or five or maybe even eight whole lives before this life, can remember all the details from the square in Toledo, every flower that blossomed between the cracks in the cobblestones and every wrought iron gate, while he repeats, line by line, the discussion on the lack of coherence in incoherence so that its secret — *to think reflection away* — sparkles like a diamond thrown up to catch the rays of the sun.

She lies across him on the bed, slowly massaging the back of his neck. She kisses him on the nipples.

'That's also how you used to taste in those days!' she whispers, stretching her legs into the air. She tickles him on the chin with her dangling fringe. She also happens to be so sure of what their next life is going to be like that she can see them flying through the skies, way up above the clouds, in a strange machine, over the vast expanse of land and water to their palace of glass and gold on the top of a mountain where no man has ever trodden before. Møller enjoys her flights of fancy, even though he has a sneaking suspicion that they have been partly culled from the latest serial stories which she and the other girls in the shop read so greedily when not engaged in their customary tasks, such as turning a pair of trousers for a poor bachelor like him. But when she asks him to repeat the juicy story of how a brazen actress lulled the Danish king into a sort of illicit marriage, he can only groan in dismay.

'Ah, *non*!' he replies. 'Surely not again!'

'*Mais si*! I want to hear *all* about her. Now what was that Louise Raz-muh-sayn's motto?'

'Fidelity is my honour.'

'Hmm. . .'

'What makes you say hmm. . .?'

'Well, it does seem a bit exaggerated, that's all. Now tell it again, *my love!*'

'*Non, ma petite!*'

Jeanne Balaresque playfully attacks him, and he knows that he started it all. One day she asked what those sheets of writing were, the ones untidily stacked on his desk — *Three Epistles from Hans Mikkelsen, Burgher and Brewer in Kalundborg* and *On Danner Literature, by Hans Mikkelsen, author of three Epistles*. As it happened to be just one of those days when something or other in her behaviour made it clear that he ought to go out of his way to attract her attention, he had told her, with dramatic gesticulations and using different voices for different characters, how Frederik the Seventh, a king with few equals in this world in terms of stature and power, had offered huge cigars to one and all and roared to his government: 'That woman as my spouse, or I abdicate!'

Since then she has developed an insatiable appetite for this story from the farflung snowcapped Nordic climes, and this at a time when Møller wants to forget all about Denmark which he is not to see again for at least the next six months. But then he sees the story through her eyes; sees her dream-spun Denmark with a king wearing a full beard down to his belly and the 'Countess' Danner, alias Louise Rasmussen, whom Jeanne Balaresque, throughout all the episodes so far presented, has turned into a *lorette* superior to all other *lorettes*, capable of making a stunning entrance as she marches down the curved staircase to the lower floor of the Prado, paralyzing the gentlemen in mid-sentence, freezing the glasses in their hands, leaving the other *lorettes* speechless and making the management swoon in awe. And Møller takes up the thread and describes the hundred or more trunks to be packed for the king's favourite before she can step into her carriage and begin her journey to Paris.

He makes sure to avoid telling her the truth about the physical attributes of the abominably plain Louise Raz-muh-sayn.

'I feel it in my heart. I know that things are going to work out all right for her,' Jeanne Balaresque whispers.

'How on earth have you reached that conclusion?' he asks inquisitively.

'When a man as handsome as you defends her, things can only work out all right for her . . . I mean for her and the king!'

She looks up.

'*C'est pour moi?*' she asks and picks up 'A French *ouvrière*', which is lying on his bedside table. Møller nods.

'What does it say?'

'My little buttercup, I feel like plucking you. My glittering diamond, I feel like carving a love poem on the window pane with you. Light of my life, jewel in my crown. My darling *grisette*. Jeanne. . .'

'All that?' She showers him with kisses.

'All that and volumes more, my beatific Balaresque! *Io mi voglio divertir! Vivan le femmine!*'

He laces her up, breathing on her shoulders, kissing her gently on the neck. And a new verse springs to his mind:

When cheerily and without complaint
She gets through ten hours, or more, of work
her day's labour is at an end.
Then, with her friend, she hurries
Out into town, to really have some fun.

That night Møller succeeds not only in finishing the poem, but also his pamphlet on the Countess Danner literature, that hotchpotch of pious outpourings on Louise Rasmussen, the commoner countess, and her association with the monarch.

It's the most prejudiced and turgid drivel ever written in Danish, whatever the source; an idiotic article clipped from *Kjøbenhavnsposten* or one of the bombastic pamphlets ordered from Reitzel's bookshop in Copenhagen provides fuel for his orgy of revulsion.

He decides that this is to be his latest contribution to Danish polemics, as Jeanne Balaresque wistfully falls asleep with a stack of Danish newspapers and books under her pillow, firm in her conviction that this device will help her to learn his strange language before winter comes.

'I am overwhelmed with a feeling of So-Whatness!' shouts the English major. This was the only thing Møller has heard from his next door neighbour in the hotel apart from his complaints about diarrhoea or indigestion, the exorbitant price charged by a *lorette*, the draft, the turbulence of French politics — and now all that fuss here in Paris, the night between the first and second of December, 1851. It is three o'clock in the morning, and when Møller steps into the corridor on the fifth floor, disturbed by the noise of cannon being pulled through the Rue de Rivoli, the major is already standing there, with a towel round his waist, shuffling about, fretfully clutching a half bottle of gin. 'And now this infernal racket before cockcrow!' he says, expressing his contempt and disgust, before stomping into his room and slamming the door. But before long he returns, now more martial in a braided dressing gown, and Møller is taken aback by the major's almost carefree determination: 'Should we join the revolution and have a little fun with the bloody French, Mr Miller?'

Møller declines the invitation, pleading that he is behind with his work. And for the next few days he has more than enough to do, covering events as they develop. This is his first opportunity of providing Danish newspapers with lengthy articles on Paris, and no detail escapes his eye.

The National Assembly has been summarily dissolved. Thiers has been placed under arrest. Columns of troops march up and down. On the morning of the second of

December the citizens of Paris discover that Louis Napoleon has issued and posted one decree and two appeals. The prince-president is greeted as he rides across Place Concorde, with shouts of 'Long live the Republic!' His adherents wisely refrain from adding the words 'social' or 'democratic'. Citizens build barricades at the Porte Saint-Martin. An officer is put to death with gruesome brutality. Only a few students rebel. Soon the boulevards are black with people. The occasional boom of a cannon is heard. The workers refuse to work. Møller has a meal at a restaurant in the Rue Saint-Honoré, where he hears of a nearby barricade. It is demolished by soldiers while he eats his veal chop and reads the latest out-of-date copy of Café Danemarc's *Berlingske Tidende*, which, as usual, has no notion of what's going on in Paris.

Officially, France is ruled by the war minister and the prefect of police. A *commissaire* of police and some soldiers visit Møller and check his papers. Battles in Rue Saint-Denis and Rue Saint-Martin. Courts-martial on the pavement below Møller's window, enough to make his blood run cold. The prince-president's coffers, it is said, will soon be depleted. A refuse cart is halted and all the barrels are lined up across a street to form a barricade. When the bullets begin to fly, the defenders flee from the stench. All the journalists seem to be bosom friends of Louis Napoleon, and newspapers publishing the slightest criticism of the government are banned. Thiers has been released from custody and wants to travel to Italy. Louis Napoleon has France in the palm of his hand. The peasants adore him. The priests support his cause. 'In the Kingdom of the Blind, the one-eyed man is King,' Møller writes, much to the disapproval of Jeanne Balaresque.

'You can't write that sort of thing,' she says, angrily shaking her head. 'I'd never say such a thing about your king!'

And he doesn't know what to reply. He hasn't seen Jeanne Balaresque for over a week. At first he was so busy writing that he didn't worry about her sudden absence, her failure to send him her letters and notes. Then irritation set in, as though a midge-bite continued to itch. He visited her in the shop, and she turned her back on him. He grew uneasy. But finally one morning there was a letter for him, slipped under his door, informing him that she felt better now; the sweating had ceased; her temperature had fallen. And the letter ends: '*Vous êtes constamment dans mes rêves la nuit, le jour dans mon coeur. Celle qui ne vit que pour vous — Jeanne.*'

That same morning she is again sitting opposite him, at the other side of his narrow desk, and she has been crying for most of the night. He notices that she has lost weight. Her friend, she says, the man Møller has probably known about all along, the cheese-monger from Rue de La Montagne-Sainte-Geneviève, the place where, as Møller had once told her, Danish theology students had their college in the Middle Ages. Finally she had plucked up her courage and ended her affair with the cheese-monger. Now she belongs to Møller alone. And she smiles and fondles his inkwell and pours sand onto a sheet of paper. She puffs the sand into his hair and flings herself about his neck, her body quivering. Writing is far, *far* more important than selling cheese, she whispers, letting a finger glide behind his ear. She picks up his latest article and gets him to translate it, nodding approvingly at every sentence of his description of what's going on in Paris.

But that Louis Napoleon should be one-eyed, — '*ça, non!*'

Møller finds her logic compelling. He suggests that they visit the bourse, which he has not yet described. She thinks it's a marvellous idea. Now she will have a chance to see for herself what Louis Napoleon does to make the French people richer. Even the workers are earning money now by buying shares, she tells him. And for once Møller doesn't know what to reply. An hour later, when they enter the bourse's din and bustle, his anger grows as he constantly bumps into stockbrokers with fanatical eyes, and haughty ladies fanning their papers and simple citizens with small cardboard boxes stuffed with their savings. And on every face he can see that same dazed look, people hypnotized by the giddy whirl and the prospect of riches beyond compare, and if the bourse was initially reluctant to endorse the government of the second of December, this lack of confidence has moved to the other extreme. The prices quoted are rising sky high while more and more ordinary Parisians go home in despair to put a bullet through their heads because they have been robbed of their savings by unscrupulous brokers. And this is the stock exchange that Jeanne Balaresque believes in, as though it were the most sacrosanct temple in France, with the stockbrokers as its high priests. Now he is going to make her see the light.

And again she breaks into tears.

'I can't help being so stupid!' she says, as they walk back towards the Rue de Rivoli, hand in hand.

'You're not stupid. You just don't know what it's all about.'

'I know how to sew, I know I do. I know how to cope, I know I do. And how to save a bit of money. And I know that I love you and I know that I don't like it when you call me . . . stupid.'

'I haven't called you stupid . . . Jeanne.'

'No, but that's what you believe. . .'

His thoughts are already up on the fifth floor, at his desk, where there is a new stack of paper waiting for his devastating article on the bourse. His mood has plunged to the depths, and he hardly notices it when Jeanne Balaresque lets go of his hand, crosses to the other pavement and disappears. As he reaches his hotel, she is heading for Rue Mont Thabor. He dashes up the steps. Money, money, money, is there nothing else of value in this world? And then Catholicism? That at least is capable of staging a play, Møller admits to himself a few Sundays later when Jeanne Balaresque persuades him to accompany her to the Église Saint-Roch. He has purged his system of his contempt for the bourse, the article has been sent home, Paris once more exudes Paris and Jeanne has had another fit of crying with the tears rolling down her cheeks as she nurses her bad conscience over the way she ditched her cheese-monger.

Møller remains seated in the back pew while she goes up to the altar. 'Won't you be so pleased, Jeanne, if I tell you what an impression your church has made on me, a heathen?' he thinks, watching her move demurely through the grotto, the side chapel naively decorated with heaps of flowers and candles, and — above, against a dark background, a huge transparent cross draped with a linen cloth, waiting in lonely and solemn stillness for its sacred victim. The empty cross; the thought of the consummation not as yet consummated; the chanting of the mass and the waves of incense which seem to dance in the beams of light; the choir drawing shafts of light from above, through a row of stained-glass windows, down to a diffused patch glowing with subtle hues of rose and pink; the cupola, a heavenly vault with countless angels and hosts of spirits flitting about in a mystical twilight — no, how can he experience the same wrath here as he did in the bourse? And Møller is simply overwhelmed when the winter sun comes out and the light filters through the windows and paints the walls and the worshippers and objects rose-red. He is carried away in a blaze of colour that gradually melts his soul, and he feels that he wafts and hovers on the red beams of light, higher and higher, until he is up in the cupola among all the angels, dreaming himself right into heaven itself.

Outside on the pavement, again hand in hand with Jeanne Balaresque, he listens to all she has to say. While the snow falls in huge flakes, an omnibus lumbers past and all thoughts of revolution are dead and gone. Choosing her words with care, she tells him how she feels every time she has been to the altar to receive the host.

She snuggles up to him, forcing her way in under his arm.

'It's as though I have Jesus within me, and then nothing bad can happen to me,' she says.

'As though you have *eaten* him?'

And for this he gets a stinging slap on the cheek.

Møller writes to Matilda Leiner that he hopes to receive a few lines from her, comprising a pleasing account of her state of health and satisfaction with her *position actuelle*. 'I hope to stay here until June or July,' he concludes, signing with the rather restrained *Yours as ever*. Jeanne Balaresque paces to and fro in his room. She asks who Matilda is. And without waiting for an answer she tears the letter into shreds. Soon they are fighting like savages. Objects are thrown about and, during the lull, suddenly the voice of the English major is heard:

'So what! Chaaarge!'

Møller can't help laughing, and Jeanne Balaresque soon stops hitting him. She continues to lie spreadeagled across the bed while he begins to tidy up. Now he really sees how much she has done to add a few homely touches to this drab hotel room: the curtains she has sewn and put up, a pattern of wild red roses against a background of beech green, the little rug she has woven, Havana brown and old rose, to step onto in his bare feet on icy mornings, the blue peasant trinket box filled with articifical pearls, coloured ribbons, hatpins, hearts carved out of silver paper and dried flowers, 'his Aladdin's box', as she calls it. He puts it back in its place on the window sill, having picked up its precious contents which had been scattered in the fray. Without ever mentioning it, she has hung a little medal of the Virgin Mary above the head of his bed.

Jeanne Balaresque has now curled up under his eiderdown, on the verge of falling asleep. He goes over to her, stoops down, leans his ear against her belly and listens.

'What are you doing?' she asks.

'Listening to Jesus,' he replies, lovingly, and she smiles.

When she has fallen asleep, he goes to the window. He draws the curtain aside and looks down at Rue de Rohan. Blosine, whom he has not seen for nearly two months, is standing beneath a gaslight, wearing a brand new fur. She has probably come straight from the Prado, and she looks up at his window.

He quietly blows out the flickering flame of the oil lamp and creeps out of the room:

'*Zitto. . .*'

twelve

Yes, it is true, Møller can inform his readers in March 1852; he has actually been arrested, but has not been declared *persona non grata* in France. And fortunately the police have nobly allowed him to keep enough paper to write a eulogy in praise of their magnificent feats. Which he does while the fire splutters out. Blosine, indignant at his refusal to let her in, is amusing herself next door in the company of the English major, and Jeanne Balaresque is on duty under the yellowish glare of the gaslight, accompanied by two notorious streetfighters from Rue Quincampoix.

Møller's arrest has nothing whatever to do with his elevated status as executive officer of a branch of The European Central Committee, which has among its members a few sturdy Danish journeymen printers and cabinetmakers and a Norwegian weaver, and which has the declared aim of overthrowing Europe's monarchs and introducing communist republics in every country, including the Scandinavian countries. Møller wisely resists all temptation to win sympathy for this conspiracy, refraining from any mention of it whatever, even in parenthesis, thus making sure that the Danish legation will not set their police spies on his heels, which they are sure to do if they catch as much as a whisper of the plot. No, it was all *Berlingske Tidende*'s fault. As Møller has earlier reported, Paris has a Danish cafe. It is the Café Danemarc on Rue Saint-Honoré, visited daily by most of Paris' Scandinavian contingent, the regular hangout for political refugees and revolutionaries from all corners of Europe. To please his Danish customers and cool their revolutionary ardour, the owner subscribes to *Berlingske*.

The omnipresent and omniscient police spies who keep an eye on all foreigners and their regular haunts, happened to notice one evening that *Berlingske* is written in a language that is neither French nor German. The obvious conclusion was that it must be Hungarian and therefore seditious, and a few hours later, at precisely eight o'clock in the evening, the café's three floors were swarming with uniformed police — about two hundred of them, led by two brave *commissaires*.

Møller happened to be on the ground floor and, thinking that they were probably conducting the raid to seize a highly dangerous culprit, he went upstairs to join a group of Danes who were passing round an out-of-date copy of *Berlingske*. But before he had looked at the fatal newspaper, the *commissaires* detected the Hungarian lettering and pounced on the conspirators. With friendly brutality, Møller and others were dragged over to the billiards table where they were searched thoroughly, and when the police found Møller's treatise on *Das Gudrun Lied* and half of a tattered share certificate, guaranteed for the duration of the socialist republic to represent the sum of one franc and bearing the legend *Fédération démocratique de l'Europe — ligue des peuples*, they had no hesitation in regarding Møller as a secret, subversive agent, and he was placed in the custody of two officers until he and the other *Berlingske* readers could be taken to the 'residence', the prefecture on the Ile de la Cité. Here they dragged him about for a few hours, from black cell to black cell, without a word of explanation. Then after a while they decided to take down his name, and Møller thought that this would be the end of his torture. Towards midnight he was shoved out into the yard and compelled to stand to attention for an hour until, again accompanied by the others and now under the supervision of one of the *commissaires* and three officers, he was

stuffed into a carriage and driven away. At last, at three
o'clock in the morning, he was taken back to the hotel where
he was forced to lay out all his possessions for inspection. One
of the two *commissaires*, who set about examining the contents
of the top drawer and understood a little German, declared
Møller's scribblings to be harmless while the other turned
everything upside down and messed up every scrap of paper.
But as the stack of manuscripts grew and grew and they still
failed to reach a word they could understand, the French
police began to grow weary and it was decided to choose only
one manuscript as a representative of the whole.

And so it happened that a dissertation on Oehlenschläger
became evidence of P.L. Møller's part in a conspiracy against
the French nation.

Møller's walking stick was also arrested. It was tied to the
manuscript with stout twine, and all efforts to have it restored
to his possession have so far failed, as its tiny lead tip has made
it the subject of a prolonged criminal investigation. When
walking stick and manuscript had been bound and registered
the *commissaires* amused themselves by ransacking Møller's
wardrobe, hoping to discover secret weapons. Back at the trot
to the prefecture where Møller, now seized by terror, was
marched down endless dank corridors to a fairly large cell,
pushed in, and a heavy metal door slammed behind him. In
the dim light of an oil lamp he saw that he shared the cell with
about fifty other prisoners, mostly political suspects and
ordinary criminals. Each had a mat and a straw mattress and,
as all the beds were taken, Møller, whose senses recoiled at the
thought of lying down on a floor covered with excrement,
prepared himself to spend the night standing up.

He was fortunate enough to strike up a conversation with
two old wrong-doers who offered him a space between them,
and Møller buttoned his pockets as best he could, wrapped
himself in his cloak and lay down, but did not get any sleep
that night, as his two friends kept on entertaining him with
stories of their exploits. At six o'clock in the morning, after a
quarter of an hour's sleep, all the prisoners were awoken. The
mats and mattresses were lined up against the walls along

188

with Møller and the other prisoners, while some trustees poured a deluge of water on the floor in a vain attempt to wash away the filth produced by the preceding day and night. At nine o'clock the door was again opened, and a heap of inedible loaves was flung on the same floor, still wet, still dirty. And without further delay two huge oafs, resembling an executioner's henchmen, dragged in an enormous kettle: lunch, a sort of vegetable soup, referred to by the older inhabitants as *Julienne à la préfecture* and which to Møller bore a striking resemblance to the swill used to fatten Danish pigs for Christmas. It was served in red earthware basins, but without spoons, so that everyone had to plunge their snouts into them.

On the following day he regained his freedom, thanks to the intervention of the Danish legation, which had been notified by one of the Café Danemarc regulars — several hours after the other readers of *Berlingske Tidende*, who had obviously impressed their captors as more trustworthy members of society.

While he finishes his writing, adding a few corrections, appending his signature and carefully placing the pages in an envelope, Møller realises that Blosine is now making love to the Major, and he gives himself a hard slap in the crotch, as though he wants to remind himself that there must be limits. He can hear the major's gasps of delight, and Blosine laughs so loud that it can only be because she wants it to be heard through the wall, that all too thin wall, like all the other hotel walls that are gradually becoming a permanent feature of Møller's universe. Is Blosine straddling the major, with her black stockings rolled down below her knees, driving him closer and closer to spasms of ecstasy? Is he reaching out for the gin bottle? Will he soon suffer a stroke? Or is his sweaty face between her thighs? Is she biting his ear and pretending that she loves it — right until the blood begins to trickle down, so that she can catch it with the tip of her tongue and smear it over his face, her slate-grey eyes ablaze with passion? Irresponsible, untamable Blosine, fierce Blosine, so totally unlike the other *grisettes* in her paganism, looking one moment as though she has just emerged from the mire of Brittany, and the next, after only a few hours in front of her mirror, as though she has been transformed into the daughter of a Nubian king and whose greatest passion might be listening to music. For six or seven or eight hours she is capable of keeping the mask in place, as the incarnation of all that is noblest in this world, but then she is jerked back to reality and tears the whole illusion into tatters.

And roars.

The first night he was with her:

'I *hate* you! I'll outlive you by years and years and years!'

The next night:

'*Salaud*! I'll kill you if you don't stay with me!'

And then that evening before she charged into the major's room, furious at his rejection:

'Danish turd! Fuck me or just piss off!'

Møller goes over to the wall and listens with his ear pressed against the damp wallpaper, and he wishes there were a little hole so that he could peep and see how Blosine swallows the major's member while she bangs the floor with her feet. Møller is especially fascinated by her feet, classical feet, almost as though made of marble. She has long toes that she loves to wriggle, stare at and tell stories to about this little episode and that, without any real meaning, parading the toes like pets. Møller experiences an uncontrollable desire to kiss her feet. He is already tasting her toes, nibbling them, using only his tongue and lips, and suddenly he hears himself roar, as though the words have been projected through his mouth from the pit of his stomach:

'*Fuck him*, Blosine! Give him the works!'

And he lets out a loud laugh because he knows that in a minute she will again be banging on his door, and sure enough: there she is, hissing at him, stark naked, with her clothes in her hands, and her hair is all askew and as he draws her to him he notices how wet she is between her thighs. He takes her crotch in one hand, using the other to grab her hair and force her head backwards. He is momentarily seized by a fierce urge to strike her, with real force, on both cheeks. He conquers the urge and opens a bottle of red wine, and when they have made love and she has fallen asleep, Møller finds himself sitting calmly at the edge of the bed, studying her as though she is a being from another universe.

Now she is no longer Blosine from Rue Lamartine, but a lost proletarian waif from the countryside, with ragged nails, peeling varnish, dirt embedded in every pore, cheeks caked with cheap make-up. What does this earthy being dream of as her eyelids begin to flutter? A wretched pigsty in Gullvinec or Quimperlé or whatever heathen tract she comes from? Her toothless father, prematurely stooped and broken? Her blind grandmother, some wizened Celtic witch? Or of the first time she did it? Probably it was a bleak October afternoon when she came trudging across a ploughed field, dragging bare feet through the furrows, mud-bespattered from head to toe, and the priest — why not him? — caught sight of her, hid behind a tree with the blood pounding in his temples, waiting for her, like some earth princess, to loom up before him, and with the grin of a fourteen-year-old peasant girl, she had lifted the muddy skirts to conceal her face. . .

And Møller's hands become the priest's as he lets them glide up and down her thighs and once more feel her damp crotch. Blosine smiles in her sleep. The soil of France. Its earth.

Le pays réel.

The following day he decides to take her with him to the President's Ball at Les Tuileries, to which he has been invited, via the Danish legation, as a foreign correspondent. But first she will have to be fitted out. And even if payment for his latest batch of articles is another week late in reaching Paris, his savings will be spent on material for a new dress and a new pair of boots so that she can outshine the other women when she is presented to *le pays légal*. In her tiny attic room in Rue Lamartine where everything has been smashed to pieces, with the mattress toppling onto the floor, a broken window pane replaced by a square of stiff cardboard, and the floor covered

with dust, hairpins, ribbons and bits of old shoelaces, her
friends, the other girls living in the building which has the
reputation of being the best whorehouse in the district, help
her sew a dress that can match or maybe surpass the most
expensive that Paris has to offer. And when she has spent half
an hour in front of the mirror and turns to face him, Møller
knows that she will be the belle of the ball.

She is the object of everyone's attention and no one can
resist her as she steps into the Tuileries. With a flick of her fan
she brushes aside a grumpy old marquise who obstructs her
path, and every man in the room gazes at her in silent
admiration. With Møller by her side she continues her stately
progress through the six or seven ornately decorated halls
until they reach the magnificent buffet served with enormous
quantities of vintage wines and champagne, and tea, coffee,
cognac, punch and all sorts of cakes. Time and again the
prince-president promenades through the halls, with the
diplomatic corps and flunkeys at his heels, and Blosine,
transformed, succeeds in catching his eye too, causing Møller
a moment's worry about what she might get up to next. If she
suddenly should be transformed back to yesterday's Blosine,
she is capable of eating cake with her fingers and wiping them
dry on a marquise's hair, or untying her boots and kicking
them several metres in front of her. But then Louis Napoleon
happens to be her ruler, and as he passes close by for the third
time, with the wife of the Turkish minister by his side — a
certain Princess Kallimaki, wearing a decoration consisting of
a portrait of the sultan in a double chain of diamonds —
Blosine makes such a profound and elegant curtsy that Møller
begins to wonder if she might not have had a brilliant career
on the stage.

What if he now took her on as a *task*?

And as though Louis Napoleon is now really interested in
her, he is compelled to pass by her a fourth time, when
dancing has commenced in the halls, and now he arrives with
the famous Marquise Douglas whose consort appears in full
Scottish highland attire, with swinging kilt a few inches longer
than custom dictates.

'His little *robinet* is dangling just under there,' Blosine sniggers, pointing at the sporran, and the words are so loud that the Scotsman begins to blush and advances a few paces closer to the heels of the prince-president.

She spends the next few hours dancing with members of the Danish delegation, led by Count Moltke, and this annoys Møller. Not that he fears that she will run away with one of them, as all of them have their wives with them, but after every whirl she returns with some delegation flunkey of senior, middle or humble rank who believes he can remember Møller from the glorious days when they all met at the Student Union, and this leads to a spate of inane conversations while Blosine again whirls under the chandeliers with a new admirer:

'After all these years, Møller! Surely you miss old Copenhagen?'

Or:

'Has your literary spark been rekindled by the Parisian scene? An artist is always in quest of fresh impulses, isn't he? Haha!'

'Haha!' Møller replies, smiling and bowing and grovelling in such an exaggerated manner that even these blueblooded dunderheads must realize that they are not his cup of tea, but they doggedly persist. They might as well be standing in Spitzbergen or on a Tyrolean peak from wherever they are: they view the world as the same unimaginative stage backdrop, copied from the stodgy manor house at home in dreary Denmark. A well rolled cigar? 'Not bad.' A whiff of some noble vintage? 'Keeps a decent cellar', and what a fine chap they've got for president down here, that Bonaparte fellow, and certainly on Denmark's side, no doubt about that. After the glorious victories of the Schleswig-Holstein war, the Scaveniuses and the Knuths and the Sponneckers can already see a new Great Denmark sprawling over the map, a snap of the fingers and Sweden-Norway is again back in the fold, a tiny flotilla of gunships in the Baltic and Estonia will derive the full benefits of Danish Christianity, while the Danelaw submits a request to have Copenhagen as its capital.

'Your brilliant attacks on the Germans have not gone unnoticed,' Møller is informed, and he can only reply:

'Honourable Viceroy of Estonia! Should we fail to maintain our guard, we Danes, without being conquered, are in danger of becoming Germans, although our womenfolk remain loyal. And by the way, tomorrow I shall be sending to the delegation my bill for services lovingly rendered to the state. Haha!'

Or the conversation turns to literature:

'Doesn't it strike one that Hugo and the blessed Balzac look like a pair of bandits engaged in a foul conspiracy?' A remark that represents the lofty wisdom of Denmark's landed gentry.

'True enough, Your Excellency the Governor of Lauenborg and Ditmarsken. They have formed a conspiracy of genius to combat stupidity.'

And when Schleswig-Holstein again crops up in the conversation, Møller is asked if he derives no satisfaction at all from the continued existence of Great Denmark

'Carve Schleswig-Holstein up along the language boundary,' Møller lashes out, showing signs of the effect of his sixteenth glass of champagne. 'Ah, if only the landed gentry at the helm of our foreign policy could see even that far.'

'What ingratitude, Møller! Is that our reward for moving heaven and earth to get you out of prison? What arrant nonsense, Møller.'

He is left alone with Blosine who now shows signs of changing back. Her make-up is beginning to crumble, one foot is half out of the crippling new boot, revealing an unwashed ankle, and she is continually drying her sweaty palms on the front of her dress. Møller indulges in a brief manic wish to see her abandon all control and trip the good count or slowly step out of her gown before the horrified eyes of the assembled Danish noblewomen who huddle together in one corner of the hall like a flock of overfed hens, radiating piercing glances of disapproval on all and sundry, especially on Princess Kallimaki who has not been off the floor since her promenade with Louis Napoleon. But then the ball is over, following the stately departure of the prince-president and his retinue.

On the way home, under the arcades of Rue de Rivoli, Blosine flings herself round Møller's neck. She bites his ear, and as she has long since kicked off her boots, the opportunity of kissing her feet finally presents itself. He finds a staircase, and as he makes love to Blosine on the bottom step he imagines the scandal it will create in Copenhagen if he describes the Danish delegation as he saw it — as a bunch of inarticulate Low German peasants once summoned by chance to Denmark and elevated to the 'nobility.' And he will round off the article by letting Blosine abscond with Count Moltke, who spends most of the night in her garret in Rue Lamartine trying to achieve an erection. Møller plants wet kisses all over Blosine's body, and she lets out yells of delight, audible throughout the building. When he gets to his feet and buttons his trousers, all his fascination with her has dissipated, and it is the little jewel polisher from Rue Saint-Martin who now occupies his thoughts. She has yet to polish *his* jewel.

At home in the hotel there are letters for him: from Goldschmidt, from Jeanne Balaresque and from Matilda Leiner. Goldschmidt offers him some sound advice on the chapter of their joint story entitled *P.L. Møller in Paris*, warning him against excesses in chasing *grisettes* and *lorettes*, and against the blandishments of Louis Napoleon. Take sides, Møller, declare your loyalty! This is Goldschmidt's refrain, as he praises the plan of the good Lord and what he now refers to as 'the ethical challenge'. Jeanne Balaresque writes '. . .*il vaut donc infiniment mieux reprendre chacun notre liberté. Pour vous, votre travail ne sera plus troublé par ce que vous appellez mes caprices. . .*', and Møller doesn't know what to reply to her. He asks Goldschmidt to refrain from his Kierkegaardian attempts at conversion.

He writes to Matilda Leiner: 'But I fear that when I get home I shall be engulfed in the all-consuming maelstrom of journalism. Here in Paris, inundated by tons of material, I can hardly get a line down on paper . . . I shall spend no more than six or seven weeks in Paris, I think. However, man proposes, God disposes.'

Time passes. Møller considers a trip to Brittany and

Normandy to collect folk tales. And France has become an empire.

Copenhagen-Paris, Paris-Copenhagen; the itinerary flashes before his eyes, as huge labels pasted onto his trunks, when he has his sleepless nights.

Copenhagen: take sides! Against what? In support of what? Is there not already a surfeit of 'sides' in Copenhagen? Virtually every man has his own side, his own party, with its own quite special 'ethical challenge' based on the Hegelian principle derived from world history. Not even the most insignificant comma can be inserted in a text set at Amagertorv without risk of being misunderstood and wrenched out of its context, ending as an ink splotch of hopelessness at Kongens Nytorv, whence all scurry home to their gloomy interiors, draw the curtains and grab the pen to describe the ink splotch as though it were the veritable ocean of world politics which mankind navigates without sail or tiller while it scans the distant horizon waiting for The United Democracy of Copenhagen to come to its rescue with the message of deliverance, the golden key to eternal harmony of the soul: TAKE SIDES!

Whereas in Paris: take sides or remain aloof, play the fandango if you like, or just leave it, we couldn't care less. The world continues on its path with revolution today and restoration tomorrow, *plus ça change, plus c'est la même chose*, life is a pendulum, and nobody expects you to swing it in a direction you don't like, but 'even the most stubborn opponents of the *coup d'état* on the second of December 1851 are forced to admit that if it brought no other benefit, it has at least led to a blossoming of art and literature which in 1848 and during the perturbations and uncertainty of the following years had declined in a miasma of neglect and apathy,' Møller writes in an article for *Flyveposten*, in the fading days of summer 1853. And Goldschmidt seems to be dancing in terror before his pen.

Wherever he goes, Møller can see signs of a new upsurge in art, in the theatre, in literary workshops, among students, in printing works and in bookshops. Numerous typesetters, hitherto unemployed, have suddenly been given work and a livelihood. Lengthy manuscripts, long finished and waiting only for a publisher and readers, have been taken out of the writer's drawer, and works are now appearing whose titles alone would previously have made even the bravest publisher turn pale with fear. Surveying the new historical works, Møller is impressed by Lamartine's history of the restoration, 'the writer's best historical work' whose eight volumes appear in such rapid succession that the entire manuscript must have been complete before the first line was even set, in itself an extremely rare occurrence in France. A history of the February revolution by Daniel Stern (Madame d'Agoult) has also been published.

And the continuation of Louis Blanc's history of the decade, Berante's history of the national convention, a *Histoire de la bourgeoisie de Paris* and various historical pieces by Mignet, Thierry, Mérimée and many other less famous authors; an extraordinary literary-historical movement whose roots, Møller continues, are to be sought not only in the mood of reassurance and confidence prevailing in the business community, but in the new, strict system of government which is in certain respects hostile to the press. As Napoleon III imposed restrictions on the number of daily newspapers and on their use of their customary methods of titillation, he succeeded in arousing the latent interest in the more serious, more genuine world of books — as exemplified by de Beau-chesne's *Louis XVII, His Life, His Battle for the Faith and Death*, a work in two volumes which so excites Møller that he devotes an entire article to it, ignoring the likelihood of being branded a 'reactionary by the Danish communists in the Café Dane-marc. The work has been acclaimed as a bible by the royalists, and offers sparkling dialogue. As the ten-year-old royal child, barely clad in rags, huddles in despair, wan and desolate in his prison cell, a warder enters. 'The music of the angels is so beautiful,' says the child. 'Music, where does this music come from?' the amazed warder asks. 'From above! Can't you hear anything? Just listen, listen!' And a while later: 'Among all these voices I recognize my mother's . . . Do you think my sister has been able to hear this music? What delight she must have experienced!' That was the last thought of Louis XVII. His face radiant with pleasure, he turned to his warder and said: 'I have something to tell you!' But then his head drooped to his chest, never to rise again, and his final thoughts went with him to his grave.

The work has been reviewed in all the newspapers, even the most avidly imperialist, and no reviewer has attempted to refute or even question a single point, Møller emphasizes, as he stacks pile upon pile of newly published books on the floor of his hotel room. He packs them at random, filling five crates with the first batch, ready to be sent to Copenhagen where he can sort them and the hundreds of sheets and scraps and menus and napkins and wrapping paper and confectionery bags with his odd jottings and ideas for articles and striking words and concepts and samples of Parisian speech noted during his meanderings. 'No more incense, no more bowing to royalty, Møller! Let's have some literature, serious literature! Where is it, Møller?' That's what they're all going to ask, and he has already completed the first few chapters of a lengthy treatise — or possibly a series of university lectures — which can restore the lustre of his gold medal days.

The death of Balzac is, of course, the turning point. Another Napoleon died with him, and *la génération de cinquante* is left with the task of assuming his mantle, a task beyond the capabilities of mere mortals. Napoleon and Balzac: 'The lack of *equilibrium* between head, brain, torso and the stumpy lower part; the resulting exaggeration of the functions of thought and will, and the fall (like scales where one side tilts upwards) attributable to *the lack of counterpoise of the prosaic-material element, represented by the lower part of the body* — in an enormous expansion of mental powers and creativity, the fulcrum moved, and the colossus toppled off its pedestal. Both fell as a result of this top-heaviness at the age when genius reaches its zenith — fifty,' Møller notes, on the back of a letter, continuing his musings on the comparison between France under Napoleon and literary France in the early days of the second empire. The romantic, literary republic also achieved its *empire aux cent trente départments*, but with Lamartine's republic the empire fell to pieces. Poetic veins dried up and shrivelled: Lamartine, Hugo, Vigny, Théophile Gautier and even Alfred de Musset. It was the year when the retreat was sounded, the beginning of the end: Essling, Wagram. Sainte-Beuve and Mérimée, the new Talleyrand and Fouché of literature, feel that their time has come.

Lamartine nullified, Balzac dead, Victor Hugo on his St. Helena, just as Chateaubriand had his own during the July monarchy . . . superhuman ambitions. Now it is the moment of *la réaction de l'intelligence contre le génie*, the age of criticism where Talleyrand-Sainte-Beuve can conduct interminable dialogues with Napoleon-Hugo. . .

'*Tous les courants de la production littéraire sous le contrôle de la critique!*' as Møller heard it expressed in a literary café.

And he knows that these words are a call to arms for him too, at last he can recapture the inspiration that drove him when he produced his *Critical Sketches* and left Copenhagen, to spend the next five years or more avoiding any real commitment to literature. 'The new criticism', the term strikes a chord, no longer with overtones of a polemic intended to expose the posturing of Heiberg who, according to the latest rumour, has gone into hiding in the seclusion of his observatory, but far-sighted, matching the mood of the new age which with its steampowered locomotives, central stations, countless new industries and equally countless inventions has little time for the categorizations of the Hegelian spirit. 'Don't ever think of being exhaustive, of omitting nothing — an ill-conceived endeavour that can lead only to an illusory enhancement of perception,' Møller writes, adding: 'One can nibble here and there in life — touching, hinting, arranging and taking one's bearings on the elements that the brief human span allows us to embrace; that's all we can do, all we want to do, all we can hope to achieve with the powers granted to us.' And this applies to critics too. . .

Rue Antoine-Carême, named after Talleyrand's famous chef who invented *la pâte feuilletée*, Rue de l'Arbre-Sec with its porcelain painters, Rue Aubry-le-Boucher where Cardinal de

Saint-Eusèbe rescued a condemned man from execution in 1309, Rue Beaubourg which is only two years old, Rue Lavandières-Sainte-Opportune, which ran all the way down to the flower-scented Seine in the thirteenth century, Rue des Innocents, named after the cemetery whose bones were crushed into flour during the terrible famine of 1590 — Møller is familiar with every street and winding alley in the quarter lurking behind Rue de Rivoli, *le ventre de Paris*, and it is here, between ten o'clock at night and two in the morning, restlessly wandering, as the cartloads of vegetables are driven to the market, that he discerns the outlines of an entirely modern and perfectly unphilosophical history of French literature for Danish readers. At the same time, as he snatches a few tomatoes, peas, carrots, eggs (if lucky) or potatoes, he again hears *The Danish Tone*, that deeply melancholic and utterly un-French air, with shades of Brorson and Ewald, and the rich hues of Steen Steensen Blicher and H.C. Andersen. And with Oehlenschläger as the Danish poet-Napoleon, capable of a titanic output, like a Hugo or a Balzac, worthy of being recruited as a member of their conspiracy — if only he had written in a major language — against the crass stupidity that recognizes no frontiers. . .

Sometimes Møller has to live through days of despair and dizzy fits when payment for his *Flyveposten* articles fails to arrive, and for days on end he has nothing to eat apart from what he can snatch in Les Halles — mostly potatoes which he bakes at home in the stove. Rue Jean-Jacques Rousseau, Rue du Jour, Rue des Juges-Consuls, Rue de la Cossonnerie, a lane which can trace its history way back to 1183, and the extended Rue Quincampoix, whose street fighters Møller no longer fears now that Jeanne Balaresque has apparently abandoned him forever — in these streets, people will one day be able to say his two histories of literature were conceived and born, worthy of a Sainte-Beuve, with the added distinction of being written in Danish, a language of melancholic beauty and yet marred by German syntax, a work that will also help to put Denmark's new literature on the map and which intelligently, *realistically* and totally unencumbered by prudery will describe the entirely new reality of steam engines and crystal palaces. Rue des Déchargeurs, Rue Mondétour, Rue Pernelle . . . Rue Gerda Pernelle, Rue Gerda Petrine . . . Møller walks and walks, juggling with the street names, tightening his belt another notch and deciding to settle down to serious work at home in Denmark before his fortieth birthday, which is only six months away.

Spring 1854, a good time for making a fresh start. . .

One night the hunger pangs make him vomit. He has trudged all the way out to Notre-Dame-de-Lorette and has hardly recovered from the bout of vomiting before he collapses in front of the church. His trousers are in tatters, the soles of his boots cracked, the heels gone. He sits down, leaning his back against the wall of the church like any common beggar, and he feels that his feet will soon be nothing but two huge scabs clinging to the woollen socks. But his willpower and his confidence are still intact, considerably boosted by the news that from now on he can bank on being the sole permanent contributor for Denmark-Norway working on the enormous book project, *Nouvelle biographie général*. He has been taken on 'from and including the letter B', and can expect to be invited to revise the A section for a supplementary volume. Monarchs, heads of state, bishops, men of science, army generals — and writers, he has all known Danish and Norwegian writers in the palm of his now dirty hand, sitting here against the wall of Notre-Dame-de-Lorette, and for those among them who happen to be still living, his pen represents the key to fame throughout Europe. Five lines for Goldschmidt. Seven, maybe, for Kierkegaard. And, when all is said and done, a quarter of a column for Heiberg.

But how much space for the major figures? 'Columns and columns,' he says, laughing so loud that a girl passing by turns back to give him a closer look. It is Ernestine, the little jewel polisher from Rue Saint-Martin. She waves, swinging her glossy leather bag, she stops to tidy her hair, but Møller knows that he has no option but to remain sitting. He may be capable of reciting a few verses for her, but nothing beyond that. But when he begins, the force of his voice surprises him, and the words bounce off the walls of Rue de Châteaudun:

'Apprends-moi, ô fôret, à faner heureux, / Comme, à la fin de l'automme, ta feuille jaunie.'

'What does all that mean?' Ernestine asks.

'It's a poem, a Danish poem.'

'Well it's a lot of nonsense, and I don't want to wither in any silly forest,' she says. 'And certainly not at a time like this.'

Ernestine comes up to him and kicks the sole of his boot, indicating that she wants to go home with him, but Møller continues to sit, thinking of his alphabet. Ernestine shrugs her shoulders and disappears. He remains sitting for a while, then gets up and, standing in front of the door of the church, makes the sign of the cross, happy in the conviction that Notre-Dame-de-Lorette is protecting him because she knows that he knows her secret, and when he has thanked her for all the young girls she has sent into his arms, he regains his full vigour and runs after Ernestine.

'Des lampions! Des lampions!' the street urchins shout, and Møller feels like joining in, because money has finally arrived from Copenhagen, by almost miraculous coincidence at a time when Paris is ablaze with celebration.

It is the fifteenth of August, 1853, and in Møller's opinion the Napoleon celebration must be one of the most magnificent and most beautiful the world has ever seen. Nearly a million people, two thirds of the population of Paris, throng the streets. Without the slightest scruple, vast sums have been spent on colossal decorations and illuminations which would plunge any other city into economic ruin. 'Politics,' Møller writes, 'is possessed of an element of tyranny and recklessness, and the line from an old French play, Le Tyran peu délicat, still rings true: 'Apart from a few unavoidable misdeeds during his reign as tyrant, not the slightest blame can be attached to him.'' What, after all, are huge national celebrations but politics? No, Napoleon III doesn't quibble over a few measly francs, and the huge throng's sole concern is enjoyment.

Throughout the celebration Møller detects no military presence apart from the usual sentries, and the only police on duty are those posted at the entrances and exits of the amusement parks.

The celebration commenced with the distribution of bread and other foods at a cost of nearly a million francs among the paupers of Paris; followed by free performances in the theatres, and not just, as at the emperor's wedding, at the two opera houses and the Théâtre-Français. The two circus troupes and all the boulevard theatres admit the public to their most popular shows, free of charge, from one o'clock in the afternoon onwards. But even if up to fifty thousand people have been thus enticed indoors, Møller is unaware of any thinning in the afternoon crowds parading along the boulevards and the Champs Élysées. He is forced to elbow his way forward, and every omnibus, whatever its destination, triumphantly displays the *COMPLET* sign.

When he gets back to the hotel, late in the afternoon, to change his shirt, he finds Jeanne Balaresque sitting in the lobby, wearing a stunning new dress. She catches sight of him as he comes up the steps and leaps up to greet him, flinging her arms around his neck. Møller kisses her chastely on the forehead. Despite all that has happened, he has missed her; and he feels as though Notre-Dame-de-Lorette wishes it to be the two of them, and no other two, for the remainder of his sojourn in Paris.

'*Oh, ta belle bouche!*' Jeanne Balaresque cries. '*Il ne peut exister entre nous même l'ombre de la rancune* — my dearest.'

Pleased at the sudden improvement in his finances, Møller invites her to dinner, followed by an evening of diversion in the Closerie des Lilas on the outermost Boulevard of Montparnasse where the students from *le pays latin* dance the magic contredanse, with its whirling can-can, the dance that is now sweeping Paris like a fever, the dance that demands a sense of improvisation and infinitely supple joints. He takes to the floor with gay abandon, yelling at Jeanne Balaresque to shake a leg: 'Lift that leg! Now I can see you as nature intended! Higher, Jeanne, higher!' He hammers dents in his hat, tugs at his clothes, pulls one trouser leg above his knee, turns his pockets inside out. Then he begins to dance the dance of the liberating alphabet. A is for Hans Christian Andersen, beautiful, fairytale, awkward Andersen, leaping high into the clouds showing his huge ballet dancer's feet; and so on until he reaches H for Heiberg, and Møller assumes the shape of a scaffolding, and Jeanne Balaresque is seized by a fit of laughter. Then he dances G for Goldschmidt, and he makes himself fat and dull and holds himself virtuously between the legs, right there where the bar of the G sticks out. And again he transforms himself, now from lizard to toad, from giant insect to dwarf and from dwarf back to lizard with swishing tail until all the hatred suddenly wells up in him and he is Søren Aabye Kierkegaard with the unsated eyes and the peacock strut, a K that jabs maliciously at all the other letters. Møller twitches and kicks, hair dishevelled, as though locked in combat with thousands of meaningless letters. And Jeanne Balaresque forgets all about dancing, suffused with pride in her partner's dazzling performance, the best on the floor at the contredanse. Then, from somewhere behind him, he hears:

'*Cherchez et trouvez!*'

The woman from the Elbe has already reached the exit. She turns, looks at him, drops her handkerchief, arches her neck and smiles, revealing the sparkle of garden lamps in her teeth which seem to meet as though taking a bite from a peach. Then she vanishes through the lilac-crowned arch and for hours and hours he runs after her, through most of the Latin Quarter. He reaches the Right Bank and runs up the Boulevard du Temple where the last pantomime is being performed in the open air. Night falls. Hours later he finds himself back on the Left Bank, on the rectangular plain of the Champs du Mars, but there is still no trace of her.

No call from any hunting horn, no naiads come dancing to show him where she is.

Now exhausted, he crosses the Place de Concorde. Up along Rue Royale towards the Madeleine church it seems as though will-o'-the-wisps are hovering over the city in the pale early morning light. The rag pickers are at work. Sickly and in tatters, they scavenge among the heaps of rubbish, with a flat, open basket strapped to their backs, a lantern in one hand and a stick with a sharp-pointed nail at the end in the other. For them the celebration has long since ended, maybe it has never even taken place. Møller sees everything — buildings, the cobbled streets, church spires — through a hazy, rippling fog, and he is no longer aware of his feet. His hands are strangely numb, and from all around him he can hear strains of music, but neither chamber music nor an orchestral piece. Maybe a flute. Maybe a violin. And yet neither flute nor violin nor any known instrument. The place is populated with will-o'-the-wisps, some of them floating in front of his own face, and he has just been to an hour-long symposium. He is back in Denmark, passing through *Ottevejskrogen*, the Nook of Eight Paths, in Grib Forest. It is a warm summer's night, and he recognizes the figure walking beside him as Kierkegaard. There were five participants in the symposium. All, with the exception of Kierkegaard, have delivered a paper on woman, while the champagne flowed and the chandeliers sparkled. A raging milliner contributing the most malicious attack on the opposite sex, and Møller himself producing the most vicious diatribe on his own sex as he ridiculed those present as lovers whose amorous feats were restricted to tame, arid kisses — a chaste peck on the cheek. He incurred the greatest displeasure when he compared the eroticist who — Oh! bliss that knows no equal! Oh! beatific state! — without getting caught, succeeds in stealing the bait which, since the time of Olympus, the jealous gods have set out for him in order to rob him, the first-born sex, of all his strength while other men — Oh misery! Oh worthy procreation! — devour it like peasants guzzling a hunk of ripe cheese. And get caught.

Only Kierkegaard, with his insatiable appetite for taking notes, is still willing to suffer his presence.

'Well then, Møller, what a novel you put across in your paper! Are you soon going to write chapter thirteen . . . or shall I write it?'

They have almost reached *Ulykkeshegnet*, the Hedge of Misfortune. There is a full moon. Møller chuckles and quotes the profession of faith from Charles Lassailly's *Les roueries de Trialph*, which he intends to use as an introduction to his history of French literature.

The lines are enough to send Kierkegaard scurrying far away:

> *Ah!*
> *Eh! hé*
> *Hi! hi! hi!*
> *Oh!*
> *Hu! Hu! Hu! Hu! Hu!*

thirteen

The road leads him down to the sea. The drizzle has started to fall again. And the rust-coloured Manneporte cliff, whose reptile tentacle stretches out into the sea, is awash with spray. The sky is dark and vaulted, as it is over Børglum Kloster and Sandelsbjerg and the little wood in Skeelslund. Not a human being in sight, but clouds of smoke blowing over the edge of the cliff. It is the Normandy peasants who are burning their clothing, straw mattresses and tattered rag blankets, in the hope that this will keep the dreaded cholera away.

For over a week now he has been forced to live on a diet of mussels and shell fish, and when the pangs of hunger have been particularly severe, he has eaten seaweed or nibbled tufts of grass. On one occasion he nearly caught a sick seagull, and if he had succeeded, he would have eaten it raw. He had flung himself down on the sand, but just as his hands were about to clasp the bird, it somehow flapped off and disappeared between two rocks where the heaving waves claimed it as their victim. Sotteville-sur-Mer, Petites-Dalles, Fécamp, Yport, Etretat. He has trudged from one fishing village to another, but every time he has felt like going up to the closed shutters, or walking up the narrow streets where the thatched roofs and timber frames remind him of the villages around Aalborg, he suffers from a fit of shame at his plight, and chooses instead to sit down, exhausted. And he studies his body and what's happening to it. He feels his lips and examines the base of his finger nails. He has broken out in red spots all over his body, and the glands under his armpits seem to be oozing.

The slightest scratch . . .

The slightest scratch, and he is seized by all the horror and pain and bitter remorse, as though it is really his own fault that the world is as it is, as though the scratch that offends his flesh can come from a verse that sounds wrong, or a face that gloats too much. The scratch may have been made by his mother who screams with outrage when she discovers him with a young girl, or it may have been caused by his irritation at his grandfather's drooling at the corners of his mouth as he taps his long-stemmed pipe. It can have come from the sight of rust in the drinking water, the sugary sediment in the wine, the headmaster's dandruff or the eye of the universe which exudes foul inflammation instead of radiating beauty. And when he feels, as now, that the blood trickling from the scratch will never cease, he roars:

'I hate the whole lot of you, I despise you, and I despise myself for being in your company.'

And he turns all his anger against himself. But only the seagulls hear him as he resumes his wanderings along the beach.

The palace appears far, far away, rising straight up out of the sea. The path that leads him out to it is lined with moss-covered statues of women with bird-heads. Some of the statues have lost an arm, others have lost a fold in their gown. As he approaches the palace, the statues draw back to widen his path, the gulls scream and the stones beneath his feet come to life. But the palace keeps on moving ahead of him. It is illuminated by candlelight, with row after row of gleaming candelabras, and in the lower hall there is merrymaking. The naiads perform a sensuous chain-dance, now and then seizing a green-clad huntsman who drops his hunting horn and gleefully joins in. In the upper halls thousands of birds fly about in confusion and desperation, bumping against the crystal panes.

At the top of the staircase leading up to the palace, which has been carved out of green and blue grotto stone, the fairy stands waving at him.

He runs towards the palace, and now it has stopped moving away from him. A cloud drifts downwards to caress its crystal roof which is supported by arcs of shimmering gold. He reaches the first step of the staircase, happy now that the scratch is no longer bleeding, and the fairy smiles at him and raises her hand as though to lay it on his perspiring brow. Then the palace is shattered, because a bird has caused the slightest scratch in one of the window panes by jabbing at it with its beak. The scratch becomes a rift that spreads all over the surface of the palace, shattering pane after pane as it travels, and soon the palace is reduced to a million shards of glass that are swept away by the waves.

He looks back. The statues have vanished, and in his hand he holds a key, but it is rusty and fits no lock, and the Roman flower vase he noticed on his way up the steps to the palace, and which he decided to take with him when leaving, has collapsed into a lump of muddy clay. The bear that followed him up to the top of the cliff and over the dunes has disappeared, as though blown away by the storm now raging with growing ferocity. But later it reappears, right beside him, transformed into a dog with spiky bristles on its neck, foaming mouth and yellow eyes. It leaps at him so fiercely that he barely manages to seize it by the throat before it sinks its fangs into his neck. His fingers dig deep down into the dog's throat until he finally feels the slimy gullet. The blood spurts into his face. He lets out a piercing yell, swings the mongrel over his head and flings it like a blazing rag far into the sea.

The slightest scratch. . .

The water calls to him. He tears off his clothes and leaps into the waves. He threshes about wildly, facing the waves as they break, engulfed in showers of spray. He gets dragged down, and now he's swimming with leaden arms and legs through water that has become as stiff as jelly. He swims right under the wounded dog, which is being carried out to sea, its legs dangling beneath the surface, the blood gushing out of its throat and creating a brief patch of crimson in the swirling waters; crimson like the blood that many years ago spewed him into the world; crimson like his mother's one pair of summer shoes, which she wears only when there is a 'feast' in Aalborg harbour on Midsummer's Eve and she forgets for a few hours to scream at him or to study her pared nails in silent accusation. He swims, with difficulty, into caverns full of spherical fish with white eyes that can see both ahead· and behind through the blood-red water. At last he struggles back to the beach and he wants to wash himself clean, but there is not a drop of fresh water in sight, not even in the shallow pools between the shore and the dunes. He dries himself by heaping handfuls of sand on his body, rubbing it in as though he wanted to scrape his skin off, especially between his thighs and in his armpits, where the glands are as big as eggs. He rubs the sand into his face and smears it on his scalp, massaging it into the roots, down to that part of his brain which houses forgetfulness. Not far from the spot where he's standing, he sees the dog crawl onto the beach. Uttering piteous yelps, it limps slowly away and disappears, leaving behind a long trail that sucks all the red out of the sea.

He keeps on drying himself with the sand, but to no avail. He is covered from head to toe with red mire, and suddenly he catches sight of his grandfather, up among the dunes, in a halo of tobacco smoke, sitting in a church pew from Brorson's pious century. A while later his mother comes towards him with a basin of soapy water and gleaming white towels.

'Janus, my Janus!' she cries, smiling a toothless smile, with sunken cheeks and only a little of her parchment-like skin left to cover the frozen, bluish flesh. And she collapses right in front of him, having thrown a towel across his shoulder, and digs herself into the sand and vanishes. The shadow of a cross settles on her shrivelled frame as the last grain of sand comes to rest. Once more the dog stands in front of him, snarling and

full of menace. Now he runs away from it, up into the dunes.
 The scratch.

The wall is at the end of the sodden country lane. When he
reaches it, he leans his back against it and looks all the way
back. The sky is blotted out by clouds of smoke from bonfires
burning clothes and straw mattresses, and now voices are
raised in prayer from all the churches whose spires shoot up
from every valley as far as the eye can see. There is a rumble of
ox-carts laden with corpses. In some places the corpses are
simply dumped over the cliffs. He surveys the scene. A herd of
emaciated cows wanders across the road, momentarily
blocking his view. He looks again. In the distance, where the
road swings down to the beach from which he has come, it is
getting brighter, as though summer has suddenly arrived, and
the children are playing and pointing at the lane with
expressions of fear and horror, showing one another the way
up to the wall. The girls wear flowers in their hair, the boys are
all dressed in sailor suits with wrinkles in their stockings. Herr
Kjølstrup, the sexton, is in charge of them, continually
holding his sketching pad at arm's length and estimating the
height of the sun. Then the weather changes. Everything is
suddenly cold and barren, and the children are swept away
like leaves before a storm.
 Behind him he hears a grunt. An old shepherd with crushed
fingers and sightless eyes hops down from the wall and sits
beside him. The shepherd, who is dressed in a shaggy
bearskin coat, kicks at a tree stump with a rag-bound foot, as a
greenish stream oozes from his nose. He points towards a hut
between the trees. When the shepherd gets up, they walk
together to the hut, and go inside, where all the shepherd's
children are lying on the earth floor. The shepherd's wife, with
long, knotted hair, is sitting on a stool in the corner, singing
snatches of old ditties while staring disinterestedly at the
children, all of whom have crumpled toes and fingers, caused
by all the calvados that has been poured down their gullets
since they were newborn babes, to keep them quiet. The

shepherd lashes out with his foot at a prostrate, vacantly staring seven-year-old boy, and when the boy shows no sign of life, he puts him into a sack and drags him outside.

The other children come shuffling out to watch the burial, and from the horizon more and more guests arrive, led by a German sailor wearing black clerical garments. The sailor calls upon the powers to receive the boy in the flaming halls at the core of the earth, and there, ecstatically gyrating right behind him, is the fat trollop from the most wretched street in the most wretched district in Hamburg. She lifts her skirts.

'*Ah, mein Janus! Mein Liebling!*' she yells, in ecstasy, and from right behind her pops up Doktor Hassing with his stuffed doctor's bag. He opens up the sack and closes the boy's eyes. The shepherd grunts in satisfaction, ties up the sack again and dumps the boy into a hole he has just dug with his bare hands. They all form a circle around the grave.

Everyone — the horse dealers, the millers, the sailors, apothecaries, peasants and fishermen — stare at the stranger. The shepherd's wife serves them all a helping of potato soup. The shepherd grins at him, and when he, Janus, suddenly realizes what the old man is called, his body breaks out in a welter of new scratches while the guests puff at him, blowing him to the edge of the grave. He takes in the situation, forces his way between two sailors and runs away as fast as he can. He dashes up a hill and vanishes into the depths of a forest. He reaches a clearing. He glances back and catches sight of the shepherd and the woman from Hamburg entwined in an obscene embrace, rolling on the ground at the edge of the forest, heaping handfuls of mud and wizened leaves on each other.

Normandy or Brittany, the days dwindle and are left behind, and if he doesn't travel by coaches that rattle along at a furious pace, carrying medical herbs and ointments against the cholera to the wealthy families, or if he doesn't sit on the tail-board of carts laden with corpses, he simply walks and walks, along now sodden country lanes and out across fields and through deserted villages. He recognizes them all from a year ago when he visited them and chatted with their inhabitants at a time when they were in high spirits with full, ruddy cheeks, and the sun shone and the harvest had been rich. In one village he heard the story of a subterranean city whose portals to the world fling themselves open at the sound of the first of the twelve strokes of the clock on the eve of Whitsuntide, revealing treasures beyond all compare, but which close with a slam at the sound of the twelfth stroke, leaving the unseen riches in darkness until the next Whitsun Eve. Among the treasures to be found in the depths of the invisible city is a staff made of walnut which was once upon a time the king's sceptre and with which, if a man were fortunate enough to steal it between the first and the twelfth strokes, could transform any object or being under the sun. But if the seeker is unlucky enough not to emerge before the twelfth stroke, he will be forever transformed into a pillar of stone, with outstretched arms, as though captured forever in a cold and frozen gesture of empty embrace.

In another village he heard of the visions experienced by the peasants on Christmas Eve; in a third, the poverty-stricken Plouhinak where he was offered black pudding and wheat porridge with honey, he heard of the rocks which are as numerous in the fields as crests of waves on the sea in stormy weather and which once every hundred years go down to the stream to have a drink in the rushing waters, and how the treasures they hide from the peasant's plough are then revealed, freely available to one and all, there for the taking for as long as the rocks are down at the stream. But the rocks return so quickly to their places in the fields that it is impossible to avoid being crushed by them unless one is wearing a leaf of cardamine surrounded by five-leafed clovers. And he heard of the beggar feared by one and all who could cast spells on the cattle and blacken the ears of corn, and who — a cruel punishment for wanting to pay the rocks with the blood of Bernèz, the poor Christian peasant, which the rocks had demanded if the treasures were not to crumble into dust — was crushed instead of Bernèz who had carved a cross on the surface of the biggest rock which was the first to return from the stream, so that it was thus baptised, and neither it nor the other rocks could touch a hair of his head as he harvested the treasures.

In a fourth village he heard of the Breton Don Juan, Vilherm Postik, who on the eve of All Souls refused to hold open house for the souls that are permitted to leave Purgatory. When the festival commenced, instead of dressing in black and going to church to pray, he donned his city clothes and rode to the nearest harbour to carouse with the sailors, millers and harlots. On the way home he sang the bawdiest sea shanties at the top of his voice, not bothering to doff his hat, let alone remain silent when he came to a cross, although he knew that the road he travelled that very night was full of released souls. When he had laughed straight into the face of Death, who had met him on the road and informed him that he had come to seize Vilherm Postik, he came across two girls spreading shrouds out to dry on a bush. 'We wash, we dry, we sew,' the two girls chanted in unison, 'we wash a dead man's shroud for a dead man who still is walking, still talking. We wash for you, Master Vilherm Postik!' And he laughed even louder, and spurred his horse onwards, but only to hear the girls again swinging the death shroud close by, and soon he was surrounded by hundreds of washer-girls, each handing him a wet shroud and requesting him to help her wring it. In a fit of arrogance he began to wring a shroud with one of the phantoms, taking care to wring on the same side as the girl. But soon other spectres joined in, and among them he recognized his mother and his sisters, his wife and all the women he had betrayed in his life. And when he lost his composure and the hair began to stand on his head, he became confused and began to wring towards the wrong side, and soon the shroud wrapped itself, like a smith's tongs, round his arms and his throat.

Then he fell to the ground, crushed. And he was buried outside the hallowed ground of the cemetery, where a shadow now creeps in the moonlight and this story is remembered, word for word, as is the story of the lake with the evil eyes that lies not so many Jacobin kilometers from the cemetery; and the story of the vanished city in the sea which right up until the time of the great revolution persuaded the men of the church to step into fishermen's boats and row out to the spot where the city had once stood to celebrate the holy mass for the souls of those who had drowned in it; and the account of the vampires' castle; and the tale of the field that is illuminated every New Year's Eve. Then there is the tale of the shepherd who one day during a heatwave brought sickness and a curse down on his own head because in a fit of rage at his wretched lot he had threatened the sun itself; every time his wife and children have died, the shepherd is forced to move to a new part of the country, so that he can pass on the curse to a new wife — whom he must find in the poorhouse — and to his new children. The shepherd is doomed to wake up to a world of sheep that are all dying from some sickness; of cold draughty huts and sharp stones that cut his soles to shreds, there he is doomed to waken, always waken, and see, always see, what he doesn't want to see, and hear, always hear, the groaning from the hut that he doesn't want to hear; doomed to waken just as he thinks the peace that is to take him into its eternal embrace has finally come.

And now Janus sees with the shepherd's eyes and hears with the shepherd's ears. He feels how the sharp stones cut through his soles until he finds a stone wall to sit against and rest until the following morning.

When he wakens, he notices that it is the wall he has come from, at the foot of which he has slept, and he has hardly finished wiping the sticky film from his teeth with a withered leaf wrapped round his finger before the shepherd hops down from the edge of the wall and sits beside him, not saying a single word, while from the hut all the children chant in unison: 'We wash, we dry, we sew.'

The shepherd knows that his own words are no longer needed, now that the stranger knows his name — a name that goes right back to the days when people first began to talk about him, in the year of Our Lord 1530.

The slightest scratch.

'*Pauvre Louis* . . .,' she whispers behind him, but he doesn't listen.

He is looking up at the vaulted ceilings of the crystal palace, where the birds no longer fly straight at the windows and get their beaks caught in the glass panes. And there are no breakers crashing against the cliffs of Normandy, but he hears the cannon from the Hotel des Invalides. They are not sounding to proclaim the fall of Sebastopol but the triumphs of civilization. It is the Peace festival. A festival for a future without superstition and epidemics and plagues. A festival in which he, P.L. Møller, with his few francs in his pocket, can also participate, even though he is now forty-one years old. Jeanne Balaresque had met him in the street, while he was in the process of removing all his trunks and boxes of books from the hotel in Rue de Rohan, and she had pestered him about the black rims under his eyes, and how his hair had suddenly turned white and begun to thin at the temples, until he was forced to reluctantly admit that he had lied about his age ever since he first came to Paris and had been passing himself off as being twelve years younger. He studied himself once more in the mirror and again averted his gaze. He thought that a month's stay by the sea, in Blokhus — when he and his brothers and sisters had settled the Mariendal estate after his mother's death — might be an appropriate prelude to his return to Copenhagen. A month with good Danish food and the loving care of a fisherman's family, and he would be able to cross the country and arrive in the capital with ruddy cheeks, neither a day younger nor a day older than his forty-one years. And while he pasted the address label onto the last crate of books — c/o Marenus Laurentin Møller, The Swan Pharmacy, Copenhagen — and dragged it out of the room, he took hardly any notice of Jeanne Balaresque who still clung to his heels.

'What a rush!' 'Better late than never,' he replied absentmindedly and wondered whether *Berlingske Tidende, Faedrelandet, Flyveposten* or *Kjøbenhavnsposten* would be the best employer to approach when he got back. Jeanne Balaresque asked:

'What's better late than never?'

To which he replied: 'To be at home again.'

'*Where* at home?'

'At home with Louise Razmuhsayn. . .'

But then, as he made his way down the stairs with the crate of books bumping after him, down to the push-cart and the beggar from Les Halles who was waiting for him on the pavement, he heard all the sounds from the hotel and from Rue de Rivoli. Again he smelled the damp glue behind the wallpaper with that odd whiff of beetroot soup, and saw again that awful painting on the landing between the first and ground floors of a gypsy princess with a bouquet of violets. Again he heard the insults exchanged between the patron who was quarrelling with a *lorette* who had a striking Occitanian accent. Again he saw a cockroach running down a familiar step and finally heard again the clickety-clack of Jeanne Balaresque's high heels behind him. Then he also felt again the essence of Paris coursing through his veins. And when his last crate of books had been stacked on the cart, and as the late afternoon sun made the grime on the omnibuses glitter like golden confetti down on the Rue de Rivoli and the first heat of spring caressed him under his shirt and up the back of his neck, he changed his mind and instead ordered the beggar to push the cart over Pont du Carrousel rather than up towards Gare du Nord from where he had planned to dispatch the crates and whence he himself was to travel once the World Exhibition had come to an end.

'*The air of a great city sets a man free!*' — He recalled the maxim of the Middle Ages and instantly felt his muscles harden and his back straighten like a Roman centurion's. Møller saw in his mind's eye distant Copenhagen as a not very important market town, with red-rimmed, running eyes reflected in the countless warped street mirrors. Then he decided upon a little hotel at number eight, Rue de Bellechasse, which he had passed on a few occasions, most recently when he had vainly tried to locate the house where Gustave Doré had his studio.

'*Tous les sciences pour un sou!*' the beggar cried out to the passers-by, with an unsteady hand pointing towards Møller's crates of books. Then the tiny procession set off, led by the beggar and the push-cart, then three or four urchins hoping to earn the price of a loaf by helping to unload the crates, then Møller himself and finally a now subdued Jeanne Balaresque. He moved slowly, leaving behind him Les Halles and four years of his life. He had noted, for inclusion in an article, that the bellies of Paris were annually stuffed with over two hundred million eggs, four hundred and forty thousand Brie cheeses, a million and a half Neufchâtel small cheeses, nearly eighty thousand Montlhéry cheeses, half a million Livarot cheeses, a mere thousand Mont-Dore cheeses from Clermont-Ferrand, not to mention a million other cheeses from a thousand other parts of France. And the vegetables are not measured by the kilogram but by the wagon-load. This works out at forty-five thousand wagons delivering an annual total of two hundred and fifty thousand sacks of peas and one hundred and ten thousand sacks of beans — not in some remote surburban depot, but right in the centre of Paris — and the carrots; and the leeks; and the potatoes which an engineer believes should be driven right into the Halles on special tipping wagons, running on rails from the gates. And the fish market — but Møller abandons his fit of euphoria and attempts to calculate volume and classify the fruits of the sea, and to compile statistics that add a bit of spice to his articles, as the push-cart makes its bumpy way across to the Left Bank. Soon he is in the Saint-German-des-Prés quarter, which stubbornly resists any hint of change, so that the masonry now whispers to him the innermost secrets of centuries, cloaked in names like Saint-Sulpice, la Charité, le Luxembourg, l'École des beaux-arts, l'Institut, la Monnaie, le palais du Sénat, Saint-Séverin, Saint-Julien-le-Pauvre, Saint-Étienne-du-Mont, l'École de médecine, and the schools and colleges — Saint-Louis, Napoleon and Louis-le-Grand, la Sorbonne, le Panthéon, la Pitié, le Jardin des Plantes, and the libraries — Saint-Geneviève and Mazarine and Madame Cardinal's famous 'reading cabinet' in Rue des Canettes, where the bookworm's every wish is fulfilled by Madame herself: costly folios, out of print first editions, even manuscripts and letters from famous authors.

When Møller flung open the window of his new hotel room in Rue de Bellechasse, he felt that he had arrived in Paris for the first time. He had been away on a long journey which he scarcely wanted to recall. Had it lasted a week, or was it really a month? He didn't know, but the journey over the Seine had taken only a few hours, and those hours were like a whole day's happy journey in an upholstered coach, like the day he had travelled from Copenhagen to Sorø. *'Cette chose mystérieuse que nous nommons l'avenir!'* he yelled down the length of Rue de Bellechasse where the cats came out as evening fell, and he closed the window and walked down the new, solidly built stairs, blew a kiss at the vase of Flanders tulips on the landing between the ground floor and the first floor — and received a nasty surprise when the owner demanded a whole month's rent in advance. And, of course, Jeanne Balaresque continued to sit there, on a doll's house sofa at the reception desk.

Throughout the removal of himself and his earthly goods and chattels to Rue de Bellechasse he had not spoken a word to her because she had kept on asking him why he had lied about his age and about returning to Denmark. And was her dress still beautiful and did her hair still shine as it had done when she came to him in Rue de Rohan, could he detect signs of exhaustion in her features as he could in his own? Did little *Djinn* fail to realize that their time together was now a thing of the past? Did she still want him to dance madly in the Closerie des Lilas?

'Why did you fill me with lies, Louis?' she asked. For the umpteenth time.

'One month in advance, Monsieur Møller,' the hotel owner repeated. For the third time.

Møller looked from one to the other and suddenly he heard himself say to Jeanne Balaresque:

'Could you . . . *lend* me. . .?'

'In a week,' she replied, between the sobs, persuading the owner to grant Møller a reprieve until the opening of the World Exhibition, and:

'*Pauvre Louis . . .*' were the last words she uttered before departing, and now she repeats them as she lets the notes glide into the pocket of his jacket, but he no longer listens, no longer *wants* to listen, and rather than listen he points everything out for the benefit of Jeanne Balaresque, who snuggles close to him in the tightly packed galleries and holds his hand as the visitors edge their way forward, craning their necks, greeting acquaintances with their new toppers, agog with excitement, kissing hands, blowing kisses.

The dancing bourgeoisie has assembled in force here in the crystal palace, invited to attend a peaceful contest, and the room strikes Møller as worthy of being sited alongside the amphitheatres of the Greeks and Romans, while the tournaments of the Middle Ages could hardly boast of fairer damsels. Admittedly, there are no minstrels to laud the fair damsels on the arms of these knights of industry. The visitors are all of solid bourgeois stock, their riches have not been amassed by undertaking long crusades but from perfectly bourgeois pursuits, by the sweat of bourgeois brows, and the crosses and medals of honour worn so proudly on the breasts of the men all signify the merits of steam engines and typesetting machines, gigantic steam laundries, railways, shipyards and mining. An entirely new civilization, Møller notes, and he too is swept off his feet by the mood of the day: a civilization sprouting from centuries of blood-stained soil, the thousands and thousands of sinewy, healthy, starving children of French revolutions, brimming with enthusiasm at man's inventiveness, man's willpower, man's pact with anything that can be rivetted together when red hot, anything that can plough its path through the seven seas, or maybe even one day under their surfaces, anything made of iron and glass that can soar into the sky, anything that hammers, presses, digs, drills, stacks, *produces*.

At precisely one o'clock on the fifteenth of May, 1855, the thunder of cannon from the Hôtel des Invalides proclaims that the imperial procession is under way. All eyes are turned upon the gold brocade of the velvet canopy beneath which the emperor and his consort are to take their places. The *lorgnettes* are polished and adjusted, a strange ripple runs through the

crowd, and even the eminences and dignitaries in their gala
uniforms, drawn up in rows in front of the canopy, display a
certain curiosity which is oddly at variance with their
customary, assumed aloofness. Then there is a gasp from
every woman in the room as the empress makes her entrance,
dressed in a sea-green dress trimmed with lace which
enhances her white, Spanish complexion and her voluptuous
form, while her locks, braided with pearls, add a touch of the
childish, a touch of the majestic, to her features. Those locks,
crowned by a diamond tiara, hang right down to her gleaming
white throat, and the trace of bashfulness Møller senses in her
face otherwise contrasts oddly with her composure which
seems to combine the self-confidence of an Amazon with the
hauteur of a Castilian *grandezza*. Little attention is paid to the
emperor, wearing his general's uniform, as he can be seen any
day of the week riding through the streets of Paris. As he
enters, the band strikes up '*Partant pour la Syrie*', and when he
and the empress have taken their seats, the prince reads his
speech to which the emperor replies:

'*J'ouvre avec bonheur ce temple de la paix qui convie tous les peuples à
la concorde!*'

'*Il a de la rhétorique primaire dans ses tripes, le petit Napoléon. . .*',
Møller hears beside him, while Jeanne Balaresque shushes
the culprit, a journalist from *Le Figaro* whom Møller
recognizes and who obviously likes Victor Hugo. When both
speeches have been delivered, emperor and empress,
accompanied by the ladies and gentlemen of their retinue,
undertake a tour of the crystal palace, slowly moving along
through a guard of honour formed by the spectators, while the
orchestra plays overtures and marches by Meyerbeer,
Rossini, Spontini and Auber. It doesn't take very long for the
imperial couple to inspect the exhibits, and Møller knows that
only a meagre sample of the achievements is on display. The
exhibition has suffered a fortnight's delay; the agricultural
machinery display has been postponed until the end of the
month; the machinery section on Quai de Billy is not due to
open until the tenth of June, and *La rotonde du Panorama* not
until fairly late in June. But for Jeanne Balaresque the sight of
the empress is enough, and as they walk back along the banks

of the Seine she is so full of gratitude that she offers to *give* him the money, because he had, with some difficulty, managed to get complimentary tickets to the grand event.

Again Møller pretends not to hear what she's saying. He is overwhelmed by a sudden burst of happiness. Spring augurs a long summer and the anglers get a bite and a rowboat with two young lovers drifts round and round in blissful circles on the calm surface of the dark waters. And he thinks of his new anthology of poems, *Fall of the Leaf — Poems by Otto Sommer —* a pseudonym he has chosen so as not to rekindle the anger of Danish readers with his own P.L.M. The anthology is to be published by Bernhard Bendix, and printed at Sally B. Salomon's works in Gothic type (in contrast to the Latin type he had selected in Gothic Copenhagen for his *Lyrical Poems*), a fount which, in Roman Paris where the Latin type face is seen everywhere, in some way allows him to show his loyalty to the Nordic marshes and oak spinneys, of the dreams they engendered and the heritage of which they are the guardians. The emperor will probably find it fitting to reintroduce the Latin names for the days of the week from the great revolution, thus ending all references to Monday, Tuesday or Thursday which is named after Thor, and instead there is only *primedi, duodi, tridi, quartidi* and so on, down to the ten-day week's *decadi*, so appropriately Roman as to be chiselled into new triumphal arches erected in honour of Proconsul Piston, Tribune Steam Valve and Imperator Printing Press.

Otto, a Nordic name that looks both ways, far into the future, and back to the days when the peasants flung rags on the meadows to conjure up disease; Sommer, pronounced in Danish like a fairy-tale by Andersen, as in a taste of plums, corn and honey. And for a moment Møller is neither forty-one nor twenty-nine. He feels like the eternally young Nordic youth, an Ørvar-Od who may very well allow himself to be impressed by the Frenchman, but who can also in his poem *Queen of the North —* placed towards the end of *Fall of the Leaf,* following a commemorative poem in tribute to Oehlenschläger, a verse narrative about King Arthur, translations of Béranger and Victor Hugo and a free rendering of the poem *Mad Martha* by Jasmin, the Gascon poet — let him know:

But when warm Sun has come, although with delay,
bringing our Queen rich tint of South's summer day,
her pure white mantle's a blaze of amber.
At her feet a sea of roses, rippling hues;
on blossoming beech, sparkle of morning dews;
and when th' nightingale sings it doth twice seduce
— so tardy to come, so loth to linger.

Møller draws Jeanne Balaresque close to him, and when they sit down on the shore of the Seine she leans her head against his shoulder and, happy as the first day they met, wriggles her feet with such glee that she is about to lose a shoe. He tells her about the demented Martha, and she shudders at the lines:

Then, like a Death's Head appearing
just when all rejoice —
The Queen of Spades loudly fell, echoing
black Doom's warning voice. . .

Then the biting wind from the Seine begins to snap at them, and when Jeanne Balaresque takes his jacket and wraps it tightly round her own shoulders, Møller fears that now, despite everything, she will again believe that all is well between them, maybe even that the affair is ripening, has reached the stage where wedding bells will soon be pealing in the tower of her beloved Saint-Roch. He grabs his jacket, slinging it over his shoulder, and walks back alone, no longer in the guise of Otto Sommer, but as *Pauvre Louis* who doesn't care a damn whether his name appears in Latin or Gothic types or whether he is over fifty years old or hasn't yet reached twenty. The only thing that bothers him is *Flyveposten* which so frequently shelves his articles. And he slowly makes his way towards the Café de la Regence in Rue Saint-Honoré where in the yellowish glare of the hissing gaslight he can read the latest French papers and the long out-of-date Danish and Swedish papers. And get new ideas. For new articles, whole new series of articles. Which may also end up on dusty shelves. Until he again gets new ideas for yet newer articles. Day in and day out.

He no longer looks forward to the day when *Fall of the Leaf* will reach the bookshops in Copenhagen. The chill is piercing him to the marrow, as though it were midwinter and he were wandering about some dismal rural district.

The slightest scratch.

Summer arrives

And he asks himself: how can it be any concern of his, of *Pauvre Louis*, resident of Number 8, Rue de Bellechasse whose mastery of the French language has almost reached the point at which he can write for French newspapers, how can it in any way concern him that a Danish doctor of theology whom no one in France has even heard of, he who is forever tormented by his vivid memory of the scene when his father, then a shepherd boy, heaped curses on Heaven from a bleak hilltop on a mist-enshrouded Jutland moor, he who incurred as punishment the same disease as the eternally wandering shepherd that Møller heard about while collecting folk tales in Normandy and Brittany, and knew for certain that the disease would be passed on to his children and their children all the way down to the seventh generation . . . how can it any way concern him that this doctor of theology Søren Aabye Kierkegaard is now at war with the established Lutheran Evangelical church in Denmark? Who in the Paris of Alexandre Dumas and Théophile Gautier and Lamartine cares one whit about Bishop Mynster or Bishop Martensen, here in Paris where it is either a matter of being a strident Catholic or a brazen atheist and where Protestantism, especially Nordic Lutheranism, is regarded as a sickly negation which dare not recognize itself as such.

Despite his misgivings, Møller again dips nib into ink one dull afternoon, with the unpleasant feeling of having reverted to his role of student of theology, totally lacking the energy to tackle the second year exam. Squeak of metal nib, creak of oak desk — padded footsteps, muted speech — matters of moment are *disputed* here! Møller has ordered copies of Kierkegaard's *The Instant* from Copenhagen, and now he is working on an article for publication in *Flyveposten*: 'However, as I approach Herr S. Kierkegaard's mystically tortuous imaginings with the same mediocre sympathy that I reserve for the outpourings of all the others who nowadays try to play the role of prophet or apostle, from Ernst Mahner to the inventor of Mormonism and on to the evangelists of communism, it thus pleases me that. . .' And suddenly he is tired, but feels compelled to complete the article . . . it thus pleases him that Kierkegaard has drawn inspiration from . . . the . . . biography . . . that Møller . . . yes, *he*, Møller, contributed to *The Danish Pantheon* on that very personage . . . Bishop Mynster . . . probably in '43 or '44 . . . although *he*, Møller . . . had not drawn the ingenious distinction between Mynster's Sunday manifestation and his weekday self. 'That' . . . and he is back in Copenhagen, hearing the bells of the Church of the Holy Spirit and tasting the chicken soup from Madam Fouchanée's eating house in Vestergade. . . 'requires an isolated, existential subjectivity, contemplated with Socratic irony, Jobian guile and distorted with the pathetic . . . *madness*', the word falls from Møller's pen. . . 'of Christian asceticism'.

But instantly the thought returns: how on earth can it be any concern of his?

And how can it be any concern of his that the most highly praised exhibit in the Danish section of the World Exhibition is the array of Hornung & Møller pianos — now that Pleyel has placed himself *hors concours* — which are regarded as the best in the whole exhibition and can expect to be awarded at least a silver medal? Or that silver medals are also likely to be awarded to the makers of the Hansen bookcase, the Jürgens chronometer, Drewsen paper and to the Royal Porcelain Factory whose biscuitware castings, modelled on Thorvaldsen sculptures, were in such demand that they were soon sold out? Or that, following an utterance by the prince himself, the Sørensen typesetting machine seems certain to win one of the rare gold medals? And how can it be any concern of his that along with these products, whose merits and quality have already won praise and may soon win laurels, Copenhagen's selection committee has approved the display of a large number of dull, ill-conceived articles — which strike Møller's sensibilities as being puerile efforts — in glass cases which seem to blush with shame at the triviality of their contents.

If all these are undoubtedly matters of concern for Danish readers, he keeps on asking himself as the stack of articles in his hotel room continues to grow, how can it be any concern of theirs *that* a French *locum tenens* bishop has been admitted to the French Academy in recognition of his defence of the Greek and Roman classics; *that* George Sand's play *Flaminio* has been defended in *Le Figaro* by Alexandre Dumas; *that* green sugar, made with pistachio, is now available in Paris; *that* it has now become fashionable to copy Chinese porcelain by painting Chinese motifs on paper and then sticking the paper onto ordinary jampots; *that* Gerard de Nerval has hanged himself from a lamppost; *that* Mary's immaculate conception has been proclaimed in France; *that* Roger de Beauvoir has applied for a court injunction against his former wife, restraining her from writing short stories under her married name; *that* a letter written in gold characters has been deciphered by a child too young to speak; *that* the seventy-four-year-old Ingres has completed a ceiling fresco depicting the apotheosis of Napoleon I; *that* the *lorettes* have drifted from Paris to the camp at Saint-Omer to offer comfort and diversion to the brave Crimean heroes; and *that* the people of Paris fail to understand why the Danes for the sole purpose of scanning the pages of *Berlingske Tidende* and drinking insipid coffee persist in patronizing the Café Danemarc?

How can *that* concern anyone?

And how can it be any concern of his that Kierkegaard is dead?

Autumn has come and gone, and winter has now set in. Møller is in his regular seat in the Café de la Régence, haunt of mutually exclusive cliques of literati and journalists, each with its own exclusive table — *les illuminés, les deçus, les crypto-saint-simoniens, les anarchistes-royalistes, les pulvérisés, les revenants, les communistes-spiritistes, les pendus, les gophloramanes, les neo-scalamaniaques* and all the rest of them, those already accorded an apt designation by Møller and those awaiting his classification which will depend on their manner of speech, their gesticulations and on his intake of hashish and laudanum. Or even ether. Over there in the corner is a group that can only be called *les neo-suicidaires*, on account of the expression of sullen despair on their faces; and in the other corner a group he brands *les homo-romantiques*, his salute to their white gloves and button-hole carnations. He has a particular affection for *les yankee-doodledees* because one of them happens to resemble Georg Carstensen, founder of Copenhagen's Tivoli Gardens, with whom Møller spent a few days on the boulevards of Paris. Looking healthier and more prosperous than when Møller had last seen him on the old artillery range just outside Copenhagen, Carstensen has just returned to Europe, via the West Indies, from New York, where he had conferred upon the Americans that benefit of civilization, which is the crystal palace.

'*Yankee-bambee-winkee-wankee! Doodeeleedee!*' Møller sings, lifting up his glass to the absent Carstensen and ignoring all but the headlines of the reports of Kierkegaard's funeral in the Danish and Swedish newspapers. Seated beside him is a black girl, accompanied by two Turkish bodyguards, and Møller guesses that she must be a princess or the current harem favourite visiting Paris with the Sultan. She lets her purple gown slide down over her shoulder and puts her feet up on the chair so that he catches a glimpse of thigh reflected in the mirror on the opposite wall. She kicks her shoes off, and he realizes that yes, of course, the balls of her feet are white. Her perfume fills the room, and she ceaselessly toys with the glass beads in their velvet pouch. Møller takes five drops from the laudanum phial. Wherever he looks, he sees new quarrels brewing. But it's getting late, and the café gradually empties. Møller takes another five drops.

The church is packed with a mixed congregation. The two front rows are reserved for the family which arrives with lots of time to spare. Professor Rasmus Nielsen manages to close the door so firmly that it becomes temporarily jammed. The tightly-packed throng sways to and fro like a heaving sea, while a ring of dismal figures crowds round the tiny, flower-bedecked coffin; workers from the markets and harbour, drunkards from Christianshavn, street urchins, and all the regulars from *The Elephants' Graveyard*. Then the church door opens again and a tightly-knit group enters totally different from those already assembled — students who wish to form a guard of honour around the coffin of Søren Kierkegaard and to accompany it to the graveside.

When the rites have been conducted, the coffin is carried outside to profane Copenhagen and onwards to the cemetery where a new throng awaits the arrival of the procession. The pallbearers have difficulty carrying the coffin down the straight, broad path to the open grave. Eager spectators climb over fencing and perch on the tops of tombstones to get a better view. The pile of earth flung out by the gravediggers forms a yellowish-grey mound beside a section of fencing removed to permit easier access to the grave. 'Who is it?' the bewildered onlookers ask, and a young medical student steps forward to deliver a graveside oration. 'He's all right!' The crowd expresses its approval, and the student shouts: 'This man who is being buried today with all the honours the Church can bestow was, during his lifetime, its greatest opponent. It is only by the most devious means that the Church has now managed to claim him as one of its own!' Then the interment is over and two cemetery officials solemnly supervise the filling in of the narrow grave. One of them says gruffly to the other:

'We can go home now, Chris'ian.'

And Christian turns round and Møller sees that it is the shepherd with the tattered bearskin coat, the rag-bound feet and the twisted fingers. Møller uses all the force he can muster to dash the laudanum phial against the mirror on the opposite wall, but it fails to break, and the shepherd looks at him with accusing, milky-white eyes, as though intent on reminding him that he, Otto Sommer, who sees both forward and backward, made a mistake by omitting the poem written by

Fracastorius in 1530 from *Fall of the Leaf*; the poem which refers to the shepherd for the first time by his real name after he has threatened the sun and which describes in minute detail how the disease spreads once it has entered the body through the slightest scratch; *Syphilis sive Morbus Gallicus*.

The black girl gets up and pours all her glass beads right into Møller's lap. The Café de la Régence is virtually empty, and a waiter turns down the gaslight. Now the shepherd has vanished too. A bitter wind sweeps through the deserted streets of Copenhagen.

It's a long way from the Café de la Régence.

fourteen

The subject set for the University of Copenhagen's aesthetics prize for the year 1856 is worded thus:

'To show the merits and demerits of recent French comedy, and to examine its beneficial and less beneficial influences on the development of dramatic art in Denmark.'

When P.L. Møller one morning studies the columns of one of the two theatre reviews — *Entr'acte* or *l'Avant-scène* — to determine how best to spend his evening, he discovers that there is plenty of choice: *la Comédie Française, l'Opéra, l'Opéra-Comique, l'Odéon, le Théâtre Lyrique, le Vaudeville, les Varietés, le Gymnase, le Théâtre du Palais-Royal, la Porte Saint-Martin, la Gaîté, l'Ambigu-Comique, les Folies-Dramatiques, les Délassements-Comiques, le Théâtre du Luxembourg, les Bouffes-Parisiens, les Folies-Nouvelles* and *les Funambules,* not to mention the various establishments offering an evening of diversion with music and drama: *le Concert Musard, le Jardin d'Hiver, les Soirées-Fantastiques.*

Unfortunately, it is difficult for him to get free tickets, especially through the Danish legation where they have borne a grudge against him ever since the ball at the Tuileries, and if Count Moltke learns that he plans to submit an entry for the University of Copenhagen's prize, even this will not improve his chances, while there is hardly a Danish baron or biscuit wholesaler or minor Lusitanian diplomat who is not equipped with one of the Count's obsequious letters of introduction to the Parisian theatre. *'Ami, si tu n'as rien, n'attends rien de personne,/Les riches sont ici les queux à qui l'on donne,'* according to a popular French translation of Martial. Despite the adverse circumstances which prevent Møller from seeing all the plays he might wish to see, he can read all about the theatre — in Madame Cardinal's 'reading cabinet', supervised by Madame C. herself who regards all who enter her emporium as members of her family, sparing no effort in finding whatever volume he seeks — plays, criticism, history, theory, biography. And it is in the silence of her musty, shelf-lined rooms that he decides to go through with his plans to return to Denmark, as soon as he has filled his notebooks in order that he can complete his comparison of French and Danish comedy.

He has already written to Matilda Leiner about his travel plans, having earlier sent her a copy of *Fall of the Leaf* with this comment: 'So as to flatter the sickly-sweet, contemptible monster we call the audience, I have made it all as innocent and impersonal as possible, and as you too constitute a part of this fabled monster, you may not disapprove of this approach. I am, nevertheless, reluctant to conceal my partiality for the French form, which may very well cause resentment among the miserable, pompous nonentities we both know — they understand nothing, and have always found it more convenient to follow in the footsteps of the Germans, while at the same time still showering these same Germans with their rotund, inflated phrases, rejoicing at their happy independence of or liberation from the German yoke.'

And he continues, possessed by the thought of his imminent return: 'This, I admit, induces a shudder of fright, when I toy with the idea of settling down in the Spring, until the end of my days, among these malodorous philistines and arrogant fools who call themselves the National Liberal Party in our beloved Hafnia. On the other hand, I hope to lock myself up with my books and to be in a position to earn enough to keep the wolf away from my hermit's door. How justified you are in longing for the golden sunshine of the South. Down here, under the

vast panoply of art and in the atmosphere of that Catholicism
which is so unjustly derided and denigrated by Nordic
buffoons, the human heart is at least permitted to unfold itself
in all its magnificence and beauty, even in its amiable
weakness. . . Have you read Christian Winther's new poem
which has enthralled all Copenhagen's tea-drinking ladies
and gentlemen?. . . But I must stop. All private chatter is
burglary of my stomach and theft from the articles which are
supposed to fuel it. . . I shall not sign off as you do: *la vôtre pour
toujours*, which is rather sentimental, but: *à vous comme toujours*: I
am yours in all that is good and noble and — not all too
fatuous. . . Rest assured, I shall inform you in due time of my
departure. *Otto Sommer*.'

Furious at Christian Winther's treatment of Countess Danner
in *Flight of the Fawn* — 'King of the Danes! Lewd sot! / Shame on son
so depraved! / The most brazen harlot / Cavorts in the monarch's
bed. . .' — tired of the lengthy, unfavourable reviews of *Fall of
the Leaf* in *Berlingske Tidende* and the recently launched
Dagbladet (which has, nevertheless, opened its columns to his
letters from Paris, following his long-anticipated break with
Flyveposten) and of all the other scribblers' comments in
Copenhagen's newspapers, Møller sits, as spring arrives and
he has still not packed his belongings, evening after dreary
evening, in the Café de la Régence, drinking scalding cups of
black coffee to irritate his nerves and absinthe to calm them, a
special mixture to which he has taken a liking. Like poking at
a wound and then putting a plaster on it. First the palpitation,
then a pulse like a sleeping child's. Blazing desert sunshine
from a cloudless sky and humid, dreamy mists at the same
time. He finds some solace in the prospect of spending yet
another long day reading at Madame Cardinal's where the
distinguished proprietress maintains control of all borrowings
with a mental agility and a sense of order that would put the
public libraries to shame.
   But then, on a particularly warm April evening, he happens
to reread one of Matilda Leiner's most recent letters in which
there is mention of a mistress he was supposed to have had

and whom he treated 'cruelly',. virtually 'murdering' her, only to sell her remains as a mere cadaver — *more black coffee, more!* — 'I must thus inform you,' he scribbles down in reply, 'while expressing my appreciation of your steps to defend me that this is certainly not the manner in which I choose to defend my friends. Under such circumstances I explode and can find no words sufficiently strong to stigmatize the slander. Why did you fail to say. . .' — *more absinthe, more!* — '. . . what I believe the most elementary common sense dictates, that before selling anything one must have established ownership of it, and that, as far as is known, women in Denmark are not part of the chattels of their male acquaintances?' Admittedly, if he had possessed such rights of ownership, he adds with a grin, he might just have donated the skeleton to show his respect for science, and then he lays down the stubby pencil and wonders whether to address Matilda Leiner as *Dear Friend, Ma bonne amie, My excellent M., Mia cara, Signorina!, Matilda, my Tilda!, Sweetly naughty or Naughtily sweet* or *My dear, dear prudent Miss M!* He decides to use *My excellent M.* and he hasn't the slightest wish to add his own signature.

Even though his appeal to Countess Danner for a contribution towards the cost of extending his stay in Paris — dashed off during a bout of excessive obstinacy — has been received with monumental silence, Christian Winther is once more the target of Møller's wrath. The volume of verse, with its 'wood engravings' and all poems revolving around a single theme, has for some unknown reason been sent to Paris, perhaps as a mark of appreciation of Møller's defence of the author years ago in his *Critical Sketches*, or as a token of gratitude for writing about him in German newspapers. The volume now lies on Møller's desk, bulging with inserted sheets of annotations, exuding a sense of the mawkish Danish idyll in the Rue de Bellechasse. In the Café de la Régence it grows dark and two of *les crypto-saint-simoniens* have started to quibble about what seems to be a comma. Møller can't resist the temptation of grabbing the stubby pencil and lambasting Winther in the letter to Matilda Leiner: even though the many beautiful details in *Flight of the Fawn* may be admirable, they cannot mask the fact that the composition itself is a failure, because neither the single item nor the ensemble centres on an action or a central character, and the reader inevitably feels that Winther — upon the promptings of his wife (how women insist on meddling!) — has been eager to produce a hefty tome, whatever effort it might cost him, and that the huge success of the book can only be explained by the author's bizarre, not to say 'unworthy' idea of turning part of the poem into a lampoon against Countess Danner so as to please the virtuous ladies of Copenhagen who persuade their husbands to buy the book just for the titillation of finding *la petite bête* precisely in those four lines containing the most horrendous insult. Yes, Christian Winther has once more shown himself to be what he has always been — 'the ladies' darling'.

And Møller himself? 'I have always been unlucky with women. Not once have I achieved the happiness of unblemished skies, of tranquillity of soul, in combination with a taste of love,' he confesses to *Nostrissima*. At the same moment a woman approaches his table, dressed in a red striped dress trimmed with gold at the neck and sleeves and with a glaring red patent leather belt that sits loosely round her slender waist. Is she naked beneath, as she was when they were last together? Møller remembers her short, tousled hair, her swan neck and her sideways glance down to the floor after flinging her gloves onto the table in front of him, one glove happening to land on top of the absinthe bottle. Møller leaps up:

'*Valsons! Polkons! Sautons! Dansons!*'

Throughout *La Queue de la poêle*, staged in three acts and nine tableaux by *le Théâtre Montansier* or *le Théâtre du Palais-Royal*, as it is officially designated, the leading role is played by the handle of a roasting pan around whose magical powers the plot hangs. The action switches from hell to the island of Paphos to the palace of King Kaperdulaboula, from the Undines to robbers and criminals of every nature and description. The hero is played by the renowned Hyacinthe. His most striking attribute is his extremely long nose and his sole talent consists of delivering his lines so phlegmatically as not to detract in any way from the comic effect produced by the nose. Møller laughs out loud. Gerda Petrine, now a 'royal' actress, no less, and in Paris to study the theatre, is impassive. And she remains so, although Møller has explained to her that *Montansier-Palais-Royal* must be taken for what it is: the home of farce, of tra fa la dera and bim bam boo, and that the piece they're watching is a so-called *féerie*, a fairytale comedy that would appeal to Andersen.

'But not to Professor Heiberg,' she replies.

Hyacinthe reaches Paphos, the island of love, accompanied by his faithful armour bearer who drinks to the last drop a bottle labelled *Le parfait amour*. He discovers too late that it is platonic love he has quaffed. If he were under pressure to rush to an editor's desk that same night with his review of the play, Møller would baulk at the prospect of describing Hyacinthe's facial expression as the implications dawn on him. The nose turns, and with it Hyacinthe's face. The nose grows; sniffing around the edges of the prompter's box, sniffing in every crevice of every floorboard. Hyacinthe on a leash. A fly settles on the outermost tip of the nose, commanding all Hyacinthe's concentration while he continues to deliver his lines slowly as if he were hauling the words in on long ropes from the wings. Perfect love! Haha! So that's what it tastes like! Argh! And the nose seems to hover, out beyond the orchestra pit, above the audience who are rolling in the aisles.

Gerda Petrine can't manage even the shadow of a smile.

Møller, laughing so much that he is beginning to double up in pain, looks at her out of the corner of his eye. At the same time his eyes are drawn to the little Cupids of Paphos who hurl arrows of love to the music of the Bellman melody used in *Capriciosa*. Later on there is a *terzetto* of three of the five melodies forming the grand quintet from Heiberg's *The Critic and the Animal*; Nonpareils, Madame Voltisubitos and Ledermanns. Have the French authors been borrowing from Scandinavian sources or have they and their Scandinavian colleagues a common source? Møller feels excited as he grapples with such matters. He looks forward with growing enthusiasm to the prospect of writing his entry for the

235

University of Copenhagen prize competition. Every now and then he looks at Gerda Petrine to assess her reaction.

'It ought to be banned,' she says.

'The play?' he asks, looking down at her nervously tapping feet.

'No, to plagiarize Heiberg like that!'

'All art is theft.'

'Surely you don't mean that.'

'Of course I mean it.'

'You've always had a compulsion to hold the *opposite* opinion.'

'The opposite of whose opinion?'

'Of . . . well, of . . . what one might. . .'

'I see.'

La troupe d'Inkerman or *Messieurs les amateurs du 2ème régiment des zouaves* have been engaged by the *Variétés* to perform, in the same spirit and with the same props, one of the plays they staged in the Crimea during the siege. Before the performance commences, a Zouave with an enormous handlebar moustache comes on stage, already wearing his costume under a heavy grey army coat. He gives the audience a formal salute and addresses them briefly, reminding them that they are in the Crimea, in the la Tscheruaja field theatre. The piece is *Les Anglaises pour rire*, an outrageous farce in which the Zouaves parody the manners of the English ladies. All the men appearing in the comedy sport their incomparable moustaches under the grey wigs, even those who are dressed up as English women. Only one mistress, who looks slightly more feminine than the others, is clean-shaven.

'And you probably think it's amusing, Møller?'

'Yes, I think it probably *is* funny.'

The costumes are beautiful and impeccably cut and fitted, although they suffer from the absence in the Crimea of unlimited stocks of the necessary stage accessories, but invention and skill have been applied to produce adequate substitutes from the materials available. Fans are made of newspapers, and women's belts fashioned out of sword belts. One final surprise, which does not fail in its impact, is reserved for the audience: as the play nears the end of the last act, those dressed up as women lose their skirts in their burst of frenzy to reveal their naked limbs to the horrified father of the 'female' lead, but instead of the prescribed finale, a warning shot is heard backstage. Gerda Petrine, terror-stricken, clasps her hands to her ears while the rest of the audience either stand up or lean forward to get a better view. In the twinkling of an eye the stage is empty, all the actors have vanished, and out of the prompter's box crawls a uniformed Zouave while the props are transformed into a trench in the Crimea. There is a flurry of shooting from a tiny group of Zouaves, firing from behind their parapet, and this group is gradually joined by the entire troupe. There is the good father who has merely swopped his grey wig for his turban; and there is the chambermaid who has had to shed her skirts; and there is the female lead with her skirts gathered in one hand and a pistol in the other, preparing herself for a leap of which no woman would be capable. In a final address to the audience an appeal is made for their forbearance, and Møller sees that there is no element of exaggeration when the perspiring *monsieur l'amateur* who delivers the verse says that he is tottering like . . . a raw recruit. And the Zouave stares Gerda Petrine in the eye.

'I *really* think it's ghastly,' she whispers.

'What? Why?' Møller asks, now irritated.

'To use the theatre like that. . .'

'They have, you realize, been to the wars, *madame la Marquise!*'

They walk through the lobby. Møller has not yet touched Gerda Petrine's hand. They have been to the theatre together now, evening after evening, for almost a whole week, and after every performance he has walked her to the omnibus which will carry her home to her hotel with its arcade entrance in the Rue de Rivoli. In the theatre lobby there is a display of original theatre posters from the Crimea, with small drawings done by a Zouave, shoddily copied, which Møller regards as obviously deserving of greater recognition as masterly examples of the art of the caricature. All of the drawings are obscene: soldiers in the latrines, soldiers running after hens they imagine to be women, two generals who have lost all their decorations in a latrine barrel. Not a single drawing fails to mock the conduct of the army, in clogs and up to its neck in mud.

'I'm against war, I can assure you, Møller.'

'And I'm all for war. I revel in gore and carnage.'

'Oh yes, I'm sure you do. You were so obviously obsessed by those vignettes, and in ecstasy when you saw real war on the stage. Are you in earnest?'

'In earnest about what, Miss Gerda Petrine?'

'About your passion for war. You, Møller, the publisher of *Gaea*? And by the way, if you don't mind, *Mrs*. Gerda Petrine Morten. . .'

'. . .sen. Oh yes, Mortensen here and Mortensen there, and *Mrs* my arse. Only in war does man show his true face. That's what I say. Boom! A severed head, a bayonet in the guts, the reek of gunsmoke, and the early morning sunshine on the battlefield with its dying horses and screams of pain from the field hospital. All else is but insipid cups of tea for pretentious Copenhagen drawing rooms, for the contemptible Consuls' wives, the *Konsulinde* Mortensens, with their philistine husbands. Good morning, *Mrs*. Mortensen, Professor Heiberg awaits you in his majestic office for a little — now what is the word? — chat. And a few little cakes; and don't forget to wipe your boots before entering. No, give me Inkerman and Sebastopol! The shit and the gangrene and the stench! Austerlitz! Wagram! Moscow! Borodino! Swept into the mire by the wings of idiocy! Pure poetry!'

'I knew all along that this would be your line.'

'Which line? You speak in riddles, Madam *Konsulinde* Mortensen. I imagine that your husband must be dean of a school of medicine. Which line?'

'The reactionary one.'

Møller controls his rage.

In the *Porte Saint-Martin* they have seen *Le Fils de la nuit*, a lengthy performance incorporating a dance. Was it really 'innovative' to give the characters names like Scylla Ben Leil, Bravadura and Montefiore, Gerda Petrine asked, nor could she see anything especially 'gifted' about the final scene which consisted of boarding a pirate vessel under Bengal lights. Are Heiberg's names one whit better, Møller asked, and then rephrased the question: was it not the 'innovative' Heiberg who could hit upon just that sort of name in one of his happier moments when he forgot his scaffolding project? Silence. At *l'Ambigu-Comique* they have seen *La tour de Londres*, a romantic drama based on a horror story about the Tower which Gerda Petrine believed should have been permanently incarcerated there. In *la Gaieté* they have seen Eugène Sue's *The Wandering Jew* which Gerda Petrine regarded as passable — just — even though the female lead was abominable; in her eyes they had no notion of how Scribe should be played in Paris. They totally failed to generate the marvellous sense of whimsy that one found in Copenhagen's 'royalty' theatre.

'How true, how undeniably true!' Møller groaned, now firmly deciding that, following the abysmal failure with Inkerman's dramatic company, Alexandre Dumas the Younger's *Le demi-monde* at *le Gymnase* would be the last play he would recommend for Gerda Petrine's edification before admitting that there are moments when even the bravest Zouave might just as well sheath his weapon and beat a tactical retreat with his tail between his legs from the losing battle fought in the trenches of the Parisian theatre.

They manage to get seats in the stalls, right beside the first violin who stares at Gerda Petrine with unabashed desire, as though she were naked beneath the dress and as though, in an hour or two, she would invite him home to share a bottle of chilled white wine in a staid but naughty apartment with silhouettes on the walls, in the city of Copenhagen where, according to the rumours, everything is *democratic*, so different from here in Paris with police spies and censorship of the press, in this vast imperial city where it is a matter of playing the violin until one's fingers wear out and the strings snap — and all for a pittance.

'*La gloire est en vers, mais le vrai bonheur est en prose!*' the first violin exclaims, quoting Scribe and making a conspiratorial half bow to the unconcerned Møller after blowing a kiss to Gerda Petrine whose features remain frozen.

The overture; a vague rumbling behind the curtain; tickets and bonbon bags scattered all over the place; the smell of garlic which makes Gerda Petrine's nostrils quiver nervously; the ceaseless chattering of the audience who reveal their advance knowledge of the plot which they have gleaned from the papers; the sniggering, especially from the *lorettes* who occupy the cheaper seats; the bonbon seller who slips on a banana skin and tumbles into the orchestra pit, leaving a trail of sweets and toffees and peaches and candied apples. At last: the curtain goes up.

'Impossible to stage this sort of thing at *Det kongelige Teater*,' Gerda Petrine whispers, before five minutes have passed.

'Withdraw your critical fangs, my gracious Bravadura. Give your King Kaperdulaboula a chance!' Møller is fully aware that everything in the play from now on will incur the displeasure and disapproval of the 'royal' actress. Where others might laugh, she will, perhaps, raise an eyebrow. While the rest of the audience is gripped by the tension, — especially when the former demi-monde and current baroness of Saint-Ange is confronted with de Nanjac, an officer from Africa who regards as real the world into which he is plunged until he is convinced that the object of his untainted affection has been the mistress of another man, has had carnal relations with his best friend — Gerda Petrine will blithely study her carefully manicured nails, wondering how Johanne Luise Heiberg might react to such a coarse manifestation of the human spirit. The reaction of the professor himself is too horrible to contemplate.

Dumas portrays a depraved, corrupting world of countesses and baronesses rubbing shoulders with an aristocracy to which they do not belong by birth and with the bourgeoisie from which they are forever excluded, ever since they made the mistake of dancing at the Prado or the Mabille or the Closerie des Lilas; and the expression used by one of the main characters, Lalin, who refers to these fallen women as '*les pêches à moitié prix*,' 'peaches at half price', evokes jubilation from the audience. The stage seethes with the obscene prompts issued from the wings and the outright bawdiness of the dialogue so excites some of the men in the audience that they stand up and shout their own contribution to the script:

'Let her have that sword up her arse, de Nanjac!'

Or:

'I'm standing on three legs, *ma comtesse*! Do you have need of one?'

. . . And again the garlic, and the heat which grows more and more intolerable; and the *claque*, paid for by Rose Chéri who every year ages by two years, but whose talent, in Møller's opinion, grows at the same rate. She has no equal in Paris when it comes to playing Dumas the Younger's noble courtesans, driven by calculation and by love in search of a husband, and with so much refinement in the presence of her enemies, and who — even at the moment when everyone in the audience believes her to be defeated by her finer feelings — remains sufficiently coldblooded to keep one escape route open. And there is more din from the *claque*, and more bonbons flung from row to row and the *lorettes* giggle and the men shout out. Gerda Petrine has broken out in a rash at the horror of it all and, with the perspiration rolling down her neck and one heel wrenched askew, she constantly runs her splayed fingers through her boyish hair. During the last intermission she no longer addresses Møller with her dark voice, so full of irony, so practised, so controlled, so appreciated by The Royal Theatre. Instead she hisses:

'And you're infatuated with this rubbish too, aren't you, doctor of philosophy, Møller? Or whatever you pretend you call yourself . . ! Just as you are with war and bloodshed! That vile war and this vile theatre. . . That's the way you want to see things: men are men and women women. . .'

'Whores, you mean.'

'Your word for it.'

'All real women are whores. Madonnas or whores. There's no in-between, or rather, there are some odd neutral creatures who are nothing but a pair of legs with a barrel for a body, yes, *a barrel*, Fru Mortensen, filled to the brim with impotent professorial chitchat and plagiarisms from the *Berlinerstadt*. And the whole tawdry mess is held together by a sordid calculation that's ten or twenty times worse than a whore's. Our excellent monarch is well aware of the fact!'

'Now Louise Rasmussen, *that* woman. . .'

'Yes, *that woman*. . .' Møller replies, and tells her, while grinding his teeth, about Céleste Mogador, the queen of the Variété, dancer, *fille publique, femme de lettre* and comtesse after her marriage to Monsieur Gabriel-Paul-Joselin-Lionel de Chabrillan and to whom Dumas is supposed to have said, '*Merci, ma bonne Céleste, c'est vous qui m'apprenez mon succès!*' A complete whore to satisfy King Frederik's lusty desires! Johanne Luise Heiberg could have been like her if she hadn't been sidetracked by snobbish provincial ambitions. . . And as for Heiberg, he could have been a Dumas if only he had followed his . . . *lustings*, is that not so?

'What a vile beast you are, Møller, God knows!' she shrieks. 'Just imagine . . . here I come like a fool, hoping that you're going to give me a few hints about the Parisian theatre. Well, I've paid enough for my foolishness. . .'

And while Møller sees how she now stands there, shuddering with sheer hatred, surrounded by the audience as they jostle and heave, glowing with pride as they recall their success as joint authors of the evening's piece, he feels that everything about her is repulsively clean and has no idea if she can really be the Gerda Petrine he once visited in Bredgade, and his rage wells up. The small hairs on the back of his neck stand on end, a cloud of blood passes before his eyes and his pulse begins to race. For a brief moment her tight, embittered lips are his own mother's, and her eyes, now burning with rank disapproval, are those of all the Aalborg women from the 'fine' houses gossiping about the woman with the Wendic eyes.

Deep within he knows that he is exaggerating; that this is not the right way to react and that the lightning flashing through his brain has been caused by the clash of dark clouds from two different worlds. Deep within, he knows that Gerda Petrine may not at all be what he's making her out to be; that the bit about her vile cleanliness is only a figment of his imagination. Deep within, it occurs to him that she may have actually *enjoyed* certain performances, although in her own discreet, indirect, ironic manner, until he, by his mere presence, forced her to react so negatively. But he can no longer control himself. And when the confectionery seller passes by, he snatches a peach from his basket, splits it into two and smears the flesh on Gerda Petrine's face. She collapses on the floor and bursts into tears. A few *lorettes* dash to the scene and try to help her to her feet.

'Frozen northern fruit! Full price!' Møller shouts.

He stands holding the two peach halves, now bruised and oozing. Then he tosses them away and runs towards the exit.

Relieved.

The next day she sits in his hotel room. Please, oh please! He must understand. He must forgive. She didn't really mean it. At least not like that. If only he knew, if only he could imagine what it's like to be in her place. . .

'As Mrs. Mawr-tön-sön, the wife of a coffee wholesaler?'

'You guessed it all, didn't you?'

'Who *are* you, in reality, Gerda Petrine?'

Møller is quite calm. He sharpens a pencil. He glances at the papers on his desk.

'The same person that I was then . . . *Pauvre Louis*. When I used to get the shakes as I finally worked up the courage to write to you.'

'You mean when you woke me up in the middle of the night and hammered away at me like a silly schoolgirl and spoke like . . . like an echo of the powers that be at the Royal Theatre: *Leave, get out!. . .*'

'Hit me. I deserve to be hit.'

'Like this?' He smacks her on the face, twice.

'More.'

He hits her on the face again with his full force. Gerda Petrine flings herself onto his bed, unbuttons her dress and hides her face in her hands.

'Whip me,' she whispers.

And as though it is the most natural thing in the world, as though it is a humdrum daily matter like sharpening a pencil end or putting an article into an envelope and addressing it to *Dagbladet*, 82 Brolaeggerstraede, Copenhagen, he takes off his braces, rolls Gerda Petrine onto her belly, strips her of her dress and corset and whips her until the blood begins to trickle down her beautiful, supple back. She says nothing. Then, feeling his excitement grow within him, he tears off his trousers and spreads her legs over the edge of the bed so that he can have a better position to make love to her from behind, the way he prefers it, and he keeps on and on until Gerda Petrine, clawing at the bedclothes until her fingernails are bloody, screams with pain and pleasure. When he is on the point of orgasm, he turns Gerda Petrine round, kneels in front of her and forces his member in between her narrow lips and spurts his seed deep down her throat. Moving the tip of his member to and fro, he rubs the last few drops on her cheeks. Using both hands, she spreads the semen all over her face.

'If you want to rinse it down, Mrs Mortensen, I'm afraid you'll have to pay for the champagne yourself.'

'Yes, I'll pay for anything you ask,' she blurts out, amid the tears.

He snatches up a copy of *Entr'acte*.

'Offenbach!' he suggests, as he buttons up his shirt and grabs his jacket.

'Who is he?'

'Just about everything that's *new*, that's all.'

From as far back as May 1855 Monsieur Jacques Offenbach has enjoyed the right to his own theatre on the Champs-Élysées. The licence was issued to him by the Minister of the Interior with the following description of what might be seen and what might not be seen in *la Salle Lacaze*: 1) harlequinades, pantomines with five performers, 2) comic scenes and musical dialogues for two or three performers, 3) *physique amusante*, conjuring tricks and vanishing acts, *fantasmagorie*, Chinese shadows and *fantoccini*, 4) *tours de force et d'adresse*, 5) exhibitions of curiosa, 6) no dancing with five or more dancers and 7) *chansonettes* for one or two performers with or without costumes.

'*Mon théâtre che l'appelerai les Bouffes-Parisiens!*' exclaimed the happy Jacob alias Jacques Offenbach. Møller imitates his Cologne-Jewish accent while he and Gerda Petrine sit on the upper deck of the omnibus which for two sous takes them along the Champs-Élysées, out to the Bois de Boulogne where Møller has proposed that they spend the afternoon before attending the Offenbach evening performance. Gerda Petrine is now thrilled with everything about Paris, even the small glass lamps hanging lopsidedly and untidily on les Champs-Élysées. Many of them are shattered; the paper balloons and stars have faded; the decorations — vases and antique columns — have been defaced by soot, and the tricolour hangs limp against the walls, without a whisper of a breeze to create a ruffle. When they have passed l'Arc de Triomphe, the road out to the woods stretches ahead of them in a long uniform empty line. The only living things they see are members of the watering brigade, fastening hoses to the water pipes along the curbs and sending showers of rain all along the road. In the shimmering rainbow of the downpour Møller is especially inspired so that in the politest possible manner, as though requested by the Danish foreign ministry itself to conduct a tour of Paris for the 'royal' actress on the occasion of her first visit, he tells Gerda Petrine about Offenbach's first successes with the short musical pieces — *Les Deux aveugles*, *Violoneux* and *Madame Papillon* — which made him famous in the capital for getting the violin to sound like any musical instrument, especially the flute, up to the time when *le directeur-auteur-compositeur-chef-d'orchestre* moved across the water to the Left Bank and achieved his breakthrough with *Ba-Ta-Clan* in which, contrary to the stipulations issued by the Minister of the Interior, he had five dancers on stage.

'*Ba-Ta-Clan, Ba-Ta-Clan*, Fru Gerda Petrine von Mortensen, simply *is* Paris, just as much as le Bois de Boulogne out there in front of you! Enjoy it all now that you're here! The whole world will soon be thronging to Offenbach's "operattas" . . . *Souvenirs charmants . . . d'une vie . . . qui suivait gaiment . . . la . . . folie. . .*'

'*La . . .?*'

'*Folie* . . . madness . . . *Ba-Ta-Clan! Rantanplan! Fenihan! Ficheton Khan! Ta-ta-ta-ta!*'

He notices how the woods have been improved since he was last here: a long artificial lake with swans, gondolas and even a schooner; in the northwestern corner, to which they stroll arm in arm, the new pleasure gardens, Pré Catalan, with its puppet theatre, panoramas and buffets and bands rehearsing. When the music starts up, the rain that has been threatening Paris since early morning comes pouring down, and all the visitors, mostly soldiers and English tourists, escape the deluge by rushing to the cafés or their carriages. Møller and Gerda Petrine seek shelter under a tree where they are joined by an old man. Grinning, he points out something between the trees with such an unpleasant look on his face that Gerda Petrine buries her face in Møller's shoulder. A mist forms before Møller's eyes, and while he thinks of the difficulty he is having with his entry for the University of Copenhagen's prize, he puts the laudanum phial to his lips. He is tired of Gerda Petrine and intends to present her with a huge bill before she leaves — for all the time she has stolen from him. She still rests her face against his shoulder as she clings to his neck, twirling a lock of his hair, and with her very deepest voice tells him that she knew that they would meet again and that the future will be theirs if he wants it that way, if he wants it as sincerely as she does.

The airy, spacious apartment they're going to live in, overlooking lawns and flowers and trees and the palace. All the books he'll be able to afford, even the oldest and rarest folio editions. And when she comes home from the theatre and she will make dinner for him, while he has bought flowers for her, leaving them in the hall for her deft fingers to arrange. And when she wakens in the morning she stretches so that her breasts flatten out. If he can only submit an entry good enough to win that gold medal, the world will be his oyster, everything he has ever wanted will be there for the taking. She knows that. Her woman's intuition tells her that. And he thinks of all that has happened in French writing for the past many years . . . Chateaubriand and all the others . . . *le salon rouge . . . la génération des années vingt . . .* the young Lamartine, the child prodigy . . . *les enfants du siècle . . . les poètes mourants . . . les Byroniens . . . Rolla . . . Alfred de Vigny . . . Mémoires d'Outre-Tombe . . . les poètes de la ballade . . . les poètes du mythe . . .* a truly gigantic amount of material, never yet richly described for a Danish readership . . . yes, French writing has made progress since Napoleon . . . Oehlenschläger will appreciate his entry for the competition . . . if he now succeeds in tackling it . . . in the proper . . . manner. . .

'Grimur Thomsen will come too . . . and Holst . . . and Kierkegaard, if he wants to . . . if he dares . . . wants to. . .'

'Møller?' Gerda Petrine raises her head.

'Yes? I mean to the party . . . the party to celebrate the gold medal . . . maybe we can hire Rosenborg Castle from the king. . .'

The pigeons fly right in front of his face, the pigeons he has always liked. He breathes in the smell of salty waves and the seaweed of the sound.

'Come on,' he says, 'let's dash over to the University Library in Copenhagen and read together. There's shelter there.'

'My poor mad poet!'

The old man looks him straight in the eyes, and Møller notices that he's not a day older than forty-five, maybe he's even in his late thirties. He has difficulty standing upright, and the madness is written on his face; the sores from the time he caught the disease are like small craters, and it is as though huge chunks of his lips have been skinned, creating holes all the way to where his teeth are fastened to his skull. The wreck stumbles off in the direction of Pré Catalan where the children, afraid of coming into contact with him, steer clear of his path, as he utters loud shouts of abuse. He lashes out with his stick, lost in his own world of jumbled fragments of memories from the bright summer when the disease conquered his body, through the slightest scratch, until now, when, in its last stages, it has finally crippled him. Møller wrestles himself free of Gerda Petrine's embrace and begins to walk back, all the way to l'Arc de Triomphe, down the Champs-Élysées. Now and then he breaks into a trot so as to reach the Left Bank and his hotel without delay, hoping to be able to get sleep, just sleep, for twenty or twenty-four hours at a stretch — to waken up to a fresh, new world. But when he reaches Rue de Bellechasse and enters the lobby, Gerda Petrine is already sitting there. She would simply love to invite him to dinner. She would simply love to spend every second of the rest of her time in Paris with him.

'*La Fontaine des Innocents!*' he replies.

Gerda Petrine is radiant. Møller allows himself a contemptuous smile; she fails to realize that the restaurant he suggests is virtually a poorhouse kitchen. Never mind how arrogant he may be now, never mind what stratagem he invents to humiliate her, she will say yes, yes — I love you; and when they're finally sitting in front of the fountain where all the vagabonds from Les Halles come to fill their bellies, Møller feels that he is on the verge of asking Gerda Petrine to get down and crawl on all fours among the dogs and the filthy pauper children who beg for a potato — and she will obey.

'Did you *really* sell her skeleton?' she asks, biting the tops of her fingers.

'As a matter of fact, yes — several times over. I kept the skull for myself. You may inspect it in all its splendour at my brother's place — the Swan Pharmacy.'

'What a play it would make for Dumas. By the way, is it true that he's a mulatto?'

'Dumas *père*, yes. Why?'

Møller suddenly gets the idea for the motto he's going to use for his competition entry: '*Les décrets du destin ont voulu qu'Appollon / Fut le meilleur des Dieux pour la race mortelle.*' Things are no longer as they were in the twenties and thirties. The gods have long ago abandoned Olympus and have turned into humans. The gods want to *amuse* themselves, dressed up as coffee wholesalers, cheesemongers and railway engineers. Oehlenschläger would turn in his grave if he knew what Scribe has had placed as an inscription over the main entrance to the magnificent house he owns amid acres of parks and rolling countryside on the outskirts of Paris:

Le théâtre a payé cet asyle champêtre,
Passant, merci, je te le dois peut-être.

That's how Scribe — in an unguarded moment — has revealed the secret of the new age, thanking the theatre and theatregoers for having paid for a country retreat, befitting a man of his station with a fortune of four million francs and an annual income of two hundred thousand francs. Why should such a man care if young revolutionaries accuse him of feuding with French grammar and of writing French like a junior officer in 1823?

'Simply because it's all so exciting. . .' Gerda Petrine replies softly.

'What? *What's* so exciting?' Møller asks, and thinks of staying in the confines of his hotel room for months on end with healing mercury and ether, laudanum, hashish, wine, bread, lots of coffee and all the plays he can borrow from Madame Cardinal. From Denmark he's going to order Hostrup, a writer of definite talent.

'To be a mulatto . . . negro blood in our *white*. . .'

'Why is it exciting?' he asks dispassionately.

He looks her in the eye as he orders two bowls of potato soup. A Zouave with forehead shaved in an attempt to look oriental seats himself beside them and unabashedly grabs Gerda Petrine and takes her on his knee. Møller knows that the Zouave has a reputation for beating his women, and he casually lets her know this, implying that as far as he, Peder Ludvig Møller, is concerned, there will be no fuss should she happen to feel like subjecting herself to a sterner hand. And it all works out the way he knew it would, as though he is now finally capable of manipulating all the strings. After the soup, Gerda Petrine disappears with the Zouave, 'in love with Paris' as she, while flinging her arms about, tells all the scraggy, unwashed denizens of *La Fontaine des Innocents* who, sitting at the roughly hewn tables remind Møller of a heap of silhouettes she has decided upon some odd whim to scrap.

He doesn't see her again until the following morning when he arrives at her hotel to submit his bill. She is carrying her hand luggage out to the hired carriage while two boys are dragging her huge trunks down the steps. Wearing heavy make-up which barely conceals the cut on her forehead and the bluish swollen cheeks and the inflamed yellowish patches under her eyes, she is once more the Gerda Petrine who came to him in the Café de la Régence and flung her gloves onto the table in front of him. The same embittered lips; the same distant gaze; the short-cropped hair once more brushed and combed; and her way of looking sideways at the ground, as though nothing could bother her. Møller wishes her a pleasant journey home to the linoleum floors and puts the detailed bill into his pocket as he knows that he won't get as much as a *sou* from her. From the Café de la Rotonde on the corner he hears the shouts of the jostling waiters:

'*A gauche, pavillon! Deux tasses et un demi! Demandez "le Figaro" Troisième ballustrade! "Le Tintamarre"! Annoncez "le Figaro"! Deux vanilles!*'

Gerda Petrine's eyes burn with contempt for all that is Paris and, before stepping into the carriage she orders the driver to brush the seat clean, to remove every speck of dust.

'Give my best regards to Christian Winther!' Møller laughs.

'Certainly, *he* is a writer!'

'If you say so, *Fru konsulinde*.'

The driver cracks his whip, and while he whistles the bolero from Offenbach's *Les Deux Aveugles*, he sets off towards la Gare du Nord with Gerda Petrine.

The verdict issued by the panel of adjudicators reads:

'. . . Despite the fact that the author of this treatise may have restricted himself to a shorter conclusion than might have been expected following his exhaustive treatment of the premises, he has nevertheless amply demonstrated his ability to apply his mental powers to treating all relevant aspects and his ability to concentrate on factors that lead to a solution. He has satisfied the adjudicators that he has accorded his material a detailed study without allowing himself to be overwhelmed by it; he combines a thorough grasp of the prescribed material with an independence of mind, and we take pleasure in declaring that in our opinion the treatise fully deserves to be awarded the University's prize.'

Copenhagen, the 16th of September, 1857

F.C. Sibbern   C. Hauch

The author turned out to be P.L. Møller (in Paris).

fifteen

He pours himself out in long tirades. And some of his repartee takes up a whole page in Goldschmidt's novel. He's called Schiøtt.

He pops up suddenly, like a Jack-in-the-box, independent of the others in 'the company', because he sets up beauty as the sole law governing life's allurements. In the novel he is born with immense talent, with a capacity for joy and happiness. His first conscious glance into the world settled on an aura of affluence and the most beautiful sight of all: a tender, loving mother. But when the child was five or six years old, dire tragedy hit the home. A bankruptcy in the mother's family had swallowed up her fortune and this loss induced black, choleric fits in the father, dark moods that dragged the home down, from affluence to poverty, from a life of peace and happiness to a welter of despondency and strife. The father took to beating his wife. The boy, who witnessed it all in a state of profound distress and paralysis, used to scream, thus informing his parents of his existence. The tearful mother swept him up in her embrace, kissed him on the eyes, as though to kiss away what they had seen, and wrapped her arms about him, burying his head in her bosom, as though to keep the sound of the blow away from his soul. But the blow had fallen.

Schiøtt is not, however, a melancholy child. Bursting with

vigour and zest for life, he cannot allow any pall of bitterness and sadness to cripple him, and he is seized by a deep desire to add to his knowledge, to broaden his perception. Through these he gains the force of intellect that enables him to forget what he wants to forget. His feeling for the ideal, for the beautiful, leads to his creation of a system of bliss, an outlook on life embodying an ideal which seems to lead upwards to the very pinnacle of ideals, and he understands how to transform minor pleasures into major experiences. Against the world's many vicissitudes and reversals he hurls his innumerable arrows of barbed irony. His forte is dialogue:

'Hell: well, if there really is such a place as hell, then the conditions prevailing in society are responsible for sending an awful lot of women to this hell. Droves of them, God only knows how many, who, bereft of love or cherishing another love, have squandered their essence on a man simply because the formalities — the marriage rituals — were duly observed, and further droves of them who neglected to publish the banns or failed to obtain the licence and thus lost their self-confidence, their love and the idea, and ended up by taking to the street. Why do the so-called tales of seduction usually end in such misery? Because they are the fruits of 'I want to, no, I don't want to', because one of the parties involved lacks enterprise while the other lacks gratitude for something offered in a spirit of confidence. Nothing but uncertainty, fear and accusations. . . "*Wir alle sind verliebte Natur*"_..'

And later:

'Nature speaks to us, the grass chirps to us in springtime, the birds warble, yes, even the muslin smells, the glove that has brushed against a woman's hand, and the most treacherous sighs of all are those beneath the corset. It's not a question of saying: "Don't do this and don't do that!" It should be: Do whatever you please, with beauty and respect for the gods! It's a question of idealizing Nature.'

'But where have you learned this?' asks the terrified main character, Otto Krøyer. Much of what Schiøtt has to say causes him 'a pain in his heart.'

'Through intuition. . .' the smiling Schiøtt replies. 'We

252

have all of us in our souls a master key that opens the door to other people's souls, if only we have just a little experience of trying it on ourselves.'

At one point Otto Krøyer asks: 'What then keeps the world from falling apart?'

'Centripetal force, centrifugal force, the law of gravity and the law of equilibrium, the balance of interests. A certain system of interests clings to every ideal concept, just as every shellfish in the sea clings to some submerged object. And the greatest sum of grave, coarse interests clings to the most superior ideal concepts . . . the world moves forward towards infinite perfection by means of the shellfishes' weight.'

The novel, whose final volume was published in 1857, goes to considerable trouble in working towards an understanding of Schiøtt who speaks with the sort of irony whereby a man appears to stand so many times above or behind himself that he is like a room whose walls, floor and ceiling are covered with mirrors. The eye pursues his image into infinity without ever focusing on a permanent point, being constantly drawn inwards and onwards by its own self-defeating search. Schiøtt's childhood fate should thus have pursued him into love. He made the acquaintanceship of a family with whom a distantly related, extraordinary young girl, a year older than he, happened to be living. He was eighteen years old at the time. It created quite a fuss when she suddenly disappeared — some said with a circus riding master, others with a diplomat. No one knew that Schiøtt had loved her, and that she had left him amidst all the passion and all the bliss which she had aroused in him, to untangle the mystery of whether she had known of his feelings or not.

So far, so good. Up to this point Møller finds himself in agreement. Not so difficult to recognize what he himself had once told Goldschmidt, either in Store Kongensgade or in the home of the budding young Jacobin, although undeniably more poetic. At one with the natural riches of North Jutland which took her to its breast, the girl ran out like a naiad or an elf, across the meadow with a little heart-shaped mother-of-pearl box tied with a silk ribbon, containing the poem that the

swooning Møller had given her. Two months later she broke
the engagement off, at the promptings of his mother whom
Goldschmidt, fortunately, has not sufficient imagination to
portray as she really was; 'the maidenly' Georgine Sofie
Magdalene Kanneworff Møller with the wrinkled hands, the
all too closely pared nails and the eyes downcast in fear of her
husband's moods. And later, the girl's virginal lustre had
faded after her engagement to the landowning twit in the
green uniform high boots and Bavarian hat — diplomat or
circus riding master neither of which was that far from the
truth. So far, so good.

'One must guard oneself against the tragic,' Schiøtt says in
another passage. Møller recognizes that line too.

'What exactly do you mean by that?' asks the novel's
ambitious 'good' man, Otto Krøyer, 'almost scared by a
sudden shadow.'

'One must have happiness. Somewhere in life there is a
secret; there is something that cannot be measured or weighed
on any scales, because justice has nothing to do with it,'
Schiøtt replies, and Møller is on the verge of becoming fond of
him because of his ability to infuse life in the other characters,
expecially Otto Krøyer. But when he reads what Meïr Aron
— in his seemingly endless, chatty novel (*Entwicklungsroman*,
he can hear Goethe whisper from the shelves in Goldschmidt's
study) with the oddly anonymous title *Homeless* — has called
Schiøtt's mystical, lost and actually quite shrewdly observed
youthful love affair, it strikes a decidedly farcical note, not
only when evoking memories of all Goldschmidt's troubles,
but also Møller's own memories from Aalborg: *Ottilie* . . .
Angelika . . . *Damm*, the master's pen has plucked them from
the goldplated inkwell, without as much as a tremor, or a
single shameful blot.

As a migrant Frenchman and former plantation owner
from the Antilles, François André, who on the pages in which
he appears, abetted by Schiøtt, succeeds in slightly raising the
level of the novel, obviously struggles in vain to teach the
callow Otto Krøter:

'Judge every young housewife by her tablecloth and every

young girl by her handkerchief and you won't go far wrong!
And learn to parry an octave — look at that parry — the
opponent jabs a deep tierce after a deep quart feint. Don't do
as your fencing master does because he has grown stiff, do it
with spirit, with elegance, always with a smile — one has to be
born a *gentilhomme* to do it. . .'

And then all that Jewish stuff, Møller thinks. Now we know
that much: despite the *Gemütlichkeit* with which Abraham
prepared himself for the sacrifice of his son, Goldschmidt is
against the idea of the Jews having used children as human
sacrifices. But what entitles him to assume that his forefathers
should have been more philanthropic in that respect and so
differently constituted from all others, from the Celts or from
the Scandinavians to whom also Goldschmidt can of course,
in a way, trace his ancestry? Why is it so improbable, Møller
muses, that the Jews of the Middle Ages, when they saw an
opportunity presented, now and then ate a Christian child
during the Christmas celebrations? 'Nothing,' he writes in a
draft of a lengthy critical essay on *Homeless* which he hopes he
can complete when he gets back to Rue de Bellechasse, hearing
himself speak like Schiøtt in the novel: 'of course, nothing but
the sickly sentimentality which modern Jews, especially
literary and artistic Jews, often display in dredging up
anything that will serve to reflect glory on the Jews and gain
for them the sympathy or public esteem previously denied
them.'

And in his rough draft Møller lets Schiøtt play a trump: 'To
steal legally, that is with the approval of the law, in itself
constitutes legal art, at least as it is consciously or
unconsciously practised by Otto . . . by *you*, Otto Krøyer. . .'

Møller searches in the novel for a passage where he can
insert his new lines. He flips through the novel at random, and
again finds himself impressed by Schiøtt as he was so many
years ago, as a young man in Copenhagen:

'What is the resemblance between you and the Marble
Church of Copenhagen?' asks the 'demon'.

Otto Krøyer guesses wrong.

'You want to hear it — well, put up your shield!' Schiøtt continues.

'Go ahead and shoot!'

'*Messieurs*, you have both become ruins before being finished. . .'

And Schiøtt heads for the door as Møller places *Homeless* on the bedside table.

Etretat. The knarled, rust-coloured La Manneporte cliff that sends its tentacles stretching out into the waves. The beach. Stones and more stones, encrusted with seaweed and scales. A wrecked, abandoned skiff. A tattered sailor's cap that is constantly filled with surf, drained of surf. Seagulls. Snails, mussels. A rusty knife stuck, as though in anger, into the porous sandstone. The smoke drifting over the cliff at a predetermined point. The hut from which the hardly varying smoke drifts. The place where one can make one's way up to the path leading to the hut. The path, muddy and with deep wheel tracks from the time the cholera raged and the carts carried the corpses to the edge of the cliff, to be committed to the mercy of the churning waves. The hut, warmed by the fire in the hearth, fire constantly stoked with spluttering logs. The duck being roasted in its own fat, the mulled wine, the calvados to be served after the meal; the bed freshly made with aired linen; soap; sparkling water from the spring; the mornings when the clouds drift and the gulls seem to hover in the same place facing the wind, and there is a smell of burning hay. And he hears a snatch from Baudelaire's *Les Fleurs du mal*:

Je veut bâtir pour toi, Madone, ma maîtresse,
Un autel souterrain au fond de ma détresse. . .

It will take Jeanne Balaresque at least an hour to get the dinner ready in the tiny fisherman's cottage they have rented for a few weeks, long after the season has ended, and as Møller walks along the beach he forgets for a while all the things he feels like forgetting. The pains in his arms and legs have disappeared, and it is as though his stomach is functioning normally for the first time in years. His skin is smooth and tanned, and the salty wind makes his skin tingle with pleasure while the winter sun makes the blood pulse in his temples, throbbing at being one with Nature. When he fills his lungs with air, it is as though he once more — in a sudden glimpse that goes all the way back to his childhood — can see without glasses, and he finds a spot where he flings himself in a giddy swoon onto the sand and studies a stone at close quarters. He can follow all its bluish green, wavy rings, formed throughout the aeons; the pain in his eyes from the time when — with his cheap glasses temporarily mended in makeshift fashion with a piece of string — he lay and read *Homeless* has gone, and he hasn't a notion why he should spend any energy at all on the novel. In his pocket he has a letter to Matilda Leiner, and he doesn't know if he will even bother to go out of his way to get to a mailbox in Etretat to send it on its way: 'You speak to me of *fantaisies des poètes*, but apart from a few theatre tickets and the purchase of a few books I have never indulged — especially in Paris — in others than those that can be enjoyed free. And as in any case women are to be regarded as life's great luxury, a life's *agrément* that demands much time and usually means expenditure rather than income, you will probably understand that my philosophy has dwindled, from observing this expensive gender, as from observing all other luxuries that life has to offer, into almost total indifference, bordering on contempt . . . I shall send this to you when an opportunity presents itself, as I don't believe that this particular letter is worth the postage. Farewell. And I hope to see you again under more fortunate circumstances.'

She lays the table, choosing the rustic plates with the floral motifs. She has lit the candles, one red, one green, in flickering tribute to heart and hope. She brings in the duck, simmering with desire to be consumed, garnished with fried potatoes and carrots and she has already drawn the corks to allow the wine to breathe. The fire; the fragrance of her perfume; and the final line from *A une madone, ex-voto dans le goût espagnol* which Jeanne Balaresque is especially fond of, because from the seven deadly sins Baudelaire has fashioned seven sharp knives, which, to add the final touch to the role of Maria and to blend love with barbarism, he plants in her bleeding heart, in her ebbing heart: *Dans ton Coeur sanglotant, dans ton Coeur ruisselant!* . . . she hums, again and again, while drawing the chairs up to the roughly hewn table, and she runs her fingers through her hair and invites him to take a seat. A while later she says in a low voice that with all that kinkiness in her hair and that lighter colour on the soles of her feet, lighter than the rest of her, which is always darkish, even when there is snow on the ground, she must surely, like Baudelaire's mistress, the Creole actress Jeanne Duval, have negro blood in her veins. Her mother had spoken to her about it on one occasion, just that once and never again, hinting that her father was a dark-skinned man from the southern region of Algiers, and when Jeanne Balaresque loses her temper she does so in a manner that is not like that of the other girls in the milliner's in Rue Mont Thabor. She laughs, sits down at the table and draws Møller's attention to the fact that it is the gentleman's duty to do the carving. When angry she says it is as though drums are beating in her head, and she experiences an irresistible urge to run barefoot through the African savannah.

'That helps, you know,' she whispers, looking at him. 'If you only knew how many times you've forced me to get up and run. . .'

Words that have long ago ceased to have a meaning; words that stick like boils in his throat every time he is about to answer Jeanne Balaresque. Words as slag, words as gravel, as broken glass in the throat: conversation has long since ceased to be Møller's forte, and he grows tired at the mere thought of all the pages in *Homeless* which he has infused with life. He feels like quoting several lines from *Les Fleurs du mal* for Jeanne Balaresque, the way she loves him to do it, if she hasn't taken the book herself and flung herself onto the bed to read and read. She thrills at every line, as though Baudelaire had personally plucked the entire bouquet for her, and even the most evil flower is clasped to her bosom as though it is the colour of innocence and its scent lacks all trace of anaesthetic poison. Words that have a meaning; words that are sin and putrefaction; words that are purple, gold, temple dances, the male sex deeply thrust into the female, knives in the chest, blood and the radiance of the resurrection, God and Satan in the one and same person; words that sound, sing, threaten, lure, strangle, caress, dance, words that throb in the blood and run like fever and fire through the savannahs of the soul.

'*La poésie de Baudelaire, c'est la poésie de Sainte-Beuve plus la poésie,*' as Møller heard it described in the Café de la Regence as far back as 1855, when eighteen of the poems were published in *La Revue des deux mondes*. In the Café de la Regence *Les Fleurs du mal* was the subject of conversation at every table, following the release of a set of proofs and the guilty verdict of an offence against public decency, and at each table they selected a favourite poem from among the six removed from the collection at the insistence of the public prosecutor. Some years before Baudelaire himself might just have turned up, the first thing one saw of him were the enormous bronze buttons that fastened his greyish overcoat, cut by the tailor to resemble a sack, with blue socks jutting out from the hunting boots with the glossy military shine, the ungloved hands with the carefully manicured nails and the expensive lace shirts with the distinguished folding collars that redirected all attention to the wearer's face; at the same time the face of a devil and the face of a hermit monk, Møller remembers, so smoothly shaven that not a single whisker remained visible, with the small, vivacious, distrustful eyes, the sensuous nose, the narrow, virtually hidden upper lip, the square jaw and the short-clipped hair, as though he wanted to look like a convict just released on parole. And the voice: high, penetrating:

'*Messieurs, j'ai soif.*'

And when the waiter suggested either a bottle of Burgundy or a bottle of Bordeaux:

'*Si vous me le permettez, je boirai de l'un et de l'autre.*'

And when he suddenly came too close to a carafe of water:

'*Messieurs, veuillez faire enlever cette carafe; la vue de l'eau m'est désagréable.*'

To be Baudelaire; to dare acknowledge oneself as a sinner; to be capable of carrying the burden of original sin on one's shoulders, even though it weighs as much as a cartload of shellfish, handed down as it is from generation to generation in an unbroken chain; to carry it without complaining; to know that woman is nature, '*c'est-à-dire abominable*', and possibly most despicable of all when as the most natural thing in the world she places, as Jeanne Balaresque from Rue Mont Thabor does, all the Flowers of Evil in a glorious array of radiant innocence. To know, in every fibre of one's body, back to one's earliest memory, that every idea concerning the naturally good human being is an insane idea from the eighteenth century, exacerbated by all the insignificant Hugos and Georges Sands and Meïr Aron Goldschmidts of the age; to know it and to enjoy knowing it: '*La nature ne peut conseiller que le crime*'. Then to be relieved, to be lost in the anonymity of Paris and the bottle, in nooks and crannies where the gaslight does not penetrate, in the worst gutters from the cowl-clad Middle Ages, up in the coldest attic rooms, in back yards at the back of other back yards where the rats with tails entwined to form ribbons dance their bewitched toe-dance under the foul glare of the moon, to get lost at the end tables in kitchens for the poor where the wretched skin-clad skeletons crawl between the legs and stretch out their disgusting hands to grab a little spittle from the palates of those a little less hungry, to be lost down in the sewers where the rats are white through lack of sun, hideous sun, appalling sun, sun beyond the sun beyond the sun. To be lost, lost, best of all down in the catacombs among the throngs of the dead from the past, throngs of victims of original sin, *ha ha*, sin visited upon them by Lord Satan because you are all evil, evil — evil as I myself who am what I am. And down there, among the piles of skulls and bones: to see it reflected in the eyes: '*Le spectacle ennuyeux de l'immortel péché*, and then fortified by power flowing down from primeval times, from the time when Old Pan ruled, wielding his even more pernicious evil, to break out towards the light and to shatter the yoke of sin by sinning even more, by sinning, sinning — and never, never repenting,

in an ecstasy of new and different colours, with words that say
the opposite of all other words, ugly, misshapen, even
appalling words that become more breathlessly beautiful the
worse they are: horrifying sights that become divine in their
horror. To sin one's way to salvation and immortality; to
reject Christianity and its mother Judaism, yoke upon yoke,
with words that at the same time caress and strangle, tripping
up old ladies, stabbing youth in the back, flaying the
rich, heaping derision on the poor, bringing an end to all
weeping, gloating over sympathy, emitting jaw-breaking
yawns of love; words that throb in entirely new constellations,
with violent sentence breaks, unfolding with the unseen,
incessant but sweet, sweet pain of evil. To be lost, lost, as on
that night in the streets of Copenhagen when he, Pennyless
Peter, *Pauvre Louis*, the young ironist Schiøtt, Johannes the
Seducer, dreamed of a new literature that brought the town's
street signs tumbling down on the heads of the readers, rooted
up cobblestones and sent them hurtling upwards from their
gravel bedding to hit inquisitive eyes, turned night into
day and day into night and made the rats squeak as never
before and made Oehlenschläger's snores beneath gold-
embroidered sheets sound like the raging hammer of Thor
pitted against the Salt of the World. And he walks and walks,
now with feet so cold that he feels as though fire is coursing
through him, Lavendelstraede, Knabrostraede, Nytorv,
Gammel Torv, Vimmelskaftet, and three steps — always
three steps — ahead of him walks Janus, who turns round
and. . .

'Catch me,' Janus says with his wolfish smile. 'Catch me for
your novel, *Hramor!*'

'Wait a moment, wait, wait. . .' Møller replies, increasing
his pace on the path that leads him and Janus from all the
literature that has been long dead and on to the magical
poetry and prose of the new age where the seven deadly sins
become seven knives thrust into the heart of the loved one.

'*Mais qu'est-ce-que tu murmures?*' Jeanne Balaresque asks.

Møller recovers.

'Something in Danish. . .' he replies and steers the

conversation back to Jeanne Duval whom Jeanne Balaresque is sure she has seen dance several times at the Mabille and the Prado, and she smiles again and insists that he quote from Baudelaire . . . and write new poems in the same genre for her. He must make them as ugly as he can, *as long as they are pretty!* Then she falls silent when she sees that his thoughts are still scattered to the four winds. She begins to clear the table while he pushes his plate aside and — in a state of confusion and for the umpteenth time — has a tentative go at a draft for an article for *Dagbladet* on Charles-Pierre Baudelaire. But he knows that it's no good. 'Obscene', 'blasphemous', 'perverse'; 'insane and epoch-making'; 'revolting and inaccessible'; 'Black Mass' — no, he fails to find the word or the words for *Les Fleurs du mal* around which he can weld his article together. However much trouble he takes in translating some of the verses so as to give Danish readers a sample of the 'evil', they will never get into print, not with the galloping prudery that has seized Copenhagen. Things that could have been stated openly in the thirties and forties — Møller even remembers having seen Baudelaire's *On wine and Hashish* from 1851 reviewed, possibly in *Kjøbenhavnsposten* — are now, at the end of the fifties, banned, as all signs point to the likelihood of a new war with Germany, and the Copenhagen intellegentsia anaesthetize themselves with the latest national romantic reverberations which will never be able to rhyme with a true *poésie du pécheur et du péché.*

Instead, he scribbles an incoherent draft for a travel letter from Normandy, so that when he returns to Copenhagen from Paris there will be some money to be picked up, but it is sheer gibberish.

Møller drains the dregs of the bottle, tears every sheet of paper within reach into ribbons, flings himself onto his bed and falls into a deep sleep.

'Do you write, Otto Sommer?' the grandmother asks from her armchair. She looks like a peeled egg while everything around her is neatly stacked and measured off, from the year-old biscuits in tiny bowls on her sewing table to the mussel shells on the scrubbed floor. He sits at the back of the class, and all the pupils have to write a poem. He keeps on chewing his small pencil stumps and can't decide whether to choose the *terza rima* or the *ottava rima* or the difficult Gregorian stanza.

> *Sharp is the pencil*
> *The pencil sharp*
> *Sharp. . .*

. . . is all he manages to get down and, as punishment, he has to sit in detention for several hours after the others have run off. The words become smaller and smaller on the sheet, and soon he can't read a single letter he has written because the piece of string holding his spectacles round his ears is about to snap. His head swells like a balloon and soon turns into Schiøtt's who is speaking incessantly to Otto Krøyer who, with pockets full of gold coins and with the Mosaic Law worn like a schoolbag over his shoulders, returns from the beach dragging two sacks full of shellfish which he puts on his, Otto Sommer's, frail young body where the shellfish cling like leeches and drink all his blood.

'By the way, what distinction do you make between a writer, a great writer and a truly great writer?' Schiøtt shouts so loud that his ballooning head is about to explode. The shellfish have now worked their way all the way up to his throat where they are beginning to gnaw into his windpipe, but he doggedly continues: 'One is a few octaves greater than the other; during the happy moments when the muse decides to drop in, she plays on the instrument, and when she has departed, the writer is as dejected or as vapid as a recently emptied wine bottle.'

He struggles to get rid of the shellfish, but still more come, crawling, clinging, gnawing. Every single one of them is a prohibition, brought to Europe by another people, another race, to oppress him and all the other Normans and Celts and Scythians and Danes and Angles and Saxons, forcing them down into eternal passivity and misfortune, down to regions where only the bottle can bring a little solace. Dragged down by shellfish, he will forever be doomed to move forward via the centripetal force, unable to find the magic formula which will make all the shellfish fall off his body and turn into mother-of-pearl dust at his feet.

For a brief moment Otto Krøyer looks at him with horror in his eyes because he senses that a writer like Otto Sommer, whose pen is capable of writing the most beautiful, the most gruesome poems, will soon find the magic words·that will send him and all his shellfish and his gold coins extorted as interest and his clay tablets inscribed with the Law back where they came from. And Otto Sommer leaps out of bed while all the pencils grow like killer knives between his fingers. He is sure to hear someone whisper the formula from some remote place, and there is blinding sunshine when he runs away over the meadow, now finally wearing his own head and not Schiøtt's. One by one the shellfish fall off his skin, every fibre of his body breathes with a totally new life, and in the distance he catches a glimpse of the woman from the steamer on the Elbe. But then she's gone again. He finds a path that leads to the town and on his way in he stops. A fisherman is sitting in front of his hut, and Møller chooses a particularly big lobster from his catch, big as original sin itself, which he is about to take and pay for and crush into tiny pieces when, from just behind him, he hears the woman's voice:

'*C'est pour moi!*' And she lets a gold coin drop into the fisherman's gnarled hand, snatches the lobster and walks over to a group of intrepid winter bathers, togged out in modern bathing apparel, styled as sailor suits.

He runs after her, grabs her shoulders, swings her round and peers with growing horror into her ugly face, addled with greed as though she is a washer woman who has undeservedly reaped honours and power as a marquise.

'Where did you get that voice?' he shouts, 'It's not yours! It's *stolen!*'

She wrenches herself loose and hurries over to the other bathers who are now indignantly threatening him.

Møller turns round and walks back to the fisherman's hut. He notices that his boots are unlaced and that his trousers are not properly buttoned. His legs are tired, as though he has had no sleep at all. For the first time he entertains fears about Jeanne Balaresque. If she has left the cottage in the meantime it may be the best thing for her. For him.

P.L. Møller writes at his regular table in the Café de la Régence to *Dagbladet* while at the same time in his little notebook he makes an entry under the letter G for a new volume of the Didot brothers' *Nouvelle Biographie générale*, due to be published in 1858. Now working on Grundtvig, the most important name, he has got it into something like Cartesian shape, so that the great blusterer can only be satisfied if he understands as much as a single word of French. 'Death in Paris has wrought such destruction in its war against celebrities that it sometimes even seems that its labours would be reduced if it chose to do its grim reaping in alphabetical order.' Within the past year, Møller calculates, it has thus snatched to its cold bosom Adam Béranger, the composer, and Auguste Comte, the philosopher. From M (Alfred de Musset) it skipped a few letters and grabbed Eugène Sue. When it apparently became aware of its lexicographical inconsistency, it returned to L and M and picked up Lherminier (a talented philosopher and critic) and Mordret, a promising young writer. Then it got as far as the 'P' volume and ran off with Eugène Pradel, the poet, who managed to improvise several hundred tragedies in addition to his output of thousands of short poems and epigrams and who on his journeys to the provinces and Belgium is supposed to have improvised up to thirty-five thousand francs a year. Following 'P' the scythe moved on with merciless logic to Quatremère, the orientalist.

So as to return to life and to reality, Møller swoops upon the letter C and informs his readers that Carteron the chemist has discovered a substance that will soon make outbreaks of fire a sheer impossibility: all sorts of material can, at very low cost, be ironed with this substance, and all over Paris allegedly successful experiments are being conducted with domestic curtains, theatre curtains, shop and office curtains, tent canvas and wooden huts. Møller can also report that in the south of France, under the auspices of church dignitaries, a quasi religious ladies' association has been formed with the aim of imposing a ban on crinolines.

If Møller is visited by Danes or Norwegians who, for one reason or another, deserve inclusion in the Didot brothers' biography, he has no hesitation in demanding twenty-five rigsdaler — or an equivalent sum in French francs — for his trouble. Usually he gets his reward, and again he can afford to eat. He also considers sending transcripts of the entries to Denmark and Norway, hoping to receive payment by mail, but when he reaches Grundtvig's name he abandons the thought, perhaps because he is reluctant to have the old eagle make a big issue out of the fact that one can never rely on anything to do with France which translates as 'that runaway Pierre-Louis Moeller'. And as though the powers that be want to thank him for his astute move, the G leaps back one notch from Grundtvig to Goldschmidt whose biography Møller has not yet tackled. From the moment he sees, from his window, a dark figure in a fur coat, on the far side of Rue de Bellechasse, and especially from the moment the knock sounds on his door from a restrained knuckle shielded by soft leather, he knows that it must be Meïr Aron who after an absence of many years has returned to Paris, possibly in the hope of achieving his earlier London success at Hachette's or Lévy's with *A Jew*. Or maybe with *Homeless*? Or maybe with his collected works. . .

'Well, well, well — so you've finally come all the way down to Paris solely to pay me my hard-earned remuneration, Sir Gulbenkian, or whatever you call yourself when hobnobbing with the barons of English industry,' is Møller's greeting as he flings the door open.

'I don't owe you a single sou,' Goldschmidt replies. As far as Møller can make out, he's still the same Goldschmidt. 'After all, old chap, you've neither ploughed nor sown for me.'

'No, I must admit I have not harnessed your horses, but I've driven them and kept them in check.' Møller sees how Goldschmidt politely avoids staring at his nearly bald temples, and he continues, still standing in the doorway. 'If I have provided *Homeless* with all too many of my brilliant lines which, considered in a purely pecuniary context, can only have benefitted you, since, as far as I know, your major opus is read by all classes but the lowest. In the past I nevertheless removed many of your lines, tortured them and massacred them. Don't you place any value on my lesson to you, that wise maxim: "What has been deleted cannot be ridiculed"?'

'Confound it all, Møller!' Goldschmidt takes him warmly by the arm. 'There was a time . . . I mean, after all . . . can't we just. . .'

Møller instantly withdraws his arm:

'Heiberg once wrote a treatise on inappropriate touching on stage. Your touching me now is inappropriate or superfluous. . . But tell me, do you know *hadchi*, spelled as pronounced?'

'You're referring to Hadchi Baba's fairytales?' Goldschmidt looks down at the floor when Møller still fails to invite him in to the room, to the piles of manuscripts and the bookshelves he has himself hammered together and which look as though they are about to collapse under the weight of the randomly stacked volumes.

'Baba? Bah! I mean the culinary delight which is probably the most brilliant, or the *only* brilliant delicacy that the ancient Israelites passed on to humanity . . . the delicacy called *gelée hadchi*. . .'

'But that's a sort of opium!'

'Yes, just as a diamond is a sort of stone. Opium is a brute who seizes you by the throat, *hadchi* is an oriental waiter who casts a veil over the world and over the happy guest. . .'

'And you take *hadchi*?'

'In moderation, of course, as in all things. When the opium rush becomes unpleasant, one must indulge in a brief retreat to the beautiful Parisian reality.'

'Oh, Schiøtt!'

'Oh, Krøyer! Would you, perhaps, care to inspect what I have bought for a song down by the Seine? A Diderot and Sainte-Beuve's *Causeries du lundi*.'

Møller changes his mind, grabs his coat and dashes down the stairs, followed by Goldschmidt: 'Let's go to the Prado!'

While they get seats and watch the dancing couples, Møller produces a blank sheet of paper from his pocket. His hunger is so great that his knees are shaking. He feels another attack of nausea coming on. He smiles, opening his hand.

'You, Sir Aron can return in style to Copenhagen and pocket a tidy sum for adding another chapter to our joint opus, whereas I, and then only if I'm lucky, can earn the price of a few meals by filling this virgin-white paper with *my* impression of *you*. Might I be granted the journalistic privilege of access to some information concerning the subject of a forthcoming article? Dates, locations — that sort of thing. And which aunt you are currently staying with to have your oatmeal soup and matzos served on a white lace tablecloth. That sort of trivial detail.'

'What are you getting at?'

'You happen to be in the land of Diderot's birth, the home of the encyclopaedia, or to be more precise the place where mere names are turned into celebrities by giving them a column or two in the huge, indestructible biographical encyclopaediae.'

Are you referring to *Nouvelle Biographie générale?*'

'Precisely, Golle. I have reached the interesting letter G.'

'And you think that. . .'

'*Shema israel!* I think nothing! To start with, I haven't yet made up my own mind as to whether or not you deserve to be placed immediately preceding the good Grundtvig, who, thanks to my few well chosen words, is now the subject of conversation in this great metropolis. And then there is the little matter of the editor's fear that the inclusion of two Goldschmidts, both authors, and one immediately following the other, might impose an undue strain on the reader's gullibility.'

'Who's the second?'

'You mean the first! None other than your English namesake and Hebraic cousin, Oliver Goldsmith. His brilliance, in spite of his origins, entitles him to a rather lengthy entry. Two foreign writers with the same name, in the ignored opinion of the editor, might easily cause some confusion, misleading those trying to locate Goldsmith, and resulting in his mail being addressed to you, my dear Meyer. Do you follow me?'

Goldschmidt pretends not to have heard a thing.

'Kierkegaard — will you be writing about him too?'

'I may get round to him some time in 1884, Goldschmidt, and with greater sympathy now that I have reached the stage where I can, so to speak, see him as a whole person.'

'Do you mean as a cadaver?'

'If you choose to put it that way.' Møller's stomach is now beginning to ache with the pangs of hunger. He has already drunk over half the bottle of wine placed on their table while the *lorettes*, to Goldschmidt's acute distaste, swarm about the fur coat draped over a chair by the foreign tourist come to town. Møller raises his glass and proposes a toast:

'Twenty-five rigsdaler, or a corresponding amount in francs. Is that an exorbitant amount to demand for my contribution to your immortality?'

'You won't get a sou, I've told you.'

'Not even when I now inform you that this is perhaps the last decade, or shall we extend it to the last half century, when people like you will be included in biographies of civilization? Oh, Otto Krøyer, thrifty friend, don't be all that sure! Times change! Innovations are waiting in the wings! A great genius addressed himself, without being able to claim any real success, to the philosophical question: When the Law forbids me, on pain of severe punishment, to poison a grocer like . . . shall we say you, Krøyer . . . how can it be that the grocer who attempts to poison me risks only the mildest punishment, a mere fine, or at the most a few months in prison? Perhaps because your Law has one set of rules for you and another for us Danes, Scythians, Celts. . .? When the Law with such rigidity and strictness forbids everyone to administer poison to the bodies of other persons, how can it be then that virtually all you so-called Mosaic friends of freedom and of the advancement of humanity with such enthusiasm and zeal demand the right for all sorts of grocers, without let or hindrance or risk of incurring any charges, to poison the souls of their fellow human beings? Does it not, Krøyer, state in the scriptures, which your Christian disciples edited over eighteen hundred years ago, that one shall not fear him who only slays the body as much as one shall fear him who seeks to kill the soul. . .? Verily, I say unto you, Krøyer, the night of the Lord shall come like a thief in the day . . . no, nonsense. The thief of the Lord shall come like a day in the night . . . no, the thief of the day shall come like a lord of the night . . . twenty-five rigsdaler, is that asking too much . . . *Jew*?'

Goldschmidt, upset, grabs his fur coat:

'Be on your guard against tragedy, Schiøtt!'

'What do you mean?'

'What you yourself taught me, *Hramor*, fool: one must have happiness in one's life; that is something which cannot be measured and cannot be weighed because justice has nothing to do with it. . .'

Goldschmidt has left. Like that time in Berlin.

Møller feels he is becoming bigger and bigger as he walks through the streets. He knows that Goldschmidt did not succeed in his attempt to snatch the magic ciphers from his palate, the ciphers that have enabled him to grow as tall as the rooftops in a few minutes. He is constantly forced to proceed with caution, as if he as much as brushes against one of the lampposts, it will snap like a twig, and if he should happen to lash out with his boot at the kerb or some other obstruction, it would crumble to dust. If he thumped the wall with his clenched fist, the fist would go all the way through, leaving a gaping hole, and he has to hold himself in check as he passes the trees for he has an urge to tear them up by their roots and send them flying over the rooftops of Paris.

The beggars flee from his path. They know that they will receive nothing from him, and if they dare to ask, he will attack them, viciously and without mercy, just as Baudelaire advised his closest friends to do and which he may soon include in a new compilation of breathless hymns in praise of evil. Oh, these imploring eyes, these unforgettable, indelible stares, which would have brought thrones tumbling down if the spirit had only been there — and it would have been if only enough people had wanted it. Only he who can actually *demonstrate* it, is truly his neighbour's equal. Only he who can actually conquer freedom, is truly entitled to it by piling up sin upon sin, by allying himself with all the slumbering powers from the age of Old Pan! Oh, to hurl himself at the beggars, to attack them with such ferocity that their eyes bulge; to knock out their teeth, to pull the hair out of their scalps, to crush their fingers, to break their arms, to throttle them — until they begin to kick back — oh! what bliss for a philosopher to see his theory confirmed — to see life pulsing in that old pile of bones and rags and corpses, to see them rise with a power that outworn organisms can never muster; to look straight into their hateful eyes when they finally pluck up the courage to defend themselves with tooth and claw: *'Gentlemen, you are my equals!* Let us together shape the new age, an age without mercy! Let us never again experience the pain of begging for alms!'

To walk across the Seine bridge realizing that it is only a short part of the road, via a brief stay in Rue de Bellechasse, towards the new age; to walk up the steps and into the hotel and to be constantly on guard so as not to trample the steps into dust — to know that the steps are a foretaste of that decisive step up, towards immortality. The road will soon lead him, and anyone else who wants to march onwards, to Turkey where the wolf-people live and still worship the same wolf-god that the Wends worshipped before the Christians thrust the cross into their breasts and the women in Aalborg chased the woman with the yellowish-green eyes to the city gates. From there the road leads to the Aryans' Persia where the magic ciphers for putting up into the palate are tossed about in the bazaars. Many will fall by the wayside on the long trek, especially on the last stage where the road passes through India on the way to the foot of the Himalayas and from there

on to the nine thousand nine hundred and ninety-nine steps
leading up between the mountains, up to the city of spirits
where immortality beckons in the scintillating crystal palace
for all who have persevered, who, suffering excruciating pain,
tore the gnawing shellfish from their bodies, who burnt mercy
out of their bodies with glowing tongs and plucked all the
flowers of evil in a bouquet ablaze with the colours of horror,
of blood and ruthlessness.

Jeanne Balaresque arrives in his hotel room too late to
snatch the ether bottle from him. She has come with a letter in
which she says that things have now gone far enough, that
although their love had died even before that Danish actress
turned up, she had until now at least regarded their friendship
as valuable, but obviously that too is of little significance to
him — '*Hypocrite lecteur — mon semblable, — mon frère!*' She
wishes him all the best; she hopes that the Danish papers will
print many more of his articles, including the ones about
Baudelaire and Jeanne Duval. She will always remember
their few happy moments together, when he went with her to
mass in the church of Saint-Roch, when they sailed on the
Seine, and all the times he gave her good books to read while
he was living in Rue de Rohan. Oh yes, she will remember all
the good things, but to put it plainly, as far as she's concerned,
he can pack his bits and pieces and travel home to Louise
Razmuhsayn tomorrow, if that suits him, because he couldn't
care less if she, *Djinn d'autrefois* ends up as an old maid, or
marries the cheese-monger from Rue de la Montagne
Sainte-Geneviève or commits suicide like so many others like
her. And she does not omit a few other points — stressing each
'that' as she lambasts him the way she has so frequently heard
him doing while working on an article — *that* she will
no longer disturb his work with what he refers to as her
caprices, that she has again annoyed her *patronesse*, simply
because she spent all that time trying to get him on his feet
again in Normandy, *that* he has probably now finally
extracted his revenge for whatever it was all about back in
those days when their relationship flourished and *that* she has
only two and a half francs left to live on. She has dated the

letter *minuit moins le quart*, and on a separate sheet she has written a quotation from *Les Fleurs du mal*:

> *Car ce que ta bouche cruelle*
> *Eparpille en l'air*
> *Monstre assassin, c'est ma cervelle*
> *Mon sang et ma chair!*

She lays the letter and the poem against his chest. Møller is spreadeagled on the floor, with the ether bottle in his hand. On a scrap of paper which she has flung away in terror he has drawn the secret password sign which he has so often told her about, although always just for fun, she thought: the password sign to the Himalayas and immortality: the Christian cross and the Star of David dangling from Old Pan's oak gallows.

sixteen

Everywhere they are knocking things down, everywhere they are building. Clouds of brick dust hover over the streets, houses come crashing to the ground, leaving gaping holes, and when the dust settles it is possible to see what Paris was like in the distant past. The number of amateur archaeologists grows daily, and huge rewards are offered for the best Roman and Viking artefacts. Thousands of families are driven from their homes, with landlords waving eviction notices issued by the highest authorities. Exhausted fathers push carts carrying the family's possessions, all their bits of furniture and pots and pans, vases, curtains, bric-à-brac, cots, books and clothes, in the hope of finding a new place to live, even though the rent will be twice as high, if not more. At the same time all the richer quarters are celebrating, drinking toasts to the new Paris, the imperial city which will soon outshine all other capitals. 1858: Boulevard de Sebastopol is inaugurated; 1861: Boulevard de Malesherbes is finished, soon to be followed by Boulevard du Prince-Eugène. Towering new pavilions of iron and glass loom above Les Halles. One man decides everything; Haussmann, the architect — shrewd, with the energy of a regiment on the attack and the appearance of a Scottish drum-major, great in his faults, great in his visions, and with direct access to the emperor.

On his lonely channel island Victor Hugo is indignant
about the dissolute goings on at court which stand in sharp
contrast to the virtuous, tea-drinking English court of Queen
Victoria. But more and more Englishmen make their way
across the Channel to Paris on 'business trips' or to attend to
'military matters', hoping to find an amorous *lorette*. The
lorettes now live in the new quarters being built just off
Haussmann's boulevards, and they bring ruin on the heads of
many gullible sons of wealthy families, young men known to
Paris as 'Arthurs'. When Arthur has concluded his afternoon
visit to his 'steady' Ernestine, Blosine or Jeanne, the creditors
visit the girls, sometimes even tearing the cashmere shawls off
their shoulders in the middle of the street. The *lorettes* get
younger every year, and the rustle of their silk dresses with
volants tantalizes their admirers in the cafés. The older girls,
those who had their hour of glory ten years ago, have become
marchandes de toilette, run illicit gaming houses, procure young
girls for the merchants, the stockbrokers and the Englishmen,
or commit suicide, like one of the prettiest whom they fished
out of the Seine and whose body was tattooed with the names
of her lovers and the dates of the commencement and
termination of each affair.

The court decrees a new fashion every month. There has
never been such a brisk market in forged securities. 'Show me
the man of any standing without his own carriage! A unique
society in which everyone seems bent on plunging to his ruin,'
is the lament of the Goncourt brothers: '*Jamais le paraître n'a été
si impérieux, si despotique et si démoralisateur. . .*'

Wherever one goes, the music of Offenbach is heard.

The Café de la Régence, the established rendezvous for
Italians, Poles, Russians, Hungarians, Germans and Scandinavians, is visited by the Angel of Death. The owner's wife
has died of consumption, shortly afterwards the big waiter
died, a man who looked the picture of health and who served
coffee to Møller and the others as though he were performing
an act of grace. And finally the owner has died at an early age.

But the café continues to exist — in fact, apart from the hour it took to get the funeral over and done with, it never closed, 'as is the customary practice in sentimental, unpractical countries like Germany and Denmark,' Møller notes. He is properly dressed for the first time in many months, wearing a new pair of glasses that present reality with a new sharpness, with new boots, and smoothly shaven and smelling of Eau de Cologne and with most of his bags at the hotel packed and ready to be sent off. Perhaps the rumour circulating in Copenhagen is really true — that they want to take him on as Lecturer in aesthetics at the University. Hauch's wish. And Sibbern too is interested. Heiberg died a peaceful death. And if he is not to travel northwards, his alternative destination — and possibly even better chosen, possibly the very solution — will be westward. No, not Carstensen's savage United States, but to the free communes which, it is said, are being created in Brazil where emperor Dom Pedro, an admirer of Voltaire, is interested in all sorts of experimentation with new, free, open societies; societies of the future in which all are equal, where money has been abolished and where everyone gives according to his ability and receives according to his needs — a society on the fringe of the jungle and within reach of the beach that stretches into eternity. Animals. Sunshine. The rivers. The fish. And the red, miraculously healing earth which they are all talking about in the café. Three Poles, two Russians and a Basque who sailed across the ocean have written home about Brazil, even going so far as to include a little sample of the earth which mixed with water in a crystal glass and held up to the light reflects the future for anyone who cares to look into it.

And Møller studies his hands at length: they can deal with manual labour. And he feels his thighs: firm flesh, supple muscles. And he looks at himself in the mirror on the opposite wall: the sun will banish those black rims under his eyes. The tropical sun will free him from the chains that bind him to his desk, from the supporting cushion at his back, from the pain in the small of his back, from the candlelight, the scraps of writing on scraps of paper, the bits of wrapping paper. To grow, born again, away from literature, to get his eyes back and finally to be able to use and apply all he has read, all he has learned, as the first person after a long examination in front of the gods' green table. The coral reefs. A canoe up a river. A circular fishing net joyously flung out over the dancing waves. They say that in certain parts of Brazil one can live up to the age of eighty or ninety by following that sort of life.

And he taps his feet and massages his legs: he will be able to stand the daylong treks.

But until then: the Paris machine grinds on relentlessly, just as the earth and the planets, despite the destruction each moment of millions of lives. It is all just like that famous distinguished hotel in Fauborg Saint-Honoré where the master of the house died on the morning of the very day on which a splendid evening ball was to be held. The distraught widow felt that it would be far too much trouble to cancel all the invitations, thus wasting all the money spent on the preparations. And so she had her husband's body placed in the attic, told her guests that he was slightly indisposed, and then they all ate, drank and made merry until the crack of dawn — including two police spies whose job is regarded by all, with the exception of Copenhagen world reformers who happen to be passing through, as perfectly decent: *il n'y a pas de sot métier, il n'y a que des sottes gens*, as it is said man to man.

In the Café de la Régence they are on the point of believing that Møller must be a police spy, now that he is so elegant and rejuvenated. Wearing a toupée, a handsome young man on a study tour!

To get it all over and done with as quickly as possible, before the final disintegration. The preface to *La comédie humaine* in Danish, an edition he has dreamt of publishing for years. Articles on the French troubador poets; on the critics, Chasles, Planche, Champfleury and Taine; the essay on race, climate and literature; tidying up and editing of the Breton, Norman and other folk tales he has collected; French translations of Blicher and Andersen; entries for the French biography on Danish and Norwegian writers, and, for the *Nordisk Conversationsleksikon*, notes on French writers, from Balzac to Eugène Sue, with Dumas especially, whom he loves most of all: 'untiring, entertaining, dramatic, spiritual and lively . . . he is the most marvellous phenomenon that has ever existed'.

And a pile of new articles for *Le Siècle*, *L'Illustration* and *Le Constitutionnel* on the eternal Schleswig-Holstein problem, in which he launches yet another bitter attack on Germany, even if he feels more like attacking Denmark and the increasingly hair-raising futility of the National-Liberals: deaf and blind, inflated with academic arrogance, stuffed with Christmas goose, with jaws ambitiously thrust forward, they stride, tottering and rocking around in Copenhagen, which they have persuaded one another is the capital of a Valdemaresque major power. *'Partition . . . along . . . the language boundaries. . .'* the words ring in Møller's ears, but whatever he writes it elicits no response in France, nor in Denmark where the foreign office continues to refuse to send him the sum he needs if he is to entertain any serious hope of making any impact in the French newspapers which are *limited liability companies* and thus exist on every form of bribery.

And *The Danish Tone*; all his literary portraits for the German newspapers and those he has had printed or has planned to have printed in French. One thing is still missing. The heart of the book. The major essay on Oehlenschläger. And one October evening in 1861, after Bissen's bronze statue of the poet king has been unveiled at Skt. Anne Plads in Copenhagen, Møller walks over to the dark, narrow Rue des Bons Enfants where Oehlenschläger wrote *Palnstoke* in the now crumbling Hôtel de Hollande. In the course of three days and three nights he writes *Adam Oehlenschläger — in memoriam.* He is happy. Clean. Fresh sheets, entirely new wallpaper, an entirely different carpet on the floor, no sheets of paper flying about the room, no stacks of books threatening to engulf him; clear desk. The best thing, he believes, he has ever written. It all comes easily to him. He needs no aids. He sees Baggesen go

down on his knee to Oehlenschläger and beg for forgiveness.
He hears Oehlenschläger cry.

Møller cries.

(To Matilda Leiner) 'What do you wish me to tell you about?
That I'm still sitting in my Parisian cage where I can neither
live nor die in any decency, neither stay nor cut myself free. . .'
Months later: 'The hunt for a measly hundred sous makes a
man wild and unpleasant. . .' And still later: *Dearest Tilda*, I
am wrestling with my departure. . .' 1863: 'My Parisian
incarceration will be prolonged until July, as I have allowed
myself to be engaged as Danish tutor to the minister's bride, a
daughter of the Saxon minister, Baron v. S. The wedding is to
be held at the end of June. In the meantime I pack a few things
every day.'

It might very well be on the path linking Nørreport and
Østerport. It's about half past six in the evening. The sun has
lost its strength, but still manages to send a broad shaft of soft
light over the landscape. The lake is placid, smooth as a
mirror. The air is less charged. The buildings are mirrored in
the water, which is as dark as metal in the middle of the lake.
The path and the buildings on the other side are bathed in the
fading rays of sunshine. The sky is pure, with only a single airy
cloud gliding imperceptibly, a cloud that is best viewed as it
floats and then passes out of sight on the surface of the barely
ruffled waters. Not a leaf stirs.

It is she. It is her smile. And she smiles again.

She is not conscious of thinking, but the steady trickle of
random thoughts stirs a picture of longing in her soul, a
picture of longing shaped by the foreboding that is as
inexplicable as the long sighs of a young girl. She is at her most
beautiful age. She stays at a remote distance and absorbs the
picture. She moves slowly, nothing disturbs her peace, nor the
calm of her surroundings. By the lakeside a boy sits with a
fishing rod. She stands still, surveys the surface of the lake and

the trickling stream. She unties the scarf knotted round her neck beneath the shawl; a gentle breeze from the lake caresses a bosom, white as snow, yet warm and full. Then she walks on a few paces until she reaches Quai aux Fleurs, where beside the Palais de Justice there is a daily market selling all sorts of flowers. And as he follows her, he feels himself surrounded by a heavenly, revitalizing smell, not just the smell of the thousands of flowers but of the remembrance of a former existence, from his childhood when he ran across the field and picked forget-me-nots and made wreaths of cornflowers and every day paid a visit to the hedge to greet the arrival of summer in the first bloom of the first rose.

A human figure, or something resembling a human figure, is sitting on a pedestal. A large crowd has gathered, and she is there too. He sees her from the side, and observes that her finely turned nose seems to be pulled into her forehead, making it seem shorter, and more spirited. Now and then rapid pistol shots can be heard, followed by silence. He watches a cripple who demonstrates his various skills. He was born with one arm, one leg. With the aid of a crutch and his wife who fires the pistol, he manages to get along at a fair pace. Fortunately the arm is on the opposite side of the leg so that there is a certain symmetry about his misery. When the first unpleasant impression has been absorbed, Møller examines the cripple more closely, and is surprised at the strikingly intelligent and cheerful expression on his face. Everything is dear to him. He has a wife who brings him lunch, who often stays with him and picks him up every day around five or six o'clock.

She walks on, and he follows her while the pistol shots reverberate behind him. She walks in the direction of, could it be, Østerport in Copenhagen? He again wants to see her at a closer distance without himself being observed. At the corner is a house from which this should be possible. He hurries past her with rapid steps and gets a long way ahead of her, knocks on the door of the house, greets everybody inside, including the tea-drinking guests, and walks over to command the view from a window overlooking the path. She comes, and he

watches and watches while at the same time indulging in
chitchat with the guests about the Greek attitude to woman —
that she is born of the thought of man. From the window he
cannot see very far down the path, but he can observe a bridge
that juts out into the lake, and to his great surprise he sees her
out there again. She turns and faces him. Again that smile,
that smile:

'*Cherchez et trouvez. . .*'

There is a terrible scream. The house's dog dashes up to
him. He has accidentally knocked over the teapot into the lap
of the hostess, who runs out to change her dress. He stands
there with his hat and stick, his only worry being to get away
from all this. And to change matters swiftly and justify his
retreat he states, with considerable pathos:

'Like Cain, I shall remove myself to exile from the spot that
saw this tea spilt.'

But as though everything and everybody back in
Copenhagen were in league against him, the host gets the
bright idea of protracting the discussion on the attitude of the
Greeks to woman, and declares in a booming voice that he will
not be permitted to leave until he has enjoyed a cup of tea,
holding it in the one hand he owns, standing on the one leg he
owns, without the support of the crutch, after hopping about
and making due atonement for the spilt tea, before the flannel
blanket of darkness settles over the Quai aux Fleurs.

She has disappeared from his dream. If it *was* his dream,
or just the pages of Kierkegaard's *The Seducer's Diary*; old, old
pages that are confusingly merging with his own immediate
impressions. He must find his own words. Back in the hotel,
he writes to her:

'. . . *But when I deliver a eulogy on that magical, infinitely
enthralling smile, which you do not possess, but which possesses you, I do
so without fear. . . How often have I not studied that peculiar lighting
effect, but hardly dared to mention it so as not to be seen as a lowly
flatterer, when you stepped across the threshold and that smile,
emanating through the blue veil, suddenly illuminated the whole room. I
am certain that it is an utterly spontaneous smile, which never crosses
your face unless your soul is in a state of candour and goodwill.*

Nevertheless, I state this because I can no longer remain silent. On the last occasion it was all too striking, a veritable miracle. It happened quite recently, when you drove past Rue de Bellechasse, which I had just entered at a point some distance away. The carriage was travelling at a rapid pace, I caught no glimpse of any face, but one of these magic smiles greeted me and emitted a radiance that immediately illuminated the whole street, and thus I instantly knew, although it had swept past, who the carriage's passenger was. That smile, believe me, is an adornment far more precious than the most glittering diamonds, more precious than the most costly, most alluring hat. . . That smile, permit me to write this to you as an aesthete, is the highest beauty of all, being, as it is, solely the essential beauty of heart and soul. . .'

Countess Marie von Seebach desires the pleasure of the company of P.L. Møller, for the first time at her own residence. And without the Danish grammar book. Without anything at all.

She is in the salon, in morning apparel, casually seated on an elegant sofa. She holds his letter in her hand. How many times has she told him that he must not send them to her home address? But as always, he is a master of the beautiful phrase. Her hair, which dissolves in flowing locks, is bound with a simple ribbon; a rose on her breast, from a breed of roses from her homeland, Saxony, seems to be the only clasp preventing the morning gown from falling open. She is even more attractive than when he last saw her, in his hotel room, and he had gone down on one knee in front of her and had apologized for the dingy surroundings, which in due time . . . in due time. And he had spoken in torrents. About beauty. About literature. About her body which he sensed beneath her clothes. About her feet. And had got her to laugh the whole time. Every time he sees her she becomes more and more beautiful, and now he can see the touch of gold in her skin, now that she has just returned from the carnival in Nice which she has attended with her future husband, the recently appointed Danish envoy, the young Gebhard Leon Moltke-Huitfeldt who, in Møller's eyes, is little more than a boy who can hardly have any profound knowledge of literature, of beauty, of woman.

She holds his letter like a fan, and a shadow of tiredness falls over her face:

'How on earth am I going to tell you that after all these months, how am I going to make you understand that between you and me there can. . .'

He interrupts her with a gale of laughter. He knows that she is struggling against him in vain, as on former occasions, usually at Lapérouse on the Quai des Grands-Augustins, where she always pays for the luxurious *chamber séparée*.

'So you came, after all,' she whispers, reaching out a hand, and continues: 'Never allow any word or any allusion to betray my folly in showing you my inner sanctum. I am relying on your discretion. After all, you are my teacher.'

'No more than that?'

He feels ill at ease when she gets up, slings a shawl round her shoulders and takes him by the arm.

'We must make the most of the time,' she says. 'My little envoy may very well arrive within a few hours. I must show you more. . .'

She leads him up a low staircase in the mansion on Faubourg Saint-Honoré, up to a mezzanine. They walk down long corridors where one could easily get lost without a guide. At last she opens a door. They are in an antechamber with a few choice items of furniture. In an armchair one of her chambermaids has fallen asleep. His sense of uneasiness grows. Then she opens a secret door in the panelling and puts two fingers to his lips and pushes him in. He is standing face to face with all that wealth and the desire for magnificence can display, and he feels that he has seen it all before, has been in precisely this mansion, but when? When he was a boy and dreamed it all at that woman's place down by the harbour in Aalborg? As then, he feels that it is like an initiation into the Orphic rites: he has hardly entered the room before all his senses begin to swim. He doesn't know if he is surrounded by paintings or if he is the middle of a landscape whose avenues and prospects are repeated and extended into infinity, but soon he sees how the illusion has been created. All the walls and the ceiling, apart from a few bays covered with expensive paintings, are mountings or frames for magnificent mirrors, thus infinitely magnifying every object. Then she shrieks with laughter, coarsely different from anything he has heard before, as though she wants to tell him that, if he kneels before her and beseeches her, all this will be his. There is nothing he desires more. And there is nothing he feels less like doing, at this moment. And he no longer understands his own mood which vacillates from one second to the next. Even without glasses he sees everything with crystal clarity. Something is wrong. But she smiles, letting him know that . . . soon. . . And she runs her fingers through her rich, dark hair, producing sparks of electricity.

> A legend you should hear
> in ancient runes cut sharp:
> Lend me, friend, but an ear
> while I stroke th' golden harp. . .

'Your beloved Oehlenschläger. Through him, through you, I shall soon master the intricacies of your strange tongue,' she replies and continues while his eyes roam from view to view: 'I see doubt and wonder written on your face, Louis. Is it wonder at the fact that a lady should have spoken the truth? Has she kept her word? Is it so incredible? Do you still doubt?'

'No, *ma comtesse*. It is wonder only at the fact that so many conditions for true *joie de vivre* and bliss can have been fulfilled in one place without bliss itself being present.'

'Yes, it's true, isn't it? Bliss is malicious. But, as you so rightly say, one must be philosophical.'

Along the lower rim of the lowest mirrors there is, following the oriental fashion, a divan upholstered in crimson silk, and in front of all the windows there are *jardinières*, decorated with palms and rare growths and all sorts of flowers artistically arranged in groups and pyramids that prevent daylight from fully revealing all the objects in the shrine. And yet the light has been so cunningly contrived that it hides only that which

should not be seen and yet there is still enough to light up
every point of the room as one approaches it. She walks by his
side. She walks right behind him. She vanishes. She is there
again. The wall through which they entered is covered with
creepers which form portals and festoons and groups of
flowers. The fresh greenery of the niches conceal here and
enhance there the white marble of a Cupid, a Venus or a
Hymen. He wants to turn back. He wants to proceed. He
wants to turn back.

'What a surprise, *madame*,' he says and suddenly wishes
only to run along the quay in Aalborg. Run in the mud. Hurl
himself down into the mud. Get the taste of earth, sand and
iron in his mouth. Cover himself in mire, and then cover
himself again. But he speaks as beautifully as he can:

'We should actually just be sitting down there in the
legation going through the day's quota — the use of the
passive in Danish. It is as though Pygmalion is looking at his
divinely beautiful. . .'

'Statue. . .' she whispers. She is once more right up close to
him. She plays with a lock of the hair on his neck.

'. . . come alive in front of his very eyes. What we like in the
kingdom of ideas must in some way or other become alive and
breathe upon us. But I'm letting the cat out of the bag.'

'Never! Never when you speak so beautifully.'

'As now?'

'As always, Louis! Since our first meeting you have spoken
to me only as a true poet who created palaces out of mud huts,
and that both in French and Danish, and now in my own
German. You will get your reward.'

It all repeats itself, as though from a remote past. Cupid
hides his bow and strews garlands on an altar on which
various crystal figures, golden chalices and costly jewels
glitter so that his eyes smart. The fireplace, which is itself a
work of art, has also been covered with a multitude of works of
art and *bagatelles* in alabaster and bronze; often cavorting
animal and human figures. And there are several rosewood
cupboards lined with magnificently bound volumes. Before
actually seeing it he already knows it: above the altar there is a

sort of temple, designed with a light touch and decorated with flowing arabesques. He remembers it: just opposite the temple where the light almost disappears, in the gloom he catches a glimpse of a grotto whose background is sealed off with a heavy drape. It is the entrance to the holy of holies, she tells him. To the right of the grotto the wall is decorated with a canopy of crimson velvet borne aloft by Cupids depicted in the gayest postures and under which there are low chairs with lots of silk cushions, bouncing with elasticity. He knows it: that she has intentionally let him, without intrusion, make his way to the assault on the senses exerted by the room and its trappings.

She now sits under the canopy and invites him to sit beside her. A moment later she takes his hand and asks if he can find an element of pleasure in this work-room. He loses all control over the words, saying yes when it should be no, no when it should be perhaps; his left hand has assumed the position of his right hand and it is as though his shoulders have become locked. When she becomes aware of his confusion, she lays — as if out of compassion, as if to prevent him from further verbal stupidities — her fine hand against his mouth, leans over him and kisses him on his brow. She makes a gesture, as though to show him something, and a thrill runs through him when he suddenly sees the couple reproduced a hundredfold, in the flickering lights, in all the mirrors and their thousandfold reflections. His blood races, and he lunges out to seize her, but she always manages to elude him, leaning backward and forward and sideways. At one point she loses the morning gown, at another a shoe, at a third the ribbon binding her hair so that it tumbles in rich profusion down her naked back. At every point she looks at him with that same smile, as she finally eludes him just as he is about to catch her. Now she is again wearing the morning gown, and when she gets tired of his grabbing lunges she whispers right into his ear:

'Forgive me, *mon bien cher Louis*. It was merely to show you the aesthetic and optical effects of such a couple that I took the liberty of showing you this room. It lives up to what your spirit demands, doesn't it? There is, as you yourself would put it, something magnetically stimulating about this infinite replication of a picture or a posture at the very instant of its creation.'

'True enough. I'm bound to concede that you've learned. . .'

Her laughter rebounds from the dazzling surface of one of the mirrors, of all the mirrors:

'*Learned*, is that what you're saying! And from you, are you going to tell me that too? Or am I again letting the cat out of the bag?'

'Certainly not, far from it — when you speak so beautifully.'

'As now?'

'As always,' he replies, now grown weary. And freezing.

'But you haven't seen everything yet,' she says. 'Come quickly, we haven't all that much time!'

She takes him by the hand and leads him to the grotto and draws the curtain: they find themselves in a tiny boudoir where the style is totally different. This is the real bedroom. There are very few pieces of furniture, only divans, a couple of small tables and a huge four-poster bed. Everything here is ornate in style, as though done in gold and ivory.

'You are the first man to whose profane eyes this secret has been revealed. My future husband who admittedly has sufficient taste to have all this installed and fitted, but who is not sufficiently lovable to occupy it himself, I naturally regard as a nonentity. Oh, I know, I detect a trace of suspicion in your smile, but what I'm telling you happens to be true. By nature I'm far too proud to indulge in petty lies when there's nothing important at stake. I shall not, however, attempt to deny that I've had many lovers — what woman in our noble Faubourg has not? But I haven't dared show any of them in here. The French are fiery, they burn with passion for a woman, or should I say: for the pleasure a woman is assumed to be capable of giving, but they are extremely indirect. With you, on the contrary, my Nordic hunk of marble whose heart is of ice which refuses to thaw at any temperature — it's a different matter altogether. But you don't know everything yet.'

And she holds her breath, herself excited about what will happen. He is in a state of total perplexity. Just opposite the bed is a chaise-longue, covered with bulging cushions finished in ornate gold embroidery. With a movement he hardly notices she ushers him towards it, and as he bows with his final burst of courtesy to examine a Venus hanging above the chaise-longue, he suddenly feels himself hurled aloft as though by an invisible force. A spring hidden in the floor is released, triggered by his hostess with her toe, and he is instantly tossed head over heels into the sea of cushions where he feels he is being suffocated. His confusion and his ridiculous efforts to free himself from this embarrassing predicament fill his distinguished pupil with mirth. She bursts out in a fresh gale of laughter:

'Don't let this little joke embarrass you, *mon cher Pygmalion!*' she says when the laughter subsides and she is again coherent. 'You've already made me accustomed to swopping the obvious roles we're so stupidly meant to play. But what am I saying? I do believe that you have mud or something like it all over your face. I must have those cushions cleaned at once.'

Just then there is a sound of footsteps nearby. It is the chambermaid who has awoken and now enters with the information that the master's carriage is in the courtyard. When they leave the boudoir all the Cupids, obeying the same mechanism that earlier propelled him gracelessly into the pile of cushions, have turned round. Hymen has lowered her flambeau.

'It's true, isn't it?' his hostess smiles. 'All this is perfect rococo.'

Then she casually stretches out a *plaisir de vous voir, mon petit Arthur* hand to be kissed and an embroidered cloth to wipe his face clean. She gives him a book and makes a sign to the chambermaid who leads him quickly down the back staircase which leads onto the garden where a covered passage swallows him up. A door in the wall swings open, and he finds himself in an unfamiliar street, without a single ten-sous coin for the omnibus home to Rue de Bellechasse. In his hand he is holding a bound copy of Victor Hugo's *Le Roi s'amuse*, and he notices that it is the same copy with which he slapped his thigh when he stood on the rear deck of the steamer on the Elbe and she came to him and asked him from behind the fan:

'*Vous êtes français?*'

Nestling between the pages is a lock of her hair.

Hans Christian Andersen has reached Paris, coming from Spain, and the young Norwegian poet, Bjørnstjerne Bjørnson has also arrived, coming from Italy. Andersen is morose, and lives alone, in Cité Bergère between the two operas, with the *angst* in his heart that always signals his imminent return to Copenhagen. Bjørnson is living on the Left Bank, and has heard of Andersen's arrival by the merest coincidence. Now he plans to pay tribute to Denmark's greatest writer, and along with some other Scandinavians arranges a huge dinner party for him at the Palais-Royal. The table is lavishly decorated with flowers, a picture showing Andersen surrounded by his fairytales is prominently displayed. *The Angel* hovers in the heights, *The Wild Swans* fly past; here is *Thumbelina*, and over here *The Butterfly*, *The Next-door Neighbours*, *The Little Mermaid* and *The Steadfast Tin Soldier*. Even the mice who tell the tale of the miraculous soup are here. Bjørnson himself delivers the main speech of welcome, placing Andersen above all other Danish writers.

Andersen feels as though he is hearing his own funeral oration and when thanking his hosts states that he hopes he can prove himself worthy of the honour bestowed on him, by composing new fairytales capable of fulfilling such great expectations. He is, after all, not yet an old man, and as the evening wears on he no longer suffers from the week-old attack of Parisian spleen that is like fog seeping through his bones, as though by day there was a dark rim around the sun and the moon had grown to the size of the sun without adding any brightness to the night. His wolf-mood.

But now the dinner party is in progress, and a beautiful young woman, without herself doing a thing to encourage it, is attracting everyone's attention: the evening's other sun. Her

smile is the sort that inspires Andersen, even if he has
difficulty in finding the words amidst all the noise and the
bottles being opened. 'Its enigmatic reflection, a reflection of
another world.' No. Perhaps. No. He immediately trusts the
woman, although he has not yet exchanged a word with her.
It's because of her face. A beautiful face may very well lie if it
has been artfully adjusted in front of a mirror. No, 'it is the
smile over which she has no control, but which has control
over her, a smile that does not permit itself to be sealed with
padlock and key'. No. Better words. 'A smile that — like a real
traitor, without as much as a by your leave, reveals a beautiful
soul'. Still not the right phrasing. The right words won't come
till he gets back to Nyhavn, in Copenhagen.

Andersen hears only the highest recommendations about
her, and only praise of her beauty. Countess Marie von
Seebach, bride-to-be of the new Danish envoy, the affable
young Gebhard Leon Moltke-Huitfeldt, is the flower of the
von Seebachs. She is the daughter of the Saxon envoy in Paris,
granddaughter of the Russian chancellor Nesselrode. The von
Seebach mansion has for years been the rendezvous for the
Russian and German nobility in Paris. The old French
nobility, who stay well clear of the court of Napoleon III, go
there, to discuss matters of import with politicians like Olivier
and Thiers. Thiers and the Countess Marie — now that's
another story! And the Countess and that other man, what's
his name? But every time it is as though she succeeds in
obliterating all traces, in leaving the slate clean, before
enchanting the next worshipper with her smile. Franz Liszt
and his artist friends all carry her in their hearts. As does a
certain Danish literary gentleman who is best left unnamed.

And suddenly she has disappeared. Perhaps she was never
here, Andersen muses. Perhaps she is a fairytale he has heard
the day before, from some Scandinavian or other who wanted
to banish his despondency. And the merrymaking continues.
With more speeches. Most of them boring. But one of them
moves Andersen deeply. It is by P.L. Møller, delivered in
perfect French. It is read aloud by an anonymous guest. Every
word goes to Andersen's heart, even the passages where he

can't fully understand the difficult French which he has spent years studying.

After the speech he enquires about this Møller. We'd rather not discuss the man, is the answer he gets. And they all begin to talk about the man. His old friend from that time back in Copenhagen when they were known as the odd couple that might suddenly enter, called Amadis and Verner who shocked people by using the familiar *du* form when addressing one another. The young literary gentleman and the writer, older by ten years. Both from humble origins, *den Spydige og den Krukkede*, as they used to call them — the sarcastic and the affected — or 'the good and the evil', as they also used to say, Andersen could never quite make out why. He could only ever see the good in Verner, with his hearty masculine bursts of laughter, his sheer delight in making fun of the others, his predatory smile that shone with pleasure at any line of pure poetry . . . his old fried Verner: he doesn't exist. Must not exist. Malice, they say — 'to put it mildly.' Master of intrigue. Can't leave a skirt or blouse alone. Full of rage at Denmark even though he still receives remuneration for writing his anti-German articles for the French newspapers. Would have the Danish government shot by court-martial and himself appointed as minister in sole charge of all European affairs. Believes that he is the Marquis of Occitania after spending a few disastrous months as tutor to the future Fru Leon Moltke-Huitfeldt. Has taken to spitting at people in the streets. Snatches money from their pockets. Is often seen without a winter coat, with a virtually naked torso. A gorilla. Recently smashed a baker's window.

Andersen fails to understand.

And the party goes on, and Andersen reads some of his fairytales.

And perhaps she too was a fairytale.

Møller sits in the Café de la Régence with the letters he has received from her, all signed 'Anna Hutton' so that no one will ever know that they knew each other. The letters are full of secret signals; one sentence tells, behind the words, of their forthcoming trysts, another refers to her progress with Danish — but really describes all the nights she looks forward to spending with him, in Rome, in Naples, in Florence. He knows it, knows it well. But he is no longer able to interpret the signals, not since she suddenly changed her mind, tossing him amongst the cushions and sending a cloud of diamond dust flying into his eyes as he groped for his new glasses. Clumsily he puts the letters into an envelope. Now it is all in the past, he tries to tell himself, as though nothing has happened. If nothing else, he can at least write articles on the back of those sheets, with the aid of his glasses and magnifying glass and candle stumps.

He orders a cup of coffee, knowing that he will probably not enjoy it. She has also stolen his sense of taste, without his noticing it, by placing her index finger under his larynx. Two cups more and his credit will have run out, and the worst thing is that she has promised to cover his expenses. 'Just send me the bill,' she lets him know through one of her footmen. Every cup of coffee he drinks, every glass of absinthe is on her account. If he wishes. For three days he has had nothing to eat — that's how she wants it to be. If, on the other hand, he is capable of eating to a state of repletion — that too will be as she wants it. If he gets up: that too will be as she wants it. If he crawls: that too will be as she wants it. If he lives: oh, that will fulfil her heart's most earnest wish. If he dies: oh, well, that will be how she wants it too. Three days without eating anything but the lumps of sugar he has stolen from the café. The first two days were the worst, as on all the previous occasions. Now it is as though the hunger has devoured itself. That's how she wants it to be, because, after all, 'she wishes him all the best'. He thinks of Brazil and has made enquiries about the cheapest routes. On a little shelf behind the counter there is a crystal glass with water and some dissolved red earth from the kingdom of Dom Pedro Segundo, a permanent fixture which is now and then taken down and studied by someone who wishes to interpret what the future holds. He walks over to the glass, returns to his table, sits down, opens the envelope and again reads her letters now that he feels that his eyesight has suddenly improved. He reads them again and again. Then his eyes begin to smart worse than before.

A hypnotist who has a regular table opposite Møller is of the opinion, firmly based on established scientific principles, that only the past, and not the earth in the glass, is capable of saying anything accurate about the future. And the past is made up entirely of sounds, which must be especially pleasing to the blind, as Møller is about to become. Everything, absolutely everything, according to the hypnotist's theory, which he will soon publish in a major work, is *sound*: every chair in the café, every table, every glass, every window pane, every coffee cup is 'solidified sound', and if one bombards these objects with the proper electrical waves they will all yield the secrets of the past. Thus, for example, every sigh in a wine glass, every discussion over a bottle of Bordeaux, will resound anew. And if properly interpreted the sound of the past will, with mathematical precision, reveal all about the future, thus enabling the expert listener to predict what will happen throughout the universe in all its marvellous complexity, right down to its tiniest component, such as the Café de la Régence — because everything moves in accordance with these curves of sound determined long, long ago, just like a great symphony. Precisely the way she wants it, precisely the way she has determined it.

And Møller looks down at the coffee rings on the table, at all the places where he has scratched and doodled, and it is as though he can hear everything that has happened and been said over this table during the past twelve years, from the very first time he sat at it. And it is as though he knows already, before the huge shadow falls over him and a shiny toecap makes contact with a table leg and a briefcase comes flying over him and lands on the shelf behind him, who it is who has successfully looked him up and is now sitting in front of him. With his eternally drooping, slavering lower lip, it is the dimwitted, abominable Slamberg, the worst of the lot in the school in Aalborg. With the years swelling him up like a barrel, eyes bloodshot from excessively rich living, in a brand new fur coat, wearing silver rings set with amber on every piggish finger and a hat from Strøget's most expensive hatter's. That's how she has dressed him.

'Well, well, well, *pauper Ludvig*, surely one isn't going to miss the Andersen festival down in the street?' is the first inane question, echoing the sounds already transmitted to him by the table.

'No, one surely isn't,' he replies, without looking up.

'They certainly know how to have a bit of fun in Paris, don't they?'

'Yes, they certainly do.'

'We're going to win, Møller, let me tell you that much. The Germans are going to get it where it hurts!'

'Are you sure?'

'As sure as wheat grows in Denmark, Paris is worth a fortune and the Danish infantryman is full of fight! Good old Polemicus! You yourself have also hit the kraut down there between — ha-ha — the stilts! Still studying theology?'

'Still studying theology.'

'Not many shekels in that, is there, Møller?'

'No, Slamberg, not many shekels in that.'

'But enough for a stringy lamb chop, I take it. Lots of fun in Paris. And the small *mamselles* with the glad eye! How about a little glass of something?'

And then the question Møller knows is coming, like a hammer blow during a violent attack of migraine. Just as she wants it:

'*Do you ever run into any of the others?*'

Kaarsberg, Testrup, Rovlund, Brix, Hastrup, Hoffmand, Schack, G. Hansen, Bock, Mørch, Steenstrup, Schierup. And Slamberg's lower lip, still the same as that time back in Aalborg when it took four of them to beat him up; as though nothing has changed, nothing will ever change and everything is doomed to be drawn down in a swamp of *the majority*. The strip of saliva running down the middle of that lower lip, the way the lip seems to tilt slightly to the left. The tongue waggling over it. When he hears that Slamberg, in addition to running a flourishing grain business, has also been elected to

Parliament, Møller can no longer restrain himself. He will have to throw up or lash out at that lower lip so that it can never again give utterance to a single word in parliament, beating it into bloody pulp that even the dogs from Les Halles would reject. And he pushes the table to one side and strikes out so that Slamberg topples backwards. He pounces and lands squarely on top of him and keeps beating until the blood flows from the toadish lower lip and runs down over Slamberg's throat, with chips of a tooth, and on down under the collar of the fur coat.

The waiters come dashing to the scene, but it is as though Møller's blow is the spark that ignites the whole conflagration, the spark that the Café de la Régence has been waiting for, for years. Within a few seconds they're all at each other's throats; anarchists, royalists, saint-simonistes, social democrats, communists, imperialists, Hungarian rebels, Neapolitan Garibaldistes, German refugees and the usual police spies. The chairs fly through the air, tables are smashed, domino pieces are hurled from one end of the café to the other. Not a glass is spared, bottles are dashed against the mirrors and even the glass with the mixture of water and Brazilian earth is smashed, bringing the future tumbling down with it as it falls. Some seize the opportunity of snatching a few bottles and running off with them, others with dazed eyes attack the innocent coffee pot as though it and it alone is the cause of all the misery. The *lorettes* come up screaming and depart still screaming. And the police arrive at full strength. Those who fail to escape are arrested, Møller among them. They are to be taken to the 'residence' on Île de la Cité, to the abominable soup and the slimy bread. Better than nothing, Møller thinks, while his temples throb with the pain. He is carried out by two policemen and looks back groggily to catch sight of Slamberg who is lying unconscious, like the assembled Danish democrats, in the middle of the floor, legs askew and gold watch trampled into smithereens while two beggar boys from Les Halles just manage to empty his pockets before slipping away from the clutches of the policemen.

Exactly how she wants it.

There is snow, lots of snow. On the way to the police wagon Møller detects a tall figure approaching on foot.

'Amadis!' he shouts, stretching his arms forward in wild confusion before being hit on the neck so that he can no longer see a thing.

'Verner, Verner. . .' he hears, spoken softly, as in the gently falling snow in Copenhagen many, many years ago.

'To the Royal Theatre'.

'Yes, Amadis, let's go to the Royal Theatre where she's been waiting for us so long,' Møller continues the dialogue while the police wagon proceeds at a gallop towards Île de la Cité and he holds his hands up to his eyes to wipe away the diamond-dust.

seventeen

The wind is blowing. The road leads him away from Paris, and Denmark has disappeared. He often dreams the same dream when, having run away from the bill at an inn or *pension*, he has fallen asleep in an outhouse or in one of the new railway's waiting rooms, trying to get a seat next to the warm stove: he has died and is being punished and tortured for all his sins. After this has gone on for a long time, he begs to be allowed to see Denmark again for a few moments — a brief return to Copenhagen and the river of old memories. His plea is granted, and he easily raises the rotting coffin lid and scrapes aside the loose earth. And now he's standing in human form at his own graveside, not all that far from the avenue that leads up to the sombre Kierkegaard family monument, or from the pathways of Andersen's eternally green meadow, ringed with wild rose bushes, straight across from Heiberg's collapsed scaffolding which continues to attract odd creeping flowers from a distant planet, otherworldly growths that unfold their petals in the pale moonlight, and not all that far either from Blicher, Aarestrup, Hauch and Oehlenschläger who have formed a huddled group, while Grundtvig has his tumulus far beyond. But there is no trace of Goldschmidt who has elected to return to his own people instead. It is early in the morning; little birds hop from treetrunk to treetrunk, making the earth seem at ease, even the patch above Søren Aabye Kierkegaard. Dawn covers each graveyard flower with pearly dew, but it is over Andersen's grave that the effect is most beautiful. The only living soul within sight is an old man. He trudges from grave to grave, watering the flowers, tidying the oblong plots.

He turns pale when Møller looks at him.

'Don't be frightened,' Møller says, 'I'm not an evil spirit. I shall not do you any harm. I've just come for a few brief moments to see how things are here on earth.'

The old man regains his composure, steps forward and with a trembling voice says:

'If what you tell me is true, then tell me what you want to see and where you want to go.'

'I wish to catch a glimpse of the Denmark of old that I cherish, I wish to enter the old royal capital, Copenhagen, inside its old ramparts, to see the state of things as they are now, to learn who is king. I wish to be reminded of those I admired, those I loved. And of my enemies.'

'Oh, great heavens,' the old man exclaims. 'What is it you're saying? If you were a living human being and not the resurrected dead, then the rigour of the law would demand your head, then swords would be drawn and blood would flow.'

'Why so? What have I *now* said that's wrong? What sin have I *now* committed?'

'If you don't know, then I'll tell you, now that there's nobody listening. You have named Denmark. Well, when I was a child there probably was a country by that name, but not any more. You ask who is king. Anybody would regard your words as outrageous blasphemy.'

'What do you mean? Why so? Doesn't Denmark exist any more?'

'I can see,' the old man replies, 'that you're from those happy days when Denmark still existed, when peace prevailed in. . .'

Møller races round the cemetery, from tombstone to tombstone, and now he sees it: not one of them has a Danish name. He can vaguely discern where Oehlenschläger's name used to be chiselled, but the stone is now heavily embossed with iron lettering spelling out the name of a German headmaster's family. Andersen's blooming summer meadow belongs to a Saxon lineage. A giant eagle flies over the cemetery, then swoops downward, seizes him in its clutches and bears him aloft, carrying him over Denmark where all is changed, utterly changed. Every house with any trace of memories of Denmark has vanished, every field has been ploughed past all recognition. The landscape is dotted with barracks for the German army. On every road soldiers are tramping. Then the eagle releases him, and he falls to the earth and then down a black hole. He whirls on and on, and is soon back in Germany's gut, the gut he had so happily banished to oblivion, and he is now forever doomed to fly round inside it, with bloodshot eyes and skin that hurts, bones that hurt, and with the worst hurt of all: an everlastingly hurtful memory. Over there he catches sight of Hauch and Ingemann with their vacant sockets and mouths frozen in an eternal scream. And beyond them all the others, floating. The gardener from the cemetery too, as punishment for speaking Danish to him.

And the gut encircles the whole earth.

The road leads him away from the hottest summer he has ever experienced in the imperial city, the summer of 1865, and from an autumn during which he has written next to nothing, suffering new, violent attacks of sickness, each bout leaving him stretched out on his bed like a worn-out cadaver. Opium, ether, quinine, iron; quinine, ether, opium — with the money he has collected by begging from the Scandinavians and the regulars in the Café de la Régence. Someone who has been especially helpful is a journalist from *le Figaro*, a radical socialist, who is ready to build barricades for a new world order where not greed but talent and conversation and humanity will be to the fore.

The journalist, Jules Andrieu, is one of the few people in

Paris that Møller misses, as the wind now blows from the four corners of the earth. For the past few years he has cultivated the friendship of this man, as much of a friendship as is possible with one of those honest writing and thinking and creative Parisians who turn a deaf ear to the allurements of Napoleon III because luxury bores them to distraction. They always avoid any personal note in their conversations, always manage to pursue a line of thought to its most extreme and stimulating point, but without toppling over into German abstractions; never smiling in ordinary, total relaxation; never squandering time on the trivia regarded in other parts of the world as the most important factor in friendship, such as an invitation to a dinner at home. And yet each can remember what the other has said, can recall passages from conversations conducted years ago, and politely, without drawing any attention to themselves, they help those they like, with a good quotation, a useful reference, elaboration of a concept . . . or they help by paying for the hotel room or the medicine. Until as lean, sinewy agents for a better world they get up and go home to their studies where the books are resting on the shelves, as security against tomorrow's needs.

And now the road leads him away too from Jules Andrieu, always turning up in the café when Møller least expects him, always on his way to the newspaper office when he would most like to share his company — and away from others of his kind, from the scholars beside the crates of books along the quays and from Madame Cardinal's 'reading cabinet'. But then he consoles himself with the thought that the road is leading him away from *all the rest*: from the wall of icy hostility surrounding the Danish legation, to which no house tutor will ever again be admitted; from the Rue de Bellechasse and the postman who never tires of bearing him ill tidings from Denmark, from the university and from the Copenhagen editors. He is not to entertain any great hopes one way or the other if he is thinking of popping up one bright morning in Copenhagen — to become at best maybe a puppet in the hands of certain vengeful landowners by editing their Junker rag *Danmark* and thus ending up as a reactionary joke. The road leads him away from the unwashed coffee cups, from the empty ether bottles, the books he is no longer capable of reading to the last page, the newspapers that make his whole body shudder if he merely looks at the headlines; from the socks full of holes, the trousers that are so frayed that they slide off the hanger, the thick layers of dust on the shelves and the dirt on the floor, the rickety armchair, the constant draught that chilled him to the marrow even during the worst heatwave of the dog days — from all this too the road is leading him away.

And from *aesthetics* in three volumes. To be rid of that at last. Not to have to explain beauty. Not to have to ponder over the deduction from a concept, but to stick to the notion of or feeling for beauty whose laws are laid down by an unknown God. To say goodbye to the three volumes with a scrap of paper inserted here and another scrap there, flung on top of the pile of articles both published and unpublished: 'Can you think of any more ridiculous and deplorable a figure than a professor of aesthetics who gets up on a platform and says: Now I'm going to teach you about the most beautiful being in all its sections and subsections. *I write aesthetics, my friend!*' To stay away from all school classes, to roam in the woods, to sit down by a pond and not lift a finger, apart from jotting down fantasies on scraps of paper, not crude and ill-phrased, but dressed in the finest raiment the language has to put on parade, in limpid, harmoniously constructed and rounded phrases that glide without breaks or strain through the eye and the ear to the heart, phrases which are ignored by the great multitude of readers and writers, but treasured by the one who knows the secret that no textbook or professor has ever revealed, the secret placed by god or demon on the infant's cradle: '. . . so as to understand or speak with insight about beauty, it is of no use to possess philosophically exercised comprehension, an imagination schooled through study and works of art; the first and most important condition is to have a natural understanding of beauty: *to be yourself an aesthetic personality.*'

And the road leads him away from the irritation, while the wind gains in force — all that irritation he has suffered just because he is an aesthetic personality, and without any intellectual understanding other than that which he gleaned from Jules Andrieu and a few other denizens of the Café de la Régence, and which with his final burst of writing energy he got down in two volumes of satirical verse without any reward whatever, the first volume printed in the barbaric dialect called Danish, which will soon disappear, *The resurrected Paars, a truthful new ballad by the Honourable Sgr. Hans Mikkelsen, erstwhile Baron and Squire, now shareholder in Elysium,* in which he flays the Danish drivel mentality, the boastful rubbish, the hopeless Danish newspapers which outdo one another in political daydreaming, the Danish ravings and the Danish 'godliness', borne aloft for all to see by 'the prettified and perfumed piety' which is nourished by 'Biblical toffees, sweet soup and devotional whipped cream':

> *It's no use any more, continuing the pretence,*
> *deciding if hyphen or comma cause least offence. . .*

is *Pauvre Louis*'s final message to the readers who are no longer there because their heads have been chopped off in that meaningless war with Germany which, in perfect German, he mocks in the other book of verse, the Heine parody *Der neue Atta-Troll, heroisches Epos aus der Gegenwart,* with verses such as:

> *'Aufwärts, immer höher, winkt und*
> *ruft mein sterngekränzter Genius*
> *'Präsident sei, oder Kaiser*
> *in dem Weltstaat Pangermanien!'*

And the road leads him away from the intertwinements and entanglements of the Kanneworf Møller family. Whenever he made enquiries at home about the possibility of his eldest brother, Michael Marenus, the farmer, paying back the loan Møller had made to him shortly before his departure from Copenhagen, it was as though the entire family, the living and the dead, with the grandfather at their head, arrived in Rue de Bellechasse to issue the blunt refusal, fully aware that if the loan were repaid with interest, and interest on the interest, he could take it easy for at least a year. Indignant and elbowing their way in, the members of the family were downstairs, demanding to be told his room number, and then they were all trooping up the stairs, crashing into his room without once knocking, loud in their defence of his brother who for the eighteenth year refused to pay back as much as a single rigsdaler.

His mother: 'You must show some understanding for Michael Marenus! He has *invested* the money! You only spend it!'

The sisters: 'It's true, it's the truth Mother is telling you!'

The grandfather: 'It's true, not a word of a lie in it!'

The grandmother: 'There you have it now. . .'

'But it's you who fail to understand — *a loan's a loan!*' he replied, his mood aggravated by the heatwave, so vindictively that they would have held their hands to their ears if he hadn't just then — wild with hunger, fainting from the heat — danced round the room, threatening them with his bare fists against their throats so that his grandfather lost his long-stemmed pipe, his grandmother collapsed into his armchair, his horror-stricken mother laid her scoured forehead against his father's threadbare shoulder while the sisters gathered their skirts, ululating in chorus, and the brothers formed a ring around him, with Michael Marenus' triumphant smile adorning the lips of all three.

'You shouldn't have done that,' the grandmother said.

'What should I have done then?'

'You should have kept your money in a sock under your mattress, my dear Per.'

'That's not what you should have done, my son,' his father said.

'What should I have done?'

'You should have bought yourself a little ship to ferry cargo to Norway.'

'That's not what you should have done,' said his youngest brother, Marenus Laurentin.

'What should I have done?'

'This, brother.' And Marenus Laurentin took out a bundle of notes, holding the money out in front of him, and set fire to it, laughing hugely at the jest — Marenus Laurentin who had nevertheless been good enough during his last few years in Copenhagen to help him get his articles published, collecting his fees, then sending him news while he was abroad and now finally accepting delivery of the first three crates of his books and papers. And the sight of each burning note made him so furious that one by one he flung the family out of his room, even the grandmother, who toppled headlong down the stairs.

And he always ended up flinging himself on the floor in a vain attempt to save the notes from the flames, to rescue the price of a meal.

The wind whirls him away from Matilda Leiner and all her wool. Far, far away. From her knitting needles, her bags of wool, her finished and half-finished stockings and sweaters, made for him, the woollen caps she made for him, woollen mittens, gloves, knee-warmers, woollen vests, woollen long-johns, scarves that would go four times round his neck, tea-cosies for the teapots he hasn't got, egg cosies made of wool, pencil sheaths made of wool and quarter finished woollen rugs — all the things she has brought to Paris with her, eternally knitting, and has placed in his cupboard, on his chair, over the end of the bed and in bags along the walls, even though it is so hot that the air becomes more and more unhealthy day by day so that even in the richer districts one can't walk along the streets without holding a hand to one's mouth and nose, to avoid breathing in the dust and the stench from the sewers which has poured over into the water pipes so that the water smells and tastes of filth.

'But I think you should say yes to the offer — after all, you must excuse me, but you're *fifty-one* now!' she cries and starts work on a new scarf for him. Or for one of the poor she takes pity on every day.

'Matilda or Constance, or whatever you now choose to call yourself: can you see me going from Junker to Junker bowing and scraping and saying: of course, yes, Baron certainly, Count, I shall behave myself and write pleasing articles for

Danmark, dancing to your tune, causing universal satisfaction. We may soon reintroduce an aristocracy with absolute powers, thanks to this innovation, this ushering in of a new epoch in Danish journalism, and who can tell, maybe in addition to hammering our own peasants into grovelling submission we can challenge Germany to a new war, to wreak our revenge, and with the Sealand Dragoons, that unrivalled and gigantic corps of mounted stalwarts, we may well succeed in wresting back Charlemagne's kingdom. The Amager Infantry Regiment wearing outsize clogs will display new heights of gallantry and win back Sweden and Norway.'

'That's a sensible attitude, Møller, and you know it.''

'Know it, know it! Now what do *you* know, my dear sweet fire-scarred Aunt Knitting Needle, my good fairy, *chère bonne*. . .?'

'Oh, Møller, would you really like to know?'

'No, may I be allowed. . .'

'That I love you now as I did then, P-e-d-e-r- L-u-d-v-i-g. . . And that with all my heart I wish that you were back in Copenhagen.'

'My poor thing, there's going to be no packing, no journey home. All I can manage to do is try to look after my health, with all possible fortifying remedies, the mere sight of which would make the worthy Miss Leiner swoon, and by going soon on a trip to the countryside before the Evil takes a turn for the worse. This summer has shortened my life by several years — that and your visit. Look at me, *mia cara*, teacher in distress: anaemia, general nervous prostration, as the doctors call it, shortage of breath, no nutrition! Every quarter hour I have to take a rest and dab my head with cold water. At best I can write for only ten or twelve minutes a day. . . Are you listening? Constance? Sorry, Matilda. . .?'

'Yes?'

'There are moments, sometimes they last as long as half an hour, when I . . . can't even . . . *see* . . . you. Then you become a dark outline, a few sounds, that's all. Are you wearing flowers in your hat right now? Have you brought your parasol? As long as you don't lose your hearing, that's what wise people. . .'

Yet he again saw her in the sharpest detail on that last
morning they spent together. And with sudden horror he
thought: why has this woman from the forgotten forties in
Copenhagen come to Paris? Malice? Officiousness? Female
love of mollycoddling? Desire for revenge on behalf of her
frivolous, capricious sex? Why? Wasn't she aware of his state
of health, of his poverty? He saw the reflection of her eyes in
the shaving mirror, surveying him, now sitting down after
finishing her compulsive bout of fussing about the place when
she had first arrived, arranging the flowers she had brought in
a vase, straightening the curtains, drawing up the bedspread.
And her eyes betrayed a puzzled curiosity he had never before
noticed, a cold, determined inquisitiveness, as though he were
an object from another world which she wished to enmesh in
all her wool and pack into a box and send home to experiment
with, to play with and cuddle and caress and amuse with
meaningless words all day long throughout the Danish
winter.

She abandoned the knitting as soon as she began, and her
eyes moved slowly from his tattered slippers up to his legs, and
he felt as though they were covered with boils. The eyes
moved upwards, to his thighs, his back, as though she were
measuring his spinal segments with the professional eye of a
doctor or nurse, and they moved on to his neck, and from there
to his balding temples, before gliding, at the same pace, all the
way down again. Then he knew for sure. He couldn't stand
her company for another hour — however unchanged she
herself might be, not a day older than when they went to see
King Réné's Daughter at the Royal Theatre. Anything that he
had felt for her on their first day in Paris together was now
dead, the glow of that first afternoon they had spent strolling
through the Luxembourg Garden and it had occurred to him
that . . . perhaps . . . perhaps . . . if everything now fitted
nicely into place and things worked out properly and they,
perhaps, wanted him, after all, at the university. . . She meant
it literally: that bit about getting married. Her apartment in
Store Kongensgade. He could have the biggest room for
himself. She would get Copenhagen's best cabinetmaker to
put up the bookcases, painted red for Danish literature,

brown for German, blue for French. And the knitting needles would be ignored while he was around. . .

He kept on seeing her eyes in the shaving mirror. Then he put the razor down and turned to face her. He hurled the basinful of shaving water into her lap, showering her in flying suds. He was forced to muster all his self-control to restrain himself from flaring up and pummelling her with his bare fists.

'*Leech!*' he roared. And held the door open for her.

In his last letter to her, sent a few months after her departure from the Hôtel Byron, he made no attempt to conceal that his brutal farewell to her had been seriously meant: '*O Sangsue, ja, veritable.* A leech you are, who would still suck my blood or compel me to write at a time when I might be short of blood just then and rob me of the strength I need for a hundred other tasks, never mind the packing. . . If I had not been expecting you this summer, I would have fled from this intolerable heat at the end of June. . . If I had moved then, a fortnight of fresh air would have prevented the Evil. . . If you had urged me vehemently to look after my own health instead of packing, you might have secured my happiness, whereas now (probably involuntarily) you have signed my death warrant.'

His final words:

'If you hurry, you can send the money to Dieppe, Hôtel de Newhaven, where despite the cold and the howling gale I shall stay, perhaps until the end of the month — on account of the disturbing reports of cholera in Paris. And yet the earlier outbreaks of cholera in '48 and '56 were less dangerous for me than this heatwave in '65. . . I shall probably not be sending any more news.'

The wind leads him away from the sunshine streaming through the windows of Saint-Roch church, colouring worshippers, walls and objects a rosy red. But not his thoughts. That last Sunday in Paris, he once more felt what it was like to be in a world of colours that slowly made his soul yield, after a sleepless night when he had wandered about in his old haunts. It was as though he were rocking to and fro on the waves of light, constantly moving higher and higher, until he reached the cupola, up among the angels, and dreamed himself right into heaven. The hymns and the incense that appeared to dance with the beams of light; the cupola like a huge heavenly vault with choirs of angels and hosts of spirits seemed to move about in a mystical twilight. And the very moment when, in the midst of it all, he caught her glance — when she, who knew that he was present in the church, turned fleetingly before demurely walking up to the altar with the cheese-monger from Rue de la Montagne Sainte-Génevieve. He is so totally different from what Møller had imagined him to be; despite being ruddy-cheeked and wearing a jacket that was too tight a fit, and with hands like shovels, he is also erect, almost with an air of military pride in his bearing, with broad shoulders and rich, curly hair.

Once more he thought of all the shades of female blushes that are to be found, when she cast her glance downwards, like the girls in Madame Fouchanée's eating house he had described, when he was a young man, so that all present, even Victor Eremita, refrained from eating and drinking to listen to his words. There is the coarse redbrick blush, there is the one that novelists always overdo when they let their heroines blush *über und über*; there is the subtle blush; there is the aurora of the spirit. In a young girl it is worth more than gold. The fleeting blush that accompanies a happy thought is beautiful in a man, more beautiful in a youth, ravishing in a woman. It is the flash of lightning, the summer lightning of the soul. It is at its most beautiful in a youth, ravishing in a girl because it reveals itself in a veil of virginity, and has thus also the modesty of surprise. As one grows older, this blush gradually fades. . .

And yet it was not just the stained glass windows that coloured her cheeks, and she blushed most ravishingly when, walking beside her cheese-monger, she left the church and pretended not to see him. She had grown older; there were rims under her eyes and in the eyes themselves a streak of pain that no Parisian woman of the people escapes as the years march on. Suddenly she was once more the Jeanne Balaresque who so many years ago filled him with the urge to invent endless rhymes to go with her surname, his *Djinn* who felt that it was Jesus she had in her stomach when she had been to the altar. He had at least hoped to be able to whisper a word of gratitude; from the others in the Café de la Régence she must have heard how things had turned out for him since the morning the envelope with the hundred francs had arrived. All the money she could manage to scrape together.

When he came out of the church, she had vanished. For an hour or two he rambled round the new Halles.

'My Cordelia, my Cordelia...,' he thought, as he succeeded in stealing an apple, a pear and a loaf, '*laisse-moi appeler quelqu'un qui me confesse et qui me puisse absoudre!* Cordelia, Elvira! *Soli saremo e là, gioiello mio, ci sposeremo!*'

Then he noticed the wind blowing. It hurled him without mercy from street to street, from the Right Bank over Pont Neuf to the Left Bank. He fell a few times and had to be helped to his feet by passers-by. In the hotel the wind had blown all his windows in, creating further chaos in his room. Sheets of paper were still flying about. The wind gave him yet another sleepless night, and the following morning sent him headlong to the station where he took a train that carried him deep into the countryside.

The wind is about to grow in force. Soon it will be a hurricane, and it carries with it the words from the distant Elbe:

'*Cherchez et trouvez...*'

eighteen

'What do I hope to achieve by moving among you? I hate the
lot of you, I despise you, and I despise myself for being in your
company,' he roars in Danish, so that some of the others at his
table in the dining room clasp their ears in horror.

He gets up and wants to go back to his room. They all
look at him. Those who can see. One of them keeps on banging
his spoon in his gruel. Another is being fed by an orderly, and
it trickles down over his chin. A third is seized by a fit of manic
laughter. Every time the door is opened at the far end of the
room the wind plays havoc with the tables. When he is
half-way to the door and the long corridor to his room, three
men jump on him. They twist his arms behind his back, tie
him up and carry him off. Not until late in the afternoon, when
he has been lying for hours, tossing and turning on the bed
with its sackcloth sheets, do they come to release him and ask
if he wants his gruel. The mere thought of it makes him vomit.
He has a board brought in so that he can sit up and write by
the last rays of daylight filtering in through the barred
window. He writes to them all. Short notes; quotations that fly
through his brain, exclamations. Often he forgets when half
way through who it is he wants to address. He had started on
some of the notes in the Hôtel de Newhaven in Dieppe, when
he lay on the floor in the candlelight and roared with pain.

310

One of the letters from Dieppe is to an old acquaintance in Copenhagen: '*Hélas que je ne peux écrire un poème sur l'éther, quel thème. . . — j'ai attendu la mort pendant trois heures sans message — . . . Vous devez mettre dans mon nécrologue quelque chose sur ma grande malédiction comme disposition de caractère*'.

He again feels the urge to write poetry. He thinks of Baudelaire in Belgium, sick and broken. It is not Otto Sommer who guides Møller's pencil stump:

Seul —
L'Ésprit tout sain je vois venir. . .
Écrivant à la lumière première fois depuis longtemps.
Point de chance!
Voulant mourir avec un prêtre je n'ai trouvé que
des imbéciles — renvoyés avec dédain.
With what heart remains, copy this poem and send it
to my brother.
I write on my deathbed, in full consciousness.
Prends le sac and autres manuscrits pour Matilda Leiner.

The mental asylum — l'asyle des Quatre-Mores in Sotteville-le-Rouen — collects patients from large areas of Northern France and Paris where the psychiatric hospitals have long been overcrowded. The train stops almost right in front of the new red and yellow brick builings. All methods are applied here, from boiling baths, hypnosis, medicaments of all sorts and anaesthesia to strait jackets, isolation cells with walls padded with cork and rubber and boxes with air vents which allow the patient no freedom of movement. L'asyle des Quatre-Mores is situated in a pleasant, recently laid out park, and it is here that P.L. Møller was brought one morning in the beginning of December, not knowing what has happened to him in the many hours that have passed. They said he had been running about the harbour in Dieppe, almost naked. They said he had been screaming and shouting.

What he can remember is the candlelight in the hotel room, one candle going out after the other, the mouse droppings all over the place, the soot-encrusted, tattered wallpaper and the stench of sweaty feet nauseously trapped for years in mouldy carpet. And that fat Flemish landlord, sprawled in his bed two floors down, emitting snores that resound in the farthest nook and cranny and that malicious jackal, Monsieur Lachambre, the quack pharmacist, who has deliberately given him an overdose of quinine. And the priests he had sent for and then dismissed from his sickbed, in a fit of fury, telling them to go back to their god, when he realized that they were incapable of offering a single word of inspiration to usher him over death's threshold. The letter he wrote to Jeanne Balaresque: *Madame Jeanne, 36, Monthabor . . . il est difficile de mourir à Dieppe. . . Je meurs d'insomnie, empoisonné par un pharmacien. . . Pardonnez mon crayon au dernier moment de la mort. Jeanne! Matilda Leiner!'*

He forgot to lock the door when he raced down the stairs; driven frantically onwards, downwards, by the pain; as he passed the snoring landlord's room he lashed out with his foot at the mangy mongrel curled up in front of his master's door, kicking so savagely that the slobbering brute snarled and bared his teeth before retreating; he wrenched the glass door open with such force that one of the greasy panes fell out of its cracked putty casing. Streets, market squares, church squares. The crêperies, the boucheries, the bistros and the cheese-sellers' flimsy stalls that had all been smashed. The storm that carried him off, past two drunken English seamen, staggering out of a brothel and a priest, muttering to himself on his way home after administering the last rites; the pain that relented as he neared the harbour, the storm that abated, the clouds that settled into a coherent formation — as though the world were smiling at him again. A world smelling of newmown hay. And over there . . . no . . . over there he thought he could see her, catching a glimpse of her, lurking behind the fish crates. Her purple cloak. And the steamer that drew alongside the quay and was transformed into a palace that imperceptibly rose and then, glowing and shimmering, gently sank to rest, over him, round him, with walls and pillars like pure crystal.

The naiads' song.

Monsieur Dumesnil, physician: 'Have you had epileptics in your family?'

'No.'

'Maniacs?'

'No.'

'Derangement of the faculties?'

'No.'

'Mental disturbances?'

'No. Yes.'

'Yes or no?'

'No and yes.'

'Profession?'

'*Littérateur.*'

'That explains everything.'

Monsieur Dumesnil leaves him, having placed his midnight medicine on the bedside table. He turns in the doorway for a moment, uncertain as to whether he should order Møller to be tied to the bed again. Then he is gone, just as indefinable as when he entered, just a pair of enormous eyes behind thick-lensed glasses and two narrow white lips behind a huge beard with a grey streak. Møller falls asleep, wakes up, falls asleep. Around him he hears all possible sounds from the other beds — the death rattle, the shrieks of anguish. One of the patients lies there, sniggering into his blankets. Another sits at regular intervals on the edge of his bed and stares, lost, down at the stone floor. And the stench. Like a sewer in Les Halles. And the clock above the entrance that will soon strike three. The wolves that howl by night in the park. Now he is wide awake, and the wolves are drawing closer. They're standing right outside his window, and the clock strikes three and the patient that sat and stared, lost, at the stone floor gets up, walks three times round himself, bows three times in deference to the moon that sails past the barred window, sits down again, says *mo-ma-mi*, tousles his snowy hair and resumes staring at the stone floor while Møller feels the pains getting worse, getting constantly worse. Now no medicine helps. He screams as he has never screamed before. Not a single part of his body is left in peace. A patient sits up in his bed and laughs at him, in rapture. Only the wolves can help him. He gets up, white with pain. He crawls to the door, on all fours. Then he feels stronger than he has ever felt, he wrenches the door open and runs down the corridor that stretches on and on. The more he runs the stronger he becomes. He brutally brushes aside the orderlies who come towards him. The moon is on his side. The wolves are on his side. He runs, runs. The screams he utters are cries of victory. He knows it: the lane awaits him.

The lane that will lead him back to the castle in Dieppe. First there is the narrow path running between the thorn bushes, then it gets broader. Behind him the wolves frighten the orderlies away. Straight above his head the moon is racing along, maintaining the same pace, away from this place that may not even exist, maybe just some houses he imagined when he was questioned in *The Elephants' Graveyard*. The lane? What does it look like? The house? What does it look like? The vase? What does it look like? The key lying in the lane, what does it look like? The bear that's coming towards you, what does it look like? And what will you do when you meet it? And the water, you see water, but what water? And the wall at the end of the lane, what does it look like? And what do you see on the other side of the wall?

The vases are all over the place, and he can't make up his mind. He knows that one of them is the most beautiful. The key is lying there too somewhere, shining, and now he sees it as the sun rises, and there too is the most beautiful vase. Then the huntsmen approach, their hounds snapping at his heels. The wolves can no longer help him now that the moon has turned into the early morning sun, and he runs on while the huntsmen's horns ring out between the trees. Having run through all the forests of Normandy and bashing his head against several hanging branches, incurring scratch after scratch, he notices that the lane again broadens. It leads over to a meadow that leads down to a lake. At one point there is a white village church built on the site of an old ruined castle, and the melancholy surroundings ensnare him and drag him down into a bout of reverie, now that all the huntsmen have abandoned the hunt for a while. As he looks out over the lake, which is coated with ice, he hears his own voice. All the swans and ducks are trapped in the ice.

Retain, Lord, alone Thy Heavenly Realm,
If I may but retain my Esrum!

. . . He heads for the shore. He detects a rustling somewhere in the reeds. He thinks it's a hedgehog, or a water rat. It's the bear. It grows and grows. The storm grows in ferocity. He again hears the baying of the hounds and the blare of the hunting horns. He gets up and runs along the shore of the lake, through fields and copses — to the wall. As he climbs the wall, his nails begin to bleed. Pain meets pain. He combats one pain with the other as he crawls and crawls up the stones, and at the last moment he escapes the clutches of the bear which jumps up to grab him, three times in a row. Then the storm is over. A deep silence prevails. He is standing on the other side of the wall, and in the distance he sees the outline of the palace. He quietly walks up to it. The flowers around him are white as snow. The blood on his body dries, changing into a porous scab that he brushes off. His shirt has resumed its proper shape, his trousers are fitting properly, and his dress jacket, from Fahrner's, the most expensive tailor's, with gleaming bronze buttons, fits perfectly at the shoulders.

There is a burst of brilliant sunshine when he finally reaches the palace, and he knows it: that she will be standing there waiting for him in a gown of the same purple as her cloak, that she will show him the stone steps and that when he has wandered through all the apartments in the palace quite alone, she will come to him in the innermost hall of mirrors. The Cupid statues again survey him, and Hymen has once more raised her flambeau; no bird has got wedged in the crystal vaults of the palace, not the slightest scratch is to be seen. Everything is smooth. Everything is clean. And when he reaches the innermost hall, all the mirrors sink to rest around him so that he sees himself endlessly reflected. He is young. He has got his hair back. He has firm cheeks, the black rims under his eyes have gone, his beard is neatly trimmed. He smiles as he did that time when he drove back from Sorø to Copenhagen on the freight wagon.

Then one of the mirrors opens, and out of it steps the old shepherd with the crushed fingers and the feet bound in rags, and behind him is the bear, on a leash.

The bear attacks him, and he knows that there isn't a thing he can do. His new jacket has been cut to pieces, and the bear's breath is hot against his face. He lunges at it with a sword that was lying on the marble floor, but none of his thrusts hit the bear, which is now gathering itself for the final pounce on him while the shepherd looks on, laughing. With the tip of the sword he accidentally hits one of the mirrors, right behind the shepherd. Immediately a bleeding scratch appears on the shepherd's face. He runs from mirror to mirror, cutting them to pieces while the shepherd rages with pain every time a new scratch appears on his face and over his body. The bear, now frightened, backs off. Finally, all the mirrors are shattered. The shepherd is lying dead on the floor, under a white shroud.

With the tip of the sword he raises the shroud. There is nothing. In the shattered mirrors the bear has turned into the howling dog from the beach in Etretat, and it's running away, leaving a long streak of red in its trail, dragging all its reflections with it.

Now utterly exhausted, he flings himself onto a Greek marble bench. He brushes his trousers. Then she comes to him, and she is carrying the most beautiful vase and the most beautiful key. And now the huntsmen and the naiads throng round and sing:

> Here shall you dwell, and here remain
> Here shall you find lost peace again!

The nymph's pale hand presses against his forehead, it is as though she is about to lose her balance, one knee already touching the floor. Her arm slides down, round his neck, and the blush fades from her cheeks. Her gown turns into a transparent film of ice, and through it he sees that she is as cold and as stiff and as pale as one of the statues in Fredensborg Gardens. He melts in a state of bliss he has never before experienced.

He feels as if he too is turning into a pillar of ice. The chill creeps slowly through his limbs, and now he doesn't waken before it finally reaches his heart. Janus has found his way home.

glossary of names and places

Note

Danish literature is not very well known in the Anglo-Saxon world. Yes, 'we' have produced Hans Christian Andersen, Søren Kierkegaard and Karen Blixen. Not bad for a population of five million. In the 19th century Denmark had little more than one million inhabitants. Those three names should 'do'. But the fact is that behind, and beside, them stands a long line of excellent poets, novelists storytellers (especially) and playwrights like Ludvig Holberg, father of the Danish Enlightenment and often referred to as one of our 'Four Greats' — the other three being Kierkegaard, N.F.S, Grundtvig and not only Denmark's but Europe's greatest turn-of-the-century critic, Georg Brandes (1842–1927).

Not all the Danish writers mentioned and quoted in this novel can be exalted to world-fame, but some deserve more than just Danish fame, and amongst them is Meïr Aron Goldschmidt who plays such an essential part in this novel: to him I have devoted the most attention in these notes.

H.S.

Aerestrup, Emil (1800–56): The most 'pure' and most erotic of 19th century Danish poets. His poems and *ritorelles* were ignored when first published. He translated Byron, Burns and Thomas Moore.

Andersen, Hans Christian (1805–75): It is impossible to do justice to his genius in a note. By far the most translated Danish writer of fairy tales, he ought to be better known for his Gothic romantic novels and his courageous travel books. His *In Spain*, recently translated for the first time and with great success into Spanish, contains descriptions of bull fights which match the very best in Hemingway. It was Henrik Hertz who first called Andersen 'Adamis' to P.I. Møller's 'Verner'. Some of Andersen's plays, which were rejected at the Royal Theatre of Copenhagen by Heiberg, could be transformed into fairy-musicals on Broadway. Andersen would have loved this, as he often dreamt of going to America and was thrilled with railways, steamboats and everything modern. Andersen never forgot that P.L. Møller was the first to recognize him.

Baggensen, Jens (1764–1826): As a (moderate) revolutionary, and a classicist in his writings, he opposed Oehlenschläger and the rising German–Danish romanticism. His famous reportage on Europe in the 1790's, *Labyrinten*, was inspired by Sterne's *Sentimental Journey*. A violent opponent of 'romantic' anti-semitism.

Bakkehuset: 'The house upon the hill', owned by writer and critic, K. Rahbeck and his wife, Kamma, it was one of the top literary meeting places in Denmark at the beginning of the nineteenth century.

Blicher, Sten Steensen (1782–1848): Together with Andersen, Goldschmidt and Karen Blixen, he is our best storyteller. Inspired by *Ossian* and Scottish romanticism, he described 'dark' Jutland in his stories as nobody had ever done before.

Brorson, H. A. (1694–1764): Bishop and writer of well known psalms.

Danner, Louise Christine (1815–1874): Born Luise Rasmussen, she was an unsuccessful dancer in the royal ballet. King Frederick VII married her to universal public outrage and against the wishes of his government.

Eckersberg, C. W. (1822–1870): Painter and professor of fine arts, he greatly influenced the development of Danish painting.

Ewald, Johannes (1743–81): Excellent pre-romantic poet. Together with Goldschmidt, Karen Blixen's favourite Danish poet.

Goldschmidt, Meïr Aron (1819–1887): Goldschmidt was born in Vordingborg, and after going to school in Copenhagen, planned to study medicine, but became a journalist instead. In 1840 he founded *The Corsair*, a satirical weekly expressing his radical republican ideas. The feud between P.L. Møller and Søren Kierkegaard caused him to leave the paper in the hands of Møller and to go abroad in 1846. His first novel, *En Jøde* (1845) was translated twice into English (*A Jew* and *The Jew of Denmark*). Later Goldschmidt abandoned his radicalism and founded a new, more 'serious', periodical, *North and South*. He visited England several times and planned to settle there, but ultimately decided to remain in Denmark. His knowledge of the customs and pyschology of the orthodox Jews in Denmark forms the background to many of his novels and short stories.

In the 1860's Goldschmidt was regarded as Denmark's most important novelist and storyteller, but his growing conservatism created a gulf between himself and the new radical movements led by young Georg Brandes. Goldschmidt's finest descriptions of Jewish life are to be found in *A Jew* and another outstanding novel, *Ravnen*, and in his novellas, *Maser, Avromche Nattergal* and *Mendel Herz*. But his 'Gothic tales' not only deal with Jews, they are also an expression of the best of Danish romanticism with all its beauty and horror. Karen Blixen's writing was deeply inspired by the exquisite craftsmanship shown in Goldschmidt's work and his philosophy of retributive justice, or *Nemesis*, which he expressed fully in his memoirs.

Grundtvig, Nikolaj, Frederik, Severin (1783–1872): Poet, priest, hymn writer, historian, philosopher, dreamer, manic depressive fantasist, founder of Denmark's famous and radically democratic *folk highschools*, always in love with some fine woman, he was an advocate of free and tolerant

Christianity. His influence on the Danish national character, then and now, for good and sometimes for bad, has always been profound. His psalms have an everlasting beauty. They are sung at every church service in Denmark.

Hauch, Carsten (1790–1872): Born in Norway. A naturalist of the romantic school like his colleague Peter Wilhelm Lund (see *The Road to Lagoa Santa*), he was a poet of quality and later a professor of aesthetics at Copenhagen University. He had one of his legs cut off in Naples, and has described this operation (he was fully awake at the time) in some unforgettable pages. ·

Heiberg, J. L. (1791–1860): Son of exiled Danish Jacobin writers P.A. Heiberg and Thomasine Gyllembourg, Heiberg started out as a radical but ended up as the theatre censor and 'know it all' critic as well as the director of the Royal Theatre. He established himself as the doyen of Danish literary aesthetics in the decades 1830–50. Relying heavily upon Hegelian principles, he singled out the superiority of light comedy in which he excelled. His wife, the famous actress Johanne Luise Heiberg, collaborated with him. Their home was Denmark's great literary centre. A much more sympathetic portrait of him as 'a man of taste' is given in *The Heibergs* (Fenger and Marker, New York 1971). His sketches contain some funny moments, but the rest of his work is pure Hegel.

Hertz, Henrik (1798–1870): Poet, playwright: faithful to the Heibergs and a member of their circle.

Holberg, Ludvig (1684–1770): Historian, novelist (*Niels Klim*), moralist, philosopher and a superb comedy writer, inspired by Italian *commedia dell'arte* and Molière. Born in Norway, Holberg is the father of Danish 'common sense' and moderation in politics. Radical when supporting women's liberation and opposing colonialism, conservative when opposing any kind of uprising, he is present as the good teacher, if not in our hearts then in our minds. *Erasmus Montanus*, about a young student who comes home from university and wants to prove to his 'stupid' village that the earth is round, but because of his arrogance is forced to admit that it is flat, is a masterpiece, as modern today as it was in 1723.

Ingemann, B. S. (1790–1862): Admirer of Walter Scott and author of several successful historical romances (*Valdemar Sefr*, 1826).

Kaalund, H. V. (1818–85): Sympathetic poet, known mostly for his children's fables.

Mikkelsen, Hans: Pseudonym for Holberg, when publishing his comic/heroic poem, *Peder Paars* (1719–1720).

Oehlenschläger, Adam (1779–1850): The first and greatest of the Danish romantics, his *Aladdin* (1805) is a dramatic entertainment which completed *The Golden Horn* in which the poet, totally revitalizing the forms of literary expression, exalts poetic genius as a divine spark, a gift from nature. If Holberg is everything connected with the Enlightenment, Oehlenschläger is romanticism incarnate. With him a completely new tone was heard in Danish poetry which still vibrates with great beauty even today.

Paludan-Müller, Frederick (1809–1876): An ascetic poet of great moral rigour which found its fullest expression in his verse drama *Adam Homo*. He is an example of how a great Danish writer and a universal poet can be consigned to oblivion because of the language in which he wrote. Nothing was ever available by Paludan-Müller outside of Denmark until a few years ago when *Adam Homo* was published in America where I was moved to find this Danish classic, in a superb translation by I. Klass, on sale in a leading bookstore in New York.

Regnensen: Foundation attached to the University of Copenhagen for the accommodation of impoverished students.

Sibbern, F. Christian (1785–1872): Philosopher, known for his *Spekulativ Kosmologi*.

Schleswig-Holstein: Denmark had won a half-victory after the Schleswig war of 1448–50, when Holstein revolted and wanted to separate not only German, but also Danish-speaking Schleswig from Denmark — referring to an old treaty from 1460 where the Danish king Christian I, in order to obtain sovereignty over Holstein, had accepted that Schleswig and Holstein should 'for ever remain together'. During the 1850's our newly democratically elected politicians, the so-called 'National Liberals', wanted all of Schleswig, including the German-speaking parts, to remain Danish, ignoring the fact that Germany was being united under Bismarck who didn't mind a rehearsal for his upcoming wars with Austria and France. The old-fashioned, badly equipped Danish army was defeated in 1864 at Dybbol. Bismarck not only took all of Schleswig, but also Southern Jutland. Had he wished, he could have conquered the rest of Denmark, turning us into a kind of German Brittany. Denmark was reduced to a fifth of its natural size — and nearly disappeared. *Pauvre Louis* had predicted this to deaf ears from his hotel in Rue de Bellechasse. We got back part of Sønderjylland in 1920, after a referendum, more or less in the manner Møller and other intelligent Danes (and the pro-Danish English!) had advocated between 1852 and 1864. Spilt Milk.

Steffens, Henrik (1773–1845): Danish-German romantic naturalist and philosopher who profoundly inspired Oehlenschläger.

Tausen, Hans (1494–1561): A convert to Luther who became the most important Danish herald of the Reformation.

Tordenskjold, P. W. (1690–1720): Celebrated Scandinavian navigator.

Wessel, Johan-Herman (1742–85): Danish-Norwegian satirical poet and rebel of great wit. He was a staunch defender of classicism in the second half of the eighteenth century.

Winther, Christian (1796–1876): The poet just about every Dane loved to read. Nice and sweet and romantic and idyllic and Danish. But when read with the eyes of a Baudelaire. . .